RANDOM
TRUTHS

Jan 27, 2022

Dear Marti,

I hope you enjoy this book a trip back in olden days through my characters

Best Regards,

Joanne Hardy

Joanne Hardy

Other books by Joanne Hardy

The Girl in the Butternut Dress

ISBN 9781729170106

ACKNOWEDGEMENTS

My critique friends who tell the truth.
My husband who always believed in me.
My children who keep me diligent.

and

To the real John Malvern
Who found his own truth.

CHAPTER 1

Illinois
June, 1938

"Here she comes," Malvern shouted, squinting up into the metal lattice of the Lone Star oil derrick. "She's a good one." Black splotches of oil shot up and fell back hitting his felt hat and his shoulders, and then it began to patter harder and drip off the brim onto his barrel chest. He ripped his hat off, tilted his face up, eyes closed, and the slick crude pelted him, dripping from his nose and chin. The spirit quickened in him until he was dancing about the derrick platform slapping the soggy hat on his knees and laughing.

Joey was beside him, screaming over the noise of the drill. "We gonna be rich, Papa?"

Malvern grabbed his twelve-year-old and swung him about. "We ain't gonna be poor no more - no more, Joey, boy." And they laughed, hugging each other. John Malvern jumped down from the platform. He looked out at the circle of cars and trucks parked in the light of the derrick and found his other sons. "You boys, get over here! Glenn, Kurt, this here's your day, too." The boys still in their dusty overalls came to the edge of the platform under the splatter of raining oil. John Malvern's arms reached around his three sons. "Boys, it's manna from heaven. Feel it. Remember it." He looked over Kurt's shoulder to his wife and younger daughter Eva Mae, laughing and clapping.

Only Annie held back, his first-born, set apart, her arm linked to Willis Porter as if joined already with the Porter family, even though the wedding wasn't for ten more days.

Maxwell Porter, sober faced, stood by Annie and his son. John Malvern knew Porter had grown bitter, vindictive even, when his well didn't come in. But Malvern didn't spend much time on that. He was sorry about Annie marrying into that Porter family, awful sorry, his "first-born baby doll," he always called her.

"Better clear the platform," the driller called over the noise. "We're gonna cap her off soon as we can."

Malvern moved away a bit, but the oil still rained down outside the derrick, and even beyond the platform. He watched the narrow pipe where the oil would come out, channeled to a dugout pit. It came. Gushing. Then in spurts, sputtering with mixed gas. Then it came hard.

"I'm gonna get me a hatful of crude," he said to Joey, and he put his soaked hat to the pipe, but the pressure blew it out of his hand across the expanse of light and against the tires of old Porter's Ford truck.

Porter let out a ridiculing cackle. "Things turnin' out real pretty for you, Malvern. Some gits, some don't."

Joey was by his father's side and he looked up at his sister standing by Willis Porter. "We's gonna be rich, Annie. Us Malverns is gonna be rich."

Maxwell Porter leaned back on the hood of his truck, "What do you know about being rich, Joey Malvern? Your pa don't know nothin' but how to make do."

Joey looked at Porter and seemed not to have an answer. Annie reached forward, ruffled her brother's hair and smiled.

In Malvern's darkened field, the derrick towered in the center of an island of brilliant white light. Parked at random at the edge of that glow, were dusty cars and trucks dirty from fieldwork.

They had heard that afternoon that an oil well was about to come in on the Malvern farm. Maybe tonight. Word spread like a contagion, down country roads, house-to-house, amplified by the party line and encroaching even into the world of town people. After chores and supper, they came. Men congregated, leaning against cars or sitting on their haunches, talking crops and unsettled weather – stealing glances at the derrick. Waiting. Women gathered in cars and talked of gardens, and illnesses they'd heard of. They did not talk of the larger subject pressing most dearly, a desperate hope they held close in their hearts, that it might be them sometime.

Two years before, Carson Garrett had come to Illinois from Texas, and drilled a wildcat well. He hit four strikes and knew he had found a pool. Then came the duster—a dry hole on Maxwell Porter. Since that dry well, a silent question hovered before them. If Malvern's well was a duster like the one on Porter, might Carson Garrett and his Star Drilling Company move on? And others not get their chance? So they came. They had watched Malvern on the platform, waiting too, nearly a silhouette against the light, thick arms, wide shoulders, ragged overalls hanging loose on his square frame. The familiar brim of his felt hat pulled too often over his work-browned face. He was the neighbor they had always known, had sat by in church, had taken meals with and tonight they shared his joy as his gusher came in. And now there was hope again.

Cooler night breezes whispered across the cornfield outside the island of dazzling light, and pale pink remnants of the day rippled low across the western horizon. Children frisked about, chasing lightning bugs, their giggles drowned in the incessant grinding of the drill and indifferent to what an oil strike meant.

Then something else caught their attention—a shiny new 1938 Buick 8 moving slowly over undulating furrows of a road cut through the field, coming they knew from the well on the Patricks' farm. They watched as he pulled ahead of the circle of cars and trucks. The door opened, and Carson Garrett stepped out. Foreign-looking to them with his wide hat, big silver belt buckle, and boots with heels. They had wrapped him in an aura of magic. When he had come to lease their land to drill wells, they eagerly signed. He could change hardscrabble poverty to wealth.

Garrett strode over to Malvern. "Congratulation, John, looks like we got a good one this time."

Malvern could hardly get a grip on himself, hardly contain his joy, hardly keep from crying out that what had just happened would change his life forever and he would never forget this night as long as he lived. Didn't Garrett understand that? But Malvern steadied himself and spoke like the man who would shortly be doing business with an oil company. "Congratulations yourself. This ain't gonna do you no harm, neither."

Garrett stood back, towering over Malvern. The Malvern family, every one of them covered with black crude, moved closer, all except Annie, to reverently listen to what this miracle man might say.

"It'll be a good one, but this is what they call a McClosky, got a lot of gas mixed in. That's the pressure. We can expect, maybe, two-hundred barrels a day for a while, but it'll simmer down, later. Don't get me wrong; it's a good well. The Cypress well comes in easy and flows out steady a lot longer. We have to get a pump on them right away to bring it out. You see the difference? But we found the pool again and that's good after that duster on Porter. I'll be talking to you some more, if you're interested."

"You bet I am." Malvern offered him a wet slippery hand.

After Garrett left, Malvern stood, his hands resting on the platform and looked up at the derrick that pierced the black sky. Like a jeweled lady, he thought, who could bestow or withhold. He tried to understand that tonight she had poured out her treasure on him. "How could it be," he whispered, his heart so full he could hardly breathe.

"How could it be?" Then his great shoulders began to heave, tears burned his eyes, and ran down his blackened face.

Later, when they came home, the car crunching over a graveled drive, up to the back porch, the moon high, Malvern turned to his family as they left the car. "Before we go in or even clean up, we're goin' out there under that oak, and we're gonna give thanks for this day."

They stood about, dappled in moonlight through the tree branches, black splotches on each of them. Crickets sang their night song under the porch and the smell of new crops growing in the fields filled the hot night air. After a moment Malvern bowed his head.

"Lord, I don't know we deserve what You gave us today, but we are humbly thankful for Your grace to our family." He fell silent. He didn't mention the disease that went through his cows, forcing him to destroy the whole herd. Nor did he speak of Liza, their little girl who had died when they thought they could bring her fever down and not have to bear the expense of a doctor. It was not Malvern's way to rail against God.

Finally he finished, raised his head and looked at his wife and his children, each one so much a part of him. He was just sorry Annie wasn't there.

CHAPTER 2

Sarah Emma Anderson didn't like to think of herself as envious. Envy was wrong – a sin. Four months ago, she would have been glad for Sophie Malvern and her family - getting that oil well and all. Four months ago! Was it just four months? It was another life. She had felt the lucky one then – a pretty home in town, wife of a railroader.

She sat down in her usual place, arm on the roll of the quilt frame. She looked out over the sea of quilting, the wedding ring pattern it was called, done this time in blue and green and white. They had made progress since she'd been here, she could see that, but Annie's wedding was tomorrow, and the quilt would not be done. It was her fault it wouldn't be finished, but of course it wasn't her fault. She tried threading the needle, but her fingers trembled and she couldn't get the thread in the tiny eye.

She wet the end with her lips and made another stab. "The light is so bad in here," she complained.

Hattie Stamper bounced over. "Lemme do that for you, Emma." She took it from her, threaded it expertly, handed it back, and then gave Sarah Emma a hug. "We missed you somethin' awful."

A fan and a row of light bulbs anchored to bare rafters on the ceiling had come along when the church got electricity the year before. On a table at the end of the quilt frame a lazy fan creaked and served to blow out the musty smell of the basement more than cool the four quilters.

Sarah Emma had met with the quilters in the basement of the white clapboard Bethlehem Church every Friday afternoon for twenty-three years. It, with Sunday visiting, was the only time she took for herself. Monday was washing day, Tuesday, ironing and Wednesdays, mending, Thursdays she baked and Friday morning the house was cleaned in time for quilting in the afternoon. Saturday was left for shopping, a schedule designed for the solemn punctuation of the week, church on Sunday and visitors in the afternoon. During those twenty-three years she had brought seven babies into the world, buried one, married off four, with two still at home —but now that solid orderly world had come apart, unglued. The nightmare began. She couldn't sleep or think or hardly even move. Her mind was still too distracted now to listen to Dora Cook across the table. Talking the oil talk. Everyone talked oil like they were expert, she thought, even if they had no real knowledge and, of course, Dora loved to be the expert.

"Looks like the heavy oil activity is coming this way. They're setting up a derrick on our property and one down on the Owens farm." Dora squinted her eye as she put the thread in the hole of the needle and pulled it through, smug with her inside information. "They said they found a deep run of sand at around 2,470 feet on Gibson and they're doing a drill stem test this afternoon."

Hattie reached for her scissors. "Guess we'll hear."

"They say it's one of the Cypress series," Dora took back the conversation. "And they say," She leaned forward as if revealing a secret. "that regardless of what, they'd go on drilling to test the McCloskey formation."

"They talk this Cypress one." Sophie Malvern spoke softly. "And this McCloskey one and some other names ... I don't know what they're talking about." They all looked up, because the truth was only the Malverns really had a producing well on their land.

Hattie Stamper squinted, punching the air with her needle.

"We're all gonna know about it pretty soon."

"Your well," Dora explained to Sophie, "came in with two hundred barrels a day." She continued to look exclusively at Sophie. "They say the deepest point of the basin is on the Patricks' land and yours is right beside that. I read that in the paper," she added quickly for validation. "That's where them companies are rushing to drill."

No one answered because no one seemed to have the inside information that Dora Cook had and that was only because the Cooks were waiting with bated breath to see if their well could be a good one.

Sarah Emma closed her eyes momentarily, and then went back to stitching. It wouldn't be human not to be envious, she thought.

Sophie Malvern kept stitching without looking up, "I just don't know if this is a good thing or not."

"Oh, Sophie, you sweet old soul." Hattie stopped and leaned across, twisting a lock of hair behind her right ear, in the way she always did. "It'll help – money comin' in. You can have things you never had in your life – do things."

"I don't know. It's like... like things are movin' on ahead of me. John likes it, spendin' money already and he's not seen so much as a penny of the oil money."

"You just let me have a look at one of them oil checks," Dora Cook piped up. "I ain't gonna question nothin' about it."

Sophie smiled. "Well, one thing's sure, my little Annie's gettin' married day after tomorrow." Sophie clearly wanted out of this uncomfortable conversation. "We're all ready and Willis is a good boy, I think... "

"But you don't like his family, the Porters, do you Sophie?" Hattie dug down in her sewing box for a new spool of thread. "Old man Porter is nothin' but a drunk and blowhard. Always was."

"But that's no reason to fault Willis, Hattie," Dora shot back. "He didn't pick his Pa."

"Annie is such a pretty thing." Hattie kept at it. "I can just imagine her standing out there ankle deep in sawdust at old

Porter's sawmill—like a lily in a mud hole."

Dora glanced over at Sophie. "Hattie, I just wish you'd get a handle on that tongue of yours."

"Willis is a good enough boy," Hattie plowed on, rethreading her needle. "What makes people detest old Porter is he owes everybody in the county."

Sarah Emma looked down at her stitching. Would people be talking about her like that, too? The wedding ring pattern lost its focus as tears misted her vision. Sarah bent close to her work to hide her tearful eyes. "Well, at least she'll have a husband." She hardly realized she'd said it out loud.

Conversation stopped. The fan creaked in the silence.

"How are you getting along, Emma? We should have asked." Sophie said.

"Fine. Just fine." Her shoulders began to shake. Tears came in spite of herself. "No-o, things are not fine. They're just awful. I'm worried sick. I can't sleep. I can't do anything but walk around and cry. I had no idea Albert was so sick. He never told me he had heart problems or how many times he'd gone to the doctor. Not a thing. There's a big doctor bill and I didn't know. There's the funeral expense. And this week I found in the desk that there are two notes due up soon. One is for $200 at the end of the year and another for $800 in February. I don't have money like that. I don't know where to turn."

Sophie came to her, pulled a chair beside her, and took her hand. "I'm so sorry, Emmy. Here we're talking all this oil talk foolishness without even thinking."

"Yesterday, Mr. Allison stopped me..." Sarah put her hand across her mouth trying to control herself, get hold of her emotions. "He said I couldn't buy anything more until I paid something on that bill and ... I didn't know we had a bill."

She calmed herself, but it had filled her head all spring until she hardly knew anything else to talk about. "And worst of all," she turned to Sophie, "I had been carefully saving all this year to make the final payment on our place. Forty dollars! Just forty dollars and it's paid for. I thought that was all we owed on the face of this earth and now... what if I lose it? I don't know where I can go."

"Didn't the railroad have any kind of insurance or death benefit?" Sophie asked, her elbows on the quilt frame. No one was stitching.

"Yes," Sarah Emma whispered. "$750," she said finally. "But my husband took out the policy when all the children were small and at home, so each one, including me would get $93.00. I asked my four married daughters if they would send back their share to help me pay off these bills and one of them has, one sent part and says she'll send more if she can, but she's so strapped herself with her little family and her husband out of work. The other two refused. They said Daddy intended them to have it, and they need it, too. And now," Sarah Emma swallowed hard, sat silent for a moment. "There's trouble between the children. What can *I* do? Even men can't find work and..." She looked across at Hattie. "I'm an old woman who has never worked out."

The women around the quilting framed looked on. Not one of them had anything to give her, not even Sophie Malvern, yet.

"Had you thought of selling some of your acreage, Emma?" Dora asked.

"Well, there's not much. Four acres. Albert was not a farmer. He never wanted land."

"Land don't bring nothin' anymore." Hattie sat back, twisting her hair, "You'd be lucky to get $20 an acre."

Sarah Emma sat up straight, dug in her purse for a handkerchief, couldn't seem to find one, and closed the purse. "I think I may take in boarders."

Dora came to her with a handkerchief. "You could do that. Roustabouts are always looking for a place with good cooking."

"Oil men!" Sarah sighed. "I don't know. I have a daughter at home and of course, Bill, too."

She shouldn't have told all this. It was why she had stayed away so long. She hadn't trusted herself. They couldn't know the nights she had walked the floor in despair. "I'm so sorry," she whispered, looking at her dearest, oldest friends. "You have your own..." The words drifted away as she wiped tears from her cheeks with Dora's handkerchief.

No one said anything. Cooking three meals a day for oil crews, taking care of a family, a garden and farm, even a small one, was... they understood about hard work.

Hattie looked at Emma, and then turned away. They had nothing themselves to offer except maybe eggs or potatoes or side of ham. Nothing in the way of money.

As late afternoon sunrays came through the rectangular basement windows, they put away their needles and scissors, put away the fan and pushed the quilt frame to the side of the room. Sunday school class would meet in the basement in a three days.

"We'll see you at the wedding," Hattie called out to Emma.

Sarah Emma didn't answer. How could she go among her old neighbors? Maybe they had spoken of her husband as they did about Maxwell Porter and his debts, and she had just never known.

CHAPTER 3

More than a week had passed since that night when Annie Malvern watched the spectacle of oil shooting up in an oil derrick on her father's farm. Since then, life in their house had been a whirl of activities. Tomorrow, though, would be *her* day—her wedding day—and she would become Mrs. Willis Porter. Perched in a chair before a mirror in Belle Dorsett's Kozy Kottage Beauty Shop, she wore her blue and white checked dress that hugged her lithe figure, and Willis said, brought out the blue in her eyes.

"I've been saving up for this, Aunt Belle. I want a permanent for the wedding but," she ventured with a timid smile. "I want something that will look good for a lot of mornings after." She looked at her aunt in the mirror. Belle Dorsett was forty-two, with just enough padding coming on her figure to make her look ripe and comfortable.

"I'll fix you up good, darlin'." She pulled out two curved brown combs and Annie's dark hair fell loose over her shoulders. "You'll look so ravishing your husband'll grab you, take you back to bed and have his way with you."

Annie giggled.

Her aunt had been a widow for as long as she could remember and was like her second mother. Annie loved to come to the shop, with its flower box of African Violets under a wide window with lacy tieback curtains. There were lotions, permanent solutions, wave-sets, creams and shampoos on the shelf that did wondrous things for very plain faces. The room was filled with chemical scents and perfumed creams, which somehow in combination made the room smell fresh as spring in the woods.

"It's a good idea, honey," Belle was saying, "to get these cosmetic things done before, because after you're married the money goes, you'll just wonder at it. Getting a permanent will feel like you're being selfish or vain or something. Course..." Belle glanced at Ella Donnally sitting under the dryer by the window. Ella Donnally was an Allison, sister-in-law to the matriarch of the Allison family. Belle leaned close and dropped her voice. "Now that your daddy's got some oil...."

"That oil won't help me none. Willis Porter won't take a dime of my daddy's oil money. It pains him already that we'll be living in that house on Daddy's land. I just told him that Daddy and Mama went to housekeeping there and then it was on her papa's farm. Did you hear they're drilling another oil well? Daddy just leased the land yesterday. Oil's all he talks about."

"I can't hardly believe my own brother's gonna get all that money. We were both born in that bed yonder." She motioned to a room across the hall from her shop.

Belle adeptly cut Annie's dark locks, applied pink solution and rolled them into curls.

"They're bringing in another derrick on the Patricks' place. Now tell me, what would those two old bachelors do with a lot of money?"

"Chase women?" Belle answered.

They both laughed.

"You know what, Annie? There's prostitutes in town." Belle whispered as if the shop was full.

Annie swung around in the chair. "Who told you?"

"Now you sit up. I want to get this right." Belle straightened the chair. "I'll just tell you, one of them came in here."

"How did you—mean, how could you tell?"

"I couldn't. It was just when she was coming down the walk one of the ladies in here told me about her."

"What was she like? I mean, what sort of thing did she talk about?"

"She was just like anybody you'd meet. Real easy to talk to. She had a good figure. They say they follow the drillers. Wherever there's oil and money. Somebody said they saw her going to Carson Garrett's hotel room."

Annie sobered as she thought about it. "I suppose you need a good figure to do ... that kind of work."

Belle set Annie under the permanent machine and clamped rollers around the curls. "I'll go to the truck stop, sweetheart, and get all of us some donuts. You'll be there for a while."

Belle hurried down the walk. As she crossed the highway to the graveled drive of Dutch's Truck Stop, she saw the shimmer of summer heat on the blacktop. Dutch's parking lot was full. She opened the door and a row of truckers and oil men at the counter turned slightly to see who had come in. Overhead were four fans, spinning full speed.

Dutch met her at the cash register. "What can I do you for, Lady Belle?"

"Three donuts, today."

Almost lost among Dutch's collection of steins, a radio poured out Spade Cooley's "San Antonio Rose." The parrot in a cage by the cash register, Roosevelt by name, began his usual rasp, "Pretty Baby, Pretty Baby, come and let me..."

At the end of the row of stools sat Carson Garrett, his hand wrapped around a cup of coffee. "That bird's got good taste, Dutch."

"He says that to all the girls, believe me." Belle fished out a dime for the sack of donuts.

"He sounded like he had conviction this time."

Belle stole a glance in the direction of Carson Garrett as she left and was embarrassed to see him turn on his stool frankly watching her. She hurried out, back toward her shop.

The Belle Dorsett Kozy Kottage Beauty Shop was in the front room of her house, an old, single-story wooden structure where and she and her brother, John Malvern, had grown up. It sat by the highway where the road made a lazy curve before going onto the overhead and dropping into town. Old things, family treasurers that had been passed down, filled the house. Indeed, as Belle walked the long hall from her shop to the kitchen, five generations of Malverns looked down on her, sober of countenance in their dark and heavy picture frames.

It was late afternoon when Annie Malvern stood before the mirror of the beauty shop, her dark curls cascading down to her shoulders. Belle carefully captured them in a thick hair net "until tomorrow."

"Just a minute, Annie. I have something for you." Belle came back with a string of pearls. I want you to wear these. Your Uncle Steven gave them to me when we were married, and I know he'll be looking down on you tomorrow."

"Oh, Aunt Belle... something borrowed." She kissed Belle's cheek. "Thank you."

While Annie held the pearls to her throat, Belle Dorsett, looked in the mirror, turned sideways, considering her figure. She pulled herself up erect and tightly tucked in her stomach.

CHAPTER 4

Somewhere creeping through deep sleep, a soft melody came into Annie's dream. A warm breeze tickled over her bare legs, and she realized that sunlight was streaming into the familiar room, poppy wallpaper, white curtains - and the music wasn't in the dream. It was outside the window and... Today was her wedding day! She hopped from her bed, shoved the window high, laughing at the sight of her father, violin under his chin, singing— just outside her open window.

"The bells are ringing for my little girl, the parson's waiting..."

Her sister Eva Mae came up beside her, and leaned out the window, too.

"... and for weeks we been knowin', to a weddin' we're goin'." Malvern sang.

"Oh, Papa," Annie cried, "you are the sweetest ..."

"... every Susie and Sal. They're congregatin' for my little girl ..."

John Malvern lowered the violin from his chin; his eyes glistening as he came closer to the window. He reached in and gathered both his daughters in his arms. His voice was hoarse when he whispered in Annie's ear. "I hope with all my heart you'll be happy."

Eva Mae pulled back, "Papa will you serenade me on my wedding day?"

"Course I will. I do that for all my daughters."

Later, Annie and Eva Mae sat side by side on the bed they had shared all their lives.

Annie tilted her head back, looked at the ceiling, her hair still encased in the hair net. "Tomorrow I'll wake up in my husband's arms, in my own bed."

Eva Mae moved to the middle of the bed and sat, legs crossed. "I want you to tell me about it, Annie."

"Tell you what?"

"You know. What's it like when you *do* it."

"Eva Mae!"

"Well, how am I gonna know? You know how Mama is. I can't believe she spread her legs to get us."

They laughed, and then Eva Mae sober-faced, leaned toward her sister and whispered, "I want to know..."

"Eva Mae! No-o, I won't tell you that!" Anne drew back. "That's special between me and Willis."

"Please, Annie."

"Maybe, but just generally."

The sisters faced each other, Eva Mae desperately serious. "Okay. Generally."

Later, Annie stood before the mirror, her thick dark hair falling over her shoulder. She wore a blue and white flowered wedding dress, princess style with a sweetheart neckline. Aunt Belle's single strand of pearls and a white hat with a three-inch brim framed her face. Her mother had just this morning assembled six white rosebuds from the garden, added some ivy streamers and tied them with white ribbon on her grandmother's New Testament for her to carry. Eva Mae stood beside her, in a pale blue dress made from the same pattern. Sophie Malvern prided herself on always getting several dresses from one pattern.

Annie could hear voices outside her bedroom; waiting for her, neighbors and family she had known all her life. The reality of the moment—her wedding ceremony—rushed through her and made her tremble. All morning the family had carried assorted chairs from the bedrooms and basement and placed them around the living and dining rooms. She and Willis would stand in the arch between the rooms to say their vows. Outside, long tables covered with starched white tablecloths were set for the wedding supper. A soft knock came to the door and John Malvern stepped inside. The clock chimed four. Annie's heart began to pound.

Eva Mae looked out, and then turned. "This is it." The door opened wide and Eva Mae walked slowly out.

Conversation stopped. In a distant corner, her Aunt Belle played the organ. Then to the halting cadence of Lohengrin, on her father's arm, Annie walked to the arch where Willis Porter stood waiting. She saw only Willis looking down at her, smiling. She had loved him since they were children in the country school. The preacher before them spoke and Annie was hardly aware of what she or Willis said until they turned, Willis holding her elbow, and the preacher presented them as husband and wife. They were rushed to the front door, down the steps in a blizzard of rice.

The house emptied quickly, and people surrounded the bride and groom, showering them with hugs, kisses and well wishes. When they were seated at the bride's table under the great oak, John Malvern raised a glass, and the others joined in the toast.

"To my beautiful first-born daughter that I give away... both sadly and, yet, happy for her to become the wife she wants to be. Happiness through the years." They drank the toast.

Maxwell Porter rose and raised a glass. "I am proud to claim Annie as our own, and I want to say, she could do no better than to become the wife of Willis Porter."

Hattie Stamper looked down the table to her quilting friends, Dora and Sarah Emma. Would they drink to that? Their glasses were raised so she raised hers, a little tentatively, and then drank to that toast, too.

Kurt seated by his father, stood glass in hand, "To Annie who I played with and fought with as long as I can remember. It's good to get you out of the house." Everyone laughed. "No, I'll miss you but I want you to be happy. Miss her... hell, she's just movin' down the road, not even out of sight." He tipped his glass once and they drank to this.

Twelve-year-old Joey stood up across from the bride and groom, his glass filled with wine for the first time. "I wanna say something, too. You're the best big sister a guy could have, but it don't matter if you are married, one of these times I'll beat you racin' to the beehive tree and back without gettin'stung."

Malvern smiled down at his son as they drank to his toast. "Well, now, folks, my wife's been cooking on this for two years. We got to dig in. Help yourselves."

The bride and groom were seated at the center of the long table and the rest found seats around them. Dozens of dishes were passed and passed again, for second helpings. Then the cake was brought out, a three-layered creation from Sophie Malvern's largest baking pans, using a full dozen eggs, she said. The bride and groom took the first piece and other pieces were passed down the long table.

The music began inside, fiddles and the organ in the living room. The bride and groom rose and the crowd surged about them as they moved to the front steps.

"Throw your bouquet, Annie, before you go in," Eva Mae called. Annie slipped the ribbon holding the bouquet on the Bible and, standing on the top porch step, turned her back on four screaming girls and tossed it. But it was Belle Dorsett who caught it.

"Aunt Belle," Eva Mae yelled, "that was supposed to be mine."

The bride and groom went inside and began the first dance and soon others joined them. The evening grew dark and the older ones sat outside at the table, drinking Malvern's cider and wine and listening to the music. Across a wide field, a flare of light filled the eastern horizon. Malvern's second oil derrick was being put in place.

CHAPTER 5

Kurt downed his last glass of wine, walked through the house, past the dancers and the crowd of visitors, to the back door. Across the porch and backyard, light poured from a window making shadows all the darker.

"You leavin'?"

Kurt turned abruptly. Maxwell Porter sat in the semidarkness of the porch, nursing his own bottle.

"Don't look like your party's in there." Kurt said.

Porter stood, raised his bottle. "I'm drinkin' to the joining of two fine families, the Porters and the Malverns."

"Listen, old man, Annie may of married Willis, but I ain't joined with the Porters in any way, shape, or form. You got that?"

Porter teetered, reached for a post, looked down at his empty bottle, hesitated for an instant and threw it at Kurt.

Kurt jumped aside, then grabbed Porter by the lapels, "You're so damned happy about this match, go in *there* and celebrate." Kurt opened the screen door and shoved Porter into the kitchen. He watched Porter already drunk find a kitchen chair and drop into it. Kurt slipped out into the darkness of the yard and ambled down the road. Near the Patricks' lane he'd left his truck. He started it and drove slowly away, lights off. No point in rushing; Malcolm wouldn't be gone yet, but God he was anxious.

He lived all week for these two nights. It was with him all the time, eating at him. He couldn't get enough. There'd never be enough. Lillian!

He drove through town, out to the park and circled the lake where he always waited for Malcolm to leave the house. The moon was up and light sprinkled across the lake like a million floating diamonds. Fireflies whirled about as he watched intently for Malcolm to come out to his big boat. Kurt's lip curled a little in contempt at the fool Malcolm Powers was. With all his money. He was a fool to leave a woman like that alone every weekend, a woman half his age. But Kurt reflected, maybe Malcolm had forgotten how it was, that drumming, consuming hunger. He didn't know how men like that felt. That age. A lot of money. He didn't care. He didn't give a damn. He just wanted Malcolm gone, gone for the night, so he could live his own ecstasy and somehow make it until the next time.

Malcolm Powers came down to the dock behind the house, climbed into his boat, and started the motor. He'd be off fishing with the Sheriff Logan Webb and Bucky Allison until Sunday night.

Kurt started his truck and drove, lights off, around the lake to the dark patches of the grove near her house. Then he walked to the back porch.

She was waiting, moonlight on her white robe, barefooted, her long hair loose, hanging to her waist. She said nothing as he came to her. Then she was in his arms, and he held her to him. With all the driving passion of his twenty-two years, he wanted to absorb her, devour her. He slipped the robe from her shoulders and she stood before him, a perfect white marble goddess. She touched him only with her wet probing mouth as he caressed her breast. She lay down before him, at his feet, arms raised above her head. A sliver of moonlight lay across her, and he could see her face, her drowsy eyes, begging. He slipped down to her, touching her, feeling the realness of her flesh – warm and supple. Anticipation began to pound through him as his hands moved over her thighs, to the silken flesh of her inner legs, finally to wet crevices and folds.

Then he was drowning in her, always drowning, wanting all of her until he could stand no more and still drinking in more and more until, exhausted, they pulled apart and lay, damp from their own fever, staring into the darkness.

"I live for *this*," he whispered after a long time.

"I live for *you*," she answered in the darkness.

It was always the same, the first time, a savage, desperate meeting. Later, there was tenderness and lingering.

As they lay there, she turned to him, "I've heard your daddy got an oil well."

"Yes, and they're drilling another one."

He noticed she didn't answer.

"I suppose," he said, "if we get enough wells you might even speak to me on the street."

Lillian Powers was quiet for a long time. The night sounds of crickets whispered though the screened porch. "This is the most precious thing in my life, Kurt. The rest," her voice was throaty, "is just window dressing. You are my existence."

"So you tell me."

He knew what he was to her. A farm boy she used. He should get up and leave, but he couldn't. He just couldn't. Her soft palm moved over his leg and inside. He turned on his side and with his index finger began gently, feather light to draw designs across her stomach and he could feel her quicken under his touch.

CHAPTER 6

Lillian Powers stood at the podium, her committee seated before her at a long table inside the empty ballroom of the Allison Hotel; a hotel her grandfather had built. Cool October breezes floated across the room through open windows. She had called a special meeting of the City Council's Steering Committee of Social Events. She knew, even if they didn't as yet recognize, that there was much to be concerned about.

"The Harvest Ball is next week," she began. "There's something important we need to consider. As the standing committee for our town's major events, we have obligations. What we put on the calendar and how it is conducted is our responsibility. People look to us; depend on us. We've been a guiding force in this town for three generations. We shape activities for our children, our oldsters and plan the galas..."

Lillian looked at her husband, Malcolm, slouched glumly in his chair. He'd rather be out on the lake fishing, she thought.

Malcolm stared past her, watching leaves drift gently down from the great oak outside, now clothed in rust and yellow fall regalia. Four other members of the committee lined the table. Ella Allison Donnelly slipped her white gloves off and searched in her purse for a pencil. Her husband, The Honorable Judge Fredrick Donnelly Retired sat by her side. Willa Logan, Lillian's sister, nodded in agreement. But, of course, she usually did. Marthursa Allison Preston, a cousin who had received the honor, or maybe it was the burden, of carrying their great-grandmother's name, sat at the far end of the table. She absently toyed with a new diamond ring her husband had just given her. An appeasement trinket, Lillian thought, for his latest affair.

"We may need to look over our bylaws," she continued. "Our town, our circumstances are changing as we have not seen before. The oil strikes have brought in an amazing influx of," she searched for an appropriate word, but found none. "... people."

Ella Donnelly shifted in her seat and smiled glowing approval on her beautiful niece, a statuesque brunette swathed in a custom-made red suit.

"We're grateful, of course," Lillian went on, "for the help the oil gives the poor people out in the country, on the farms." She paused. Thoughts of Kurt were so lively, so intrusive, she could hardly keep them away. She swallowed hard, stepped to the wide arch and motioned to a waiter from the Garden Tea Room across the hotel lobby.

"Could you bring us a pot of hot tea, Arthur, and maybe a tray of sandwiches?"

She went back to the podium, feeling discouraged. They don't really understand, she thought. They don't grasp it...what's happening. How could they know what she knew, that the boy who came to build a boathouse in the spring—some anonymous boy who came to fill her lonely days and satisfy her hunger, now wanted to be somebody different, and he was going to be somebody different. His father's oil had made him want to be different. This would happen a hundred times over, she thought. And where would that leave the Allisons?

"Even their good fortune filters into the merchants and professionals." Lillian focused on her aunt as she continued. "But Amsley is our town and we cherish it, so we must guard it."

At that moment, Carson Garrett, the very symbol of the unknown, the questionable, stepped up on to the wooden porch that curved around the outside of the Allison Hotel ballroom. He sauntered along the porch to the hotel entrance. Garrett, above all, was responsible for the rough mysterious oil people who had come in uninvited and threatened the old fabric of the town. As everyone had said at one time or another, Carson Garrett was "from away from here." His wide hat and high-heeled boots said he was foreign and although he might not know it, he would never be one of them.

They silently watched through the wooden arch that opened into the lobby as Garrett picked up his key at the desk and climbed a wide curved stairway behind the Tea Room.

Lillian glanced down at her husband and went on. "Yes, well, the Harvest Ball is next week, and we'll raise some money for the following year, but we must discuss who will guide our future events."

The tea arrived.

Lillian had hardly seated herself, when she saw a woman walk past the windows. Her hair was matted and piled high, her eyebrows darkened. The purple dress she wore was fashionable and hugged tight about her stomach, showing her slightly rounded belly.

Ella Donnelly's eyes widened. "That is a prostitute! I know it. I know everybody in this town and I don't know her. Look how she's decked out. I've heard they're about."

Judge Donnelly looked at Malcolm Powers, then to his wife. "They've been here for a while, dear, a year or more. There's a place two blocks from the train station where the roustabouts go."

"And, ladies," Malcolm said, his interest finally awakened, "there'll be more."

Brows arched, Lillian looked down at her agenda "My grandfather built this hotel. I'm going to speak to the Sheriff. They are not going to do their business in here." She made a note in the margin.

"See there," Ella whispered, "she's going right upstairs. I'll bet she's going to that Garrett's room." Six sets of eyes were riveted on the purple dress as the woman walked up the stairs and the last glimpse of purple vanished.

Ella Donnelly poured tea all around. "We have the Gala next week, and the Thanksgiving Turkey Shoot at the Grove will be upon us in a few weeks, then Christmas. It's really time to make a new calendar now. Something must be done."

The sandwiches arrived.

Willa Webb turned to Ella Donnelly. "I can't imagine having Fourth of July without the fish fry and fireworks or the Christmas sleigh ride at the Country Club. I grew up with those things."

"But, my darling," Ella patted her niece's hand, "that is not the point. Those things won't cease unless..." she paused, looking into the lobby, "new people think they can... come in, change things. Even then the events you love, may continue but what makes you love all those things would change... in character. The people of this town have always tried to get along. We all know where we're comfortable, but now..." Her words drifted off as she glanced toward the wide stairway. I propose we write in our bylaws that this committee be open only to members whose parents have lived in Amsley."

Ella quickly echoed her niece's sentiments.

"No," Marthursa spoke quietly, "grandparents. It should be grandparents." Her opinion carried much weight. Her husband's father had donated land to the city on which the Country Club was built. Many of the year's events were held there.

"But some of those getting new money from the oil," Willa Allison Webb, Lillian's sister and wife of the sheriff, looked about uncertainly, "will see themselves... in a new way, and their grandparents certainly lived here." In her naïve way, she often seemed to hit on the very nerve of the matter.

The group fell silent. Control could be a fleeting thing. No solution felt right.

Lillian reached for a sandwich. A band tightened hard across the back of her scalp under her freshly coiffed hair. She had been in Belle Dorsett's beauty shop just this morning listening to Belle tell about the charming country wedding of her niece to the son of Maxwell Porter last summer. Kurt's sister! She usually liked to hear Belle tell about Kurt's family, but this morning Belle had said the Malverns were getting still another oil well. She shrugged it off. Why should that disturb her? Kurt would never be anybody. Just a farm boy always.

Judge Donnelly cleared his throat, tapped the table with his index finger. "It should be grandparents. That would be best."

Lillian smiled indulgently at her uncle. His little "fix" would be a ripple in the water when the deluge came.

"Yes. Grandparents." Ella smiled up at her husband and clapped her plump little hands in glee. "I just had a mental picture of Maxwell Porter wandering around our yards on the Spring Garden Tour?"

Lillian didn't laugh.

CHAPTER 7

John Malvern looked again at his oil check as he paused before the door of the First National Bank of Amsley. Six-hundred, twenty-three dollars and fifty cents. He wasn't sure about these banks. The Patrick brothers wouldn't go near one. They'd lost all their savings when the banks failed. But he'd decided, so he went in. Malvern looked around as he stood at the teller's window, hoping no one watched him as he learned about this banking business.

He shoved the check beneath the grate. "I want to open an account, but I want some back. To spend."

The pretty young girl smiled at him. "I think we can do that. How much do you want back, sir?"

He cleared his throat. "Give me $25 back." Two drillers were cashing their checks at the next window, but they had paid no attention. It was Friday, payday. The girl soon counted out two tens and a five and placed them on top of a tiny black book. Malvern took it up, scratched at the back of his head as he studied the figure on the pristine first page of his new bank book. Five hundred ninety-eight dollars and fifty cents. He quickly did the math. She'd done it right.

Afterwards, Malvern walked down to Allison's store. He knew what he wanted. He'd been studying on it all week--that bicycle in the store window, he was going to give Joey for

Christmas. This would be the first thing he bought with the oil money, a present for his son. He could picture Joey's face on Christmas morning when he wheeled it in. He thought of other Christmases, good ones, but there had never been presents. It made his heart swell to think of this year. He could do something special this time for his family.

Inside the store, he motioned for a clerk. "Reckon you could help me out here? Get that bicycle out of the window?" The clerk stood the bicycle down, inside the store. "Gonna give that to my boy," Malvern said proudly. He slipped down on his haunches and looked it over, the shiny, bright red bike with a thin white stripe over the wheels. He'd never had one, never even sat on one, but that didn't matter. He was gonna make Joey's heart sing when he brought it out.

"How much did you say for the bicycle?" Malvern asked.

"It's twenty-two dollars and eighty cents."

The clerk took up a small pad and began to write. "Is that all for you, Mr. Malvern?"

Malvern pulled out his billfold, opened to the section with the two tens and the five. He started to pull out the two tens, and then he thought of something.

"There might be something else. You got some white boots, something with fur? My girl was talkin' about 'em."

"I know the ones. Follow me."

Malvern had never been in this part of the store, shelves of shoes lining the wall higher than his head. At the end of the aisle he saw a table with white boots in the midst of other shoes. He reached for one—a lace-up boot that folded over to show a fur lining.

"This is just the thing, now," the clerk said.

"My girl's gonna be sixteen next week." Malvern smoothed his hand over the fur, then turned the boot over to see the price on the sole. One dollar and ninety-five cents. He was instantly taken aback. They sure as hell knew how to hold a man up without a gun. A dollar and ninety-five cents!

He put the boot back. "My wife never held with giving

birthday presents," he explained.

The clerk nodded. "So the bicycle is all you want?"

Malvern was figuring. "Twenty-two dollars and eighty cents for the bike and a dollar, ninety-five for the boots. That would use both tens and cut into the five and leave twenty-five cents. Then it came to him in something of a rush. He could buy them both if he wanted to! There was money enough. "I'll take the boots."

"Your daughter's going to have a very special birthday."

"I reckon so, at a price like that."

He followed the clerk to the cash register. By the register was a tray of pins--ladies pins. He picked up a three-cornered one with rows of pearls covering the triangle, and scalloped gold around the edge. It was a pretty thing. He ran his fingers over it. He'd never given Sophie a Christmas present. He studied on it for a second, couldn't remember if he had ever given her a present. She'd probably think it was just foolishness, anyway. He put it back. Then he saw another one, a dragonfly, with some sparkling stones on the edge of the wings. "How much do you get for these pins?"

"They're a dime each, Mr. Malvern."

He looked at the clerk. "Which one do you like?"

"They're both nice. The triangle one goes at the throat and the other is worn on the shoulder. Both very pretty."

He figured some more. He could buy Sophie a pin and still have a nickel coming.

"I'll take both of 'em." He almost didn't believe he'd said it after it was out. *Both of them*, his mind echoed. Sophie would wonder what on earth had taken hold of him. He could see her face now as she turned them over, looking puzzled. He opened his billfold again.

"That's going to be twenty-four dollars and ninety-seven cents. Mr. Malvern, two cents tax."

Malvern slapped down the twenties and the five on the counter. He wouldn't even get the nickel back.

It made him feel good though, as he left the store—happy.

Kind of free like. Not careful and sparing. As he covered up the bicycle in the back of the truck, he remembered one time his mother had made a raisin pie, his favorite, and said that he could have his piece and since his two brothers were away helping with the threshing, he could have their pieces, too. He ate his piece and one more. He didn't want the third piece, but it was there if he wanted it. It was the only time he could think of when there was *more* of something than he wanted.

But that was before the oil! That was before he had a bank account with six hundred twenty-three dollars and fifty cents, ready money to put in it, before he could take out twenty-five dollars and just spend it. Things were different; they had to be. If you could put that kind of money in the bank all at one time, maybe baubles weren't such foolishness.

Malvern sat in the cab, letting it warm up, beside him wrapped in brown paper, were the boots and pins. As the truck warmed, steam fogged the window and Malvern thought to himself what he had done. He'd gone into that store and in less than thirty minutes spent nearly twenty-five dollars. He'd never done that before in his life. He often sneered at people who he thought just let money pour through their fingers.

Somebody knocked on the window, but he couldn't see through the steam. He wiped it away. Maxwell Porter. Malvern rolled the window down.

"Let me buy you a drink, John. We need to do some celebratin'."

"Naw. I got to get on home."

"Now, John, it ain't ever' day we can celebrate havin' a new baby comin'."

Annie and Willis had just last week announced they would be a little family come summer.

"Well, I guess it won't do no harm." He slid out of the truck and locked it. They ambled a couple of doors down to the Blue Moon. The weekend was beginning and the saloon, hazy with smoke, was filled with oil workers getting ready for a long night. Malvern followed Porter to the back where it was dark, and settled at a table. Bluegrass music, nearly drowned out by the chatter, poured from a radio behind the bar.

After they'd had a drink, Porter leaned forward and motioned, "Let me show you somethin'." Malvern followed him up a dark enclosed stairway along the back wall. At the top, Porter opened the door to a room over the saloon where only dull gray light of a winter day came from the front window. A sea of tables filled the room, and a row of slot machines lined the wall. By the window, Malvern recognized three drillers from his own wells, hunched over a game.

Porter found a table, "You got money now, John. Oughta give me a chance to get a piece of you."

"You got my daughter, Maxwell. Ain't that enough?" Malvern still stood, taking it all in.

"Come on. Let's get in a little poker," Porter coaxed.

"There's no gaming in this county. Don't the sheriff do nothin' about this?"

"Sure. He comes by, but he lets 'em know in advance when he's comin' and then there ain't a thing to be seen."

Malvern rubbed his hand across his mouth and slid down in the chair across from Porter. "I reckon it's bound to come—followin' the oil."

Porter leaned forward, looked about as if he had a great secret, "This ain't the only place. There's another one here and a couple in Clay City. It's them hoodlums comin' in from Chicago. That's what I heard it was."

"All I know is, I want to keep my boys outa here." Malvern pull off his hat, put it on the table, then turned to the ring of a slot machine and watch it disgorge a handful of coins. "I hate what's happening here. I been walking down that street out there since I was holding my Mama's hand. Now Belle says there's prostitutes comin' in her beauty shop."

One of the drillers walked by and grasped Malvern's shoulder as he passed. "I never expected to see John Malvern up here."

Malvern laughed, a little embarrassed.

Then the driller came back, turned a chair around and sat astraddle it, his lanky frame hunched over the table near Malvern. "You know, John, we're gonna be getting a little competition." Malvern enjoyed the soft Texas drawl of the oil workers.

"All the talk is that a new wildcat well is being cased today. You know what that means--if that one comes in? It'll mean there's five different wildcats scattered around three counties, and every one of them is opening a new pool." The driller leaned closer. "We're hoping, Mr. Malvern, you stay with Lone Star Drillin' and don't go signing up with some other company."

Malvern looked at him, surprised. "Don't need to worry none about that." He had a fleeting sensation that people were treating him with defference. It felt good to be courted.

"What I'd like to know," Porter cut in, "is when are they gonna put one of them wildcats on my place again."

"Well, Mr. Porter, that wouldn't be a new pool." The driller turned his attention to Maxwell. "You're in one that's already been opened, with the first Patrick well. That's why there's so many drillin' in here."

"You shore been missin' my patch of ground with your drillin' rig," Porter shot back.

"Your time's comin'."

Porter looked away in disgust, then got up and went over to one of the slots.

The driller pushed his hat back. A strip of white skin showed along his hairline. "These farmers are the most pessimistic lot I ever seen. They don't seem to recognize that the oil development is just starting, wildcats openin' new pools to be drilled to."

The slots whirled and clattered behind them. The driller leaned over the table close to Malvern again. "The farmers are gonna make more money in two years than farmin' their whole life, and they don't have to do a lick of work to get it."

Malvern didn't answer for a while. It felt things were moving like a runaway team of horses.

"I'll tell you about old Porter over there." Malvern nodded, and then turned back to the steady brown eyes of the driller. "He got his hopes up once but it was a duster. Made him feel like a fool in front of folks to get that dry well. When Garrett and his crew came to plug the well, Porter run 'em off with a shotgun. They're not rushi to tangle with him again."

CHAPTER 8

Kurt sat across the lake from Lillian's house. The sky was rippled with rushing clouds, first splotching the water in shadows, then bathing it in bright moonlight. Tall trees in the park behind him swayed and crackled in the wind. He had not seen her for two weeks and he was desperate for her. Last week, he had parked here and watched as she and Malcolm went to the car dressed in some kind of costume for the Harvest Ball. He had heard of the Ball, knew of it, but it was not something his family would do.

Later, he had driven slowly by the Allison Hotel looking through the wide windows of the ballroom until he spied her in a sleek black dress, cat ears anchored in her black hair and the half mask of a tiger. The truck had come almost to a standstill, as he watched. A tiger! Like her fierce love-making. She could devour a man if—he thought of Malcolm—the man wasn't up to her. But she knew, and he knew she could never exhaust the raging passion of a twenty-two year old. He smiled, she would never devour him. He drove on, longing for the next week to pass and he could have her again.

And now that week had passed, and he waited for her to walk Malcolm to the boat pier, to return to the sun porch for him.

He drove around the lake, parked his truck in the deep shade of her garage. Picked up the flowers he'd brought and went to her. She came to him immediately and he could feel through the robe her naked body. She probed his mouth, clinging to him. Finally, he pulled back.

"I brought you something." He handed her the flowers.

She didn't take them.

"My mother grows tiger lilies in the summer, but I got these from the shop." He tipped her chin up and gave her a gentle kiss. "I saw your costume at the ball. I thought the flowers fit you."

"What am I going to do with them?" She turned away, disdainful.

"Put them in something. Water. A vase. That's what you do with flowers."

"I don't want them. I don't want presents from you, Kurt."

He came to her, put his arms around her shoulders and kissed her neck. "Isn't that what men do when they have a woman they make love to, have tender feelings for?"

She turned slowly in his arms. "Do you have tender feelings for me, Kurt?"

He suddenly felt awkward. "I don't know."

"Tell me if you have tender feelings for me."

"I suppose. I think of... This...all the time."

"This!" she motioned to the rug on which they usually made love. "I can't take the flowers. Take them back." She dropped her robe and lay naked before him on the rug.

He put the flowers in a chair and came down to her, but the edge had been taken off his hunger. She began slowly kissing him, unbuttoning his shirt, opening his belt buckle, then warm fingers were reaching beneath clothing, touching skin, stroking until nothing filled his mind but consuming her.

Later, as they lay quietly beside each other, he gathered her in his arms. The wind poured through the screens of the sun porch, and he pulled the robe over her, tucked it under her chin and held her. Soft pattering of rain sang on the tin roof of a wishing well in the yard. She cuddled close to him, warm against his bare chest.

"I understand that you can't take my flowers." Kurt kissed her forehead, but she didn't answer.

"Let's go inside," he whispered. "Have some coffee. Talk a little." Rain was beginning to blow through the screens.

"No. No, we can't do that." She pulled away from him.

"Why not? Malcolm's gone. Do you expect to get laid out here when the snow flies?"

"We'll think about that when the time comes."

Kurt got up, buttoned up his jeans. Pulling the robe tightly about her, Lillian stood before him, nearly shoulder high to him, barefooted.

"I'm going in. It's ridiculous to stay out here half naked."

She ran before him, blocking the door. "No. You can't come in."

"And why not?"

"You just can't."

"So the farm boy can't come in your fine house?" A chilled mist blew in on them. He held both her shoulders. "Now, let's see, what do you want the farm boy for, Lillian? Courtship? No. Friendship? I guess not that, either. The farm boy must stay on the back porch." He reached past her for the doorknob. It was locked. "The farm boy's locked out!"

"You don't understand."

He could barely see her in the dark shadows.

"Oh, I do understand, Lady Lillian. I know my job."

He scooped her up, took her again on the bare damp floor. When it was over, he stood up, buttoned his jeans, grabbed the flowers, and tossed them on her. "I don't need these in my work."

"Kurt, you don't understand."

He drove slowly through town, the window down, rain cooling his fury. As he went home, out through familiar road, gas flares from the oil wells wavering in the wind and illuminating the countryside in an eerie golden hue, he could still hear her words. "You don't understand." But what *she* didn't understand was, who *he* was.

CHAPTER 9

Annie woke slowly, to the dim morning light. There it was again. She hadn't imagined it. She laid her hand over her stomach, where she had felt the tiny feather light movement. She touched Willis.

"Honey. Feel this."

He turned to her, eyes heavy with sleep, as she guided his hand under the warm comforter. "Feel that?" She whispered.

He smiled, still drowsy, and propped himself on his elbow. "Well, I'll be dammed. That little burger's gettin' busy in there."

They laughed, and Annie slid into his arms. He kissed her slowly, his hand cupped over her stomach, waiting for the thrill of that indistinct flutter that says a new being is awakening.

"I love you, Annie." He held her for a moment then abruptly threw back the covers. "Get your duds on, sweetheart. We're gonna tell the world."

Annie and Willis walked through the stubble of a cornfield to the new oil well behind her father's shed. Malvern stood a bit away from the platform, buttoned up against the blustery winter day, talking to Carson Garrett.

He put his arm around Annie and spoke close to her ear. "The driller says it'll come in this weekend." Malvern shook his head as he looked up at the derrick silhouetted against a grey sky. "Number seven, Annie."

Annie kissed her father's cheek.

"I was just telling Garrett here, I don't think I'll farm next spring."

Willis stood back, sulking. "Gonna be one of them gentleman farmers, huh? I reckon you can do that when you're growin' oil wells in your fields."

"Papa," Annie quickly cut in, "I got something to tell you. Let's go to the house." She linked her arm inside her father's. "It's moving, Papa. Your grandchild is moving. I felt it this morning."

"You did!" He hugged her ferociously. "Your mama's gonna want to know this. My baby doll's having a baby."

Annie sat at the kitchen table, her father leaned against the door, glowing as he looked at his daughter. A blue enameled coffee pot sputtered and spit on the ancient black cook stove. "This is a great day, and it's gonna to be a great day when I get to hold my first grandchild."

Willis hung on Annie's chair, but Sophie came around and hugged her daughter.

"I'll give you some of my birthday cake, Annie, if you let me feel it?" Eva Mae bargained, then giggled when she felt it.

"Well," Willis began awkwardly, "we knowed you'd want to hear about it."

Annie took her cake and followed her mother into the dining room and sat down.

A square white box rested on the dining room table. "What's this?" Annabelle asked.

"Boots." Eva Mae opened the box and handed her one. "Papa brought them from town yesterday—for my birthday," she said.

Annie pushed the cake aside. She turned the boot over, studying every detail, the tiny heels and white fur at the top. "They're pretty, Evie." Hurtful tears burned behind her eyes. I can't cry, she thought. I mustn't cry. "Real pretty," she felt like a spoiled child, jealous of a pair of boots.

"Are you sick, Annie?" Eva Mae asked.

"No-o" She still held the boot. Something tightened in her chest. She felt she was suffocating. Eva Mae knelt down in front of her, looking at her. How could Evie understand, she had been a baby then. "I know it was a different time. I know..." It made her feel cheap to resent these silly white boots, but something in her just couldn't meekly accept it.

The clock ticked in the silent room and then struck nine.

"The first day I went to school, Evie, I didn't have shoes. I wore Glenn's old shoes." Annie twisted the handkerchief in her hand. "You should have heard them laugh at me because I was wearing boy's shoes. I ran off. I couldn't go home; what could Mama and Papa do?" Annie averted her eyes. She had been too ashamed to tell her parents. "The next day, I hid Glenn's shoes in a log and went barefoot. The girls were waiting for me. 'You wearing boys' shoes, again?' They called to me. I didn't answer them."

"'She's barefoot,' one of the boys called out. 'Hey Annie, you got on matchin' panties, too?'

"I walked right past 'em all, inside to my desk, and sat on my feet all day. I kept doing that 'til it got cold and I had to wear Glenn's shoes."

Annie got up and put her arm around Willis. "Willis was the one who told 'em to stop tormenting me."

"What's any old pair of shoes, pretty boots or boys' shoes compared with a real live baby?" Eva Mae was always bored with family stories that happened before she could remember.

"Annie," John Malvern stood before her, his face stern. "You're a woman now, a wife, soon to be a mother. It's time to look to the future. Forget those sad days. You're to be woman enough make a home for your family, no matter where, even if it's under a tree, and lead your family. I can't put fine things in your childhood memories, it's too late. That's just the fact of it."

"I came here to tell you my big news," Annabelle burst out, "the best day of my life when my baby showed me it was going to be a real living child and..."

"I'll buy you boots like Eva Mae's." There was disgust in Malvern's voice. "I'll buy you whatever you want."

"No, you won't," Willis flared. "She's my wife. You'll not be lordin' it over the Porters with your oil money and what you can do with it. I'll get Annie whatever she needs."

"Oh, Willis." Annie took his arm. "Let's go—go tell your family."

Malvern stood immoveable as the oak in his front yard, his eyes steady on his daughter. "I did not raise a whiner, Annie."

"It's not boots." Annie looked about the rooms, so familiar, where she had played and grown up, but now seemed so strangely changed. It's not exactly any *thing*, it's something different. It's ..." She sensed a new energy, and excitement in this her childhood home, but she was not part of it. They had not wanted her to marry Willis Porter. She knew that. Were they ashamed of her now? She felt left behind. Her eyes met her father's. "I was not raised to be a second best child in this family, either. If you want to see me, you'll have to come to *my* house."

Willis held the door for his wife. "Yeah, she might feel like whinin' if she comes over here."

"Annie," Eva Mae followed them to the car. "I don't mean harm to you – getting things," There was smugness as she tossed back a lock of dark hair. "But I didn't cause your childhood to be poor, so I'm not gonna carry guilt about it."

Annie glared at her through tears then turned away as the car moved out of the drive.

She was still shaken as they turned down Maxwell Porter's lane.

Porter came around the house and met them at the car window. A week's growth of whiskers sprouted on his chiseled face, the bill of a blue and white striped cap pulled over his eyes, his eyes constantly darted about, Annie thought, like a cornered rat.

"Git out. Come on in. Warm up."

"Can't stay, Pa but we got some news to tell you," Willis said.

"Old lady's not here, but come in. It's damned chilly today."

Willis bailed out of the car and Annie followed. "This little critter in Annie's belly's been movin' around," he said.

"Well, I'll be, let me feel." Maxwell Porter started to run his hand over Annie's protruding abdomen. She drew back, at the touch   of   his   hand   on   her.

"You been cryin', girl!"

Willis put his arm about Annie's shoulders. "Oh, well, Pa, the Malverns are gettin' kinda the big head. It's like they're wantin' to ferget Annie 'cause she's a Porter now."

"It wasn't like that, Willis. It was..." Annie stared at her husband, protesting.

"Looked that way to me."

"No, Willis," she said.

Maxwell put his hand on Annie's stomach again. "This here's a Porter. Malvern ain't gettin' this."

"It's a Malvern, too," Annie flashed.

"But they're pushin' you out, Annie girl," Porter patted her on the shoulder. We're proud to have you--and this here little package, too. We'll just make you a Porter all the way."

"No, it's not like that—I mean, it's not like they turned me out or," she was gasping in the cold air, "it's just that things are changin' so fast for them... we were so poor when I was a little... my papa didn't mean..." She dropped down in the seat of the car. Everything seemed to be happening outside of her, other people putting her in *their* place, for *their* plans. It had started out to be a special day and now she felt lost, like she was cut away from everything solid and certain.

Maxwell took his cap off, ran fingers through his grizzled hair and readjusted the cap on his head. "John Malvern always did have the bigitis." Porter looked across his winter-dead field, his eyes hard. "Just never had nothin' to back it up, till now."

Annabelle felt sick. "I think I want to go home."

After they drove away, Willis pulled the car off on the frozen shoulder and took her in his arms. "Annie, I won't never let you be sorry you married Willis Porter. I promise you, and I'll make sure that John Malvern sees that."

"But, Willis, honey, no one except the Patrick brothers has more wells than Papa. Our old farm looks like it's sprouting derricks."

CHAPTER 10

Malvern drove past his seven oil wells, out into the woods on the back of his property, looking for just the right tree. He spied one, got out, sawed down a small cedar for a Christmas tree and loaded it in his truck. It would fill the front corner of the living room, he thought. Even as he did it, one thought filled his mind, Joey's face when he wheeled out that bike. This would be a Christmas like no other, the best ever, that is, if Annie came back. His whole family had always gathered around the table for Christmas, him at the head and Sophie at the opposite end.

It was clear and cold on Christmas day, the kitchen window covered with frost except for a small patch in the center and the house smelled of roasting turkey, raisin pie and hot cider. He waited by the kitchen window as he sipped hot cider, looking for Willis to drive in with Annie. Maybe, he comforted himself, they had gone to Maxwell Porter's for dinner and forgot to tell him.

Malvern looked up at the clock as it struck twelve but said nothing.

Sophie noticed John looking to the clock as she brought in the turkey and placed it in the center of the table. There were two vacant places where Sophie had set the table for Annie and Willis. Maybe they would still come, all be together—like always. She returned to the kitchen and looked through the small space in the window not covered by frost and prayed they would drive in. She'd take her time, she decided, putting the separate dishes on the table, giving them time, laugh when they came bounding in, making excuses for being late, then everything would be alright again. She carried in the cut glass dish with sweet potatoes and set it before Glenn, his favorite. She made sure they all had full water glasses, and she thought once again that her children were like two halves of a whole. Glenn, quiet and bashful and Joey, mild and pleasant as a summer breeze. But then there was the other two, Eva Mae with her quick tart words. She'd spoken to her often about her sharp tongue. "Child, have a caution with them words," she had told her. "For you, to think it, is to say it and words can be hurtful." But there was more to it than that with Evie. She had a self-serving way of making everything turn to her own advantage.

Sophie brought in the corn casserole Kurt favored. Kurt. When she looked at her handsome son, her heart simply melted with pride, like a restless bridled colt he was, like she'd seen sometimes in their corral, impatient and quick-witted. But he had a temper, too, ready to boil to the top in an instant. The blue shirt he wore made his corn silk light hair look all the brighter. She'd smiled at the division of her brood. But she had once held all of them as babes at her breast. They were all hers and John's.

In the kitchen, Sophie stopped again at the window hot tears smarting in her eyes; she hoped God would forgive her. You can't help who you love the best. "Annie, please don't break my heart," she whispered. But Sophie knew, as she reached for the silver dish of pickle relish, it was not her husband's way to recant from his position and apologize; and that Annie had had reason for resentment. What was once amusing differences in her family; now was a wall formed by a wound from hot bitter words. It was the oil. She knew Annie would not come.

Finally Malvern decided they were not coming and so he put them out of his mind.

"Sit down, Sophie," he said, "it's time to have grace."

Through the meal, with singleness of thought, Malvern waited on his surprise for Joey. He had planned it out. He would give Sophie her pins, and then when Joey had finished his dessert, he would bring the bicycle out.

Sophie hovered about the table, filling coffee cups and water glasses. Kurt fiddled with his food and stared out the window at the dead remnants of Sophie's summer garden.

"You didn't eat much, son. Is everything all right?"

"Good meal, Mama. Always is." There was impatience in Kurt's voice, Malvern noticed and thought that the boy would like to be somewhere else.

"I don't know." Sophie came back with the coffee pot. "The chocolate cake didn't turn out so well this time."

"You never can take a compliment, Mama." Kurt said. "The cake is fine."

Malvern reached behind his chair, into a drawer of the breakfront. "Here's something she'll have to take." He laid the two pins before her.

Sophie looked at the pins as if they were a couple of strange little bugs she had stumbled upon. "What's this?"

"They're for you, Sophie." Malvern pushed the plate aside so they lay before her on the white tablecloth.

"What for?" She still looked at them curiously.

"To wear, Mama." Eva Mae picked up the dragonfly and Sophie took up the other.

Sophie shoved back a graying blonde lock from her forehead as she leaned over to study the pin, then looked at her husband, puzzled. "What in heaven's name possessed you, John, to put out money for the likes of this?" Malvern laughed as she turned them over in her hand.

Kurt got up and hugged his mother. Sophie had cooked all morning and still wore her apron. "Let me pin one on for you."

"What am I gonna do with fancy pins?" She looked up at Kurt as he put the pearl pin at the throat of her dress.

Kurt kissed his mother on the cheek. "You deserve it. You're the goodest person I know."

Sophie picked up the dragonfly pin, turned it in her hand. "I think I might be partial to this one."

Malvern could hardly wait for Kurt to sit back down and this pin business to be over.

"Now then, Joey," Malvern stood up, an expansive feeling lifting him. "I see you're about done with that pie. I want you to stand right over here." He pointed to a spot in front of the tall clock. "And keep them eyes closed."

Joey looked up surprised, as if they thought he was more interested in dessert than his mother's gifts. "I like Mama's pins."

Eva Mae glared down at her brother. "Just stand over there like Papa said."

Finally Malvern wheeled the bicycle in and stood it before Joey. "Open your eyes, son."

The boy was silent, all eyes on him. He seemed unsure it was his, or what to say.

"It's yours, boy. Yours." Malvern stood back. There had never been presents at Christmas before and now his heart was full for what he could give his family. It was a celebration for them of the new oil, he thought.

Joey moved cautiously to the bike, walked around it eyeing it carefully.

"Well, if he's just gonna to keep circling it..." Eva Mae spoke up impatiently.

Joey worked his mouth, his tongue pushing his cheek out to one side. He looked about at all of them, a smile wanting to burst through. Slowly he reached for the handlebars.

Malvern picked up the bicycle. "Let's take 'er outside, son. Let you get used to ridin' it."

Eva Mae bundled up and followed them. Sophie went to the front window to watch Joey struggle to control the wayward wheels, her hand at her throat nervously fingering her new broach.

Kurt sat with Glenn, not talking. He pushed away the crust of his pie and leaned back in his chair.

Finally Malvern came back. "You see that? The boy got the hang of it right away." They watched Joey riding a bit wobbly down the hard-packed, frozen road in front of the house.

Kurt got up. "That's a real nice thing you done for Joey. Something he's always gonna remember."

Glenn's eyes were averted. He twisted his fork in the pie.

Malvern turned back from the road and looked at Kurt. "What's the matter? Joey likes the bike."

"It ain't nothin', Pa." Glenn said. "You made a real fine day for Joey. That's all that counts."

"Sure I did. I aimed to." Malvern looked from one to the other of his older sons.

Kurt bumped the chair, and it clattered backwards. "No, Glenn, that's not all that counts. We got memories too, Pa. Like you bringin' home a rusty bicycle with no wheels. We remember you hangin' it up and sayin' you were gonna get wheels for it—but you never did." Glenn pulled at Kurt's sleeve, but Kurt ignored him. "No, Glenn, I'm gonna say it. I wanted a bike till I could taste it. We'd take that old thing down, Glenn and me, and try to make up something for wheels but we couldn't. We just couldn't do it. When we'd ask you, you'd always say, 'I'm gonna get you boys them wheels when I get the money. But you didn't."

Malvern turned full to face his two children. He guessed he hadn't thought about them when he bought the bicycle. "Well, I couldn't a done it for you. That's the sum of it," he said at last.

"You didn't have to lead us on." Kurt face was flushed. "Glenn, here, with his little boy ideas worked out a way to fix up some wheels with cardboard. He talked how it would ride with them wheels—worked on it for weeks. Course when he tried it, they crumbled, and he fell off. He just sat down against the garage and cried, Pa. I know grown men oughten to see it this way. We ought to see Joey having fun, and be glad for 'im, but Pa, we got some raw memories."

"You need to understand. It was ..."

"It was the promise that was the lie, Pa. You kept it hangin' up there like you was gonna do it, but you never did." Kurt's eyes flashed as he looked across the table to his father. "I used to hate you because you even brought it around. Like taunting us. Make us wish for something we couldn't have." He picked up the chair and slammed it down. "I'm goin' to town. I've been thinking about movin' out. It's about time."

He looked down, softened. Sophie was crying. "Thanks, Mama, for the meal."

Glenn said nothing. He followed Kurt but headed for the barn, alone, which was his way.

Malvern dropped in the chair saved for Annie. She'd have memories, he knew, like Kurt and Glenn. He couldn't buy back the time, to make Kurt and Glenn and Annie's young years full of treasures like new bicycles. Why couldn't they see that? Why didn't they understand? The oil made things different. He looked out the front window. Only Joey and Eva Mae were having fun. He turned his attention to them and went outside.

Later, Malvern went down to the new oil well, the one in the woods of the fifty acres. This one had been the sixth. He stood for a while, watching the drill going up and down. Then he walked away from the well, plodding through dried underbrush, and sat on a fallen log. If he leaned to one side and looked through the trees, he could see his first well pumping.

He had planned this to be the best Christmas. His family was his life, and now a grandchild was coming, but there was this heavy feeling, like dread, that came over him. Life seemed to be moving too fast for him and he couldn't stop it or understand it. Malvern sauntered back toward the house. Joey was helping Eva Mae ride the bicycle. Kurt's truck was gone. Annie and Willis had not come. As he neared the garage, Glenn carried out the old bike with no wheels.

"I reckon we kinda outgrew this dream, Pa. I'm givin' it to you to take back to where you got it."

John Malvern took the bike from his taciturn son and held it dumbly. He felt sick inside. He had never known Glenn to say a sharp word.

CHAPTER 11

The next day Malvern met Claude Briscoe out by the big silver mailbox. Another royalty check had come. Malvern sat down on the back step and opened the envelope. Three thousand, seventy two dollars, and forty-six cents. More than he made in eight years of farming. He studied the figure, trying to get his mind around it. He paid seventy-eight dollars for seed last year. It cost him nearly ninety dollars to get his F-12 tractor fixed last spring. He wouldn't forget that for a while. It nearly cleaned him out. Sophie got three dollars and fifty-four cents for eggs last Saturday when she took them to town and bought that turkey for Christmas. But three thousand seventy-two dollars and forty-six cents. What would he do with it? It created a vast landscape before him, one he didn't know. There was something else hid in that figure, too. What he saw in Kurt's face yesterday disturbed him. Sometimes trouble comes between children, he thought. He'd seen it happen. Malvern slipped the check inside his red mackinaw and studied on the situation. An idea came to him. He smiled as it began to take shape. Malvern took the envelope out again and looked at the check. He could buy each of the children twenty acres. Give 'em a stake. That would be just the thing. He rubbed the stubble just coming on his chin. Yes sir, that would be just the ticket. Twenty acres apiece. None of them would be left out. A great load melted

off him. He could do that with $3,072.46. He looked at the figure.
His mind began to encompass the amount.

Malvern went inside. The kitchen was warm and filled with
smells of cooking. A kettle of stew simmered on the stove and
Sophie had just pulled a loaf of cornbread from the oven. Boiling
coffee spit on the hot stove. He stood by the cabinet while Sophie
sliced leftover pie from Christmas, and he told her his plan. She
smiled and nodded as she set the table. After the meal Sophie
began putting the dishes away. He went out to the garage, backed
his truck out, and left it running to warm up for her. She slid in
beside him. They smiled at each other like teenagers with a secret.
She wore the dragonfly pin on her coat lapel. He'd seen that grey
coat a thousand times, but now it looked worn, the buttonholes
misshapen, and there was fraying on the edge of the lapel where
the pin rested.

It was three in the afternoon when John and Sophie left the
second of the two real estate offices in town, that of Elwood
Nellison. Malvern's plan to buy twenty acres for each of his
children had hit a snag. No one, Mr. Nellison said, was selling
land, even land so poor it had never been put to farming, on the
expectation that one of the drilling companies would come around
and want to lease it. So that was it! They'd heard the same story
both places.

They stepped from Mr. Nellison's office onto the sidewalk
and began an aimless stroll around the square, past the Roxy
Theater and Vivian's Ice Cream Shoppe. "I don't know nothin'
else to do, Sophie."

"We can keep looking, maybe somebody will want to sell."
She paused, glanced at her husband. "You can't change what was,
John. Kurt and Annie are grown, Glenn nearly, too. They're fixed
as people. After you bake a cake you can't go back and put eggs in
it. We've got the chance to help the other two comin' up. No
reason why not to."

Their breath fogged in the cold air as they crossed over to
the west side of the square. John tipped his hat to Jimmy Bob
Franklin standing inside the wide glass front of the Allis-Chalmers

Implement dealership. The town square around the courthouse had little traffic, just two days after Christmas. Clethis' Café, they noticed, was nearly empty.

"Bound to be somebody wants to sell land one of these days. Them kids know we didn't love 'em less just because we gave 'em less," Sophie soothed.

"Knowin' is not the same as feelin'."

They started to pass Allison's Department Store, then Malvern said, "Let's go in."

Sophie stared at her husband. "Why would you want to go in there?"

"We're just lookin' ."

There was a welcome warmth from the sharp air outside and a ring of a cash register in the back, but few people. He took Sophie's arm and led her through the shoe department and the lady's dresses to a section in the back where a couple of dozen coats hung on a rack.

"There, Sophie. Pick one out."

She stared at him as if he'd lost his mind. "I hadn't thought anything about buying a coat today."

He reached up and pulled one off the rack. "How about this one?"

"Mr. Malvern." A voice came from over his shoulder. He turned to face Clifton Allison, owner and operator of The Allison Department Store, as well as several other ventures in town. "Pleased to see you." Mr. Allison beamed on them. "Your wife looking for a coat?"

"Well, I thought maybe..." Malvern had never talked to Clifton Allison before, never really expected to, if he'd given it any thought.

Allison turned his radiance on Sophie. "If these don't appeal to you, I've got a new shipment in. Haven't been unpacked. You just sit right here." He pulled a chair forward. "I'll see if we can't get something special for you. Something right up to snuff, like you'd see the ladies wearing up there on the streets of Chicago."

Sophie sat down. "Well, land sakes, John. I don't know about this. I didn't think about buying a coat today."

Malvern looked up at the rack. The same thought came to him again. He could buy *all* them coats on the rack if he was a mind to. He smiled and looked across the store at the two dozen or so little counters with displays on top and below.

"I don't know that I ever saw Mr. Allison down here on the floor waiting on people," he whispered to Sophie. "Usually see him up there in that glass office." He had never seen people cater to his wife, either. It was a pleasant feeling.

Allison returned, with a clerk carrying an armload of coats. He helped Sophie slip into a maroon coat with an A line that flared out when she turned. Malvern watched her closely. He knew her frugal ways. Then he saw a little smile play on her lips.

Allison reached for a camel-colored coat with a brown velvet collar. "I want to see you in this one. This is a real beauty."

Sophie didn't say anything, but her eyes sparkled, and she seemed about to burst with excitement. Then, she looked at the price tag and sobered.

"I don't think this is what I want, Mr. Allison." She quickly slipped out of the coat.

"Well, of course, you know what you can do." He turned to Malvern. "I just wanted to give your lady a special showing."

"We'll take it. That one with the velvet collar. I see Sophie likes it," John said.

Allison beamed even more. "You'll be the most fashionable woman to show up at your club meeting."

"I don't belong to no clubs," Sophie said.

Malvern cleared his throat trying somehow to erase that remark. "There's another thing, Mr. Allison."

"Call me Clifton."

"Well... Clifton..." Malvern looked at Sophie. He knew that frown.

"John, I really think this coat is a Lord's plenty for now," Sophie protested.

He nodded to Allison as if the two men understood each

other. "We'll just take the coat."

"I hear there's a lot of oil activity out your way," Clifton Allison said as he totaled up the amount. Allison wrapped the coat in sheets of brown paper he ripped off a roll and tied them with twine. He clasped Malvern's shoulder as he handed the package to him. "I'd like it, John, if you came into our Men's Prayer Breakfast at the Presbyterian Church. Be my guest. It'll be the 12th of January. We meet at seven in the morning."

Malvern stared at him. Clifton Allison looked sincere. Malvern didn't know what to say. He'd never held with joining town things.

"I'd be honored to have you...I could introduce you around." Allison smiled.

Malvern decided it wouldn't be best to sound too eager. "I'll have to give it some thought."

They got in the truck and started home. "I never knew Clifton Allison to wait on people hisself." Malvern savored the idea.

"I'm sure sorry we can't buy the land for the children now. That was a fine idea, John."

"And he wants me to come to the Men's Prayer Breakfast." Steam began to creep up on the windshield. "Clifton Allison!"

Malvern's mind was alive with a new energy; wide vistas opening in his imagination. He'd sit down among the merchants of the town, the banker, lawyers, doctors—people he'd always known, yet didn't know.

Sophie clutched her brown package. "We never went to town church, John. We go to Bethlehem Church. I do my quilting there and have for twenty years. Why would you think of going in there with that Allison man?"

They topped the overhead that led out of town, a train rattling along below them on the Baltimore & Ohio tracks. At the bottom of the rise on the left was his sister Belle's Kozy Kottage Beauty Shop and across the highway, Dutch's Truck Stop, with its sign blinking night and day, a horde of oil trucks in the parking lot.

Beyond that, farms stretched in the distance, land now covered with dried winter stubble and little patches of snow against old furrows. But John Malvern wasn't thinking of land, anybody's land. Nothing had ever made him feel the way Clifton Allison's invitation did. "A person of consequence," he remembered reading about someone, somewhere.

"Them Allisons make dollars where we make pennies, John," Sophie said.

"Not anymore," he answered.

CHAPTER 12

The first thing Willis Porter saw when he got to the top of the stairs over The Blue Moon was seven tables of cards in serious use, and plenty of action on the slots against the wall. The noise was horrendous. It went through his mind what his father had said, "Sittin' downstairs at the bar and sayin' there was no gambling in the county was like sittin' in a thunderstorm and swearing' it was a clear day." Cigar smoke burned his eyes. Slots pouring out coins almost drowned out laughter and shouting from the bar below. He tried the slots for a while, lost, then sauntered to a table and watched a poker game. The deal ended and one of the players got up. A player from another table slammed down his cards, walked away, yelling obscenities at a player who laughed as he raked in a pot.

"What's the game?" Willis asked a grey-haired man he had been watching.

"Draw poker." Grey Top didn't look up. "You gonna sit in?"

"Yeah, sure." Willis slid into an empty chair, "Used to watch my dad play."

"A kibitzer," another player mocked.

"You got money?" Grey Top was a man about fifty, thick-set. Willis admired the way he handled himself with the cards.

"Sure, I got...let's see." Willis dug in his pocket and pulled out a wrinkled bill. "I got twenty bucks." Somewhere behind him a slot dropped a handful of coins.

One of the players glanced at the other, scratched the back of his neck. "Lay out your twenty, son."

Willis knew everybody around town, and these men were not locals. They didn't have the grime on their knuckles and under their fingernails of the oil workers, either. He put his twenty on the table. Chips were provided, and he stacked them before him.

"Now, son, it's played like this..." Grey Top spoke with the seasoned authority of a grandfather.

"Maybe if we just play around once 'til you get the idea." The other player winked at Willis and tossed out three chips. "Everything's possible in the game," he said. "Name's Lee." He shuffled the cards, cut and dealt five. Willis figured him to be in his late forties, twenty years older than himself. A cut across his left eyebrow kept hair from growing in that spot. His dark curly hair was oiled back over his skull where curls fell low on his neck.

Willis was dealt three nines and two threes. The first bet was made and Willis called. The other players took three cards. Willis took two and pulled a four and another nine. The second betting interval was made. Willis called without raising. They laid out what they had. Willis fumbled, a card stuck to his clammy fingers, but he got them down on the table.

"Maybe we don't need to help this kid," Lee laughed. "He might have the touch."

Grey Top nodded. "Could be."

They dealt the cards again, this time for money and the attitude got serious. Willis had an ace, nine and seven of hearts, a duce of spades and a three of clubs. Bets were made. Willis requested two cards. So did the others. After a long pause Grey Top raised. The other two folded. Willis stayed in and got two more hearts. He called Grey Top who then slowly turned his cards over one at a time announcing, "a straight."

Willis laid his over all at once and looked at Lee who had folded. "That's a flush?" Willis looked for a response

Lee nodded approval. "That wins over a straight."

Grey Top frowned and muttered something about 'beginners' luck'.

Willis smiled as he raked in the chips. He felt giddy. He began to count his earnings. When he looked up the others were watching him. His face was hot with embarrassment.

Willis did his best at shuffling, but felt he needed practice. Then he dealt the round. All four were in. Willis pinched out the cards he had in his hand. Three fives and two aces. He raised and counted out eight more chips and tried to push them over with the same indifference Lee did. Grey Top and the other player folded. It was Lee and Willis. Willis laid down his cards. Three fives and two aces, to Lee's two pairs. He raked in the pot.

Willis threw out his ante and another game began.

Grey Top and Lee kept lining up their cards. Lee looked sour. The third player said, "Where'd you dudes pick up this one? Just because he's some hick don't mean he can't have the gift."

"Why don't you shut up," Lee grouched and frowned at his cards.

"You can find a natural anywhere," the player persisted.

"Gift?" Willis spoke up eagerly, "Whadda he mean, 'gift?'"

"He didn't mean nothin`." Lee studied his hand, scowled.

"It means nobody's gonna want to play with you because you always take 'em." Grey Top answered.

"I'm not out to take nobody," Willis said.

"That don't make no difference. It's that some people are naturals," Lee explained. "Out there in Nevada, there's these gamblers that the casinos won't even let come in the door because they'd break 'em."

"They got the gift!" Grey Top parsed out resentful words from thin tight lips.

Willis sat back in his chair. He felt like somebody punched him in the stomach. This was some stunning revelation to take in.

"You fellas willing to have another go around with me?" Willis felt almost apologetic.

"I'll stay in tonight." Grey Top nodded his head. "I ain't

sure about sitting down with you after this."

Willis was beginning to like this game. He looked about the room, saw the intense concentration of players at other tables. He guessed he was like them. Only better. He turned his attention back to his own table. "Yeah, deal them cards." He rubbed his hands together. "What the hell, it's your money I'm playin' with."

They tossed in their ante. "It not personal, lad," Lee began to deal the cards, "but that don't mean I'm gonna lay out my money for you after this."

The third player picked up his cards, squeezed them out into a fan, took two cards and folded. "That's all I'm in for. I didn't bargain on this guy."

They played a round and Willis won the pot a third time.

He looked at the others. There wasn't much joy at the table.

"Look fellas, I just come in here for a drink and stumbled upstairs...I didn't intend no harm."

"Tell you what," Lee leaned forward a few inches from Willis' face. He spoke low. The eyebrow with the slash arched. "You lighten up a little on us right now and we'll keep quiet about what you got." Lee's eyes veiled, he leaned closer, looked about to see who might be listening and dropped his voice lower. "With all this oil money floating around, and the workers looking for a little action, you could be in here every night lining your pockets, and they'd not even notice. I been at this game a while. You're a good kid, I can see that. I like you, but you're too good. Tell you what to do. You move around, table to table—not often with the same guys, then don't show up sometimes—all so's they don't pick up on what you got." Lee leaned back in his chair and clasped Willis' shoulder. "I always like to see an expert in action."

"Well, sure, I'll lighten up, but I don't know just how..."

"Just deal the cards, and we'll see if you want to play fair with us or not." Grey Top muttered.

Up and down all evening on his winnings. Willis noticed he never had to get back into his own twenty dollars. In fact, he tripled his earnings. He felt better. He felt a lot better. His future had been saved and that future looked mighty damned good.

He stood up after playing for three hours. "I wanna buy you guys drinks."

"That's about the least you can do, son." Grey Top finally loosened up a bit, "I gotta say you're one hellava poker player."

Gladness swelled in Willis and the compliment melted down through him, warming him like whiskey. And Pa didn't think he was much good at anything! And what would John Malvern have to say when he got wind of this.

Sharp night air hit Willis' face when he walked out of the Blue Moon. Snow was falling. He resolved he would never take advantage of anyone just because he had the gift. He'd try to be fair. But hell, it's cards. You gotta win if you can. He shook his head and smiled. Wait 'til he told Annie what he had. The blinking red sign of the tavern made a rosy tint on snow building on the sidewalk. The Blue Moon was warm, so he ambled back in. The world, Willis felt as he opened the door, was literally at his fingertips.

CHAPTER 13

Annie woke slowly from a nap. The house was cold. Her toes curled against the bare wooden floor. She pulled back curtains from her bedroom window. It was snowing! She looked through the three small rooms, the shotgun house they called it. You could shoot a gun through the front door to a target out the back door. Where was Willis? He hadn't come home all day. She opened the door to the heating stove. A few feeble embers lay in the back. She started to the porch for wood and switched on the light. No lights! The sky was gray when she stepped outside, snow flying, dusting the ground. Willis had not chopped wood. Where was he? The old car was still in the drive, but the truck was gone.

Shivering, she lit a candle, pulled a blanket off the bed, and wrapped it around her thick body. It's going to get colder, she thought. Why were there no lights? Maybe she should go to the Patrick brothers. They'd have fire in the cooking stove.

She slipped her coat off a hook by the back door, the button almost refusing to meet over her new belly.

Annie turned into the drive of the old Parson place where the brothers lived. She drove down their long lane, past a dozen oil pumps and two lighted derricks in the distance, standing tall and bright in the grey wintery twilight. She parked alongside the house, went up and knocked on the back door. The brothers lived in the back room of a three-story decaying mansion that had belonged to a Civil War general. In winter, they closed all but the one big room in the back, the kitchen, and put cots in the corner on each side of an ancient black cook stove.

She pounded on the door a second time. They would have finished chores, she thought. She knocked again. They were shy. It was well known that when someone drove by their place or even turned in their drive, they ducked quickly behind trees, and watched until the car was out of sight. She had been taking their eggs and cream to town to sell for them. Even so, they would not come out from behind their tree until she got out of the car. They had never invited her in the house.

The door opened a few inches. A slice of Otis's wide plump cheeks showed. "You comin' in?"

She leaned into the narrow opening. "Do you have a fire?"

Hesitant, he finally said. "We got heat."

He let her in. A single light cord hung over the table with a naked bulb at the end. Still there was a lamp on the table that splashed light over a worn green oilcloth. Behind the stove, was a wood box and by the back door a water bucket with a dipper and a strainer. "To strain out the flies and germs..." Otis explained brightly. He was no taller than she, round and thick in the middle as a plump roasted turkey.

"We got coffee on." Henry was even rounder than his brother and no taller. His eyes slid timidly down where a protruding coat button was pulled over Annie's stomach. "Can you drink coffee... like that?"

"Sure." She tossed her coat across the back of a rocker.

As night came on, the storm grew worse. Snow piled against the ledge of the kitchen window. Annie looked out the window into the dark and began to worry about Willis. A wooden phone on the wall rang out, two shorts and a long. Henry picked up the receiver and listened. He put his hand over the mouthpiece, which meant the call was not for him. "Power lines is down," he whispered. "May last a couple, three days. Phone lines may go, too." Henry replaced the receiver.

Otis rubbed his hand over his mouth. "Well, I knowed somethin' was wrong." He handed Annie a cup of coffee. "You just sit right there, and I'll whip us up some ham and fried potatoes."

"No-no, I'm fine. I'll make the dinner. You don't need to fuss over me." But the coffee did feel good going down.

"Otis'll make up a good meal." Henry hitched up a strap of his overalls. "Your feet warm?"

"I'm fine...It's just Willis I'm..."

"There's a draft that sometimes comes in from those forward rooms." Henry didn't seem to want to talk about Willis.

"You've got plenty of rooms here?" Annie asked.

"Nine. Some way up there." Henry waved his hand and looked up.

"I don't want to put you out, but if you've some room I could stay in..." She searched from one to the other.

The brothers looked at each other. A woman in the house! At night.

Otis stood, an apron tied around his girth. "Well, I don't know." He looked at his brother.

Henry walked to the window, peered into the snowy darkness, then turned and looked at Annie's thick body. "No. You mustn't go out."

"That's right," Otis echoed. "That's what I thought."

"What we'll do is just open up that bedroom under the stairs. It's close, and there's a little stove in there." Henry decided.

Otis nodded. "We can do that."

"Where's your husband?" Henry's indignation finally burst past his bashfulness.

"I don't know." Annie wrapped a hand around her coffee cup and raked fingers through her loose hair. "Willis talks a lot about that gambling room over the Blue Moon. I think it fascinates him."

"My," Otis stood, spatula in hand, turning the fried potatoes. "I heard about that room. Sure won't go in there, let them get at my money."

The brothers were silent for a moment. "The oil people came in and," Henry shook his head, "the likes of what they brung with 'em, I can't believe."

Otis scooped out potatoes from an iron skillet into a dish and forked out three pieces of ham onto a platter. "I've said that all along."

After dinner, Annie made hot chocolate and they drank it as they sat by the stove. The wind was rising outside. The clock ticked in the quiet room. They talked about how good the chocolate tasted.

"The baby's due in March." Annie broke the silence.

They nodded and smiled slightly. Henry seemed embarrassed, and Otis looked away, as if something so intimate should not be mentioned.

"It's a healthy one. I feel it moving."

The brothers said nothing. Otis shuffled his feet and looked deep into his hot chocolate cup.

"Would you like to feel it? It's moving right now."

"No." They answered in unison.

Silence again, interrupted by the ticking clock and wind rattling the windows.

"I think I'll go to bed," she said. "I hope Willis doesn't try to come home on such a bad night."

Neither brother answered her.

Otis held the lamp high and opened the door to a hallway just outside the kitchen. It turned into a small bedroom by the stairs that led to upper stories. In the shadows of a big room to the right, she saw bales of hay stacked to the high ceiling.

In the bedroom, centered on a yard square sheet of tin, was a small stove. Otis opened the door, chucked it with wood pieces, kindling, poured on kerosene and tossed in a match.

"It'll warm up right quick in here. Best place for tonight— small room." Otis slammed the stove door closed. "This place is a drafty old thing. General Parsons built it. Looked to me like he had more money than sense."

"I guess he had sense!" Henry turned impatiently on his brother. "He run the headquarters for the trains that took food and soldiers to the camps down south during the war. Had to have sense to do that."

"Thank you, Otis." She took the lamp and placed it on a square table by her bed.

He stood awkwardly at the door, not knowing how to finish off his errand. "Well... good night."

Alone in the dim room, wind howling outside the window, she began to worry about Willis. Was he at home? She hoped he was not out on the roads looking for her. She was almost sure he was in town at the Blue Moon. Almost sure. Finally, fatigue overtook her anxiety.

In the night, she roused from deep sleep. Through drowsy eyes, she saw two round heads, a candle between them, standing in the doorway, peering into the dark room.

"She's sleeping," one whispered.

In a few minutes a short, fat figure came tiptoeing in and dropped a chunk of wood on the fire and tried to silently tiptoe out.

Annie turned in the cocoon of her covers, smiled and went back to sleep.

The house was quiet when pale morning light crept in the room. She looked about at the high ceiling, and faded wallpaper. The long window had been chinked with rags against the invading cold air. Cobwebs covered the window near the top. She got up, opened the little door to the small stove and stirred the embers, then put in a couple of pieces of kindling and a piece of wood to get the fire going again. She slipped back, sitting up under the comforter.

On the side table by the bed was a big book with a brown leather cover, raised scrollwork and letters that said, "Holy Bible." Annie opened it to the page headed Births, Deaths and Marriages. The first date entered was 1820. An Oscar Patrick. She ran her finger down until she found Otis's name and then Henry's on the line below it. Born two years apart. She did the math; Otis was eighty-three and Henry eighty-one. The names above, Andrew and Sarah, most certainly were their parents, and there was an older sister, too, Harriett. She was the only one of the brothers' siblings with a name under Marriages. There were two children listed for her. Below the brothers' names was another sister, Nora and two brothers, Jacob and Ezra. None married. Then she read the death dates, written by a shaky hand, she noticed. "Mother died November 21, 1918." Eight days later, "November 29th father died." Nora died December 10. The next death came December 19, 1918 for Ezra, and Jacob's death followed seven days later.

All 1918. It was the influenza epidemic! Twenty years ago. She had heard her parents talk of it. Kurt was a baby, then, and they had been afraid.

Annie sat up on the edge of the bed and took the Bible on her lap. She ran her fingers over the dates. The sickness had come into the Patrick family and taken away five people in six weeks. Otis and Henry were left, and the older sister who had married and moved away.

Annie closed the book. The crackling fire was warming the room. She thought of the brothers, little boys born two years apart and together now for eighty years, hurt deeply by the sickness that had carried away most of their family. She began to understand them. They wanted to live in a small tight space and let no one in; and never let something come in and take away what they loved. Of a sudden, she wanted to gather them to her, protect them, like the life growing inside her. She crawled back under the load of quilts they had provided and sunk deep into their featherbed. It felt lonely in bed without Willis to turn to. Wherever he was she hoped he was safe and warm too. She balled herself up, her arm across her rounding belly, and felt again the feathery movement.

The towering lights outlining two distant derricks showed through the mist of gray dawn. The oil companies had electricity, their own power. Nothing stops the drilling, she thought. The little pot-bellied stove was warming the room.

When she heard noises in the kitchen she got up, and dressed to join the brothers. The storm was gone and the world outside was wrapped in snow. Only oil pumps and derricks marred the unending white serenity.

It was a dark morning when Annie came into the kitchen; a kerosene lamp glowing in the middle of the table. Otis was frying bacon and freshly brewed coffee waited on the back burner of the stove by a pan of hot biscuits.

The telephone rang. They looked expectantly to each other and waited to see if it was their ring. "Johnson's," Otis said. It rang again, two longs and a short. Henry got up, carefully lifted the receiver, covered the mouthpiece with his hand and listened. Finally, he placed the receiver back in the cradle. "There's no lights over most of the town," he told them, "and some out in the country lost their power, too."

"I'm so worried about Willis." Annie said. "Maybe he came home and he's looking for me or…"

"You shouldn't drive out on the road until the oil trucks open 'em up," Henry answered quickly.

At mid-morning, Otis and Henry went to a radio sitting on a great square battery. Otis turned it on and they both moved chairs nearby and sat listening. The farm report came on at 8 a.m. followed by the news. Hitler had addressed his generals in Nuremburg.

She made lunch and afterwards both brothers settled down on their cots for a nap. Otis lay snoring, his hands folded over his middle, and Henry with a blanket pulled up to his chin.

She quietly opened the door into what Otis called the "forward rooms", looked in, and then closed the door behind her. Probably this was once the parlor, she thought. Along one wall the brothers had laid out pumpkins and onions, and a long hog trough was filled with potatoes. On shelves along another wall, were bright glass jars of canned raspberry jelly, peaches, blackberries, green beans and tomatoes. Near the front door a long cordon of wood stretched along the wall, and in the center of the room were bales of hay stacked nearly to the fourteen-foot ceiling. Across the hall was another enormous room. That ceiling boasted a prouder past, with molded plaster designs that radiated from a central hanging gaslight, now dripping with gauzy cobwebs. The bright squares in the wallpaper seemed like ghosts where once beautiful, important pictures had probably hung. Only one piece of furniture stood in the room, an oak breakfront near the hall. There were stacks of papers, brooms worn beyond use, empty boxes and a corn sheller.

Outside the front entrance, a porch stretched before the dining room and curved around the parlor to face the drive and what she imagined was once a carriage house but now held the tractor. Spindles that had formed an intricate fan design on the front posts were rotting and crumbling away. One section of the porch had caved in.

Annie shivered in the cold as she wandered up the stairs, steps covered with worn carpet, nailed along the edges. Each step creaked and the whole house smelled old. Musty. Worn out. She turned on the first landing and looked down. The baby moved and maybe it was that, that made her feel the vibrant presence that once filled these rooms. Maybe children had chased through the rooms and pounded up these very steps, laughing and teasing. She went on to the cavernous rooms on the second floor. One room had only a bag of nuts in the corner, and an iron bedstead in it. Had the sweet whispers of love been heard on that bed? Had lullabies been sung by that fireplace? She sat down on the straw tick that covered the bed. Tears burned her eyes.

For the first time she questioned her own judgment about Willis. He was gone so much. She had been told not to marry him. He was his father's son, they had said, but she had defended him. Willis was Willis. She couldn't have married any other; she'd loved him since she was a child. But already she was beginning to sense there was something taking him away from her. She had known in her heart of hearts Willis had spent the night in the room over the Blue Moon. He talked about it constantly. The baby moved again, and she shook away her doubts. They were soon to be a family.

Annie climbed to the two large dormer rooms on the third floor. There was a bed shoved against the wall in the south room and an old trunk under a window. In all the upstairs rooms, wide plank floors were covered with woven strips of carpet nailed at each seam. She felt the crunch of thin straw matting under her feet. Peering down from the high window, it looked as if some giant hand had sprinkled black dots across the white landscape, where oil pumps continued their rocking motion. Annie slipped back down stairs and found the brothers awake.

"Have you heard anything from Willis?" She asked, but they looked away and said nothing. She doubted they approved of gambling.

"I walked around in those front rooms," she finally said in the awkward silence. "You don't have lights in there."

Henry yawned and rubbed at his eyes, trying to shake off his nap. "One day the Rural Electrification Company come around here, tried to get us to have the whole house wired. We just told 'em, it wasn't necessary."

"No, I told 'em that, Henry." Otis spoke up. "I said we don't need to electrify this whole big place." He looked at Annie, as if she would understand. "People always figgerin' some way to get your money."

Annie looked through the kitchen window. Three pumps were rocking slowly up and down. "You could electrify the whole neighborhood, Otis," she said.

They were silent for a moment, and then Otis took out a red handkerchief and blew his nose.

"We don't use none of those forward rooms," Henry finally answered.

"Well, Henry, we do store things in 'em in winter." Otis shoved the handkerchief in his hip pocket.

Annie nodded and decided this was a subject not to pursue further.

CHAPTER 14

The same day Annie went to the Patrick brothers' house and spent the night, Belle Dorsett went to St. Louis. In mid-afternoon she left the city, but now three hours later, snow swirled around her windshield, early darkness coming on. And it was getting cold. The newer model cars had heaters, but she hadn't felt she could afford one yet. She should be getting near Amsley but she couldn't tell. She strained over the steering wheel to see the edge of the road but there was only a wide white blanket before her. She fought to keep the car to the left, hoping to stay on the road, but it was slick. She hit a strip of ice under the snow. The car skidded. She pulled the wheel to the right. The car twisted sideways in the road. She stepped on the gas, turning the wheel frantically left. The car flew forward off the road into a ditch and came to rest on its side.

She tried to open her door, push it up, and get out. The car was tilted into the ditch and she couldn't raise the door. She looked at the other door. It was pressed against the ground. She turned off the ignition. Someone will be along. Still she kept trying to push against the door with her shoulder and arm. It wouldn't budge. She stopped and waited. Be patient, keep calm.

There seemed to be no traffic on the road. Belle looked through the snow building against the ledge of the windshield, into the darkness and pushed again on the door. She tried to open the the window but it was jammed. The interspaces of the car felt small, tight. She looked again in the rear-view mirror. No lights on the road. None anywhere, she realized – not even houses along the road. Belle tried to sit up in the slanted seat but slid to the passenger side. Where was she, anyway? Everything was white as far as she could see in the darkness. With no lights to identify, she wasn't sure. It was getting cold. Really cold. Her feet and hands were numb, and her teeth chattered. How long would she be here? She was getting scared.

She turned the ignition key and moved to step on the starter. Better not. She might flood the thing. Just wait. Then panicky, she pushed the handle down once again, and pounded hard against the door. The full reality of it came to her; she was trapped in this machine. She twisted to look in the back seat. Was there something more to wrap around her? Nothing. It was filled with supplies for the beauty shop. The little space began to narrow in on her. She sat back, trying to settle herself. She'd been in fixes before. She would get out of this. She blinked heavy lids, pushing back drowsiness. Mustn't sleep. Someone would come along. There was always traffic on the highway. She felt calmer, even peaceful, a sweet lassitude stealing over her.

Beams of truck lights rounded the curve, lighting the white landscape. Headlight beams high. One of the oil trucks! She fought sleep. Her arm felt wooden. Her fingers found the horn. She honked and honked. The truck came to a stop behind her car.

Distant voices outside the window interrupted her drowsiness. "Gus, over here. Give me a hand..."

Nothing seemed so comfortable as to let go, drift off. She sensed they were trying to pry open the door.

They pulled her out and took her into the truck. "You okay?" the driver asked.

She nodded.

The truck was no warmer than the car. They pulled out a dirty blanket and wrapped around her, but she couldn't stop shaking and she was so sleepy. "How long you been in there?"

"I don't know." She was so cold. "Been on the road for..." She couldn't think how long.

"Might as well go out to the truck yard, electricity's off all over," the driver said. "We got auxiliary power and a stove in the shack."

He pulled up before the shack, helped her down the high step and rushed her inside. A glowing stove warmed the room and a pot of coffee sputtered on top. She found a chair as Gus poured her a cup. She wrapped her hands around it and life came back to her fingers.

Gus yanked off his gloves and held his hands, palms up, by the stove. "Where's the boss?" he asked the dispatcher.

"Out. Lookin' over the Johnson well. One's about to come in on the Patricks'."

"Just like a baby," Belle whispered, teeth still chattering. "When it's ready to come, it comes, even if there's a snowstorm in the middle of the night."

The men looked at her blankly. "Yeah, I reckon." The one they called Gus turned back to the dispatcher. "We're gonna need that truck. This one's due for the shop."

The door opened, snow breezed in and sizzled as it hit the hot stove. A man she recognized as Carson Garrett, was almost obscured in the haze of the storm.

"What happened to her?" He said as if she wasn't there.

"Found her out in a snow bank. Near froze to death."

Garrett looked at her for a moment, then silently poured whiskey in her coffee, and brought out his fur-lined leather jacket and wrapped it around her. He put a chair by the fire and helped her walk to it. Then he zipped up the jacket. It was large on her but soft and warm inside like a baby's blanket. She felt awkward, like she should apologize for troubling them.

"Did you feel sleepy before they got to you?" Garrett asked.

"At first I was angry with myself," she still shivered under the jacket, "for going off the road. Then, I realized I couldn't get out and...it was so cold, I couldn't think. I got drowsy."

Garrett looked at her briefly. "Let me feel your hands." He unzipped the jacket and massaged her hands, rubbing her fingers, rubbing his thumb over the knuckles. "You know electricity is off all over town." Then he held her hands clasped together, enclosed in his. "It would be off at your house."

He had a nice smile. "I have a coal-burning furnace," she said.

"But no lights and you're there alone in a dark house." Steady blue eyes met hers.

She started to point out that she had candles and lamps but instead she asked, "How did you know I was alone?" He had the beginnings of grey mixed in his hair. He again zipped her in the leather jacket.

"I believe it was Dutch's parrot that told me," he said in mock seriousness.

"Oh!" Warmth from the stove and coffee made her feel mellow.

"That parrot knows all about you. Knows you run the best beauty shop in town and he said you're the prettiest woman in town, too."

Fire of the whiskey had hit, coursing through her, warming her from inside. "The parrot said that?"

"And more."

They looked at each other and laughed.

"You stay put here until this storm passes and the electricity is on, and I'll take you back. We'll get a fire started in your furnace."

She settled into the furry shell of the jacket. It had been years since someone had taken care of her. She wasn't sure how she felt about it.

"We've got trucks out helping people to the school gym. Those big rigs with chains are good with this kind of thing, but I can't spare any more. There's a well just about to come in on Patricks'."

"What of the men working out in this?" Belle thought of how cold she had been in the car.

"It's rough work. It's hell climbing up on the top of one of those rigs in a biting storm, been there myself. Most of 'em wouldn't do anything else. They follow the oil strikes wherever. There's that rush when a well comes in...hard to explain. When have you eaten?"

"I guess ... this morning."

"I made soup yesterday. I'll warm it up. Keep your arms inside that jacket...keeps the warmth in." He fed her bite-by-bite and wiped her lips with a handkerchief.

She felt awkward being cared for as if she were helpless, but still it was nice.

The door opened, and a driver came in with a blast of snow and cold air. He pushed the door shut behind him. "You need to come, Mr. Garrett. They're needin' you out on the Patrick site."

Garrett nodded. "Keep close to that heat, Belle. I'll be back, We'll get your car out later." The door opened, and he was gone.

CHAPTER 15

Lillian Allison shuffled upstairs in her satin house slippers, stood by the bedroom door marked "Babe's Room," knocked, then reached for the knob. The door opened to sunshiny-yellow, flowered wallpaper, wicker furniture and crisp tie-back curtains, a space that seemed to belie the bleak winter day outside. The room was cluttered with dolls.

"Breakfast is ready, Coralee. Come on, baby."

Coralee sat on the edge of the bed and shoved her long hair back from her face, "Okay, Mama."

Downstairs, Lillian slid into the dining chair opposite her husband and poured herself coffee.

Malcolm opened his paper. "What was she doing? Arranging her dolls?" He shook his head then took a sip of coffee. "She lives up there in a make-believe world... sixteen years old! It's not normal."

"We are not going into that again, Malcolm. When she wants more, she'll show us."

He leaned forward and looked pointedly at his wife. "She'll never show you, Lillian. She wouldn't dare."

"Just eat your breakfast."

"You'd lose a piece of yourself, if that helpless little thing ever tried to grow up."

"Hush. I won't listen to this. I won't have it. Anyway, you're quite wrong. She's a fine young woman. That's what everyone says."

"Of course, they say that. You trot your toy child out to show off. What else are they going to say? It's wrong, Lillian, the way you hold that girl back."

"I protect her, Malcolm, she is not like other children. We know that."

"You don't protect her. You cripple her!" He looked over the top of his black-rimmed glasses. "She can learn things."

"Oh, Malcolm..." Lillian stared at her husband and turned away in disgust. There was no point in arguing with this arrogant old man. She thought again of all the things she wasn't getting in her marriage, no sex, no attention, no interest in what she did. She looked across at him and smiled in contempt, thinking how unimportant he had become. Kurt had made him unimportant. Kurt counted. Malcolm didn't know about Kurt. That secret counted, too. Malcolm was outside her sweet, delicious world with Kurt.

But Kurt. She had wandered the house in desperation for days after their argument. He could find younger women! But he wouldn't. He would come back. She was sure of it, but an aching doubt haunted her.

Lillian looked out the window. Some snow had melted, and the streets were clear now. Hunting season had opened, but the snowstorm kept Malcolm at home on the weekend. If Kurt had been across the lake in his truck last Saturday night, she couldn't have seen him.

Coralee appeared in the doorway. Her bare toes peeked from beneath a long flannel gown. The outline of full young breasts bulged through folds of cloth.

Lillian frowned. "It's cold, Coralee. Go upstairs and put on your slippers. You'll be sniffling."

Coralee shrugged. "I came when you called, Mama."

"Try remembering things, Cora, like that for yourself," Malcolm spoke gently to her. She turned and ran up the stairs.

Coralee came back and kissed her father on the cheek.

"Good morning, Daddy."

"I fixed your oatmeal, Coralee. Good for a cold morning. Do you have a kiss for Mommy?" Lillian held up her cheek. Coralee yawned, dropped into her chair, and tasted her oatmeal.

"So Coralee," Malcolm took up the newspaper but looked over it to his daughter. "What are you going to do today?"

"I don't know. Mama says I should clean my room."

"I've been thinking." Malcolm opened the paper to the business section, folded it into quarters, "about where you might get some kind of work, now that you're almost seventeen. Maybe you could do some filing in your Uncle Logan's office, answer the phone...pretty up the place."

"She is not working in that sheriff's office, Malcolm, around all those... people Logan brings in. You don't realize what you're saying. Besides," Lillian carefully spread butter on a piece of toast. "Coralee doesn't have to work. You know that."

"She should do something. It's good for people to have responsibility, Lillian. She can't go shopping with her friends. She doesn't have any. Or haven't you noticed?"

"She's just fine the way things are." Lillian snapped,

Coralee sat with an elbow on the table, chin in hand staring out the window. She hated it when they talked about her as if she weren't there with them, but she kept it to herself. What could she say? She asked to be excused and went up to her room. At the top of the stairs she heard them still talking about her.

"Children like Coralee can do a lot—if it's expected of them," her father said. "Simple things that need doing. But Lillian, you don't want anything for her. You want a pet baby for yourself."

"She's happy the way she is."

In her room, Coralee pulled the spread over her bed and puffed up two pillows, tossed them against a white wicker headboard, then sat a doll in the center of the bed. "There Susie, it's your turn, today, to be the special one." She spread Susie's crocheted dress out into a wide circle.

"Charlotte messed up everything," Coralee whispered to herself. She reached for the dolls and put Nancy with the red hair next to Doodad and Patty, and then pushed Rosa between them on the top shelf. At her cousin Charlotte's seventh birthday party last month, Coralee's mother had made her promise Charlotte a play day with the dolls. Charlotte's mother had dropped her off the morning before the snowstorm, then later called to say she would leave her because the roads were dangerous. Coralee had hated every minute with Charlotte.

Coralee found the arm of another doll protruding from under the bed ruffle and pulled it out. "Rosa." She straightened her dress. Coralee simply detested Charlotte. As soon as she came, Charlotte took down the dolls; and not just the ones on the long wicker seat, but also the ones on the shelves in the corner and in the closet. She didn't even know their names; didn't know who they were like Coralee knew.

She moved slowly trying to decide which one would sit in the rocker today.

"You, Mimi," she whispered. It was a game she played with herself remembering how she got each one and which one she would reward. "Mimi." She picked her up. "You were never Shirley to me, not ever, not after..." She placed the doll Mimi with the ragged hair, in the rocking chair.

CHAPTER 16

Coralee had been seven, the age of Charlotte when she got Mimi. Her best friend, Ima Jean, had come home from school with her. She and Ima Jean liked to sit on a dirt hill at the edge of the playground at school and slide down, giggling all the time. Ima Jean whispered secrets to her about other kids that made Coralee laugh. When they got home that day, her mother was gone and they had played along the beach of the lake, rolling down to the water's edge getting dirty and laughing. Then they went to her playhouse and set up the dolls in rows to play school.

Ima Jean had looked about the playhouse. "You're lucky. You got all these dolls and stuff. I've never had a doll." They played for a while then Ima Jean said she had to go. Coralee picked up a doll, drum and a stuffed cat and piled them in Ima Jean's arms.

Ima Jean's eyes sparkled.

"I've got lots of them." Coralee added another one.

Ima Jean was just leaving the yard when Lillian drove up. She slammed the car door.

"What is going on here?" she stared down at Ima Jean. "And who are you?"

"She's my friend, Mama...from school." Coralee saw her mother was getting angry and that frightened feeling again filled her, making her feel small. "She doesn't have toys, Mama, so..." Her voice broke.

"Put those things back." Lillian demanded of Ima Jean.

Coralee's heart beat faster. She looked at her friend. Tears streaked down Ima Jean's dirty cheeks.

"Who are you, anyway? Coming in here, carrying off Coralee's things."

Ima Jean's lip quivered. "She gave them to me."

"Coralee, go to you room. I'm not having you drag in every stray." She turned fully toward Ima Jean, "You're...dirty. I don't want you to come here again. Do you understand?"

"No, Mama, don't say that. Ima Jean's my friend." But her mother ignored her. Coralee ran to her room, sobbing, and closed the door.

The next afternoon when Coralee came home, a box rested on her bed. She looked through the cellophane lid. A Shirley Temple doll. They were in all the stores, dressed like *Little Miss Marker*. She raised the lid and flung it to the floor just as her mother appeared at the door.

"Do you like it?"

"It is not better than Ima Jean." She spit out.

Coralee put the lid back, went to the window and looked down on the street.

Her mother came up behind her, gathered up Coralee's hair in her hand, fondling and smoothing it. "We'll make your hair into long curls just like Shirley's. Just like the doll and the real Shirley Temple," she cooed.

Coralee refused to look at the doll until her mother left. It was the biggest and most magnificent one she ever had. She went to her coloring box, took out a pair of scissors, climbed up on the bed and, sitting cross-legged in the center of the bed, cut off each of the doll's long curls. She placed the doll in the rocker and put the curls in her lap. Then she went to the mirror; grabbed hanks of her own hair and cut. She gathered up her hair and the doll's curls from the floor and put them in a pile at her mother's bedroom door.

Hours later, Lillian came into her room, holding the hair. "What is the meaning of this?"

Coralee ran her hands over her shaggy hair. "See. You can't put Shirley Temple curls on me."

Lillian stared at her as if she had been slapped. When she saw the doll, she stopped. Then she became still and calm.

"You made me lose my best friend," Coralee screamed, tears coming. "Her mother said she couldn't be my friend. I hate you for what you did."

Lillian stood at the end of the wicker bed. Silent.

"All the other girls are Ima Jean's friend and they won't talk to me, I hate you, I hate you, I hate you."

Lillian watched her daughter. When she spoke, it had been soft and Coralee remembered the cold sound of it. "Don't turn away from me," she had said. "Don't even try. You won't win."

That night after her father left for the weekend, Coralee discovered she was locked in her room. All night and into the next day she pounded on the door, crying out. Finally her mother came and spoke to her through the locked door.

"You must learn, Coralee, that Mama always knows best."

"I want something to eat."

No answer.

"I want a drink, Mama. Please."

"You need to think about it some more."

At school, Ima Jean did not talk to her. Ima Jean had other friends. No one ever came home with Coralee from school again.

Soon she found that when she argued with her mother, the door would be locked. At first, she pounded on the door, but no one came. She would run around the room, screaming and pounding on walls until terror crawled over her skin. Sometimes, when she was older, she lay across her bed crying, but as those years passed, a new feeling crowded in beyond the panic. It gave her comfort, and she began to understand. Her mother was protecting her. Yes, it was warm there and comfortable, if she did what she was told, and she was very good, as a mother's child should be.

Only with her dolls did her mind roam free, making up things in their lives.

Once when she told her father that her mother locked her in, Malcolm looked astonished.

"Your mother is devoted to you, overly devoted, I'd say. When you tell me things like this, I think that imagination of yours is getting out of hand."

The door had not been locked on her now for a couple of years. She looked at the doll she had named Mimi because after that, she could never call her Shirley. She smiled and tousled poor Mimi's hair. She felt sorry for her; she looked so ragged. She hadn't done anything to deserve having her curls cut off.

When she finished straightening the room, Coralee stood before a long oval mirror. She unbuttoned the top of her gown by the ruffle, then the next button and the next. The gown slipped off her body and lay crumpled about her feet. Slowly she ran her hand along one thigh. She turned sideways looking at the tilt of full breasts in the mirror and the narrowing of her waist. She needed to wear a brassiere, but her mother said there was plenty of time for that.

The day was overcast, a dull light shown through the upstairs window. She raised the shade to let in more light and looked down on the ground with patches of lingering snow. It came to her with the suddenness of a crash. "McAnnelly!" She cried. "She's out there!"

She looked through the dolls on the shelves. Then the ones lined up in her closet. "McAnnelly's out there." Coralee pulled her gown back on, ran down the stairs to the back sun porch and outside. It burned her bare feet when she hit patches of snow along the brick path. A table and chairs outside her playhouse showed through the snowy blanket. McAnnelly sat primly just where Charlotte had left her. Coralee picked up the doll. Paint curled off the face and arms. Her frozen blue silk dress broke when she touched it. Coralee smoothed her hand over the doll's head. Bits of paint flecked off on her gown.

"Mama," Coralee ran to the house. "Look at McAnnelly. She looks..."

Lillian sat at the kitchen table making a list. The room still carried the friendly smell of fried bacon and fresh morning coffee.

"You were outside in your gown? Go get dressed."

"Look at McAnnelly, Mama."

Lillian ran her hands along the dolls arm and the cracked paint flaked away like confetti. "That doll's finished."

"Mama ... Charlotte did this. She doesn't care for dolls. She doesn't understand them."

Lillian glanced at her daughter. "Understand dolls?" She went back to making her list. "Coralee, sometimes I wonder where you get these ideas. I swear there is not a drop of Allison blood in you. You're all your father's..."

"She stepped on McAnnelly, Mama. She did."

Lillian put her pencil down on the blue checked tablecloth. "It's you I don't understand. When I was a child, I could beat both my sister and brother to the top of any tree in town. No dolls for me."

"Dolls are make-believe people." Coralee sat with her elbow on the table, chewing the nail of her index finger and studying the sad state of the doll before her. "It's easy for me to imagine how people feel, because I imagine how the dolls might feel if they were real. Do you imagine how other people feel, Mama?"

"...how other people feel?" Lillian echoed absently as she continued with her list. Then she reached over and patted her daughter's hand. "Tell you what, we'll bury her, Cora Baby, like we buried Grandpa. Remember? And your puppy?"

"It's not the same thing, Mama."

"Look at her paint peeling off. You can't put her up there with your other dolls. You have a beautiful collection. Do you want to toss her in the garbage?"

Coralee leaned back in her chair, looked past her mother to the rows of blue willowware plates lined on the cabinet shelves. "I got McAnnelly for my fourth birthday."

"Do you want to toss her in the garbage?" Lillian's finger followed a line in the checked tablecloth. "Is that what you want?"

"Grandma gave McAnnelly to me and she didn't want to make me do anything. She just wanted to give me something, because she loved me. That's why McAnnelly's my favorite."

Lillian raised her head, her eyes sharp. "What do you mean by that, Cora? Everything I've given you is because I want to make you happy." Lillian's eyes drilled into her. "Look at me. Isn't that right? Tell Mommy that is right."

Coralee studied her mother. She knew what she must say. "Yes, to make me happy."

"All right. That's better. Go get dressed. We'll bury it and that'll be the end of it."

"Not 'it.' McAnnelly."

"Yes, yes, McAnnelly."

Later, Lillian with Coralee, carried the doll in a cardboard box to a distant corner of the dried flower garden where, a puppy and a bird were already buried. Lillian stepped on the shovel and pushed harder into the frozen ground, but it was nearly solid. Finally, she had a hole large enough for the box.

"Now, sweetheart, do you want to say something?"

"No." Coralee felt sad, but she no longer cried.

Lillian began shoveling soil over the box, as Coralee stood by. When she finished, she took her daughter in her arms. "I know you loved her like she was real."

Over Coralee's shoulder, Lillian looked up, across the lake. Kurt! Almost hidden among the trees in the park, was his truck. He stood outside, watching them. "I know you loved, ah, McAnnelly," she stroked Coralee's hair. Her mind began to race. Kurt.

"Let's go to your room." They walked to the house. How could she get to Kurt? Could she walk across the lake? Was it still frozen enough? Maybe not. Better take the car. Leave. Excitement pounded through her. Kurt.

At the top of the stairs Lillian opened the door marked,

"Babe's Room."

"You need to rest after this, darling. This has been a trying thing for you. Just rest, baby." She kissed her daughter's forehead, hurried out, closed the door, and then stopped. She took keys from her pocket, found the right one and turned it in the lock.

Lillian snatched up the list she had just made and told Malcolm she needed to go shopping.

Now driving through trees by the lake, she saw only Kurt by his truck, waiting for her. He got in and drove ahead of her on the winding snowy road to the northern edge of the park, rimmed with a grove of cedar trees. She followed him deep into the grove until the trees grew too dense to continue. They got out, he took her hand and they walked deeper into the woods, snow crunching underfoot. It was a dark winter day, the woods still and dense with cedars, boughs drooping with their burden of snow. The air was so sharp and fresh it hurt to inhale.

He stopped, turned to her and without saying a word took her into his arms and kissed her. "A long time," he whispered, his eyes intent on her, "too long."

She opened her coat, reached inside his jacket and held him to her, feeling his warmth. "I thought you might not come back," she breathed. His body was hard and alive. His eyes focused on her as a hawk homing in on prey. She wanted to absorb him into her. They leaned back against a cedar trunk, kissing, fire rising, struggling now through clothing, finding warm flesh. Her fingers dug into his back as he entered her, and she knew then she owned him. He pressed her hard against the tree. Somewhere a limb creaked and broke, crashing. Her head lay back, eyes closed, drowning in this ecstasy.

Afterward, he stood by her, his hand on the tree trunk above her head. "I can't stand...to be away so long. I...I can hardly think of anything else."

She traced his firm unlined face with her finger. Youth, she thought as she studied him, making a memory to hold until next time, blue eyes, clear and bright, that looked at her with such desire, lips that hungered for more of her. "I'll always be here for you," she whispered, and leaned forward to kiss those lips that could drive her to desperation.

"By the way," he whispered, "what were you doing manhandling a spade?"

"Burying a doll."

He stepped back. "Burying a doll?"

"My young daughter thought her doll had died, so we had a service and buried her. Made her feel better."

Kurt took Lillian in his arms, again. "That's sweet." He stroked her cheek with the back of his fingers. He gathered her to him again, closer. "I didn't realize you had a child.

CHAPTER 17

Annabella walked into her kitchen, Henry Patrick, just behind her. He had insisted on following her home over the snowy roads. The house was painfully cold. In the next room, Willis was sprawled across the rose chenille bed spread. Henry frowned and scratched the back of his neck as he looked first at Willis then curiously took in these new surroundings—a green enameled kitchen, black stove and square table centered before two windows facing the driveway.

"Willis." Annie went to the bed and shook him. "Where were you?" She looked back at Henry, who still stood in the door, stiff as a statue in this foreign place, his mouth a tight straight line. "We were so worried about you."

Willis pulled himself up, yawned. "God, it's cold in here."

Henry Patrick looked down at Willis, his shyness shifting to disgust. "Annie oughten to be in a situation like this. House ought to be kept warm."

Willis groaned and rubbed his eyes. "What time is it?"

"It's 9:30, Mr. Porter." Henry had been up since 5:00 doing his chores. "I'll be choppin' you some wood, Annie. We need to get this place warmed up."

"Annie, I..." Willis began as Henry went out the back door situated by a row of pegs along the wall which held a sea of multicolored coats.

"Oh, Willis, you got drunk..."

"No, honey, I just stayed up all night." He smoothed back his disheveled hair with both palms. "I went to call you, and they said the lines were down...and it was snowing. Were you all right? I guess you were. We gotta get some heat in here."

"Willis, I got something to tell you...I know why the brothers act the way they do. They've had..."

"I got something to tell you, too." He sat up straighter. "And you're not gonna believe it. It's the greatest thing..."

Henry interrupted when he came back in and noisily dropped a load of wood in a box behind the stove. He stood aside, apparently waiting for Willis to take up pieces of wood, to get the fire going. When that didn't happen, Henry jerked open the black disk on top of the cooking stove and slammed three pieces of wood inside. He gathered up some papers and struck a match. A tiny flame flared. He pushed the disk in place with a crash.

"Well, that's done." Henry dusted sawdust from his hands. "Be warm in here in a few minutes." He surveyed Willis once more. "I'll be goin' on home, Annie, if you don't need anything."

"You and Otis were so good to me." Annie moved to embrace Henry, but when she saw the fear in his eyes that she might try to do just that, she patted his arm. "Thank you both."

Willis stood up, the comforter wrapped about him. "I sure do thank you, Henry, for helpin' out Annie."

Henry slammed the back door before Willis finished speaking.

Annie watched Henry drive away then begin making coffee. "I know why the brothers are so backward. It's because most of the family died in the influenza..." She turned to see Willis emptying his billfold on the kitchen table. "Where did you get all that money?"

"'Member I had something to tell you." Willis huddled close by the stove. "You're not gonna believe this, but Annie, I got what they call a special gift."

"A what?"

"I can't hardly believe it myself. I played cards last night, and I couldn't do nothing wrong. Them men I played with were sharp, but they were no match for ole Willis. I took the pot time and again. Then they told me something, kind of confidential like. They said that sometimes there's these people who's got a gift."

"Willis, that is foolishness. Gambling is...gambling. You can't ever be sure."

"I can. It's different with me. Some places they won't even let people like me come in 'cause they never lose."

"Oh, honey."

"Your papa got a gift—the oil and I got a gift, too."

Annie stood up and held her young husband to her. She could feel the hard leanness of his body, his heartbeat. She loved him so much. She pulled back and looked into his eyes, pushed back his uncombed hair. "Willis," she said, "you are very precious to me." Her heart ached for him. A gift! It was not his fault he had to face the Goliath of oil money.

"John Malvern don't have to worry none about Willis Porter," he said. "We're gonna have it all, Annie."

For the next three day, Willis left the house at dusk and returned in the small hours of the morning. Each day, he came to breakfast in a cheery mood, and laid out his winnings.

The fourth morning when she got up, he was slouched in his chair in the living room, still in his clothes.

"Good morning," she said.

He didn't answer. He stared down at a braided rug on the floor. "I can't understand it. I did everything the same. They cleaned me out."

Annie fried ham and eggs while he explained the plays he had made the night before and how they had gone wrong.

"You broke?" she asked.

"'Bout the same as. I got a ten left." He looked up. "I just don't understand what happened."

She put breakfast before him, her hand sliding over her thick girth. "It's gambling. I don't like it, Willis."

"I been raking in money by the wads. You seen that."

"I wish you didn't go there."

"Don't go trying to tell me what I can't do." He absently ate his breakfast. "They say I'm a natural. That's what they call me up there...the natural." His words drifted off then he looked back at her. "But maybe sometimes...it's just not with you—the gift."

For most of the day they avoided each other, then late in the evening, he grabbed his coat off the peg by the door, tipped her chin up and kissed her lips. "Gotta get back what I lost."

After he left, she noticed the fruit jar on the cabinet was empty. She'd been putting money in it as she could, to buy flannel yardage for the baby's gowns.

The next morning Willis was angry. He had won some and then lost it all.

She listened again as he went over his plays.

"I want to see my parents," she whispered.

"You told 'em they'd have to come here to see you, and I sure ain't seen 'em show up. They're not wanting you anymore, Annie."

"I want to see them."

"Don't go tellin''em about these losses. He shuffled off toward the bedroom. "They're just temporary losses."

She had not been in the Malvern house for three months—since their argument and Willis was right, they had not come to see her. As she turned in the drive, she didn't know how they would accept her.

Her father met her at the door. "Sophie, look who's here."

Something warm and sweet melted through her as both parents gave her a warm-hearted embrace. It was as if nothing had happened.

Once in the house, Annie saw that her parents were getting ready for the weekly music party. The smell of apple pies, rum cake, and peanut butter cookies filled Sophie's kitchen. Music parties had always been part of their lives. On Wednesday nights, neighbors met at one house or another, bringing their instruments and playing music until midnight and beyond. When the musicians were settled in their usual places, there were four violins, a bass, two banjoes, a piano, and half a dozen guitars. The living room and dining room were already set with double rows of chairs, the front row for the musicians, the back row for those who came to listen and gossip.

"I got something you need to see, Annie." Malvern disappeared and came back with a violin tucked under his chin. "Got me a new fiddle. I'm gonna try it tonight." Standing in the middle of the living room, amid the chairs, he began a slow piece. Annie smiled at her mother. They all knew they were not to interrupt while he played.

"What do think of that?" he said when he finished. "Smooth as silk. Best tone I ever heard."

"It's beautiful, Papa. Just beautiful." Annie went back to the kitchen, the feast on the table for the evening party.

Sophie gathered up her apron and wiped her hands on it. "Annie, I have something I've saved since you were a baby. Come with me." She followed her mother into the bedroom. Sophie dug in a drawer and found a box.

Annie sat on the edge of the bed watching Sophie open the box. It was a tiny baby dress wrapped in an old pillowcase. "It was yours. I want it to be your first gift."

"Oh, Mama." It felt so good to be at home, to be part of things again. She hugged her mother.

"Annie," her mother began to whisper, "that's not why I called you in here. It's your Papa."

"What's wrong with Papa?" Annie leaned closer.

"Every time he goes to town, he buys something. Yesterday he come home with a big package under his arm. It was that violin and just last week," Sophie pulled out the chair from her sewing machine and sat down closely facing her daughter, "he come marchin' right in there in that kitchen in a new suit—a full suit." He just buys, buys, buys and he never used to do that."

"But Mama, maybe he always wanted some of those things."

"He never owned a suit in his life and there he stood, proud as a peacock. Vest, too."

Annie smoothed the baby dress in her lap.

"He wanted to know what I thought of him standing there, and I just told him. I said I didn't hardly know the man I been married to. He just laughed and said, "Oh, Sophie.""

Annie noticed a bright piece of material in her mother's sewing basket. "What's this? What pretty thing are you making, Mama?"

"Well, that's just more of it," Sophie said with disgust. "More of what I'm tellin' you." Sophie reached for her sewing basket and set aside a half dozen quilt blocks on the bed. "It's a dress for Eva Mae. Papa is taking Eva Mae to a father/daughter dinner in at town church. He brought that purple velvet stuff home and told me to make up something nice for her."

Annie ran her hands over the fine soft material, fabric she had never touched before. How easy it was now to cry. "It's nice, Mama."

"Don't you think that didn't set him back a few pennies?" Sophie put her arm around Annie's shoulders. "I know, darlin', you never had anything like this."

Annie kept her head down, toying with the lace on the hem of the baby dress. She remembered the quilting ladies and the farmers' wives who'd come to the music parties and brought with them washed and ironed flour sacks with designs. They traded with each other until they got three with the same pattern. She thought nothing of it; all the little girls in the neighborhood wore clothes made from flour sacks.

Annie ran her finger down the lace inserts of the baby dress. She had come to talk to her father about Willis, but now didn't seem the time. She felt something else, something larger, the ground of her childhood shifting beneath her to an unknown. Her father, like Willis, was living with the power of oil money crowding in on their lives.

"And it's not just the suit," her mother went on, "and the fiddle and that velvet dress, Annie."

She looked at her mother. "What is it, Mama?"

Sophie looked out the bedroom window, to where she had made garden for the last twenty years. She gathered up her apron, twisted it in her lap. "He wants to go to town church!"

"Town church," Annie echoed.

"We never went anywhere but Bethlehem Church. Those are the people we know – just like the ones coming here tonight. I don't know them people in town. They make me nervous." She fingered the short chain of safety pins on her apron. "I don't like 'em and I don't want to go."

"You know Sarah Emma. She lives in town. And Aunt Belle."

"That's different. Sarah Emma quilts with me at Bethlehem Church, and Belle's family." Sophie set the sewing basket down on the pedal of the sewing machine. "All my life I could look above the trees and see the steeple of Bethlehem Church over there. There's things that need changing, and there's things that don't."

The next morning Willis sat in one of the green enamel kitchen chair, a mood dark as the winter day. He had lost all his money. The baby dress Annie planned to show him was on the table, but he didn't notice. She felt so desperately sad, so helpless and bewildered.

"What is to become of us – the three of us?" she whispered.

Willis roused. "Nothin' much that ain't good." He looked across the table to the stove. "Coffee's done. Can you pour me a cup?"

CHAPTER 18

It was a busy Friday in Belle Dorsett's Kozy Kottage Beauty Shop. One of these hurry up days, Belle thought. Mary Faith was under the dryer, Lucy getting a permanent, and another customer waiting for her appointment. This afternoon she would have Ella Donnally and Lillian Allison for haircuts. Just now as Belle put the finishing touches on Donna's comb out, the door opened. She looked in the reflection of the mirror over Donna's shoulder. Carson Garrett!

He looked strangely out of place, in a wide Texas hat and high heeled boots, but not at all ill at ease as he came toward Belle. "So this is where beauty is made!"

"I do my part." Belle smiled at him and absently gave a hand mirror to Donna.

"I haven't seen you since you were pulled out of that snow bank." Most men were uncomfortable in this exclusively feminine world, but Garrett clearly was not. He seemed to own any place he stood.

"I'm thawed out," Belle quipped.

Carson smiled at Donna surveying the back of her hair, then looked back at Belle. "Are you busy this Saturday night?"

All four customers in the shop sat in eloquent silence, eyeing him like a curiosity. Lucy pushed the dryer up off her head.

She needed to hear this!

Belle felt a rush of self-consciousness flood over her. She nervously glanced at her customers. This information would be dinner conversation in half the houses in town and the phone lines would be abuzz, too. Our own hairdresser, Belle Dorsett and that oil man!

"I'd like to take you to dinner," he said.

The ladies' attention now turned to Belle. What would she say?

Belle tried at being flippant. "I think I can work you in."

"Well, that's good."

Standing in the partly opened door, Garrett looked around at the fascinated ladies. "I don't think I've been in a place like this before."

She smiled. "When you come by, they'll all be gone."

He nodded, a sparkle in his eyes. "Saturday, then. About seven."

As the door closed, the ladies each looked at one another knowingly. This piece of news was golden, and they got it firsthand.

When the last customer left in late afternoon, Belle followed her to the front step. Across the highway, brilliant red and blue lights at Dutch's Truck Stop blinked in the grey winter dusk. Cars whizzed down the highway. Oil trucks, the bottom half mud-splattered from digging their way in and out of fields, passed by or turned into Dutch's.

Now alone in her bedroom and as enchanted as a schoolgirl, she could give free rein to elation. She pulled dress after dress from the closet and held them up. Then the royal blue crepe. She held it against her. Oh, yes.

Belle sat down on the bed. A date! Forty-two years old, and I'm going on a date. She went back to her shop, picked up a comb and worked her magic on her own hair.

What on earth do people talk about on a date now? She sectioned off her hair and rolled it. While she sat under the dryer, she picked up the newspaper. There was the weekly column about the oil news. Maybe she should know more about that. She read that. There was always the war news in Europe. She read a scathing editorial about *Time Magazine* naming Hitler the Man of the Year. The editor quoted *Time's* defense as saying "it was not the figure of Adolf Hitler who strode over a cringing Europe with all the swagger of a conqueror. It was because Hitler was the man who most influenced events in the last year." There was much more but she let the paper slide off her knees. Maybe war news would not be good to talk about on a date.

At the Tea Room of the Hotel Allison, the hostess, a daughter of one of Belle's customers met them. "Why Mrs. Dorsett, it's so nice to see you here." She glanced up at Carson Garrett, then said, "Follow me, I have just the table for you, by the fireplace." As they walked across the thick carpet, two other of her weekly clients smiled and nodded.

"It must be nice to walk into a place and everyone knows you," Carson said when they were seated. "What's it like to grow up like that?"

"I don't have anything to compare with." Belle folded a napkin across her lap. "It's just the way it's always been. I suppose there's security that I don't even realize, but...old families who have lived in one place get reputations. If you mentioned a name to my father he might say, 'He comes from a devious lot, old man went to the Pen' or 'they're a flighty bunch—wouldn't put much stock in what they say' or 'knew ole man Press all my life. Turned out a bunch of fine boys—done well.'"

"So you're known by the tribe you came from? That's who you are?"

"I suppose that's about right. When I was a young girl dating, any boy I brought home, my father already knew about or at least knew his family. And there are no families without skeletons. He didn't approve of anybody."

"So how did you ever find someone he'd let you marry?"

"My father met him first and introduced us. I guess that made him all right."

"And was he?"

"Yes, we had a good marriage," She smiled at another customer who walked by, then looked back at Carson. "Apparently you didn't grow up in a small town."

"No nor a city either. My mom died. Her parents on their farm mostly raised me. Dad was sort of—here and there, mostly there."

"Is he still living?"

"I don't know."

Belle looked about the room, one wall of windows with small square panes, and a dozen fern plants before them. People she knew stole glances at the reflection of them in the window, and then turned quickly away when Belle noticed.

She turned back. "How? I mean, how—did you get from there to here? Not a great beginning considering what you are now."

"Down the country road from my grandparents' farm, this little company was putting in a well." He leaned across the table. "I was just a kid and hung around 'til they got tired of me and gave me a job. When the well came in good, I'm telling you"—he took her hand, his eyes alive—"that was the most exhilarating thing I'd ever seen in my life. It still is. I never get over it."

Belle looked into his dark eyes trying to imagine what he had seen—so many places, so many people. He was like no one she had ever known, and she wanted to know everything.

"I inherited my grandparents' farm." He still held her hand. "When they drilled a well on it, it was productive enough for me to get started with my own drilling company. I've been lucky. It's gambling, you know—with a purpose, I guess you could say."

Carson was glib, full of conversation through the meal. As the waiter served coffee, Belle, realized she had never once thought about discussing Hitler stealing Austria.

When they walked out onto the porch, a gentle rain was falling, so they walked in the rain to his car and drove to Belle's house. In her living room they sat by the fireplace. Belle found some wine and on the top shelf of her cabinets, and some glasses she hadn't used in years.

The fire crackled and outside the rain was pelting the window. "You've been a widow a long time?" Garrett asked as she handed him the wine.

"Seventeen years. Longer than I was married. What about you? Never married?"

"Yes, long ago. A Texas girl. She got tired of us moving from place to place. But," he shrugged, "that's the business of oil. You keep trying to find a new pool, drill, hopefully make a strike and stay 'til it runs out."

These were words Belle didn't want to hear, "moving from place to place—stay till it runs out."

"Some people talk deep oil..." Belle had done her homework. If there *was* a chance of the wells going deeper in the ground to retrieve the oil—Carson would not be leaving anytime soon.

"I think there's more oil here on lower strata than the drilling we're now doing, but it costs much more to drill through the St. Louis lime. The production is not worth the cost, unless oil goes up in price. We're in this to make money, after all."

His fingers brushed against hers. She didn't know if he intended it or it just happened. The wine wrapped them in a cocoon, where the slightest touch seemed warm and suggestive.

"What is St. Louis lime?" She didn't remember reading about that.

"It's an extensive layer or strata with its outcropping near St. Louis and the Mississippi River. It extends under the surface for we know at least 200 miles. North of here about 20 miles another company found the edge of it and were allowed to drill very deep, beyond the depth of the St. Louis lime. They struck fine producing wells, so we think beneath the lime strata there is much more oil."

Belle was quiet for a while. It was a comfortable silence. A sociable silence—the dancing fire, the drumming rain, the ticking clock and the enveloping warmth of wine made them feel close, the outside world a distant place.

"You have no idea how the oil business has affected this quiet little place," Belle said softly, breaking the spell.

Carson seemed totally relaxed, staring out the window at the rush of traffic on the highway and listening to the rain.

"The have-nots are getting rich and the old guard doesn't know how to take them--how to take any of it." Belle wondered as she talked, how many women in his "moving around" life had he known. Was she just another?

A piece of burning wood crackled in the fireplace.

"In fact," Belle continued, "I don't think they know how to take themselves just yet. Then there are the others like the Patrick brothers. Those ole boys just won't put up with being wealthy."

The clock struck ten.

"I'll bet these pieces of furniture are antiques?" Carson looked about. "I see things like used to be in my grandmother's house."

"They are old. I grew up in this house. Let me give you the tour." She reached for his hand surprised at her gesture. He smiled as he took it. "This clock and table have been in my family for three generations, and that breakfront since the Civil War. That rocker...I don't know... I remember my grandfather rocking John in it ...John Malvern, my brother? You know him."

"Oh, yes, I know John Malvern very well. He's makes me know why I like the oil business."

She switched on a light as they started down a dark hallway. She pointed to a large black and white picture in a wide ornate mahogany frame. "This is my grandfather, one of them. And that is our grandmother and beside her is a great-grandfather and grandmother..."

Carson stood behind her, his hand on her shoulder. "That one is wearing a Union Army uniform."

She nodded and felt the slightest touch on her hair. Was it his lips?

"This feels familiar—like home." He put his arm about her shoulder, both looking up at a large square picture. "We had a picture in my Grandmother's parlor of her uncle in his Confederate uniform."

Belle turned in his arms. "Our families used to be enemies."

"I think that war's over." He held her in a gentle embrace." *You* make me feel at home – and I don't mean the house."

She looked into his eyes, unable to believe that anyone felt anything for her, even thought of her. It had been so long.

She moved closer to him in the dim hallway. The rain was hitting the outside door at the end of the hall. She felt herself moving into him, someone she was just learning to know.

Belle touched his cheek, her eyes following every contour of his face while he talked. Could this be her, in someone's arms? Someone who made her feel again, after so many years alone, so many nights turning in her bed—restless with passion until she became numb and didn't think of that any more. She had filled up her life to keep away the aloneness.

She tiptoed up and softly kissed his lips. "I'm glad you feel at home."

He held her close, and she could feel the beating of his heart as she leaned into him, the wine and the thrill warming her.

"You've not shown me the bedroom."

"I'll show you the bedroom." She led him to a room just off the hall, where a great antique headboard stretched up near a picture rail.

"It's a very cold night, Belle. Why should I go home? I could just stay here with you."

"I don't think so. You see after I spent the night with you, I'd get up and go to church and people I've known since I was a child would have heard already from someone or several someones. They would say, "You're sleeping with Carson Garrett, aren't you?"

"That's how it is?"

"That's how it is."

"Well, the weather is still bad, I could just stay with you all night and talk."

"No, you can't do that either. Those same people will say,

"You spent the night with Carson Garrett and they will assume in bed."

"I don't give a damn what people think. It's what you do or don't that counts—not what people think."

"I care. They can crucify you if you misstep. You have no idea."

"Did you ever misstep, Belle?" He watched her, waiting, an expectant smile on his face.

She looked down at the floor.

"No, I guess not—not much anyway." His warm breath was on her forehead.

"People alienate you if you misstep."

"That's what I hate about small towns. Perception counts more than integrity."

"And, too, a hair dresser lives on her reputation." They walked back down the hall. "My family, the Malverns, have lived here for five generations."

By the front door, Carson, took Belle's face in his hands, pushed back a strand of hair and kissed her. "Belle, I don't want anyone gossiping about you, either. You are a true gentle lady. But sometime," he said as he reached for his coat, "I'm going to sleep in that great bed in there."

"Maybe." She smiled at him. "Maybe not." Did he start relationships everywhere his life led him? Was she just another?

He softly kissed her lips again. Without answering, he went out into the night.

She leaned against the door after he left, listening to his footsteps crossing the wooden porch and she closed her eyes. "Yes, yes, yes."

CHAPTER 19

John Malvern had never in his life been in the Community Room over the First National Bank, but tonight with Eva Mae on his arm he was attending the Father/Daughter Banquet sponsored by the Presbyterian Church, the very reason he had bought his new blue three-piece suit.

As soon as he came in, he started to sit down in the back, but Eva Mae urged him down front. The room was filled with long tables, separated by an aisle, and dressed in brilliant white tablecloths, gleaming silverware, with little bouquets in the center. A few feet from the first table where Eva Mae seated them, musicians, two violins and a piano, entertained guests as they arrived. The room was coming alive with proud fathers and well adorned daughters.

Malvern felt the pressure of people about him. They were people who knew what to do, what to talk about, how to say things. He looked at Eva Mae as he shifted uncomfortably. Her eyes sparkled.

"Oh, Papa, isn't it just grand. It makes me feel elegant just to be here. I like feeling elegant, don't you?"

What John Malvern felt was a vest that was too tight and a shirt collar under his tie that choked him. He smiled as he looked at his little girl. Suddenly he saw, or maybe felt, that his Eva Mae was more than a little girl. The potential of a woman was there. A silver clip held her long chestnut-colored hair on one side, which coiled on the shoulders of the purple velvet dress Sophie had made for her. She did look a wonder. Malvern stiffly glanced about the room and decided that Eva Mae was the best-looking girl there. Still, under his tightening vest, he felt proud, if a bit uneasy.

"Oh Papa, thank you for bringing me."

A tall man with graying hair leaned forward and offered his hand to Malvern. "Judge Donnelly," He said. "I just heard someone say that this young lady is John Malvern's pretty little girl. I wanted to meet the man who's getting rich faster than any of us."

Malvern felt awkward. The room was hot, his collar tight.

Eva Mae looked up, charmed and smiling, "Why Judge Donnelly, that is the kindest thing anybody has ever said to me."

Malvern looked at his daughter, astonished at her ease in talking to these people. "Well, I don't know about the getting richer part. I may just be catching up," he said.

"Ah, you're a modest one." Donnelly patted him on the back. "Can't bring my daughter. She's with her daughter who's about to make her a grandmother and that makes me...let's see, what is that word?"

"Congratulation," Malvern got out. "You know family is all that counts."

The judge squeezed his hand and moved on.

Water glasses were put before them and the music changed to piano only. Malvern had never felt so corseted up in his life. He worked his finger around the collar of his shirt. Sweat ran down his back, and he wondered if everyone felt so warm.

"What a nice man," Eva Mae whispered.

"Do you think he'd a said any of that if it weren't for them oil wells out there?"

"Papa, don't make it complicated. He spoke to you and you spoke to him. I liked him. He's a judge, you know."

Malvern fell silent. Eva Mae was just a little girl, really. A lot she didn't understand. He'd never cared much for people who thought they were important and wanted you to think so, too.

Clifton Allison came, shook Malvern's hand and smiled his acknowledgement to Eva Mae. To Malvern's consternation, he seated himself opposite them. Now Malvern would have to think of what to say to Clifton Allison.

"Glad to see you could make it. I'm sorry to say, unlike you, I have no daughter to bring, just two sons to make me proud. Do you mind if I join you?"

"Oh, please do." Eva Mae answered promptly.

"Well, John, I've been wanting to talk to you about all these oil strikes in the county and the other counties. Do you think this is like a flash in the pan, or is it going to be life around here from now on?"

Malvern stared across the table for an instant before he answered. It was hard to believe that Clifton Allison was asking him what *he* thought.

"It's sure new to me, but I expect it's gonna be around as long as we're livin'."

Allison smiled, "You got how many wells now?"

"They're drillin' the eighth one this month and two more are in the works. Course, I'm sure you know I'm quite a bit behind the Patrick brothers. Their place is sprouting derricks like weeds."

Allison lifted a water glass and took a drink. "We don't see much of them."

"No, I don't reckon you do. They're the kind that sticks close to home."

About that time a young man in a white shirt and tie stood across the table in front of Eva Mae, pencil in hand and small pad of paper locked in his other palm.

"I am to take your order, Miss Malvern. Chicken, fish or beef?"

Eva Mae started to ask how he knew her name then with a toss of her head said, "I think...fish." He wrote that down, and then started toward the kitchen.

"Danny," Mr. Allison turned slightly. "Did you, also, want to take the order for Mr. Malvern and me?"

"Oh, sure..." Danny looked embarrassed.

"This is one of my sons. The other one is at the University," Allison explained as Danny wrote down orders. "If you don't have a daughter, you're to bring your sons to serve as waiters tonight." He turned to Danny. "This is Mr. Malvern and his daughter, Miss..."

Eva Mae extended her hand and smiled into Danny's eyes. "My name is Eva Mae."

"You want something to drink, Eva Mae?" Danny asked. "We have tea, coffee and lemonade." He leaned closer, whispering. "We've got four Cokes back there, too. You can have mine, if you want."

"Oh, no, you're doing all the work. Bring me a lemonade."

"Coming right up," He wrote it down with a flourish and punched in a dot at the end.

Eva Mae followed Danny with her eyes losing all interest in her father and his conversation with Clifton Allison.

In a short time, Danny placed a brimming plate of fish and rice before Eva Mae, then handed her a Coke. "You can have mine, anyway." His fingers touched hers and she knew it was not an accident.

"Danny," His father called back at him, "Were you going to serve us?"

"Sure thing, coming right up!

The two men looked at each other, smiled.

"Now, you were talking about that Johnson well..." Allison continued.

Then Danny was back and placed two plates before the men. "Now, that's it." He rubbed his palms across his shirt. "Everybody okay? Oh, no. I forgot the rolls. Be right back. They're home baked, Miss... "

"My name is Eva Mae."

"Eva Mae." Danny grinned wide. "They're real good. I had some already." He was back again and sat them before her. "Now... Eva Mae. Is there anything else I can do for you?"

"No, I think we must have it all, including the best service in the room."

Malvern again looked at his daughter, amazed at her easy charm.

Danny left and stood along the wall. Eva Mae stole a glance at him, and then looked quickly away; he was watching her. She hardly knew what she was eating. Eva Mae determined not to look again, but when she could stand it no longer, she looked up. He smiled wide.

As they finished the main course, two women came forward. One seated herself at the piano and the other began to sing a lovely and poignant rendition of "My Buddy."

Eva Mae looked across at the wall. Danny was gone. Then back by the entrance. No Danny. Then she saw him. Behind three tall plants strategically placed to obscure the adjoining room, now set up temporally for a kitchen. He was watching her! She rather determinedly focused through the foliage at him and made a tiny face. He stepped out from behind the plants and raised his eyebrows two times then moved back behind his blind.

Just when "My Buddy" was reaching its very plaintive crescendo, Danny moved to the other side of the plants, projected his head, winked at her, and then he was gone. Eva Mae was choking a laugh down to her toes. Then Danny pulled apart a space in the foliage, put his eye in the space and gave her an exaggerated wink just as the singer hit the saddest note..."your buddy misses—you-u."

Eva Mae exploded with laughter. She put her hand over her mouth, but tears ran down her cheeks.

Her father frowned at her, everyone turned to her, the singer glared at her then snatched up the sheet music. Malvern looked across the room at the source of the mirth. Danny was bent over laughing.

The ladies were thanked for their performance and waiters began to clear the table for dessert.

Right away, Danny was back with cherry pie. "When you finish serving, son," his father said, "why don't you just sit down with us for the rest of the program. Miss Malvern might need something, and you'd be—right here."

When the evening came to a close, Malvern walked with Clifton Allison down the aisle to the back entrance. Danny followed with Eva Mae.

"I want to call you," Danny whispered. "Can I do that?"

"I have to ask my father, but I imagine it's okay."

"How will I know?"

"I'll call you."

"Okay." He beamed.

"But you have to be very careful what you say when you call me. We're on a party line and there's that awful ole Maxwell Porter who listens in. One time Papa was listening in and our clock began to strike and everybody knows how our clock sounds, because we have these silly old music parties."

She saw Danny wasn't listening. He was only looking at her.

"You ring two shorts and a long." She told him. "That is if you can call."

"Two shorts and a long."

Outside, on the street Malvern dallied, talking to people he did not know until Allison and his son pulled away from their parking place. Then he and Eva Mae walked to his old truck. He hadn't noticed how much mud was crusted on the running board when he drove it out of the garage at home.

"He is so cute, Papa. He asked if he could call me on the phone."

Malvern made the four-way stop in the center of town. "What did you say?"

"I said I'd talk to you about it."

"Well, the answer is 'no.' He is an Allison. Why would he want to see you...a poor country girl. There ain't no reason... 'cept a bad one."

"Papa, it's not like that. Why would you say such a thing? Do you want me to be ashamed I'm a Malvern? Like I'm not good enough for Danny Allison?"

"You're as good as any Allison that ever walked. It's just that it's for ... no good reason he wants to see you."

"Papa, you make everything complicated. Anyway, I'm not a poor country girl."

"We'll see." Malvern set his jaw

But Malvern didn't feel sure about anything right now. He had lived all his life like his father and his father before that, spacing his life with the seasons, growing crops, harvesting, repairing things in the cold season, mixing with people like himself. Tonight was something apart from that life. But it *would* be a fine thing, he considered, to walk down the street and important people come to shake your hand, ask what you thought and listen and consider what you said, like Allison had. He imagined they might call him on the phone and ask him to come to a meeting because they wanted his sound advice. Then when he said what should be done, they would nod in agreement. They wouldn't just pass over him like he was just one more poor farmer. Maybe Eva Mae had it right. He was making things too complicated. It had been an easy thing tonight to talk to Clifton Allison. Yes, sir, Malvern nodded as he drove along, he had to admit it, it had been a right pleasant evening.

That night Malvern couldn't sleep. He sat in his living room in the darkness. He saw his life widening into new vistas. It was that night he decided he'd make sure Eva Mae could marry anybody she wanted to. Joey would go up to that big University in Champaign like the Allison boy. He was going to get a new truck—maybe a new car, too. And Sophie would just have to come to it; they were going into town church.

CHAPTER 20

Maxwell Porter leaned across the bar at the Blue Moon Tavern listening to a conversation between a couple of roustabouts from Garrett's Lone Star Drilling Company and a driller from the Cameron Brothers' Magnolia Drilling Company. The talk for weeks was about the new well at the edge of town. The oilmen called it the Amsley well, but the people of Amsley call it Skeeter's well. The site was near the city garbage dump which had been run by Skeeter Ambrose for forty years. Skeeter was a well-known and much-loved fixture about town. Most everybody thought if the well was good, the royalties should to go to Ambrose, even though the dump was on city property. Amsley residents who had paid no attention to oil activity were seriously interested in the Skeeter well.

"I don't know," Porter looked across the smoky bar into the mirror. Just under the bar, the radio poured out *The Cowbell Polka.* "There's been two others that claimed Amsley wells and they showed drier'n a bone. People get they hopes up, then they get knocked down."

Cobin Eckles, a driller for Lone Star, looked down the bar. "Now, Porter, they say it looks good after the acid treatment."

"Yeah, I've heard about the acid treatment. They do that like they vote up there in Chicago, early and often."

"I'd about as soon Skeeter get himself a well, as anybody." Charlie Meeks said, and he spoke for most of the town.

The muted jingle of a slot machine paying off drifted from upstairs. "You're sore on account yours was a dust hole," Eckles said.

"I'm gonna get drilled on."

"That so, Porter?"

"Right upstairs—right over our heads, one of them men from Magnolia said I was comin' up. Garrett said the same thing about Lone Star."

The men gathered around. "When's this supposed to be, Porter?"

It made him nervous the way they moved in close and questioned him, like they were making him one of their jokes.

"They're thinkin' on it. I heard they was." Porter flared. "Dammit, it's my turn and you don't need to go makin' a big thing of it. There's derricks and pumps everywhere you look." He finished his drink, slid off the stool and shuffled to the door. Outside, he stood for a minute, wiped his nose with the back of his hand, then went on, hunched over against the sharp January wind.

Inside the Blue Moon, Charlie Meeks called down the bar, "Cobin, you got one of those colored flags in your truck, the ones that Magnolia uses for a stake out when they pick a spot to set up a derrick?"

"Yeah, I think...I can get one."

Conversation lulled as men throughout the room stopped talking and looked up, listening.

"Well, let's give ole Porter a big thrill and plant a stake out there somewhere on his property where he's sure to see it. See what he does."

"And says," the Lone Star roustabout yawned. "It is kind of funny how there's been good wells all around Porter's farm." He held his beer bottle up and took a drink. "I'll say one thing for him, he's burned up but he's optimistic."

"He's the only one that's optimistic," Cobin answered.

"These people around here have been poor so long, they're scared to believe they're not meant to be poor. You tell them there's oil under where they're walking and it's gonna make them rich, and they just study the ground a while, then walk away. They don't believe in anything they haven't known about for three generations."

The men in the tavern chuckled, and then went back to their drinks.

Maxwell Porter sat at his breakfast table, a coffee cup in his hand, as dim morning light came on.

"My God, Pearl, come lookie out there."

They stared out the back window. "That there is a stake. An oil stake right out there in the garden." He whispered as though the gods might hear and snatch away his prize.

Pearl's hand went up to her cheek. "Well, lawz, why'd they have to put it right in the middle of my garden."

"No matter about the damned garden. We can have that anywhere." Porter squinted out the window. "That's a stake, all right, but Magnolia's. I signed with Lone Star. Wonder how they come to switch?"

"That's where my garden's been for thirty years."

"Pearl." He looked back at her. "You can put the damn garden over there or over there, but you can't put an oil well just anywhere. That's where it's gonna be, Pearl, right out there, chuggin along while it's goin' down in the ground, makin' us rich."

Pearl took another sip of coffee. "I wouldn't be countin' my chickens before the eggs is even laid."

Porter turned on his wife, "Don't you want to get us a well, like ever'body else."

"I reckon so, but there's plenty of places besides..."

Porter looked satisfied, having won the argument. "I'll not run the Dorance Smith lumber. He can just wait. You know what I'm gonna do today, Pearl? I'm gonna plow up that garden and take down that fence."

"You're not gonna take down my fence. Everything'll get in my garden."

"Well they ain't gonna be goin' in and out of your little gate with a big oil rig. It's gotta come down."

Pearl spooned out hot oatmeal into a bowl from a pan on the stove. At the table she reached for the pitcher and poured cream over the oatmeal. "It might be a dry well, Porter, like that last one."

"This one ain't gonna be dry, Pearlie. It's gonna be just as good as any Malvern's got." Porter finished his coffee, slapped on his cap and bounded out the back door. In the garden he walked around the stake, kicked some clods by it, backed off and looked at it again.

He came back in and dropped in his chair. "I sure don't know when an oil truck come in here and put that stake down. Did you see anything?"

"Course not. I'd a told you."

Porter stared out the back window, "Well, I'll be damned if that don't beat all. Come in here and do a thing like that and not even tell a man about it." He stood up again. "You know what I'm a gonna do? After I plow up the garden and carry off that old fence, I'll gonna move the outhouse. Reckon how a man'll feel goin' out there with the bright derrick lights pourin' all over that end of the place."

"I think the men out there might just as well appreciate one a little bit close."

"Well, woman, that just shows how little you know about these things." He motioned to the bedraggled garden and the red flag with a little white magnolia in the center waving slightly in the cool morning.

For the next two days Porter prepared for the oilrig to be brought in. He got the plot smoothed off; the toilet moved a respectable distance away; and then began to wait. Days passed and became weeks. Porter kept looking wistfully at the stake with the little flag. Oil trucks often passed by on the way to some well. Each day he thought they might turn in and begin to set up.

By the middle of February, his patience was at an end. Maxwell Porter stationed himself on a tree stump near the end of his lane, shotgun propped against his knee. Every day he saw the same oil trucks go by and sometimes that Garrett in his big Buick 8. Porter couldn't figure why it was that Magnolia flag was out there, it was that Garrett that told him one day he'd be back, and Porter would have his turn. Garrett had told him that plain as day. The flag ought to have a lone star on it not a flower.

He dropped his shotgun down in the grass; maybe he'd go hunting in a bit. He heard another truck coming from that Johnson well probably, or maybe one on the Patrick boys or Malvern. The driver waved his hand as the truck roared by. It was like they were trying to make a fool of him, he saw it now, drilling all around him and leaving him out.

Porter picked up a piece of wood, pulled out his pocketknife and began to whittle. He hardly noticed what he was doing. Just something to do. He heard a car and looked down the road. It was that big black Buick—Garrett. It came closer. But it wasn't Garrett. It was John Malvern. Driving a long shiny black car. He'd heard Malvern had taken to smoking cigars.

There he sat, just like a big ape, reared back, arm on the window of his new car, smoking his big cigar like some son-of-bitch politician. Well, he was just old Malvern no matter how he strutted out and Porter had had just about all he could take. Porter raised his shotgun. When Malvern got even with the mailbox, Porter let off a shot, heard the buckshot platter against metal. The Buick instantly sped off. Down the road Porter heard a tire blow out. He smiled and nodded but kept his gun ready. The old fool might come back after him. Porter walked onto the frozen road. Malvern was out of his car, shaking his fist at him, dressed up in some fancy suit like he was going to preach somewhere. Then he watched Malvern start walking—the other way. "Filthy, son-of-a bitch." Porter went back to the stump and started whittling again.

CHAPTER 21

Sheriff Logan Webb sat at his cluttered desk. Behind him a dark February day shown through double windows separated by a radiator, which reassuringly gurgled and spit from time to time. He thought the city moved too hastily after the other jail burned. They immediately bought the brick Victorian-style edifice called the Russell place, after ole man Russell died, and they converted the house into a jail. It set just off the town square.

Upstairs where he and his wife lived was comfortable enough, he guessed, but it was the back section downstairs that didn't live up to what a jail was supposed to be. That part had been gutted, windows barred and eight by eight-foot cubicles placed at each corner of one enormous room, which left a barred common area outside the cells.

One collar the sheriff had marched back to the cells smirked he'd like a cell with lavender-flowered wallpaper, but pink would be okay, too. Right now, Sheriff Webb had a bigger problem than what the jail looked like.

Elbows on the desk, a stack of mail to go through, he rubbed his eyes. What to do with those three slot machines that lined the hall that led back to the cells? He'd taken them out of the Hotel Allison at that last raid, photographer, "Beebite" Zimmerman snapping pictures for *The Amsley Record* all the way.

Now he couldn't figure how in the hell he was going to put them back.

He took a letter opener and ripped the top envelope. It was another complaint about the gambling. Said it had taken over the town. He put it in the back of his middle desk drawer with the others. Webb leaned back in his swivel chair and looked absently out the window at the gloomy day. Guess he'd better do something before long.

The office door creaked open.

"Jake," he called as Jacob Beardsman stepped inside out of the cold. Beardsman was a little man, who came in from Chicago, like Lee, and the others. He'd been around for about two years and he knew everything that was going on. Webb guessed Beardsman was as good as any to do business with. "How you been, Jake?" The sheriff, well over six feet, half stood and shook his hand. "How're things going?"

"Good." Beardsman sat down in the brown slatted chair opposite the desk. "I'd say real good."

The sheriff tilted back in his swivel chair, held a pencil between his two index fingers and smiled. "Glad to hear it—and I'm not surprised." He didn't like the way Jake's eyes moved over the room, like he was casing the place. Or maybe, the sheriff thought, he'd seen plenty of other jails in his day and was just comparing.

Jake opened his briefcase, took out two bags and dropped them on the sheriff's desk. He pushed one forward, "The Blue Moon." Then he slid the other across, "And the Hotel Allison."

Logan Webb grasped the sacks and briefly looked inside. "Good, good. You're a fine fellow, you know that, Jake." He pushed back in his swivel chair, opened the bottom drawer of a wooden filing cabinet that sat alongside the windows, dropped the two bags in, closed and locked the drawer.

"If that Skeeter well turns out to be a good one, and it looks like it might, they say that'll open up another pool right close—just outa town. And that means, Jake, there'll be more wells, more oil workers and more rich farmers coming into our town for some fun.

We like to see people enjoying themselves around here." Webb laughed. "Right, Jake?"

Jake nodded. He sat perched on the edge of his chair, seemingly impatient to get his business done and get away.

"Tell you what, Jake." The sheriff sighed. "There's a lot of talk. The men talk... out on the job... I get complaints." Webb opened the desk drawer and pulled out a fist-full of letters. "This is a little place. Talk gets around. Not like Chicago. Everybody here knows everybody else. This is the thing, I'm gonna make a raid, put it in the paper. Show pictures. Let's say Thursday night. That'd be about right. Both places. A surprise Capone raid, one right after the other. You understand, Jake?"

Jake stood up. "I'll see to it."

"I'll have a deputy with me and a man from the paper, ready to catch anything."

Jake reached for his empty briefcase and left out the back door.

Jake Beardsman detested Sheriff Logan Webb. He hated the slow moving cordiality that covered every transaction in this little mudhole of a town. And he hated the people; like they all knew secrets no outsider would ever know. But Jake knew which side his bread was buttered on. He'd seen what Lee could do, so he did his job. He walked slowly upstairs to the room over the Blue Moon. He made his way through the crowd picking up snatches of conversation, "Amsley well looks good. Last week it was down to six hundred and twenty feet with very little water. This morning when I left it was twenty-two hundred feet." "I calculate it'll come in before the weekend."

Jake stood in the middle of the floor. "Listen up. You guys gotta get out of here. Go out there and watch that well come in. Don't come back till the Amsley well or Skeeter well or whatever the hell you call it, is flowing into tanks, on account there won't be a damn thing in here but cases of beer and sacks of feed. And keep your traps shut about you know what. Everybody out of here by four o'clock."

Sarah Emma struggled down the stairs to the basement of Bethlehem Church with a basket in one hand, her purse and quilting bag, filled with thread, needles and scissors, in the other. She sighed as she reached the bottom step. These two hours in the week were like a calm island, a time to rest and catch up on what was happening with her friends.

Dora Cook was fussing with that cranky little heater. Hattie and Sophie, still in their coats, pulled the quilting frame nearby, while they waited for the heater to take off the chill in the expansive basement.

This would be the best time, Sarah thought.

"I've brought something. I need your expertise as cooks. She put the basket on a table and took out four pies and four plates and forks, then looked up. "I'm going to start a little something, I guess you would call it." She shrugged uncertainly. "A little business on my back porch. I'll sell bowls of hot stew and cornbread, and four kinds of pies. Something for the oilmen—to stop by and warm themselves up with—and the pies, too, to spoil them. Then always keep the coffee pot going.

"Sarah," Hattie slipped out of her coat and took Sarah's, too. "You already have so much to do."

"I want you each to taste these pies and tell me what you think." She put a small slice of apple, cherry, pumpkin and chocolate meringue pie on each plate and gave them each a fork.

Seriously, thoughtfully, they savored each piece.

Finally Hattie said, "The pumpkin needs more nutmeg and maybe some cloves, but the others are masterpieces."

"I think the cherry needs more sugar," Sophie said, "but any one of them oil men would take just what you got and ask for more. They love home cookin'."

"This a real good idea, Sarah. When you gonna open?" Dora asked. "We all want to be there for the Grand Opening. I'll bring my Brownie camera."

"What are you gonna call yourself?" Sophie asked

"Sarah's Pies, I guess."

"You gonna advertise in the paper?" Hattie asked.

"I don't know about all this. It's not a big thing. I thought I'd let my boarders spread the word."

Hattie cut herself another piece of apple pie. "You ought to put it in the paper, Sarah." She savored the bite. "I guess you saw the paper last Tuesday, I don't know how stupid they think we are."

Dora sat down at the quilting frame and fished through her purse for her glasses. "That raid was a joke—a joke on us."

Sarah Emma looked up. "What happened?"

"They raided the Blue Moon, Sarah," Hattie punctuated the air with her fork, "and guess what they found over that saloon – beer and bags of feed. Now I ask you, what do they need feed for in a saloon?"

"Stage scenery, that's what. Everybody knows there's gambling going on in this town and the next one and the next."

"My boarders say gambling's going on in every nook and cranny that can be found in this town, the whole county even." Sarah answered. "The Sheriff just never seems to be looking in the right place."

"At the right time, that is."

"The oil business is alright, I guess, but it took away our quiet little town for good."

"They're expecting three new wells to come in this week. That Skeeter well is producing about five barrels an hour." Sophie Malvern looked across the quilt to Sarah Emma. "More boarders for you."

"I don't need any more boarders. I've got eight now. Two in a bedroom, there's more wants to come in, but I got no more room."

"I see by your sign you're doing their laundry."

Sarah Emma nodded. "Seven dollars a week for bed and meals. Eight dollars if they want their wash done."

"Oh, Sarah..." Hattie couldn't finish. Then she regained her composure. "How are things going—I mean, you know, with your—obligations?'

"I paid off the place. Nobody can take my home from me. And I'm paying on the notes and doctor bills." She sighed. "I guess someday I'll be clear. Someday."

"Too bad you can't get a well or two, like Sophie and Dora, here."

Sarah Emma laughed. "The boarders have saved me. They have. They help me out sometimes—washing dishes and chopping wood. They seem to like it there. I'm hoping this little restaurant idea will work for a year and then I'll be over the top."

Sophie Malvern began stitching. "Sarah, I don't know how to say this. I know how you are, but maybe a little something from our royalty checks...I'd be pleased if you'd take it. You could call it a loan if you want to."

"I appreciate that more than I can say, but Sophie, I just couldn't do that. I couldn't."

The conversation died. The room had warmed and in the silence the ladies bent to their work. Sarah thought of the long years they had met and stitched innumerable quilts. They had helped each other through the births of babies, sicknesses, accidents, unexpected deaths, hardship and now, she looked across at Sophie, wealth.

Dora broke the silence. "I don't like what I read in the paper about that Hitler over there. He says in the future he'll tolerate no interference from a third party. Now what does that mean?"

"It means he only cares about himself and power. But Germany's a long ways off from us. We got problems of our own, like no law here that's worth anything. I know as well as I know my own name, that sheriff is paddin' his pockets with a lot more'n his salary."

Sarah Emma listened. Her time and her mind were so filled with responsibilities; she didn't know what was going on in other countries, even this county or in her own town. She looked up at the clock hung on the wall between two high windows. Four o'clock. Soon it would be time to go back to work. She rested her elbow on the quilt frame, rubbed her hands over her forehead, pushing back her hair. She was so tired of continuous work, peeling potatoes, rolling out dough for pies, dressing chickens, cleaning the kitchen and bedrooms and scrubbing oily clothes for her boarders. There seemed something to do every minute, from the time she got up until she dropped in bed late at night--and there was no way out. She had to pay off her debts. It was like trying to remove a mountain a teacup at a time.

She put her thread, needles and scissors in the bag, rolled them in a cloth and put them in her purse. They were still talking about Sherriff Webb looking the other way when he needed to. She was sorry to hear that Logan was on the take. She'd known him since he was a little boy. But she couldn't worry about that now. She had to go back to work—let them talk. At least, she thought as she gathered up the plates and pie tins, she had saved her home. Her family was safe.

CHAPTER 22

Sophie's kitchen had the rich smell of baking bread. She pulled from the oven, two rounded loaves bulging over a pan. Malvern pushed back ruffled curtains at the window and peered passed his new Buick in the drive, then turned to his wife. "I see him coming. Now just act like there's nothing unusual—just be natural, like it's any other day after school."

Joey bounded through the door, tossed his lunch pail on the table and looked at the bread. "Can I have a piece of that, Mom?"

"Of course." She sat out a plate of churned butter, a thick slice of warm bread and a glass of chilled milk. Malvern took a slice in his hand and coated it with butter. "Soon as you finish, Son, I want you to go see what wandered in this afternoon."

Joey gobbled down the last bite and followed his father out toward the barn. He opened the barn door and peered into the dim interior. Sophie followed but stopped at the barn door, fingering the chain of safety pins on her apron.

"Over there, Joey. The bay pony."

Joey turned to his father. "That's what wandered in?"

"You might say that."

"Whose is it?"

"Well...it's yours. She's all yours."

Joey became silent, his tongue stuck in the side of his

cheek, as if he were trying to keep his feelings under control. He stood still, apparently trying to understand about presents, something he'd never known before.

A year ago, Malvern thought, Joey would have let a tear escape but now, there was young manliness growing up in him.

"She's beautiful, Papa," he finally got out.

"At the auction they called her Merrylegs, Joey."

He ran his hand over her mane. "Merrylegs." He whispered the name.

They began to saddle her up and when they finished, Joey rode out of the barn, into the corral.

Sophie's eyes glistened as Joey began a slow gallop back through the pastures toward the oil wells. Malvern watched, too, feeling Joey's pride. His two other sons, Glenn and Kurt, passed briefly through his mind. He'd used them in the fields when they were boys until they finally gave up on school. He was sorry he'd had to use the boys, but there was no getting around it. Annie finished high school—for all the good it did her, marrying Willis Porter. Now Eva Mae would graduate in a couple of weeks. He watched Joey in the distance, riding around the pond in the back pasture. This is the one I'll set my sights on, he thought. Malvern nodded an agreement with his own plans. He glanced at Sophie but said nothing about it to her. Joey'd be no farm boy. Not him. He was the promise. He'd give him whatever he needed to make it. Maybe he'd make Joey a doctor or something like that. Joey would be the one. Joey'd make the name Malvern proud.

Malvern leaned on the top rail of the corral. He loved his children. No doubt about that in his mind. But in the silence of his heart there was one that touched a deeper vein, one for which he felt a special love. He never uttered the words or made the gesture that would make such a thing evident. But he knew it was true. He thought maybe it was because that child was the first, but he later came to see that she with her bright mind and caring ways, was his finest child. Annie. He could still see her running from school, just like Joey had this afternoon, her deep brown hair bouncing, eyes sparkling and cheeks red from the cold. She had been a beautiful child, was still beautiful. He would never let her know how it broke his heart when it was Willis Porter she picked to marry.

Joey wheeled the horse around and reined up before his father.

"You like her, Joey boy?" Malvern patted the pony's mane as Joey slipped off the saddle.

"She's fine, Papa. Real fine. I can't wait to show Kurt and Glenn."

Malvern looked down at the ground. He didn't want to think about that.

After they put the pony away, before they walked to the house, Malvern put his arm around Joey. "Son, there's gonna be things that seem somehow out of character with who you think you are. Things you never saw or done before, things your brothers or your Papa never done. That don't matter. I want you to grab for it and damn those that's gonna want to pull you back. You understand me, boy?'

Joey looked up at his father. "I'm not sure."

"How do you expect me to get ready for the prom, Mama, if all you do is talk to Annie about that baby?" Eva Mae had hurried off to the bedroom, came back and stood before them dressed in soft-pink formal, gauzy layers of netting over a voluminous skirt.

Annie sat propped up on the end of the couch in the Malvern living room, a pillow at her back. Warm spring breezes floated through the house, as Annie stitched quilt blocks for the baby's coverlet.

"My goodness," Eva Mae twirled around. "You'd think this was the only baby that was ever born."

Annie shook her head and went back to stitching, trying to remember her little sister was only sixteen.

"Annie, what do you think of my dress? Do you think I look like an angel? I think Danny will think I look just like an angel. Don't you think so, Annie?"

"He'll think you're the prettiest girl there, Eva Mae. No

doubt about it." Annie studied the dress for a moment. "Mama, that's a store-bought dress."

"Of course, it's a store-bought dress," Eva Mae cut in. "The second most expensive in Allison's Department Store."

"My, my." Annie rubbed her hand over her swollen stomach.

"I went last winter." Eva Mae's eyes beamed as she ran spread fingers over the wide, swaying skirt. "I told them when they got their formals in, I wanted them to call me. When they did, Papa took me in there and I got first pick. First pick of anybody in town. Think of that. Daddy remarked on it at the time. A Malvern girl getting first pick. Well, when I got home and came out into the living room in the formal, my Papa's eyes got big and he said I looked just like an angel. A living, breathing angel." She fluffed up the netted ruffle that lay across her shoulder and twirled again. "I wish we had a full-length mirror in this house. I'm gonna tell Papa we need a full-length mirror. I don't know how you ever got along when you were young, Annie, without a full-length mirror."

"Eva Mae, I'm twenty."

"Well, you know." She smoothed her hands over her tiny waist.

Annie studied the slender girl before her. "I remember my prom dress. Mine was blue. Remember, Mama? We went to Bishop's store and you sold a case of eggs and three gallons of cream. Then we went across the square to Allisons' and picked out the material. Remember the argument we had about the lace on the sleeves?"

Sophie smiled, not looking up from her sewing. "I remember."

"Annie, if you are going to start on that awful song you always sing about how sorrowful and poor we were and how you never had anything…"

"I didn't feel sorrowful and poor, Eva Mae."

"That was your life. It's my time now. I don't have to be sorrowful, and I wish you wouldn't make this a sad time. I don't have to be sad." Eva Mae ran to close the front door as an oil truck went by filling the air with dust. "Why, Annie, do you always talk about how thing used to be? I don't like it. It makes me feel bad. It even makes me feel mean. I don't have to feel that way."

"All right, Evie. Only life now counts!"

"I can't imagine being seen at the prom in a homemade dress, bought from egg money." She dropped down on a footstool spreading her wide skirt in a circle about her. "The cream and egg formal," she laughed.

Annie had helped care for her sister when she was a baby, but now, she thought, Eva Mae should be outgrowing some of these selfish ways.

"Who is this Danny you're going with?" Annie asked.

Eva Mae looked up, her eyes bright. "Danny Allison, of course, of the well-known Allison family."

"Mama." Annie put her quilt block down. "You're letting her go with an Allison boy? Keith Allison asked me to go out once when we were in high school, and you said I couldn't go. You said if an Allison wants to date a farm girl, it's for no good purpose. Remember, Mama? You said that."

Sophie looked at both her girls, apparently unsure about how to answer. "Well, Annie, I said what I thought was best then." She didn't look too certain about her explanation.

"Annie, don't upset Mama. Papa is going to be one the richest men in the county. Why shouldn't I go with an Allison, or anybody else, if I want to? Tell me, why not?"

"I'm sure I don't know." Annie smoothed the quilt block out across her knee. "I feel actually like...there's new rules in an old game, and I don't know them yet."

Sophie instantly looked up, "Oh, Annie, that's just how I feel. Just like that. What used to be true may not be true now."

"I'm going to change my dress." Eva Mae popped up from the footstool and swayed toward the bedroom. "Don't want any smudges," she called over her shoulder.

Annie awkwardly seated herself on the floor. "I've finished the last block, Mama. Let's put the pieces together." With her mother, they laid out the quilt squares side by side across the living room carpet. Each block showed a print called the Sunbonnet Girl.

"Oh, Mama, I like it. Now, we'll get it to the quilting ladies."

Another oil truck rumbled past. Sophie patted her daughter's hand and kissed her forehead. "We didn't meet for quilting last week. Sarah Emma opened her new restaurant. Hattie made a sign and put it in the window, 'Sarah's Derrick High Pies.' She drew a picture of an oil derrick on it. Hattie brought her Brownie in and took a picture of all of us by the sign."

Eva Mae came back into the room and looked down at the twenty-four blocks on the floor. "Baby stuff." She dropped into a chair, one leg draped over the chair arm. "Mama, you promised to make a little draw-string purse for me to carry on my arm."

CHAPTER 23

Willis set his sights straight ahead, driving the tractor toward the hedgerow at end of the field. He would not look at the black car that followed him--over in the road. It followed him, parallel, as he went down furrows, the planter dropping beans in the row. When he came to the end of the furrow and turned around, the black car in the road turned also, moving even with him.

He told them he'd get the money! Why wouldn't they leave him alone? He told them not to come near his home. Annie didn't need to know about this. Nobody needed to know. Panic poured through him, prickled over his scalp and neck. Sweat ran down his back, dripped off his forehead. He just needed one more good night like that one last winter. That night was magic. Every card fell into place, and he cleaned up. There had been other good nights, but not like that first one. He'd never been one to take the center of attention, to feel like a real winner, but he had that night. If he could just get that back.

The sun beat down on his shoulders. He pulled his cap off and rubbed perspiration off the back of his neck. Things had gone really sour lately. In his head he tallied up what he owed. It seemed like the harder he tried, the more he lost. Finally, the car sped off, dust fogging behind it. Relief drained through him, and he throttled down the tractor right there in the middle of the field, sat quiet, pulled out his red handkerchief, and began wiping sweat off his face. He took out his thermos, poured water on his handkerchief, and laid it across the back of his neck. Damn 'em, they hang on to you like a bulldog, he thought.

That afternoon as Willis came through the kitchen door, Annie called out, "Hi honey, I got something special for you."

"I know you got something special for me." He leaned over her thick girth and kissed her lips and patted her bottom. "That's the specialist thing in the world."

She held his face between her hands and kissed him again. "Willis, what I've got that's special is strawberry shortcake. I got a crock of strawberries from the Patrick brothers."

"They brought strawberries to you?"

"Them? Hardly. They never go off the place." She put plates at the table. A tall pitcher of tea sat on the green tablecloth. "I stopped to see if the brothers needed anything from town, and they gave me the strawberries."

Suddenly, Willis looked past her, out the window. His smile faded. He went to the window but did not part the curtain. His body froze. "Annie, honey," his voice dropped low. "I want you to go in the bedroom and stay there. Close the door and don't come out. There's somebody here that wants to see me."

"But Willis, we're going into town in a little while. Tell them they have to come back."

"I'll...I'll tell them." He hurried her into the bedroom, his hand on her back. "I'll tell them." His voice quavered.

He closed the door, but the bedroom window was open and Annie watched through the lace curtain.

A big man in a long black coat crawled out of the passenger's side of the car, and ambled toward the front, but Willis met him in the yard. He pushed his felt fedora back off his forehead. "You know, Porter, you're a hard man to find." There was a scar across his right eyebrow where hair did not grow. "Especially when we got an agreement. Remember, Porter, how we had an agreement?" He moved closer to Willis. "You said you'd have something for me yesterday. I waited, but you never showed up."

"I was gonna go but..."

He gripped Willis' shoulder, face close. "You trying to give me excuses, Porter? It always seemed to me, a man full of excuses is not good for much more than excuses. Wouldn't you say that's about what you're worth, Porter? Excuses?"

"I'm gonna get you the money. I said I am, and I am," Willis stammered.

The man took Willis' chin between his thumb and index finger. "You see, Porter," his eyes fixed on Willis. "I don't like a liar, and you been lying to me."

"I'll get you the money. I—I know just where I'll get it. Just give me a few days. My father-in-law..."

"I don't want no details."

"I'll get it. You don't need to worry none about that."

"Remember what I said, 'I hate a liar worse'n anything.' They just make me sick, and I can't be sure what I'll do. You understand what I'm sayin', Porter?" He released Willis' chin.

"I understand."

Annie heard the whine in Willis' words.

"All right. Just don't give me no more of your god-dammed lies."

"I'll take care of it. You can be sure of that. I will."

The man walked back to the car. "You damn well better," he said, his foot on the running board. Then the door slammed. The driver started the car and began to move backward down the drive to the main road.

Willis came inside, and Annie ran out of the bedroom to him. "Willis, what's going on? You're in trouble. You've got to tell me."

"Annie, honey...oh," he held her to him. "Baby, I'm gonna have to go to your father and ask him for some money."

Annie pulled back and stared at him. "My father?"

"I owe...well, some money." He averted his eyes.

"How much do you owe?"

"A little over fourteen-hundred dollars."

"Fourteen-hundred dollars!" Annie breathed, astounded. She started to ask how he could owe so much, but she knew. She dropped into a chair by the window. "And the baby coming. I can't do a thing...to help pay..."

"No, no, I won't have you working. No, it's up to me. I'll figure us a way out of this. Honey, we may need to go to your Papa." The clock in the living room chimed six.

Annie bit her lower lip as she looked away from him. She wanted so much for her parents to accept her husband, believe in him. "Oh, Willis, I do hate to do that."

"There's no other way. These people mean..." Willis swallowed hard and looked out to where the car had been.

"I'll talk to Papa, Willis. Let me talk to him," Annie said.

Annie slowly climbed the steps to her parents' house, feeling more than the weight of the child in her belly. Everything in her rebelled against asking her father to help Willis. She paused on the second step...there *was* no other way.

"Annie," her mother met her at the door, opened the screen. "Are you all right?'

"No, Mama. Not exactly. It's Willis."

Eva Mae was instantly beside her mother, eyes wide, questioning. "You're not leaving Willis and coming back here, are you Annie? Just in time for the baby? Annie, you can't do that. There isn't room for you and the baby and all that stuff. Mama, she can't come back, can she?"

"Hush, Evie." Sophie put her arm around Annie's shoulders.

Annie turned to her sister. "I didn't say a thing about coming back, Eva Mae. I just need a little of Papa's time." She went to where her father sat at a new desk—a secretary desk that stretched up six feet and had two dozen little drawers.

Malvern looked up. "What is it, Annie?"

"Oh, Papa." She smoothed her hand over her great belly. "It's Willis. It's his gambling."

"I knew it." Eva Mae stood by her father. "That Porter outfit's no good."

Annie lowered herself carefully into a chair beside Malvern. "Willis has run up a debt—a terrible debt. He wants to be rich so bad, and he thinks gambling will do it. But he loses and loses and now... Oh, Papa, they're after him. They're threatening him. They came to our house. I heard them. I'm so scared. I don't know what we'll do. We don't have money like that."

Malvern searched his daughter's face. "How much is he in debt?"

"Oh, Papa... you can't believe it."

"How much?"

"Over fourteen-hundred dollars..."

Malvern interrupted, "Didn't he know he was in over his head before it got that far?"

Eva Mae toyed with a brass bell on her father's desk. "We told you, Annie. He's a Porter."

Annie gave her sister a withering look, but it was her father she answered. "Willis never had anything in his life, Papa." How could she make them see Willis' side? "He never saw anything much and people he's known all his life are getting rich and he..."

She turned to Eva Mae. "It wasn't Willis' fault he was born in the Porter family." Everything in her wanted to defend him, but the ground seemed to be dissolving under her feet.

"Why should we spend our money to get Willis out of his mess?" Eva Mae spoke up.

"He's just a boy, Papa." Annie begged, ignoring her sister. "Those people are too clever for him. He talks all the time about the night they all bought him drinks. He said he felt like he never did in his life...like everyone was his friend. Oh, Papa, give him a second chance, please"

Curtains blew out against the sofa, a soft breeze filling the room. "We'll see, Annie," Malvern answered.

Eva Mae held Annie in her accusing gaze. "I told you, you shouldn't marry a into that family."

"I've loved Willis since I was in second grade." As soon as

she said it, she wondered why she should defend herself to Eva Mae.

"Blood will come out," Eva Mae pronounced. "That's what they always say."

"Let me think," Malvern said. "Willis, it looks to me, has got the bug. Paying him out of trouble won't cure him. I want to do what's the best."

"Mama," Eva Mae sat down on the chair arm where her mother was piecing together quilt blocks. "Annie's another family now, isn't she? She can't bring her troubles back here to us. You shouldn't put up with that."

"Annie is our daughter, same as you, Eva Mae. Now be quiet; Papa's thinking."

"Well, I see plain as day, she's gonna leave Willis and come back here, with that baby and after we all told her not to marry Willis Porter. Mama, you need to do something. You're gonna leave Willis, aren't you, Annie? And come back here?"

"No, Eva Mae. I want my marriage to work. It's just that Willis has... Well, he sees people with money and he wants what they have."

"Oh, Annie, I'd just hate for you to come here." Eva Mae came close, her green eyes bright and challenging. "All you do is make us sorry for you and spoil things for our family."

"*Our* family." Annie echoed, her voice rising. "Are you trying to say *your* family, Eva Mae?"

"Well, you're another family. You said you wanted your marriage. She's another family now, isn't she Mama? Isn't that true?"

"Hush, Eva Mae. We need to be quiet. Papa's thinking what to do."

"Part of it—," Annie began cautiously, looking at her mother "—is you and Papa are getting so much money and Willis doesn't want me to be sorry I married him. He knows what people think of his father."

"But you did marry him, so you have to lie in the bed you made." Eva Mae went to the organ bench and spread her skirt wide across it.

Malvern turned to Annie and took her hands. "This is what I'm gonna to do. I'm goin' to give Willis half, 700-dollars. That will get them off his back. The money is on the terms he stop his gambling, and he never goes near them places again. He can take care of the rest himself. He's got to be responsible for the debts he runs up. He can pay off the other 700 when the crops come in. He can tell 'em that. Tell 'em they'll get the rest then."

"Half payment!" Annie felt frantic. "I don't know if they'll settle for that."

"That's my terms. They'll have to accept it, or Willis will have to take care of the other half."

"Thank you, Papa." She leaned forward and kissed her father. "I'll take it to him."

"No, Annie. I'll take it to him. Willis will hear my terms from me."

"If Danny Allison finds out it's my brother-in-law the mob's after I'll just die," Eva Mae exploded, threw herself full-length on the sofa and pulled a pillow over her head.

CHAPTER 24

By noon, clouds were gathering, the air close and heavy, with distant rumbling in the east. Annie put plates and forks in the picnic basket on the table, and deviled eggs, pickles and the cookies she'd baked this morning. She steadied herself by the table, moved into a chair, and began fanning herself—a futile effort. She was clammy all over. Would this baby never come?

The Fourth of July! The baby was due two weeks ago. She wasn't sure about going to the park tonight. What if pains started, and she had to get through that crowd of people? Still, Amsley had not had fireworks for over ten years. The city fathers said there had been too many other things to spend money on. But this year they promised a short display, across the lake. For the past few years the best anyone could hope for was some kids running around with sparklers and a couple of old veterans strutting about in overly snug uniforms. Annie blotted her face with a damp cloth and wished she had something cool to drink. Even the water was warm.

Willis came in early from the fields to get ready. After he finished his bath, she came into the bedroom while he dressed. "I've been thinking all day how good a watermelon would taste. Will you go into town and get one?" Annie smiled sweetly at him.

He leaned over and kissed her as he tucked in his shirt, "Sure 'nough. Have to keep my pregnant wife happy. Dutch's got cold watermelons."

Willis left as Annie finished packing the sandwiches in the

picnic basket. Her parents drove by with Joey in their new car. Eva Mae, she imagined, was with that Danny Allison.

She sat down at the table again and waited. The clock chimed four, then four-thirty, then finally five. Willis must have had to go several places. It was still a long time until the fireworks.

Annie took out one of the sandwiches and began to eat it. Through the back screen door, she saw dark clouds boiling overhead. Oh, I hope it doesn't rain and spoil the fireworks, she thought. Then a deep ache came in her lower back. She stood and grasped the chair. She seemed to want to stand. Water poured out from her on the floor. She tried to mop it up but another pain wrapped around her middle section. "Oh, God, where is Willis?" she whispered. She looked out at the drive, knowing the truck was gone. She'd have to wait.

Annie couldn't see the hands on the clock in the darkening evening. She turned the light on in the kitchen. 7:23! She timed the pains for the next half hour. Six minutes apart. She called the doctor. Maybe he didn't go to the celebration. The phone rang a long time before a thin voice came on the line. His housekeeper. Yes, the doctor was out. Couldn't say when he would be back. Maybe she should call the hospital.

She called the hospital. "I'm having a baby. The pains are five minutes apart. I..." She stopped, unable to go on.

"Honey, you need to get here right away."

"I don't think I can drive now...is there anybody who can..."

"Mr. Williams is usually here...he could come get you, but he went to the fireworks, everybody's over there. Isn't there anybody who can bring you in?"

"No," she gasped.

"Well, honey, I'm sorry but I don't know how I can help you."

Annie hung up. Fear crept over her. She was going to need someone soon. She walked the length of the little house and back, then went out into the yard and walked. She looked across the backfield. She could get to the Patrick brothers in fifteen minutes.

She stopped wondering about Willis. She knew!

Annie started through the newly planted furrows. She had forgotten about that. She steadied her ungainly body and stopped when pains came. Near the Patricks' land, one of the men from an oil well spotted her and came out in his truck. He helped her up in the cab. "I better get you to the hospital."

"No," she gripped the edge of the seat. "I don't think there's time. You might have to deliver it. Get me to the Patricks' house."

"Okay," the driver quickly agreed and drove as fast as he could over the undulating furrows. "Your husband's Willis Porter?"

Annie nodded.

"We'll send somebody in town to get him."

"I don't know where he is."

The driver stared at her wide-eyed as another pain came on her. "Reckon he won't be hard to find," he said softly.

"Just hurry. I'm so scared. I've never had a baby before."

The driver helped her up the porch steps to the Patricks' house.

Otis met them at the door.

Henry was behind him, eyes wide. "The misery on you, Annie?"

"Oh, Otis," she breathed. "It's time, and I can't find the doctor... or Willis." She leaned against his short paunchy body.

"I'll see if I can find Willis for you, Miz Porter," The oilman said as Otis helped her toward the bedroom.

Henry called the doctor, but he still hadn't come in.

The brothers sat on each side of the bed, holding Annie's hands and washing her face with damp clothes and saying soothing words. About nine o'clock, Annie saw from the bedroom window, in the distance a spray of light, the long-awaited fireworks. Then another and another. Behind them, lightening flared across the heavens followed by muted rumbles. In a maze of pain, Annie sensed sharp brilliant flashes mingling with crashing thunder and raindrops began to patter against the window. Then she knew the baby was coming. Otis, his face a mask of sober wide-eyed awe, held her hand almost too tightly. Annie glimpsed the brothers looking at each other. That look spoke for them. They knew what they must do.

"We'll need to get clean sheets under her."

In the kitchen Henry poured warm water from a teakettle into a white basin and as he washed his hands, he looked to Otis. "Go to the barn, get some of that twine. That'll do. Wash it good with soap and water—about a foot ought to do." Within minutes the brothers stood ready for the delivery.

With a piercing scream and a mighty push, Annie felt the baby expel from her body, Henry guiding the delivery. She settled into exhaustion.

"It's a little girl." Otis beamed.

"It's a girl, Annie." Henry wiped her face with a cool damp towel.

She heard the wail of her baby.

She looked drowsily at Otis as he handed her the baby. His eyes were damp.

"We're not quite done here," Henry barked, as the afterbirth expelled.

Then, they—all three—wiped the baby clean, and Otis wrapped it tightly in a towel.

"We had a baby," Annie whispered to Otis. He dropped his head bashfully and looked at the tiny red face peeking out of the towel.

"Aunt Belle said there's always some kind of 'Ann' in every generation of our family," Annie said. "So I'm going to call her Hannah." Henry stood at the foot of the bed grinning sheepishly through his bushy beard.

A loud knock shook the door. The doctor, dripping wet, stood on the porch. He came into the bedroom, examined the baby and Annie. "Looks like you were in good hands, Mrs. Porter." He turned toward the reticent brothers. "I didn't know you boys had it in you."

"We been through calving time for the last 60 years. I

supposed it wasn't much different."

The doctor snapped his bag closed. "I suppose not." He shook his head, and he went back out into the dark rainy night as the full fury of the storm came on.

It was mid-morning the next day when Willis came and put the watermelon on the Patricks' kitchen table. Willis' hair hung over his brow, a sleeve torn partly loose from his shirt and a pocket ripped. When he looked down at his child, tears began to flow. He dropped to his knees by the bed and held Annie's hand. "I'm sorry, honey. I'm so sorry."

"Willis!" She looked at his swollen distorted face; a bruise on one side. "What happened?" On the back of his hands and arms were round black spots in angry red bumps. She turned his hand over. "Willis? Are these cigarette burns?"

"They kept me, Annie. I couldn't leave."

"*They* kept..." She looked into his eyes and then she understood. "Why would they do that, Willis? After Papa gave you all that money? Why?"

Willis didn't answer. He stood, and walked to the window, his back to her.

"You didn't pay them the money Papa gave you!"

He turned back, rubbing his arm and looked down at his daughter,

"Did you go somewhere else and lose that money, too, Willis?"

He turned abruptly and left the room. She heard the back door close and his truck start up in the drive.

Annie turned her head to the wall and began to cry. Otis stood by, his heart in his eyes, stroking his beard.

"Otis, I want to go to my mama. Will you take me home?"

CHAPTER 25

Annie felt a soft breeze from the open bedroom window as she slowly awoke in the bed of her childhood in her parents' home. Henry Patrick had brought her parents' home yesterday afternoon and apparently the party line got busy because by nightfall neighbors came, filling the Malvern house, to see Willis and Annie's new baby.

The next morning, Eva Mae's bright voice in the living room brought Annie to sharp consciousness in her bed.

"Mama, did lots of people come when I was born?" Eva Mae was asking.

"Yes, Evie they did," Annie heard her mother answer.

"How many?" Eva Mae persisted.

"You were born about noon, Eva Mae, but what I remember most is when the visitors came that night, they sat around my bed, laughing and talking loud, shaking the bed. I was a nervous wreck."

"Why didn't you just tell them to get off the bed, to go in the other room? Leave you and your new baby with some quiet?"

"I don't know. It would have been rude, I guess." Annie smiled at her mother's answer.

"Oh, Mama, you really are too good," Eva Mae said.

"I just try to get along."

"You're too good, Mama. It doesn't pay."

Annie looked down at the sleeping baby who curled its tiny fist around her finger. Last night, her father had remarked about Hannah's long fingers, fingers of a musician, he had said. She smiled at how bashful Glenn had been when she insisted he hold the baby. It had felt like the old days, when everyone was the same, and they came together to see a newborn, or there was sickness or sorrow. Now they mostly saw each other when a well was about to come in, and they quietly tallied up in their minds who had the most, and the next to the most wells—and who didn't have any.

"Mama," Eva Mae voice drifted into her room again. "Were there more people when I was born or last night?" Annie turned on her pillow, looking at her baby and smiled at her sister's childish question.

"I don't remember, darling. I think, last night."

"Mama, you shouldn't let Annie move in here. It's my room. She's different now. She's a mother and another family...and she's a Porter now."

"Eva Mae, your sister just had a baby. She needs rest, and we have to care for her."

"Danny Allison asked if it was my sister who married into that Porter tribe. Tribe. That's what he said."

Annie sat up on the edge of the bed. She felt lightheaded and shaky.

Eva Mae's voice still carried from the next room. "I'm glad Papa told Willis he couldn't come here anymore, after Willis broke his word to him. Danny Allison said Willis is sick in the head and makes a fool of himself in town like he's one of them big shots from Chicago. He said he's getting to be the town joke just like ole Porter."

Annie gasped. How could her own sister be saying such cruel things? She had shared this very bed with her while they were growing up.

"Mama, I don't want Annie here. I hate having a Porter in

this house. She's ruining my life." Eva Mae's stinging words came through loud and clear.

"Don't talk like that about the Porters," Her mother's voice was indignant. "That darling baby in there is a Porter...our grandchild."

Annie stood, hobbled to the end of the bed, and struggled to get into her dress. She grasped the dresser to steady herself. She was not going to listen to this.

"I want to hear my programs." Eva Mae pronounced.

"You can't while Annie and the baby are here."

"I always listen to *Back Stage Wife* and *Stella Dallas*. You know that. I feel like a prisoner in my own house."

Annie looked around the bed for her shoes. The baby was beginning to stir.

"Mama," Eva Mae began again, "Don't you think those people from Chicago talk funny?"

"I hadn't noticed. Keep your voice down."

"Well I noticed. The same words sound funny. I think they sound citified. Do you think we sound funny to them?"

"I expect so."

"I don't want them thinking that about me," Eva Mae said.

"It doesn't matter how we sound, we're all the same underneath."

"Oh, Mama, you just don't see how things are. You're so good. You don't see anything like it is. Glenn's like you, he doesn't see any difference, but Kurt does. He feels it. He knows."

"What does Kurt know?"

"Oh, Mama!" Eva Mae fumed.

Annie worked her foot into a shoe, found the other, stood up, and picked up the sleeping infant.

"Mama, how long does it take to get over a baby?"

Annie walked out of the bedroom into the living room, Hannah cradled in her arms. "I'm over it now, Eva Mae. I'm going home, Mama."

Sophie came to her. "Annie, you're white as a sheet. You have to stay in bed for a while."

"I'm going home. Kurt and Glenn are out there in the yard talking to Papa. They can take me." Annie went to the screen door and called them.

They came immediately. Malvern looked at his wife, then Annie, "What's going on here?"

"I'm not staying where my family is insulted, and I'm not wanted."

"You're not leaving this house, Annie. Not now," Malvern said. "That...husband of yours won't look after you,"

"I love my husband."

The baby began a tiny, plaintive wail. Annie glanced down at her, tears burning her eyes.

Eva Mae looked about at her father and brothers. "I can't see why you're so worked up, Annie."

Annie grasped the chair to steady herself. "I might expect this from little Joey..."

"Leave Joey out of this," Malvern countered abruptly, then turned to Kurt. "Take her, if she wants to go. But Annie, if you're backing that Willis and what all he does, don't come here wanting me to bail him out again."

"Annie can't just go. She needs help." Sophie pleaded. "Can't you all see that? She's our own. Why can't we get along like we used to. We're a family."

"It's Annie that can't get along with us," Eva Mae exploded.

"Eva Mae, you really must try to be kinder to your sister," Sophie said.

"Papa," Annie winced from the torn flesh of her delivery but anger poured through her. "Why don't you rein Eva Mae in?" she pleaded. "You would never have allowed that from us...such disrespect."

"Let her go." Kurt stared at his father as he took Annie's arm. "I understand how she feels."

"No," Sophie persisted, tears brimming her eyes. "She should rest...stay here..." No one was listening.

Kurt helped Annie into his truck. Glenn held the baby as

they pulled out of the drive. No one spoke. There was rawness in what had happened, like a fresh throbbing wound.

Glenn broke the silence in his soft way. "I'll say why he don't rein her in." Again he fell silent.

"Well?" Kurt prompted impatiently.

"It's not really Eva Mae he's thinking on. It's Joey."

"Joey?"

"I heard Mama complaining how Eva Mae wants her way all the time and wants to make everything different and Papa just said, 'Let her.' Says she knows how thing are done and we don't. Then he says, 'Things will be set for Joey when he comes up.'"

"And what did Mama say?" Annie asked.

Glenn peered down at the baby. "I never heard Mama say anything."

Kurt turned into the drive at Annie's house. "So Joey's the anointed one?" Kurt hit the steering wheel with the heel of his palm. "Son-of-bitch."

After they stopped before her front door, the three in the truck cab sat in silence. Finally, Glenn opened the truck door. "I'll stay with you this week, Annie."

Kurt was on fire as he sped off down the lane. Dust from the country road billowed behind him. He pressed hard on the accelerator. He could hardly think he was so angry.

CHAPTER 26

"Willis, shouldn't you be getting the corn out of the fields? The neighbors are cutting the beans and picking corn." Annie was carving a jagged mouth in the face of a jack-o-lantern. The pumpkin was the latest little gift the Patrick brothers had brought—something of an excuse to see the baby. "We need to get the crops sold off, Willis. Pay those terrible people so they'll leave you alone."

"I'm not going out to the field." Willis rubbed his sleepy eyes.

"But Willis, you put the crops in. You've got to harvest them."

"There's...this car that follows along the road while I'm shucking corn...down the row. It moves slow and keeps just even with me."

"I can't stand them coming around here. I'm afraid," Annie said. "We've got the baby. Sell the truck, Willis."

"I can't do that. I sold the old car, the harness in the barn and everything else I could lay my hands on, and took the money, but..."

"But," she put the knife down by the half-carved pumpkin and turned to look into his eyes. "You lost more money after that. Is that right, Willis?"

"Just get off my back, Annie. I got all on my mind I can think about." He got up and went out, slamming the door.

She finished the jack-o-lantern, baked a couple of pumpkin pies, and as she put them on the table to cool, he sauntered back in and slumped in a chair.

"The Halloween parade is tonight, Willis." Annie picked up the baby, settled in the rocker, and began nursing her. "I'm going to dress Hannah in a costume." she said.

"I'm not going to that parade," Willis cut in.

"But we always go."

"You don't understand. I can't!" His voice was shrill.

"Why can't you?" The baby began to whimper.

"I just—can't." He seemed agitated, as he went to the window, pushed back the curtain, and peered out

"What's wrong, Willis? Tell me. Tell me everything, and I mean everything."

"They're into me for some... money." He walked about the room, eyes wide, staring at nothing.

Annie watched him. "How much?"

"A little over two thousand dollars."

"Two thousand dollars! We'll never be able...oh why? Willis did you...?" She cried, shaking her head. "And you didn't pay those other people the money Papa gave you, did you?" Annie put the baby in the bassinet, came to him, and looked into his eyes. "Willis, you know I can never go to my father. You broke your promise to him."

"No, no, don't go to him. I don't want him to know."

"Oh, my God, Willis." She ran fingers through her hair. "He's going to know...sometime."

"I'm goin' to St. Louis tonight. On the train. I got an uncle there. Maybe he can help." His eyes nervously darted about the room.

The baby was screaming. Annie dropped her head in her hands and began to cry softly.

He stopped before her. "Just take me to town and go on to

the parade like everything's all right." He pushed his hair back. "Don't tell them people. Don't tell nobody where I went."

"Oh, Willis!" She felt heartsick. And desperate.

A small carnival occupied the side street just off Main, which was itself blocked off for the Halloween parade. The happy calliope music of a carousel filled the air. Witches, hobos, and ghosts ambled through the crowd, along the street among the hot dogs, cotton candy, and ice cream stands. The baby on Annie's shoulder began to rouse as she juggled her purse to pay for some popcorn. The parade was beginning. She found a space by the curb. Willis must be halfway to St. Louis by now.

Hannah stared in silent, wide-eyed wonderment as the band went by. Lillian Powers and Ella Donnelly were always in the first float. For years they had planned and promoted the parade. It had been stated in *The Amsley Record* that two oilrigs would end the parade, just before Sheriff Webb's patrol car, in recognition of the oil production, which had become part of the town's culture and ultimately would be its history.

Also, Annie remembered, headlines that had shouted that Sheriff Logan Webb and his deputy, acting on a lead that illegal gambling was going on had raided the places in question. Apparently it was a rumor that got out of hand, the paper said, because when Webb and the deputy climbed the stairs to the storage room over the Blue Moon, nothing was found but some crates, a broken bar stool and a cot. Jake Beardsman was quoted as saying he sleeps there sometimes.

The next floats were by Roland's Feed and Seed, the First National Bank and the Garden Club. The Methodist Church's Dorcas Class always outdid themselves with their float, but it was, in truth, an annual covert competition with the Baptist's "Caring For Others" float. The parade would culminate with the usual gala banquet at the Hotel Allison, under the supervision of Lillian Powers and Ella Donnelly, who also supervised the guest list.

Gala banquets were not on Annie's mind. Willis must be close to St. Louis now.

She stopped by the carousel and decided to give Hannah her first ride. Annie held her baby tightly as the carousel horse moved slowly up and down. She didn't want to leave the crowd, the noise, the lights, and the carnival music and go to her empty house. Behind these happy sounds she heard, lay deep fear. Belle Dorsett and Carson Garrett waved as they passed. Annie was glad they walked on. She didn't want them asking about Willis. He must be with his uncle now.

Finally in her truck, Hannah exhausted and asleep in the seat beside her, Annie drove along country roads. Gas flares lit the vast oil fields with an eerie yellow hue, but near her house tall trees made islands of dark shadows in her yard.

That night, Annie slept fitfully. Noisy crowds, calliope music, drum beats with the marching band, gaudy floats, and a fearsome black car blurred through her mind like the changing scenes riding the carousel. She buried her head between the two pillows. What if Willis's uncle wouldn't loan him the money? So much money! And what if he did? How would they ever pay that back? The clock struck seven, ending a restless night. In the morning, she made coffee, opened the windows, turned the key in the front door, and opened it.

For an instant, she stood paralyzed, seeing but not comprehending what lay before her. Then she screamed and tore down the front porch stairs. "Willis." He lay sprawled across the steps. "Oh, God, Willis." Blood from his head had dripped off the bottom step onto the grass.

"Oh, no, oh, no," she cried and senselessly reached behind his head to stay the bleeding. He was cold! She drew her bloody hand back, sobbing, terrified. "What have they done!"

She took him in her arms and stroked his face and buried her head on his lifeless chest. "Oh, Willis." The sobs heaved up again and again.

"Willis, you stupid foolish...they got you...damn 'em! Damn you, Willis." Then she sat down on the step by him and took up his hand. "Damn you," she screamed at him. The baby was crying inside the house. "You see what you've done. You've ended *us.*"

She calmed a bit. Stared across the field, derricks protruding over a sea of unharvested corn, piercing the yellow morning sky. What to do? The sheriff? Her father? Yes, he'd know what to do. She couldn't think.

She decided she should call the sheriff. No one answered. She went out and tried to pull Willis up onto the porch but couldn't. He lay in a pool of blood and it seemed somehow important he shouldn't be in the sun. Cover him! Yes, he should be covered. She got a sheet. Her father would know what to do. She laid the shrieking hungry baby beside her in the truck and drove to Malvern's house.

"Willis is dead!" Annie stormed into the kitchen. Her parents, Joey and Eva Mae were sitting at breakfast. "He's dead, Papa" As she said it, it seemed as if it were someone else screaming the words. "He's lying right over there," she motioned toward her house. "They dumped him on our front door step. Oh, Papa we don't know these kinds of people. They shot him in the head."

"You're all bloody, Annie." Eva Mae's mouth turned down in distaste.

Malvern hurried to his daughter and took her in his arms. Sophie took the baby from her daughter. "I never...imagined they'd..." he whispered as he stroked Annie's hair.

"I don't know what to do." Annie pulled away from her father. "This is beyond me, Papa. I'm so scared I can't think...and, oh my God, Papa, Willis is gone."

"I'll call the sheriff and undertaker. They can meet us at your house. Your mother and I will go with you, Annie. Eva Mae, take the baby."

"I'm not taking that screaming kid."

"Eva Mae, now you hush," Sophie handed Hannah to her. "You take care of that baby."

"Papa, you could have helped us." Annie flew at her father.

"You could have. You've got plenty of money. We just needed..." She couldn't go on. Her father didn't know of the thousands that Willis owed. "Willis was going to get the money. Oh, God, I can't believe this." She dropped in a chair, shaking and sobbing.

"It is not Papa's fault, Annie." Eva Mae leaned forward. "You can't put the blame on us for Willis."

"I lost my husband, Eva Mae. My baby has no father. Can you understand that, Eva Mae? She'll never know her father."

"Small loss, I'd say."

Annie gasped. "You little bitch!"

"Mama, did you hear her?" Eva Mae turned on Sophie.

Joey sat, eyes wide, turning from one to the other holding his spoonful of oatmeal.

Annie took the baby from Eva Mae and sat down in a chair. "I don't even have the money to bury him."

"Go to his father." Eva Mae sniped. "And stop always bringing us all your pitiful troubles."

"They murdered him," she whispered to herself, trying to comprehend it. Murdered? It was something you read about in the papers. Something you heard about. Willis murdered. No—no. He would walk in the door this afternoon, teasing her like he always did.

Malvern came back into the kitchen. "I called the sheriff. We'll go right over and meet him where Willis..."

Images of the morning churned in her head like a fevered nightmare. Sophie took Annie's hand, "We'll certainly see he is buried proper."

"And," Malvern continued, "we'll give you what you need to tide you over, but Annie, we won't go to his funeral."

"Won't?" She whispered, staring at her father as if she had been slapped. She turned abruptly, went out the screened door to her truck, hugging her baby to her like a stuffed toy.

When she turned down her lane, she saw in the side mirror, her father's big black Buick following, and behind him the sheriff. She got out of the car, her heart pounding, as she walked to the porch where Willis lay under the bloody sheet.

Sheriff Webb uncovered Willis's body and walked around it. He lifted up Willis's arm and shoulder and turned him over. "Two shots in the back, one at the head." He wrote something down on a pad. "Body's cold. Been several hours."

Annie stood by, the baby on her hip, watching in a trance.

"I know who it was, Sheriff. That did it," she said at last, when Webb seemed about ready to leave.

"You know that for sure?" The sheriff's face was a sober mask as he looked down at Willis, and then flung the bloodstained sheet back over the body.

"Willis owed money," John Malvern said. "A lot of it."

The sheriff studied Malvern's questioning face then looked back at Willis.

Annie shifted the baby. "I don't know names, Sheriff, but they've been hounding Willis for months."

"Well" The sheriff looked across the field. "There's a lot of new people around now—oil people. These young farm boys don't know how to take care of themselves."

"They drove a new black car," Annie persisted. "They came here once. Threatened him. Willis said they were from Chicago."

The sheriff took out his pad again and wrote something down. "I'll send the coroner out to take a look. Need all the information I can get." He turned to Annie and touched her shoulder. "I'm mighty sorry about all this, Mrs. Porter." He nodded to John Malvern, crawled in his patrol car, and sped back out the driveway.

Willis was buried on November 2, 1939; at a graveside service attended by his parents, a couple of old neighbors, his wife and infant daughter, and his two brothers-in-law Kurt and Glenn Malvern. Annie had come to the hurtful realization her parents were distancing themselves from her. Why, though, did others stay away? Was it because they didn't want to be seen where someone had been murdered by the mob, or because the Porters had no oil wells? Or was it because Porters were Porters?

CHAPTER 27

Two days after Willis's funeral, John Malvern came to see Annie. He stood inside the door, holding his hat. "I brought you a check, Annie, to tide you over." He was crisp and formal—and a little awkward. Her parents' refusal to attend Willis's funeral stood between them—a widening wall.

"Thanks for that." She looked at the two hundred dollars written on it. "I'll pay you back when I can."

"No need for that." He looked past her. "The baby?"

"Sleeping."

Malvern nodded. "Another time."

They stood avoiding each other's eyes. "Annie, paying those people off might have saved Willis's life this time, but it wouldn't the next or maybe the next. It was coming."

Annie shook her head as tears rolled down her cheeks. "Maybe I can forgive you sometime for not helping us." She shook her head. "Maybe I can forgive Willis, but not now—not yet."

"Annie, you have nothing to forgive me for." He looked into her eyes, and then left.

The house was so silent. Willis had been with her since they were children, and she simply couldn't comprehend it. He would never be there again. The terrible dread of the gambling debt that hung over them was gone. Willis paid for that with his life. She walked the floor, scared and jittery. But what would she do now? She had never worked for money.

She shoved a chunk of wood in the stove. Henry Patrick had chopped enough firewood to last a month. What about that sheriff? She'd called twice yesterday and left a message at his office. She had told him who to arrest. Didn't he want to know more?

Annie walked up the two steps of the red brick building with a swinging sign on the porch that said, "County Jail." She found the sheriff in his office. "My husband was murdered a week ago, Sheriff Webb," she burst out and shifted her baby to the other shoulder. "His body was dumped on the front steps. I called you. Twice yesterday. I know who you should arrest. The oilmen know…who does things like that. Why are you waiting?"

Logan Webb got up but said nothing as he walked to his file cabinet.

Annie followed him. "I told you, I know who it was. Willis owed money. He—he had been gambling and got in debt—he lost. Sheriff, those men were too clever for him. I know they pulled him in. For weeks they've been hounding him—us. Terrifying him. Driving alongside him. One of them walked right up to our house—threatening him. It was a black car and the man had a scar on his forehead that went down through his eyebrow." She ran her finger down across her face. The sheriff sunk down in a chair before his desk. "You have got to go get them."

Logan Webb came around, pulled a chair by her and put his arm around her shoulders. An awkward mechanical gesture, Annie thought.

"Willis owed almost six-thousand dollars." She looked into the sheriff's face. "He was just a farm boy. He didn't know what he was getting into."

"Well," Webb stood up, and then went back to his own chair. "He's not the only one."

"They thought Willis could get money from my father, but then…we couldn't. I don't know what's to become of us."

"I'm gonna try to find out who killed your husband, Miz Porter, but I'm telling you frankly we got people in here that's part of the mob. They settle up in their own way. I'm just as sorry as I can be about this, Miz Porter. You got a good family—the Malverns—never heard a word against them, but now they got all that money—the oil comin' in and all. They're gonna stand by you and your little one."

Annie looked across his desk, into his eyes, "You're not going to do anything, are you? You're not. No more'n my family is."

The sheriff leaned back in his swivel chair. "Well, of course, I am. A murder of a young man with a wife and baby. It's my number one priority, but you didn't give me much of a description—a black car, a man with a scar. There was a free-for-all out at the derrick on Perkins just last week. Man all cut up. What's come to this town outrages everybody."

The sheriff rubbed his eyes. "Miz Porter, I can't say that I do know who it was killed your husband." He sighed. "Seems like everybody's got some complaint."

"Complaint!" Annie flared. "Complaint, Sheriff? My husband was murdered!" The baby flinched and began to cry. "It's not just somebody stealing from a pumpkin patch." She looked squarely at the sheriff, and she knew. He was not going to risk his life against the men who killed Willis. He would do nothing.

CHAPTER 28

Dressed in his new three-piece blue suit, Malvern was filled with some excitement and a lot of dread, as he stood before the mirror in his bedroom. He had gotten a haircut, too, so he guessed he looked good enough. He had accepted Clifton Allison's invitation to the Christmas banquet and dance at the Country Club. What's more, Allison had asked him to join. Malvern said he'd have to think about that.

Eva Mae was thrilled. She would be Danny Allison's date, "and Papa, there's going to be a sleigh ride afterward! If you want to come…" Malvern said he'd leave that to the young folks. He pulled at the corners of his vest, looked again in the mirror and nodded agreeably with what he saw.

Sophie had been the problem. She wouldn't go. Dug in her heels. They were not her kind, she said, and she didn't want to talk to them and think about every word and every move, knowing full well they'd be laughing at her behind their smiles. No, she would not go!

Malvern had gone out to his shed, sat alone with the door closed where he liked to think things out. He took out his pocketknife and began to whittle on a piece of wood he found on the worktable. He wished he could discuss with Sophie what he was planning or rather hoping—that is if he played things right, there could be a union between his daughter and the son of Clifton Allison and that would move little Joey up. He'd send Joey to the University same as Clifton Allison's son and the name Malvern would begin to mean something. He dug into the wood hard with his knife. He knew Sophie would not care a whit about any of that. But just now all he needed was to get her to go to the Christmas party.

It took three weeks for both Joey and Eva Mae to coax Sophie around to the idea of going.

To Malvern the County Club was a somewhat magical place, turned out as it was in holiday spangle and sparkle. A long red carpet between a double row of decorated evergreen trees led to the entrance with tall carved double doors. Inside, six Christmas trees lined a wide hall on the way to the dining room. A waiter met them at the entrance, ushered them into a huge room, and seated then at a round table near the dance floor. The band, already playing, could barely be heard over the chatter of people finding their tables. Within minutes Clifton Allison, his wife, and mother joined them. Clifton sat by Sophie and Clifton's mother by Malvern.

Malvern, seated uncomfortably in a gold-colored chair too small for his rump, turned stiffly as if he'd thrown his back out, and glanced over the room, finally coming to his wife in her new blue velvet dress and Joey in his new, and hated, black suit. Three wide chandeliers across the ceiling reflected light in gilt-framed mirrors on opposite sides of the room. Malvern glimpsed Eva Mae in one of the mirrors, radiant in red satin, looking completely at ease, and charming everyone. He smiled and shook his head. She was one of *them*. She just was!

Malvern's uneasiness didn't improve when the notorious Bucky Allison sat down between his mother and Eva Mae. Danny was okay, but that Bucky was something else again. His name was listed in the paper for speeding and drunk driving about a dozen times a year, but he was fishing and hunting buddy of Sheriff Webb, so nothing ever came of it.

Marthursa, the feared matriarch of the Allison clan, seated next to Malvern, turned squarely to face him, and surveyed him thoroughly. "You're that farmer that's got all those oil wells, aren't you?"

"I've been fortunate." Malvern started to pat her hand as he might have any elderly lady but drew it back.

"Well, I'm gonna tell you something just so you know. My son Clifton is cozying up to you because he smells money. He's his father's son—loved money—loved people with money."

Malvern didn't know how to answer. Clifton Allison had invited him and had shown every sign of being a friend.

She gave him another once over, opened her small black beaded purse and took out a pair of half glasses, put them on, and then looked again at Malvern. "You look like a good sort. I'm gonna tell you something else, too. Don't let anybody take you. Anytime you get two dimes to rub together, somebody's got their eye on one of 'em."

"I'll keep that in mind, Mrs. Allison."

"My name's Marthursa. I was the eleventh and last one of the brood and I think my mother was tired and mad so she hung that name on me." She leaned close to Malvern. "You know what? All my children have named one of their kids 'Marthursa.' They think I'll be flattered and put something in the will for 'em. Don't you think that's a hoot?" She took a lacy handkerchief from her purse. "That girl of yours is a pretty little thing. Red's her color." She began cleaning her glasses with the handkerchief. "Danny likes her." She put her glasses back on. "I raised two sons, Clifton and Bucky, besides my two daughters. You're not supposed to have favorites, but I do. I like Clifton and his boys and Danny's my favorite, but Bucky here, my other son, I should have drowned when he was born." She reached over and patted Bucky's hand. "I make more excuses for Bucky than you can count."

Bucky didn't notice, he was busy ogling Eva Mae.

Malvern was perspiring under his three-piece suit. He could hardly agree with her, and he felt sure disagreeing with her was not a good idea, either. Just then Bucky Allison did something

Malvern definitely did not think was a good idea.

Bucky hovered close to Eva Mae and slipped his arm across the back of her chair. "Well, this is a pretty little dew drop." He leaned close to Eva Mae's ear.

"Danny, why don't you take your young lady up there for a dance," Marthursa said.

Bucky looked sheepishly at his mother, "Now Mother, we're just getting acquainted."

"I'm not blind yet, Bucky." Marthursa's rapier-like words withered Bucky, who withdrew his arm from Eva Mae's chair.

Bucky got up. "I think that means the loving arms of the bar is beckoning me."

"Yes, go charm somebody beside Danny's date," Marthursa said. "I like this Malvern person and you keep interrupting him. He's an interesting old bloke."

Bloke? What was a bloke, Malvern wondered. Should he be pleased? He ran his finger around the inside of his collar again. The room was a mite warm.

Danny and Eva Mae began to dance and in a few minutes Bucky cut in. Malvern could hardly keep his eyes off the possessive way Bucky held his daughter.

"Danny's my pride and joy." Marthursa looked at Malvern through her half spectacles. "Clifton, his dad, is good enough, but he only wants to make money. Like his father. Gone all the time. That's what's wrong with Bucky. Bucky can't hang his hat anywhere for ten minutes."

Bucky came back, seated himself by Sophie, and away from his mother. He turned his full attention on Sophie. "What do you like to do, Mrs. Malvern?"

Sophie giggled like a teenager, as she looked into Bucky's dark eyes. "I go to quilting once a week, and I like to cook."

"I'll bet you're a good cook." Bucky rested his chin on his fist and looked into Sophie's eyes.

"Sophie's cooking is good enough." Malvern snapped.

Bucky continued, "It seemed to me it would be an endless job putting all those little pieces together for a quilt and then stitching acres and acres of quilt."

Sophie laughed, "It's not a lot of work if you're doing it with your friends. I've got three dear friends."

"I'll bet they're just as sweet as you."

Clifton Allison cut in, "Bucky, Mrs. Malvern and I were talking about our sons going to the University. Mr. Malvern says his son wants to be a doctor."

"Hey, don't let me stop you." Bucky stared at Clifton and left.

"Bucky doesn't care for that subject," Clifton explained. "Father sent him to the University. He learned to dance, drink and call prostitutes to his room. The University didn't appreciate him like he thought they should, so he quit. I use him sometimes in the store when I'm desperate. Helps Mother when she can find him but I tell you he plays a mean banjo."

John Malvern watched Sophie as she listened to Clifton ramble on about his brother, but Malvern noticed her eyes wander to Bucky on the dance floor.

Just then, Lillian Allison Powers, with Ella Donnelley following, came forward and stood before the band. Lillian was dressed in a brilliant emerald dress cut low in the back.

Marthursa leaned across Malvern to Sophie, "Lillian's my daughter. She decorated this banquet hall. You can't get too gaudy for Lillian."

Sophie looked up, wide-eyed at the chandeliers. "I think it's just gorgeous."

"We want to welcome all of you," Lillian began, "to our annual Christmas party. None of us remember when it started, but our holiday wouldn't be the same without it. Enjoy the delicious meal we've planned, then after dancing the night away, go home in a sleigh ride." Lillian looked at the table where Malvern was sitting and turned quickly away. "Have a very happy Christmas season."

Beyond Marthursa's white head, Malvern looked at the giant tree, maybe fourteen feet high, that filled the room with the sharp smell of cedar. He studied one silver ornaments, the size of a small world globe and saw in his imagination, Joey here, a grown man, a part of this. Eva Mae, a young matron, Danny's wife, welcoming the important people in the town just as Lillian Powers had. He would be old then. He would never be really accepted, he knew, but these children would.

Waiters placed bowls of soup at each place. Marthursa kept up a steady stream of conversation through each of the courses. During the dessert and coffee, Marthursa leaned close to Malvern's ear. "That daughter of mine, Lillian. I don't think she's faithful to her husband. Malcolm's his name. He's too old for her." Marthursa held a spoonful of coffee near her lips and blew across it. "The old boy's burned out and..." She swallowed the coffee. "Lillian's got the hot pants. That's a recipe for trouble."

Malvern looked at the old lady and decided this was one person he definitely did not want for an enemy. "Well...ah, Mrs...Marthursa." He scratched the back of his neck. "She seems like a fine woman to me."

Marthursa shrugged. "Life is life."

Later, while Malvern waited for his new Buick 8 to be brought around to the front entrance, Clifton Allison said, "John, I'd like you to seriously consider joining us here at the Country Club. You'll see that the connections will be very beneficial."

Malvern stared at him. Part of that rarified group. But then he thought, what connections do I need. Money that's getting me this invitation, comes from my own farm.

"We'll have to see about that, Clifton." Malvern reached down to give Marthursa a hug and in the distance, he saw three sleighs waiting. Eva Mae and Danny with Bucky were waiting to be seated.

"This is a very interesting man, Clifton." The shriveled old lady patted Malvern's cheek. "You could learn something from him, if you'd shut up and listen." Clifton smiled as he tucked his mother in the back seat, arranged a blanket over her knees, looked at Malvern, and rolled his eyes.

As Malvern and Sophie drove home, his spirits were high.

Join the country club! Be one of the town leaders! He could scarcely imagine it. John Malvern, somebody people would want to seek out. Want to shake his hand.

Sophie finally spoke. "That worked out better than I thought. That Bucky Allison is a great guy."

Malvern didn't answer. Courting the mother to get to the daughter was not exactly a new game.

Bucky led the way for a short walk away from the Country Club to where the three sleighs waited. Danny and Eva Mae were tucked in the back seat, Bucky in front between two women and four others were in the middle seat. The night was bright, air crisp, with snow lightly dusted over the rolling hills of the park, adjoining the Country Club. They rode beside the lake. A light breeze splintered the moon's reflection in the rippling water like diamonds sprinkled across the dark water.

In the backseat, Eva Mae rested warm in Danny's arms. She looked at him, his profile in the bright moonlight as their sleigh bumped over washboard ice under the snow. In May, when she and Danny walked through the trellis archway to the Prom, she was proud to be escorted by an Allison. Through the summer, as they dated, she gloried in the envy of other girls. But she had learned to laugh with Danny and tell him her secrets. He was fun, exciting and sweet. Now, it no longer mattered that he was Clifton Allison's son. She moved closer under the heavy lap robe, feeling his breath on her cheek, his warm body close as he held her. She had fallen in love. She almost held her breath—her heart full, the moment enchanted.

"Stop the sleigh!" Bucky called out to the driver, and they came to a stop. Bucky got out and came back to Eva Mae. "Come on, kids, I want to show you something." They all followed on the crusted snow and stood at the edge of the lake. "Wanna try something, honey?" He looked down at Eva Mae.

"What?" Danny put his arm around Eva Mae's shoulders.

"You'll see." Bucky pulled out a revolver. "Wanna shoot it?"

"I don't think so."

"No, Bucky," Danny said. "Don't listen to him, Eva Mae."

Bucky put the gun in her hand and stood close behind her, his arm around her. She fired off a shot in the lake, the gun recoiled, and she fell back against Bucky. The horse was spoofed, whinnied and raced forward with the empty sleigh swinging wildly behind, the driver yelling, "Whoa! Whoa!"

"You, OK, Evie?" Danny took Eva Mae in his arms.

"I want to get back in the sleigh." Eva Mae turned. "Where did it go?"

About that time Sheriff Webb came up in the patrol car. "Bucky, what in the sam hill are you doing, scaring everybody to death. Gimme that gun. You've got a snout full."

"Bucky coaxed Eva Mae to do it," Danny said.

The sheriff shoved the gun in his pocket, "I know, I know."

The driver finally got the horse settled down and came back for them.

In the moonlight the sheriff looked at Eva Mae. "You John Malvern's daughter?" When Eva Mae nodded her head, he added, "I'll be following this sleigh. I don't want any more nonsense. You hear me, Bucky?"

Eva Mae sensed the sheriff didn't want dealings of any kind with the Malvern family. No arrest had been made for Willis Porter's murder.

When the driver finally stopped before her house, Bucky said, "What a nice little house."

Danny walked her to the door, but six sets of eyes were on them as they stood on the front porch. She wanted Danny to kiss her, but it was awkward.

"Kiss the pretty girl good-night, Danny." Bucky called, and they all laughed but when Danny took her in his arms and gave her a long tender kiss, no sound came from the sleigh.

CHAPTER 29

Annie awoke in the night, found her purse by Hannah's crib, and groped into the kitchen before turning on the light. She counted what was left of the money her father had given her— fifty-seven dollars. She needed a job—soon, but the only jobs were in the oil fields. She made a fire and fixed a pot of coffee as she clutched her robe at the neck against the chill of a December night. She sat at the table, waiting for the house to warm and morning to come. By the time daylight filtered through the barren trees outside, she had decided to leave the baby with Willis's mother for the day and start looking for work.

Christmas music, golden bells, and red and green garland filled Allison's Department Store and made Annie feel all the more fearful and alone without Willis by her side. She had never applied for a job before.

"No"—the manager smiled kindly. "We haven't hired anybody new in five years."

By 4 o'clock she stood on the street corner, a sharp wind cutting across her face, making her eyes water. What could she do? She had to make some money. She had tried every place she could think of, and they all shook their heads and suggested another possibility she might try. Annie got in the car and slowly drove out of town. As she topped the overhead, she noticed Dutch's parking lot filled with oil trucks. Maybe. She pulled in, checked her lipstick in the mirror, went in and sat on the first stool by the cash register. The place was warm and smelled of hamburgers on the grill, French fries, coffee, onions and the pungent odor of oil on warm, damp clothes.

Roosevelt, the parrot in his cage by the cash register, chirped, "Pretty Baby, Pretty Baby," A couple of oil workers laughed and kept ogling her. "Jingle Bells" from the radio blended in with loud talk and raucous laughter.

Dutch left the rope of Christmas garland he was trying to drape across three wide front windows and went to the counter. He dropped a menu in front of her, a coffee pot in his other hand. "Need a cup to warm up?"

She pushed the menu aside. "I was just wondering," she squeaked out, "if you might have a job. I'll be needin' some work."

Dutch looked her over, his face softened. He put the coffee pot down and leaned over the counter and spoke gently. "I was mighty sorry to hear what happened to your husband. He just got suckered in." Dutch ran his hand over his mouth. "And he ain't the only one. You hear mighty wild things in here." His eyes roamed around the restaurant, then looked Annie over again. "Maybe I could use another waitress. Gets busy in the early mornings when the night shifts come from the sites. You'd need to be here before five."

Annie could hardly believe what she heard—the first person not to say "no." "I'll be here." She clutched at her purse and looked again at Dutch. "Thanks."

Outside, she sat in the car for a moment before she stepped on the starter. A job. She found a job! But five in the morning! She'd have to get the baby to Willis's parents before that.

The first week she could hardly think of anything but getting through the day and back to Hannah. In the evenings she got both of them ready for the next day, put the baby down, and dropped across the bed, overwhelmed with exhaustion and grief.

She felt so alone without Willis. When the baby slept, the silence of the house crowded in on her and brought back the horror of Willis lying in his blood on the front steps. The following Monday, Annie got her first check. At home, she counted out her money on the kitchen table—seventeen dollars and twenty cents. Then she poured out a sack of coins she got from tips and began to count— nine dollars and sixty-five dollars. She'd made all that in one week.

Gradually she began to enjoy the easy banter of the men who came in cold and hungry, and the compliments she got about "a woman's touch" when she added to Dutch's Christmas decorations.

By the second week, she had found a routine and rhythm to her time. When she counted out money from her second check, she put aside some for a new haircut at Belle's Kozy Cottage beauty shop and a stuffed bear for Hannah. Maybe she could make it.

A couple of weeks later, after work, when the sun was dropping low in the sky, shadows lengthening in the yard, she picked Hannah up from the playpen, and went to the kitchen to feed her. As she looked for a spoon, she glanced out the window— and froze! That black car sat in the driveway. The one that came for Willis! Her heart pounded as if it was in her throat.

They sat just even with the back door. What did they want? They'd taken Willis's life, wasn't that enough!

She held her baby to her chest, locked the back door and turned out the lights. The baby began to fuss. "Hush, hush, little one," she whispered. "You have to be quiet," Annie put her thumb in the baby's mouth to suck but Hannah was hungry and that didn't soothe her. Annie watched them through the window, as she sat on the bed in the darkening room for over an hour, rocking back and forth trying to calm the child, and even more herself. The car slowly moved back away over the frozen drive. Relief poured through her. *But they can come back, and how can I stop them?*

CHAPTER 30

Christmas afternoon in Dutch's truck stop was quiet. Outside, snowflakes drifted and melted in the parking lot. Annie, being the newest employee had to work. A couple of roughnecks sat at the counter.

"I'd shore druther be in Texas for Christmas than here. It's just too damned cold." The name "Roy" was printed in red on his gray work shirt. The other one was "Calhoun." Roy was tall, thick about the middle, and his hair plastered in a band around his head where his wide hat usually sat.

"You like sand better'n snow?" Annie called across the restaurant. "How you gonna get the Christmas feeling if there's not even snow?"

"I'll work on it," he shot back.

The morning had been busy enough to keep her from thinking—thinking that Willis was gone and today she was missing her baby's first Christmas.

"You new here?" Annie asked, refilling Roy and Calhoun's coffee cups.

"Yeah. Been working for Carson Garrett for eleven years. He called us up here last month. Been on the Malvern site."

Annie turned away and put the coffee pot back on the burner. It had been two months since she'd seen her parents. She sat down in a booth, her back to the two customers, a dinner plate before her that cook had dished up. She'd put up a little Christmas tree in the corner on a raised platform between two booths. It made her think of last year, when she and Willis decorated the house; talking about the baby they would have this year. Her vision blurred until she couldn't see the tree. She ate a few bites and pushed the plate away. Cars breezed along the highway. They had somewhere to go, she guessed. Roy's big red oil truck sat in the lot where he parked it. She hated the oil. It came in and everything changed—people changed. Made Willis try to be what he wasn't, and it killed him. Made her father try to be what he wasn't either. The thought of her father gave her an aching heart. She blamed him for not giving Willis money that would have saved his life, for not coming to the funeral. And she hated him for abandoning the children of his old life. The poor life. How could he care more for his new friends than his own   granddaughter? How could he be the same loving Papa she once knew.

Outside, a row of icicles hung along the eaves of the roof— a huge one at the corner. She watched drops form and drip off the tip, thinking of the days when her father would wake her and Eva Mae and say, "It's Christmas morning." They would run in and find an orange in the sock they had hung up. This morning she saw her father drive by in his new Buick, Eva Mae and Joey in the back seat. Aunt Belle said there was a party in town at the Clifton Allison house.

The radio was turned low, playing Christmas carols all day. The music felt like a joke to her.

Behind her, Calhoun was talking to Roy. "Malvern was decked out this morning."

People spoke of her father as if he was an important man, like someone she didn't know. She fixated for a time on the icicle. He *was* a man she didn't know. Life had changed so fast.

"Told me his daughter got him an invite to a big Christmas party at them people that run Allison's Department Store." Calhoun punched his buddy in the arm. "There's another party we missed out on, Roy."

"Hell, you can count me out on that. I been to shindigs like that in Texas. Don't nobody railroad ole Roy into that anymore. Them folks think they breathe better air than most people." Roy turned toward her booth. "Waitress, you got some pie we could have?"

"Sure 'nough. Apple, pumpkin, mincemeat..." Annie wondered what the men would think if she told them she was John Malvern's daughter.

"Apple'll be fine and some more coffee, too."

When Annie set the pie before the roughneck, she said, "You guys gonna hang around here all day?"

"Guess so." Calhoun looked through the window at the dismal winter day. "Got no place to be 'til our shift starts. Roy, here didn't get me an invite anywhere." He held out his cup for a refill.

Annie went back to the booth and sat down. The day was so quiet. Dutch's was usually abuzz with customers, but today...everyone, she guessed, had found a place to go. A truck drove in, parked. She felt relieved—some work to fill her time. She saw Kurt bail out and Glenn followed.

They sauntering in and found a booth. Glenn pulled off his brown coat, balled it up and tossed it in the booth beside him. The parrot squeaked out "Howdy, Mister," a couple of times.

"I wondered where you two were." She reached for a couple of menus stacked by the cash register.

Glenn wore his usual overalls and long-sleeved plaid shirt, but Kurt had a new wheat-colored corduroy jacket about the color of his hair. He looked sharp—handsome and as impatient as ever.

Kurt had moved into town to his own apartment, and she seldom saw him. Glenn was working in the oil fields, rooming at Sarah Emma's house with other roustabouts.

Kurt shoved a little red box to her as she put down place settings for them. "Something for Hannah," he said.

She slid in the booth across from Kurt. "I'm missin' my baby something awful...her first Christmas, the one Willis and I would have had with our new baby."

"I'm missin' something, too." Glenn said finally.

Annie looked at her two brothers and felt sorry for them. "When you guys gonna find you a girl, get yourselves married. A couple of good-looking guys like you shouldn't be eating Christmas dinner by yourselves."

Kurt hid behind the menu. "For Glenn to get a girl he'd have to talk to her first."

Annie smiled. Kurt could talk to a girl all right. He could talk her into anything.

Kurt folded the menu. "Turkey dinner's fine."

"That goes for me, too," Glenn echoed.

When she brought back their orders, they sat waiting, silent, alone, like herself—the roustabouts, lonely, too.

Kurt finally asked, "What is it you're missing, little brother?"

Glenn buttered every inch of his sweet potato, slowly sprinkled sugar over it, covering it all carefully.

"Well, what?" Kurt finally asked.

"I'm missin' understanding, that's what I'm missin'."

Annie came back with the coffee pot. "I saw Mama and Papa pass this morning—zippin' by on the highway. Guess they didn't have time to stop in."

"I got understanding about that." Kurt was sarcastic. "Eva Mae got 'em an invitation to go to the Allisons' house. Couldn't pass that one up."

Annie shrugged, "Who cares?" she said. But she knew they did care, terribly. Their parents were shedding an old life, sloughing off children, building themselves a name, promoting their young in this new world. The three sat in silence—lonely, leftover children.

"I see Papa on the street in his black suit, cigar stuffed in his mouth, walking with that judge—whatever his name is, or Bucky Allison," Glenn said. "Like some swell I don't know. The Papa I knew came in from the fields in his overalls smelling like hard work. Now he just talks a minute or two to me and acts like he's got to get going somewhere. Like he's busy."

The brightly decorated tree and the holiday music in the background seemed to mock them. Were they oddities, Annie wondered?

Glenn still looked out the window. "That's the understanding that's missing. I never knowed parents' love could be bought like that by somebody who had money."

"Guess so." Kurt finished his meal, pulled out his keys and sat impatiently fiddling with them on the table. "And if we had enough of that money, we could buy them back, Glenn." He pushed the key chain into a circle with his fingers, waiting for his slow brother to finish the meal. "Them damned wells gave Papa..." Kurt pounded the table. "Importance he always wanted."

"You know what the oil has done," Annie said. "It reached into my bed, into my baby's cradle. Took my husband and her father."

Kurt instantly grabbed up the keys in his fist, perched, ready for flight, about to say something, but didn't.

Glenn cut the remaining turkey in small bites. "Town's changing." Glenn piled on his fork a bite of dressing and turkey and chewed it. He wiped his mouth with a napkin. "They're building a new drive-in out at the Y. You're gonna be able to just drive your car in, and they come to the window and take your order."

"And *eat* in the car?" Annie asked.

"That's what they say. The men got to kidding Sarah Emma about her competition. Said she needed another name. She said she liked the one she had just fine, but they run kinda a contest. The men put a coffee can on the counter and asked suggestions to re-name Sarah's place."

Kurt settled back, listening."

"Sarah said the name she had was just fine, but the men said she needed to get attention."

"Well, what, Glenn?" Kurt asked.

"It's 'Sarah's Squat and Gobble'."

"What?" Kurt and Annie said at the same time

"Sarah said she was happy with what she had, but the men

all put in and ordered a big red sign. It says 'Sarah's Squat and Gobble Restaurant,' and it flashes all the time, like the one at the Blue Moon." Glenn took a drink of water. "Then the men put the can back out on the counter and called it the 'cuss can.' Every time somebody cusses they had to put a dime in. The can filled up real quick. So they took that money and put up a sign out on the highway so passers-by would get directions to her new restaurant. They kinda take care of her like she was their mama."

"That was nice of them, not sure I care for the name." Annie glanced up at the icicles and realized it was the first time today she had felt like smiling.

Glenn pushed his plate aside. "Sarah gets lots of new folks just driving through. They want to see what kind of place the 'Squat and Gobble' is."

"I'll bet," Kurt said.

The front door opened, and a man entered. The parrot piped up, "Howdy Mister," but he looked neither right nor left. He walked past the two at the counter and went quickly to the opposite end of the restaurant, slid into a booth, his back to everyone.

Annie went to him and offered him a menu. "The main thing today is turkey and dressing." He didn't look up. His leather jacket was worn at the cuffs, a button missing from his shirt, and hair hung over his jacket collar. He looked like poverty itself. His eyes were watery and nose red from the cold because he didn't have a hat. When she returned with his coffee, he tersely gave her the order.

She served him the plate of turkey with trimmings, smiled and ventured a "Merry Christmas." He made some unintelligible sound, picked up his coffee cup and looked away.

She nodded to her brothers as they left payment on the table and walked out. The roustabouts had stopped talking, clearly interested in this newcomer.

Later she went back to her customer. "You want some pie or something?"

"No." He didn't look up.

She felt his aloneness—or was it just her own she felt?

"You come in with the oil people?"

"No."

"You're new to me. I've lived here my whole life."

"I'm new, I guess, if being thirty-eight years old, flat broke and nowhere to go makes you new." He parsed out every word.

Annie didn't know just what to say. "I'm sorry," she whispered.

The two men at the counter watched, then Roy said, "You that guy that traded off the mules for that twelve-acre patch of ground over by the church?"

"I guess I am." He answered from the booth, his back to them.

Annie knew the land. "You musta wanted to live around here pretty bad," she said. "That land is worthless. Can't grow anything on it."

"First, I'm no farmer and second, it don't matter where I live." He concentrated on the plate before him.

Silenced, the men turned back to their coffee. Annie shrugged and looked again at the stranger. Why did she feel so sorry for him? When he finished his turkey dinner she went to the kitchen and came back with a slice of warm apple pie.

"This is kind of a Christmas present from Dutch. Just say it's for newcomers."

He returned her a brief smile with a murmur of thanks.

He ate the pie, stood up and, hunched deep in the armor of his leather jacket, walked to the register. When he paid his bill he avoided looking at her and ignored the parrot's rasping.

The men on the stools turned, following his every move until he spun out on the slick drive. "That there's one odd duck."

"What about this mule business?" Annie asked.

"Well," Roy began, "he come in town, sorry looking like you see, went upstairs over the Blue Moon and got in a game. Won a pair of mules off Joe Watson. A couple of nights later, Cameron Barton put that worthless twelve acres up for the mules. Then, this here dude took the game, so Cameron come over got the mules and signed over that twelve acres of land.

"What they said up at the Blue Moon was the original owner had about 1,000 acres…a long time ago, before the Civil War even. Said he gave up an acre in the corner of his land for a church, right there where Bethlehem Church is to this day, close by where the Malvern and Patrick oil sites are. Course the church owns that little bit of land now but that's where the twelve acres is. Right there by that church."

Annie said nothing. She and her brothers had played "cowboy and Indian" in that wooded twelve acres when they were kids. The greater part of those 1,000 acres, though, now belonged to the Patrick brothers.

"Sure is an unfriendly cuss." Calhoun said.

Annie refilled their coffee cups. "What's his name?"

"St. Pierre. Robert St. Pierre."

The two roustabouts finally bestirred themselves and came to the cash register. The parrot gave out with his "Thankee Mister."

"You going to work?" she asked, an idea playing in her thoughts.

"Just as well." Roy said, "Ain't nothing' much doin'."

Roy laid out one dollar and eighty-five cents.

"You know something about John Malvern, that rich man you were talking about?" Annie asked, as she rang up the bill.

"What's that?" Roy said.

"I'm John Malvern's daughter. Those two men were my brothers—John Malvern's sons."

They glanced at each other. "Malvern's daughter, huh?" Calhoun buttoned up his coat and pulled gloves out of his pocket.

An easy smile came on Roy's face as he anchored a cap down over his forehead. "I worked on lots of wells in my day and I'll tell you something, Missy, when a man comes into a lot of money, he right then comes into a lot of relatives."

Annie turned away as the door closed. The parrot kept screeching out "Thankee, Mister." Tears burned her eyes. On the radio, they were playing "Joy to the World."

CHAPTER 31

Belle Dorsett snuggled in the crook of Carson Garrett's arm, light from the fireplace and a lamp on a Victorian table in a corner, made the room dim—dim enough to watch through the window, cars passing on the highway, and Dutch's Truck Stop sign flashing across the way.

"Tonight we should celebrate fate." Belle leaned forward and poured them each another glass of wine. "About a year ago, I almost froze to death in the snow bank and that very night you came into my life. Everything I do now skims along so easy—like a dream because you are in the dream," she went on.

He nuzzled her hair back and kissed her neck and then her lips. Wood crackled in the fire. "I keep thinking of that antique bed in there," he whispered.

"Why?" She looked up quickly, "Do you want to buy it?"

"Maybe."

"Maybe?"

"It depends on what might come with it."

Belle sat upright and turned to face him. "What are you talking about? What do you mean?"

"I thought I'd throw out a test and..."

"Like one of your wells—see if there's anything there?"

"Something like that?"

She stared at him. Was it a proposition or a proposal?

"My God, Belle, you've been out of circulation too long. You don't know a marriage proposal when you hear one."

She sat very still, unconsciously following the scroll pattern of her rug, absorbing what he had just said. She had been alone so long, never having to answer to anyone. "A marriage between us wouldn't work," she finally said.

"Why not?"

"Because," she still followed the looping scrolls on the floor, "I could never pick up and move around like a nomad, and that's what you do."

"I'm hardly a nomad. I lived in Texas 23 years, and I may be here longer. Where there's oil production, that's what makes it the place to be."

"Is that the reason you're staying here?"

"Yes-s" he hesitated. "That's the real reason. But, my darling Belle, that has nothing to do with us. You could be with me anywhere we go."

"I don't know about that." She pulled a pillow from the corner of the couch, put it behind her neck, and stared at the ceiling. "Look at this place."

"What do you mean?"

"It's a monument to ancestors—every piece of furniture has a past—a story about some member of my family."

"Oh, well, dead people, yes, we have to consider them. I'll show you things, your dead ancestors never dreamed of."

"I've never been where I was a stranger. I know everybody here." She shrugged. "I don't remember when I didn't."

"I would be there." He pushed the pillow away and slipped his arm around her again. "We've already built our own little world—just the two of us."

"Let's don't talk about this. Let's just go on—like now. It's enough to be loved." She said and reached for a newspaper. "Anyway, we don't have to think about that for a long time. Look at the headlines. 'Fast Pace being set by Garrett Oil in Tri-county Area. And it names locations. Vernon Smith number 4, McMillan

A-3, Roy Cruse number 2. It says Garrett is drilling…"

"That's enough, Belle." Carson said.

"Here it says F. Holman number 2 is rigging up," she went on. "And Mary Campbell number 2 is completed and on the pump. Then there are two more paragraphs of reports on other wells--all your company and then here's a column of other companies, The Stiles-Martin-Texas Syndicate test on Blackwell is coring at 3,310 feet and running higher than expected. I guess that means oil content?" She looked up at him. "And you've said many times that there is deep oil, deeper than is necessary now to drill to."

"That's why I come here, Belle, for an update on the oil news."

"And there's more. Edgar Robinson's drilling a wildcat near Barnwell's. Iroquois rigging up…"

"Belle, don't. I don't to want to hear it." He took the paper from her and wadded it and tossed it in the fire. "Come on. Settle back down. It never occurred to me that a marriage proposal would scare you into reading columns and columns of newsprint."

"Oh, really, hush." She leaned forward and kissed him tenderly. "What all this tells me is the day you leave here will be long in the future and no impossible decisions have to be made now. We can just go on, wrapped in this wonderful world together."

"Impossible decision? People get married every day! All over the country. The world. They didn't all grow up in the same town."

She leaned back into his arms, staring into the leaping flames.

Finally he whispered in her ear. "Tell me a family story about that antique bed in there. I've got quite an appreciation for it already."

"It's a sad story—mostly. Are you sure?"

He kissed her forehead. "Tell me," he whispered.

"My great-grandfather Cole built this house—you really want to hear this?" When he nodded, she went on. "Before that he had married a young girl named Harriett—they called her Hattie.

Then came a little boy, Pleasant. Cole began to build his house—tthis house. It was different then. You could just cut down timber on your own land, take it to a sawmill, have the boards cut, and built your own place. He and Hattie lived in a two-room shack while they worked together getting the house built. When Hattie started into labor with their second child, Cole took her to the shack and put her in their bed, but Hattie died before the doctor got there. The baby girl died, too. Cole was in such grief; he took his little boy into the bed to sleep with him. In the summer, Cole took Pleasant out fishing, but when an electrical storm came up, they hurried to the shack. The toddler ran ahead, teasing his father. They came to open prairie. Lightning struck little Pleasant. Killed him before his father's eyes." Belle sat up and looked into Carson's eyes. "I told you it was sad."

"Go on."

"Cole went almost insane. It was like a demon in the cosmos was taking from him everything he loved. He went into the shack—almost out of his mind, took an ax and chopped the bed to pieces, the place that had given him joy and promise. He set fire to the bed and that burned the shack down. It was said he roamed in the woods like a wild animal. Finally he came back, and lived in this partly completed house. For a long time, he did nothing but work on the house. One day a couple of girls came to his door and asked if they could gather persimmons from a tree they saw in his woods.

"That's how he met Alice, who became his second wife, and my great-grandmother. When they married, he bought that great bed. He and Alice had four children. Alice had two sisters and three brothers, who eventually had families. After he married Alice, Cole's life changed. The house was filled with his own happy family and those of his wife's. He said God gave him a second chance."

Carson was quiet for a moment, and then said. "I am glad of that. It gave me you."

"Do *you* believe in second chances, Carson?"

He turned to her. Looked at her in amazement, "Belle, I just asked you to marry me."

The day was damp, rain coming off and on. Sophie had gone to quilting. John Malvern went to his basement, put on an old blue work shirt, overalls, red plaid Mackinaw, pulled on a blue and white striped cap, and headed out to his shed. He sat on a stool by his workbench and began tinkering with a pencil sharpener that wasn't working. He finally pushed it aside. He didn't have to fix it, didn't have to do anything.

Rain peppered down again. In his old clothes, looking out the open shed door as he had a million times before, rain pattering music on the tin roof, a gentle soul-satisfying comfort coursed through him. It was a feeling he hadn't known for a long time. He liked going in town to the Men's Breakfast meetings, lunches at the Country Club and poker at Allison's house, but sometimes he didn't hardly know who that person was. Here in his old shed, his mind calmed. Reasoning set things clear. Here he could find truth.

He sat for a long time, watching the clouds drift on and the sun come through, making a brilliant winter day. He'd been thinking for some time about an idea Eva Mae had. She had come in the day after the Christmas party at the Country Club, sat down on the chair arm, and hugged his shoulders. "Papa," she had pushed a lock of his hair off his forehead. "Why don't we remodel the house? Make it...bigger." She had kissed his forehead, and then continued. "We could extend the living room and dining room on this side of the house and on the other side make a larger kitchen for Mama and a sun porch, so she could keep her plants out there and then...make an upstairs over all the lower rooms."

About the time she had mentioned the kitchen, Malvern looked through the side window to see Sophie in her worn grey coat, basket in hand, gathering eggs from the hen house.

"No, Eva Mae, we can't do that."

She got up and turned to face him, "Well, why not?" A slight pout curled on her lip. "You got plenty of money. It's Mama, isn't it?"

"She would never, ever hear of it. This was her Papa's

house," he had said.

Eva Mae went to the organ and started to play "I'll talk to her."

"God could talk to her." Malvern watched his daughter's fingers move over the keyboard, but he was thinking of Joey and his future. "It's not your mother's way," he said finally. He watched Eva Mae at the organ. What a little manager she was—always calculating. He had mixed feelings about that. On the one hand he didn't think it womanly, but then she seemed so sure about what to do now that they had all this money.

Eva Mae had wheeled about on the organ stool. "When I came home from the Country Club Christmas party on that sleigh ride, Bucky Allison said, 'That's a nice little house.' He said 'little', Papa."

"I wouldn't put much stock in what Bucky Allison says. He was too drunk to think that if you shoot a gun the horse might run off."

Eva Mae disappeared into her bedroom and came back with a magazine. "Look here, Papa. We could make our house look just like this." She shoved a picture in his hands. "The address to order the blueprint is in the back. We could do it, Daddy."

"Eva Mae, your Mama would never hear of it."

That was a month ago, Christmas had come and gone, and Malvern had begun to think of Joey and the friends he would bring home from college, people he would invite from town. It wasn't such a bad idea Eva Mae had, and as he considered it, his mind embroidered the picture.

He stepped out of his shed into the sharp fresh air and looked at his little house in the distance. It could be the core of a much larger building—extended all around. There would be an upstairs with a stairway curving down into a broad entrance hall—something like he had seen at Clifton Allison's house.

Malvern left the shed, walked to the front yard, and stood under the big oak, trying to imagine his new house sitting on an acre lawn, rising among the trees, steps leading up to the entrance.

He sighed. But there was Sophie to deal with.

He could go over and talk to Adam Lightfoot. Wouldn't do no harm to talk. Get his opinion. Adam could do the job. He was the best carpenter in the county. Probably welcome the work. Maybe he could make Sophie see he was helping some out-of-work people.

He looked again at the 'nice little house.' He wanted Joey to be proud of where he lived. He wanted Eva Mae to bring home her Danny Allison if she wanted to. He and Sophie might have parties, not the old music party people. He'd invite the people he met at the Country Club. Clifton Allison, Judge Donnelly—them people. He'd turn the party business over to Eva Mae. He didn't know how all that was done, but Eva Mae was a natural.

Malvern walked gingerly across the springy winter yard to his new Buick. As he got in the car, which didn't fit in the garage like the old Model T, he realized he'd have to build on a big garage. And re-design the driveway. Pull down that old barn and the chicken house. He thought of Sophie again and sighed. It was her egg money she used for spending. This could turn into a nightmare.

At the Lightfoot house, Malvern rather nervously spread out the blueprints Eva Mae had ordered from the magazine on the Lightfoot's kitchen table

"What do you think that might cost?" Malvern looked up, the pit of his stomach tightening. He felt he was stepping out on water as he waited to hear what figure Lightfoot might name.

Adam rubbed his chin, turned the blueprints around to face him for a better look. He scratched the back of his neck by the hairline, pursed his lips, studying it.

Malvern stood by watching, waiting. "I'm just gettin' an idea you understand, Adam. There's nothing definite. I know you're a busy man."

"Well, no," Lightfoot said, studying the sketch, "it's not that. Not much carpenter work goin' on around here."

Finally, Lightfoot raised his head. "I 'low it'd come up to maybe five thousand dollars to do all that. Can't be sure 'til I go price the lumber, and such but I reckon you could get it for that. If I could get it before time to put out crops, I'd welcome the work..."

"Well, now," Sophie's face loomed before Malvern. "Got to talk to the wife, before I commit to that kind of money."

"Tell you what, I'll follow you over, take a look," Lightfoot said.

Malvern rubbed the stubble of whiskers growing on he chin. "Guess it won't hurt to look,"

Before Lightfoot arrived, Malvern went to his new secretary desk, took out the long grey ledger, and looked at the figure in the far column--all the money he had. $156,406.14. He leaned back in his chair, remembering. Sometimes in a good year his crops had brought in up to $1,200.

When Lightfoot arrived, he walked around the house, pulling out his metal tape, laying it on the ground, and retracting it, staring up at the sky, squinting in concentration, apparently making mental notes.

Malvern kept following him, wondering if he was getting in deeper than he could handle. "I have to discuss this with Sophie, you know." he said a couple of times.

"Sure 'nough. Got to humor the ladies, they do the cooking. But I think we could do it for five-thousand."

CHAPTER 32

It was late January when the newcomer they had called St. Pierre came back into Dutch's. He picked out a stool at the far end of the counter from where the roustabouts congregated. Annie was busy, the truck stop full, but she noticed he looked a little better this time, hair cut, shaved, clean. She took his order, but he didn't look up. As she moved from table to table talking and filling orders, she felt him watching her.

When she put a plate before him and poured coffee in his cup, he did finally look up.

"I want to thank you for giving me the apple pie that day— Christmas day." The words came out hoarsely, like he was not accustomed to talking aloud.

She shrugged, flustered, "It was nothing—a gesture. Christmas. You were alone."

"I wanted to thank you."

She hurried on to the loud group at the opposite end of the counter. There was never any closing time at Dutch's because the oil crews worked around the clock when they were drilling, so mid-afternoon or three in the morning the bar stools were seldom vacant and coffee always ready.

"How about a refill, Mr. St. Pierre." Annie stood poised, the coffee pot in her hand. He looked up slowly, into her eyes. It was the soberest face she had ever seen.

"You've got a nice smile," he said without a hint of flirtation. "A pretty smile."

He was so serious, she answered in kind. "I don't have much to smile about, now."

"I heard about that—about your husband—being murdered."

Annie looked away, could feel tears coming. She tried to keep all that apart from the workplace and now, here she'd gone and dragged it up herself. Why did she do that? Why did she need to tell him about it? It wasn't his concern.

"I'm sorry," he said quietly, as if just for her. "It hurts to lose someone you care about."

"Time will help, I guess."

"Sometimes it doesn't." Abruptly his manner changed. He reached for his wallet and pulled gloves out of the pocket of his leather jacket. "How much do I owe you?"

At the register, St. Pierre paid his bill. She thanked him. He only nodded, but she caught a brief warm glint in his dull eyes. When she put his change on the counter—a nickel and a fifty-cent piece, he pushed it back to her.

"A woman's nice smile lasts for days and days," he said softly.

CHAPTER 33

"Mama," Eva Mae began gingerly, "I want to show you something."

Sophie was mixing up a meatloaf. "What is it, honey?" Bright winter sunshine streamed through white ruffled curtains into the kitchen.

"I showed Papa this picture in a magazine—and he liked it." She held the magazine up for Sophie to see a centerfold of a large white house. "So I sent for the plans here in the back"

Sophie reached for a saltshaker on a shelf by the stove.

"I was thinking we could tear out the wall between the living room and dining room." Eva Mae said.

"What!" Sophie turned, the saltshaker poised in her right hand over the meatloaf. "Tear out what wall?"

"Now Mama, listen. You'll like it. We'll take out the outside wall and extend the house another twelve feet, all along the sides. The two back bedrooms and the dining room…"

"Now just you wait a minute, young lady. I don't like any of this. Anyway, where will we all sleep if we did that?"

"Upstairs—later on."

"We don't have an upstairs."

"Well, we're going to. With that much space in here, we'll have room for an entrance hall, and that's where the stairs will go after we put a second floor on top of this floor."

"You've been one busy little girl behind your Mama's back, haven't you?" Sophie spit words out through tight lips when she was angry.

"Danny Allison's house has an entrance hall and an upstairs."

"Oh-o, I see." Sophie stared down into the mixing bowl. "Allisons, again."

"Mama, it will be so grand." Eva Mae hovered close by Sophie and slipped her arm about her mother's shoulders. "You'll love it. I just know you will."

"No, Eva Mae, you'll love it. Not me. I don't want to change who I am, because of them oil wells out there. They don't make me anything I wasn't already."

When Adam Lightfoot stopped by for a friendly visit a week later, Malvern knew he wanted an answer—wanted to drum up some work to see him through the rest of the winter. Malvern artfully kept him away from the house, walking around the grounds, talking of crops, oil wells, and the cold wet winter.

As Lightfoot came near the back door, he whipped out his metal tape measure and made a note on a paper, then tucked it inside his jacket.

Just then, Sophie stepped out on the porch, wiping her hands on her apron. "Adam Lightfoot, I haven't seen you in a month of Sundays. You come right in here and have some coffee. I just pulled out a tray of cookies."

Malvern looked at Lightfoot, an unspoken understanding.

They sat down at Sophie's table. Lightfoot cleared his throat in the silence. "Sure good cookies, Sophie," he said.

"Oh, I don't know. I didn't do the best job this time." More silence. "You thinkin' of doing some work around here, Adam?" Sophie asked coolly, wondering how John thought he was going to handle this.

Lightfoot cleared his throat again, dipped the cookie in his coffee and looked at Malvern.

"Well, Sophie," Malvern apparently decided to bite the bullet. "I was just getting some information before I talked to you about...doing a little remodeling of the house." He looked uncertainly at his wife. "Not much. Just some."

"How much?" Sophie snapped.

"Maybe extending some rooms."

"Which rooms?" Sophie peered over the top of her glasses.

"Your kitchen for one."

"My kitchen's just fine." Elbow on the table, chin in her palm, she looked from Adam to her husband. "Which others?"

"The dining room, living room and the bedrooms downstairs."

"Downstairs! We don't have an upstairs, John."

"I was thinking. Actually, it was Eva Mae's suggestion that we..." He studied her closely, then spouted out quickly, "put on an upstairs."

"An upstairs! That'll cost a fortune." Sophie cried.

"No," Lightfoot interrupted, "I think about five thousand dollars. You've already got the core of the house."

"Five thousand dollars." Sophie dropped her head in her hands. She knew she was not going to win this. When John set his mind to do something nothing stopped him, and now there was Eva Mae with all these new plans. "I love every board in this house just the way it is. I was just a little tyke when papa built it, back when things weren't so hard."

Malvern tried a different tack. "Sophie, Lightfoot here, could use the work."

Sophie was silent for a moment, then raised her head and spoke. "I swear, Mr. Lightfoot, Eva Mae has got to be like a person I never raised. She wants to be somebody. The ideas she gets in her head, just bewilders the life outa me. Then she gets 'em in John's head."

Malvern cleared his throat, "I think it started when Bucky Allison said to Eva Mae that night they brought her home in the sleigh that she had a 'little' house."

"Bucky said that?" Sophie looked at John, then turned to Lightfoot. "Bucky Allison is such a fine young man."

Malvern stared out the window, shaking his head in disbelief, as he listened to Sophie's enthusiastic assessment of Bucky Allison.

"You know, Mr. Lightfoot," Sophie said, at last. "Eva Mae sees things we don't, things we been so used to. Like its just scenery,"

Lightfoot dipped another cookie in his coffee. "All I can say, Sophie, is nobody wants to be pushed where they'd rather not go."

Sophie fished in her apron pocket for a handkerchief and blew her nose. "I've turned this over in my mind night and day since Eva Mae showed me that picture. I want this little house where I raised my family. That's what I want. But my family wants something big to keep up with them oil wells out there." She motioned, the handkerchief in her fist. "And it's my family I've lived for." She looked down, one hand enclosed over the other, gripping the handkerchief. She couldn't still the trembling. "I suppose you can go on with your plans, John, if you're set on it."

Neither Malvern nor Adam Lightfoot spoke.

Finally Sophie raised her head. "It's been over forty years since somebody took a hammer to this house, Adam. I don't know it'll work. Just this morning in my Bible reading, it said that it's a bad idea to put new wine in old skins. Do you think, Adam Lightfoot, you can put a big house in a little one?"

"I think I can work with this house just fine, Sophie," Lightfoot said.

"I'll tell you one thing you can't do, Mr. Adam Lightfoot, and that's take away all the good livin' that's gone on in this little house."

CHAPTER 34

The next morning Adam Lightfoot and his two sons arrived and began to set up. Sophie left for quilting as early as possible.

When she drove into the church parking lot, her three quilting friends were standing at the edge of the church yard in a huddle. She walked over to see what was of such interest.

"Look at that Sophie," Dora said when she joined them.

It was just a little thing about a foot high with a tiny three-cornered flag waving in the breeze. The flag had a flower design on it.

"Well lands sakes," Hattie said, "that's not more'n twenty feet from the church building. They can't put a well there. You can't hear yourself think when that drill is going into the ground. How can we ever have services?"

"It's practically on top of the church," Dora said. "Who would've done that?"

"The Magnolia Drilling Company," Sophie answered. "That's their flag." She closed her eyes, trying to get control. "There's never been a time in my life when she couldn't look out the window of my house and see the steeple of Bethlehem Church above the treetops." Suddenly it was too much. She began to cry. This very day they were starting to dismantle her house. And now the oil was at her church door.

Dora, Hattie, Emma—her best friends, came to her. "What is it, Sophie?"

"I'm going to lose my house. They're fixin' to tear into it." She shook her head. "Eva Mae gets these big ideas. She wants to change everything."

The women looked at each other, at lost to say anything that would help.

"You know what, Sophie, I got my Brownie camera in the car," Hattie said. "Let's not quilt today, let's go take a picture of Sophie's house like it is now. Make a keepsake for her."

Sophie smiled. "Thank you, Hattie. It would be nice to have that picture."

"Emma," Dora said as they went toward their cars, "The Magnolia Drilling Company is not to blame for that well being right by the church, it's whoever signed the lease. Do you know who owns that land?"

"Some new guy in town. Won that worthless twelve acres in a poker game," Sarah Emma said. "That's what my boarders say. St. Pierre, they call 'im.

CHAPTER 35

Kurt parked his truck in the shadows of Lillian's garage and walked to her back porch. The moon was bright on mounds of snow that lined the brick walkway. The air was chilled. She let him in the door, kissed him.

"Let's go to the boathouse," she whispered, and took his hand. "I put the heater on out there."

They walked silently toward the boathouse, the one he had built for Malcolm Powers, the very thing that had brought her into his life. Irritation crept in with his anticipation. Why would she never let him in her house? Did she believe she was keeping her married life safe if her lover never breached the premises?

The little room was warm, a thick rug on the deck flooring. She had planned for him and he was pleased. A wide window framed the lake. The moon, glistening on the water, and light from the heater made the room shadowy. As always, their lovemaking was savage, hungry when they first came together. The next time it would be more...he thought...artful.

Later, he sat in a swivel chair by a small desk he supposed Malcolm kept some kind of records of his fishing and hunting exploits. He looked down at Lillian, still lying on the carpet, her body white in the light of the small heater, her hair damp and disheveled from their violent lovemaking. He wondered again why he should have been the one to find this wild, lusty woman cloaked for all the world to see as a proper society leader in the town. He didn't love her. But he couldn't stay away from her--couldn't stop thinking of her—couldn't even think of another woman. When he was drowning in her, drinking her in, it was like trying to consume a limitless sea.

"I can't see you next Saturday," she said.

"Why not?"

"My husband is staying. There's a Valentine Day Dance at the hotel. I have to be there. My aunt and I have coordinated the event for years."

"I guess you know, that's gonna be hell for me." Again he felt pushed aside, used, his face flushing hot, readying for a fight.

"You'll have to manage." She sat up, her body partly lost in shadows.

"I'll come to the dance," Kurt said, eagerly. "Bring my own date. We can dance together."

"No-o," she spoke softly. "That's wouldn't be a good idea."

"To come or to dance with you?"

"Well...to come, I think."

He leaned forward in the swivel chair, his mouth close to her ear, spitting the words. "You don't want your seedy lover there, speaking to you, people asking who I am and how you know me."

"Don't start with that. You know what you mean to me."

"Lillian," Kurt stood up. "I want you to know something...for you to think about. My father can buy and sell your husband ten times over. Did you know that? Do you?"

"That doesn't matter."

"Well, that's news. What is it?" He yelled.

"It's not just money. That is, money is not all of it," She turned her head away from him. "Keep your voice down."

Kurt walked to the window. The lake was calm, and on the opposite bank patches of snow glistened in the moonlight. "I don't have the name?"

"It's something like that. It's background."

"Oh? Background, is it?" He whirled about, staring down at her.

"Even more than that."

"What?" Hackles were rising in him, fire in his blood, the old frustration pounding through him. She wanted to keep him—little! Keep her boy-lover manageable.

"Your whole demeanor," she finally said.

"Demeanor!" he yelled. "You bitch. You're eager enough to put up with my demeanor on your back. Didn't you say you simply existed for me—something like that? But not, I guess for my—demeanor."

"My life is empty, Kurt." Her voice rose. "It's nothing without you—what we have here."

"What we have here is a little game *of yours.* Where you call all the moves. Part of the man you like riding on you is enough man not to be shut out when it suits you."

"Don't be crude."

"I won't be set aside when it suits you, then picked up when it pleases you. I won't put up with that..."

"Don't speak to me like that."

"Ah, well, the grand lady is sensitive."

"I don't like this situation, Kurt," she came back quickly. "But it's all we have, the best we can get."

He walked to the door, ready to go. She had lain down on the rug again, the white goddess at his feet. Light played on her naked body. He could feel her against him, soft, hot, feel again her legs coiled around him—plumbing the depths of her body, all he could get. And it was never enough.

"There's so little of the good times," she whispered. "Come back."

He came to her, lay down beside her, and took her in his arms. "I can't stop this," he whispered to her.

"Why should you?" She turned and snuggled close, her warm flesh against him.

CHAPTER 36

Belle Dorsett looked at the bottle of permanent wave solution that the salesman from Harrisburg Beauty Supplies was stacking on her cabinet shelf.

"This looks like a deeper pink than usual." Belle turned a bottle about in her hand. "Are you sure this is all right?"

"It's a new kind," he answered. "Just came out this week."

"Well, if you're sure. I have a permanent scheduled this afternoon." She looked at her appointment book and sighed. It was filled for today, Friday and Saturday.

At one o'clock, Ella Donnelly came in and sat before a mirror as Belle clipped her hair into the usual style.

"I suppose you have plans this weekend," Belle asked, knowing that the Valentine Day's Dance was tomorrow night.

"Oh yes, I do. My niece and I have worked on this dinner and dance since last fall. I think we have gone over every single detail twice—don't want anything to go wrong. You know how people can be, so critical."

Belle finished putting Ella's hair in metal curlers, saturating each curl again with the permanent solution. Then she placed her under an electric machine with long tendrils of cord hanging in a circle with clamps on each end; clamps to permanently cook curls in her hair.

Belle turned to Dora who was waiting for her regular weekly shampoo and set. She carried the paper to her station and sat down. "I was just reading here," she ran her finger along the newsprint. "'At the beginning of the war, Germany had a population of sixty-eight million and an areas of two hundred thousand square miles. Now they have ninety million under the swastika and they've added more than sixty-thousand square miles.' I hope they keep their troubles over there. My father went off to war when I was little; I don't want my son going, too."

"It's a half world away," Belle said, as she applied slick setting lotion, and inserted a long clip into finger waves she was creating for Dora's short bobbed brown hair. "And we have an ocean separating us."

"Didn't help before."

She finished and put Dora under the dryer just as a knock came to the door.

"Got a delivery from the Garden of Eden Greenhouse." The deliveryman handed Belle a bouquet of yellow roses. Attached was a note. She sank down in the chair before the mirror. "My dearest Belle, you have brought more joy into my life this past year than I ever expected could happen again. I love you. Will you accompany me to the Valentine Day's Dance? Love Carson."

Belle leaned back in the chair feeling giddy. For some reason, tears popped into her eyes. She bit her lip to keep back the foolishness of crying over flowers at her age. But she had never gone to that dance—not even when she was young. She had read about these gala events later in the paper. She smiled and winked at Ella under the machine. Ella would be there—and more of her clients.

Finally the time came for Ella's curlers to be unclamped. As her hair was unrolled from the curlers, it revealed her white hair, certainly curly—but pink as a baby's blanket.

Ella stared into the mirror. Her expression sobered, then turned to horror. Her eyes widened. She stood up and leaned closer into the mirror, then picked up a hand mirror and threw it at Belle.

"You stupid, stupid woman. You've made me a Halloween joke. How can I go to the dance? You've ruined me."

Belle stood stiffly, absorbing the assault. "I'm so sorry. I don't know how this could have happ…"

"You set out to make a fool of me."

"No. No, Ella," Belle pleaded. "We can try to wash it out. I'm sure…it'll come out…and I'll take care of your hair for years—for nothing."

"You'll not touch my head again. Pink hair!" She glanced in the mirror. "I'm ashamed to be seen."

"We could dye it. We have time this afternoon."

"No. No. Everyone remarks on my beautiful white hair. You would make me some red-haired something-or-other like I see running around town here. I'll have plenty to say about this. I'll fix you like you fixed me. You'll see."

"I don't know what else I can do." Besides being puzzled, Belle felt terrible. "We could just wash it a few times. I can't bleach it after just getting that permanent, but we…"

Ella gathered up her things and slammed the door as she left.

Dora had pushed the dryer back off her head so she wouldn't miss anything. "She ought to put on a red dress, put a fancy comb in her hair, and announce she had a new do for Valentine's Day. She'd be the belle of the ball."

"Don't be funny, Dora, and your hair's not dry yet either." As Belle put the hood of the dryer over her again, she said, "This is a true disaster. You know what that family can do."

After she finished with Dora, Belle sat down in the quiet salon, gathering her wits about her. Did she dare show up at that dance? She wanted so much to go to that party with Carson.

She finally decided. She would call Carson, thank him for the roses, tell him how much she wanted to go with him, and not mention the pink hair. Maybe the whole thing would blow over, but deep down she knew it wouldn't.

CHAPTER 37

When Belle walked into the Hotel Allison's Ballroom with Carson, it took her breath away. Flickering light from dozens of red candles filled the room. Candles were on wall sconces, in windowsills, in tall crystal holders on tables where they cast a sheen on red satin table runners. Above, hundreds of lacy valentines hung from the ceiling. At the end of the room, by the dance floor, a raised platform was also covered in red, where a small orchestra played.

Carson held Belle's chair as she looked about, stardust in her eyes.

"Pretty, isn't it?" he whispered, close to her ear as he seated himself.

"I never realized such things went on right here in town— I've read about it, but...to see it..."

Ezekiel the clown stood before them, the orchestra playing the new favorite of bands everywhere, *In the Mood.*

"The lady gets a red rose to match my nose." He took a long-stemmed one from his basket and presented it to Belle.

"Thank you. I know who you are," Belle whispered to the clown. "You're Skeeter Ambrose aren't you? I am so glad you got to keep your oil well."

"Don't know about that, ma'am. I'm Ezekiel here with a rose for the lady."

Belle smiled and turned back to Carson. "You remember Skeeter? He's the town's garbage collector and town character. Everybody loves him. One of the drilling companies put a well by the city dump, where he lives. Only thing is, the dump is city land. I think half the town signed a petition to let Skeeter claim the well and get the royalties." Belle's eyes glowed. "And guess what?

"The city kept the land, anyway."

"You're so cynical. No, they let him have it. Deeded it to him." Belle looked up as Lillian Powers with her husband, Malcolm, came in, and seated themselves at the front table. "Oh, Carson, thank you for bringing me. It's just beautiful."

He put his arm across the back of her chair, held a program up close as if he were showing her something, but his lips touched her cheek. "You're the best thing that's happened to me."

She pulled back. "I've never been kissed in public."

She could feel his warm breath on her cheek. "It makes doing lots of things more exciting," he whispered.

"You're naughty." But she smiled at his intimation.

The spell was broken when Judge and Ella Donnelly walked past and joined Lillian Powers and her husband. Belle tensed as she saw Ella had wrapped her hair in a black beaded turban. Belle looked again at Carson. Should she tell him about the pink hair? She decided against it.

Jay Murrell, both singer and emcee stepped to the microphone, center stage, and said, "We wouldn't be here tonight except for the imagination of a very special lady. This is for her." He nodded to the orchestra, and he began singing. *"Underneath the lantern, by the barrack's gate."* he walked toward Lillian Powers's table. *"Darling, I remember the way you used to wait; Twas there that you whispered tenderly that you loved me."* He took her hand and led her to the stage. *"You'll always be my Lilli of the lamplight, my own Lillie Marlene."*

"Join me for our own Lilli," the audience began to sing, clapping rhythm for Lillian.

When the applause died down, Lillian stood before them, a vision with her dark hair piled high, bright lipstick and clinging red satin dress. "Thank you all so much for coming tonight. Lots of Valentine love to each of you and, Jay, my dearest, thank you for that song. I won't say much because you're all ready for the banquet to start, so enjoy the evening. Bon-Appétit and Happy Valentine's Day."

The band began again, with everyone singing Lilli Marlene, while waiters came through with the soup course.

During the meal, Max the ventriloquist held a flouncy-dressed dummy named Ethel Mae on his arm, whose head had the remarkable capability of turning totally around. "Are you having fun at the party, Ethel Mae?' Max asked the dummy. "Yes" she answered, "but I am not having much luck."

"Why is that?"

"I am looking for a dummy boyfriend."

"And you can't find one?"

"Well," she turned her head completely back toward the band, "do you think I could find a dummy back there?"

The audience began to laugh, and the band struck up, "*I'm in the mood for love.*"

After the tables had been cleared, the band began with *Moonlight Serenade*, and Lillian and Malcolm Powers were the first on the dance floor. Soon it was filled. When Carson and Belle heard the next song, they smiled and walked to the dance floor. They had come to think of it as their song. "*I get along without you very well...* " Jay sang, as Belle slipped into Carson's arms, nestled close, and they both sang the words softly, "*...except when soft rains fall...then I recall the thrill of being sheltered in your arms...* " Belle closed her eyes and wondered why she should have been so lucky to find such happiness. "*...but I should never think of spring for that would surely break my heart in two.*"

Over Carson's shoulder she noticed Ella Donnally walking to the stage.

There was, however, another person at the dance, uninvited, standing on the hotel porch, peering in the window. Kurt Malvern hid behind a trellis and watched, although he didn't really care who saw him. Angry, jealous, excluded, he saw only one person. Lillian was dancing in the arms of Logan Webb, her brother-in-law, who towered above her. Lillian's body was so defined by the tight red satin dress that when she moved, he could tell she wore nothing beneath. Kurt watched the movement of her hips under the clinging material. The dress was modest enough in front but dipped in a fold below her waist in the back.

Kurt's skin crawled. Logan Webb's hand rested on Lillian's white flesh just below the waist. Her body molded tight against him, moving together. Kurt followed the line of her profile, her breasts pressing against Logan. A furious hunger burned inside. He owned that body! Logan had no right to her. She was Malcolm's wife, but that body was his just the same. Malcolm was nothing. He could never hold her or love her—but Logan... Kurt swallowed. He moved along the porch toward the entrance.

He was nearly at the door, when he saw a small woman walking across the dance floor, holding her hand up. Kurt stopped, intrigued.

Inside, Ella Donnelly stepped up to the podium and put her hand up. The music droned to silence. Carson and Belle and all the dancers stood on the floor, looking at the diminutive lady now taking center stage before the microphone. Short, plump, dressed in a black dress with long fringe that fell to the floor from her waist, she wore a black turban covered with beads and rhinestones.

She ripped the turban off. The hair was pink!

The audience started to laugh. Then they saw how serious Ella was, and the snickers died out. Then silence.

"This happened to me at that Belle Dorsett's place. That woman over there dancing with that—oil man who come in here—to our town."

Belle's face burned, embarrassed as all eyes turned on her.

"I just want to say publicly," Ella went on. "I will never go there again, and you shouldn't either if you care how you look."

Belle gasped as if she had been struck and began to tremble in Carson's arms. She felt everyone staring. "I have to go." She couldn't breathe. "I can't stay here," she whispered to Carson. "We've got to get out of here." He picked up her wrap and walked her out into the hotel lobby.

"She's ruined me," Belle's hand flew to her mouth, tears rolled down her cheeks. "In thirty seconds she destroyed my business—my livelihood."

"Oh, surely not." He slipped his arm around her shoulders. "Such a little mistake." The front door opened, and a blast of cold air hit them.

"Oh, yes she did. I should not have come to this dance." She turned to him, tears glistening. Behind them, the band had resumed with the lively *"Woodchopper's Ball."*

She looked about, "Let's go somewhere else."

"We could go up to my room. I live here on the second floor."

Belle took a handkerchief from her purse. "I want to go home."

"Let's go to Dutch's." He lifted her chin and smiled at her. "We'll talk it over with the parrot. He'll know what to do." She stepped out onto the hotel porch, into the cold winter night and stopped short. She almost ran into her nephew Kurt.

They looked at each other, both surprised. "Kurt? Why are you here? Are you going to the party?"

"No-o," he stammered, "I--I guess not." He turned and left. Carson and Belle walked across the moonlit street to Carson's car.

What was he about to do, Kurt wondered as he went to his truck. He zippered up his leather jacket against the cold as he sat in the cab, his senses coming back to him. What could he do, actually? He had no real claim on Lillian. She was Malcolm's wife and Logan Webb's sister-in-law. And he was a country boy. No demeanor.

He sat for a while in the cold truck unable to forget Lillian in Logan's arms, then started the truck and began to drive. What else was there to do?

"Surely, this is not the end of the world." Carson held Belle's hand across the table. Dutch's Truck Stop Café was noisy and boisterous as always with men in from the oil sites hungry for a meal and full of the usual horseplay.

"You don't know who Ella Donnelly is?" Belle leaned forward.

"The judge's wife, I know."

"Not just that. There's this tight excusive clique' and she's been in it for a century. Her mother before that and her grandmother.

"They own the hotel where I live?"

"Yes," Belle whispered.

"But they're just people, sweetheart. They can't own you."

"It's like this. Sheriff Logan Webb is married to Lillian's sister. Their mother is Marthursa Allison, wife of old Mayor Wilson Allison who owned... everything. Their son, Clifton, runs the main department store in town. My niece Eva Mae thinks she's got a prize on the string—Clifton's son, Danny Allison."

The waitress came with a coffee pot and menus. About that time four men at the corner of the counter broke into howls of laughter over some story. Carson handed the menus back to the waitress.

"Not many people are invited to these homes." Belle poured some sugar in her coffee from a round glass container. "Unless you're one of them. They own the town—but not so much with money although they aren't hurting there, either, but it's who they are—have always been. I do the hair for all the ladies, but I do not go to parties with them any more than their housekeepers do."

"But, my darling Belle, that's silly."

"It's hard for newcomers to understand." Belle stared into her coffee cup, stirring in the sugar. "But you see Ella Donnelly ruined me tonight, Carson, because she speaks for all of them. I don't know how I'll make a living. A hairdresser has only her reputation." Tears began again. "...years of building customers..."

"Surely, there are others—the ladies on the farms..."

"Mostly they don't come to beauty shops. They're too poor."

"They're not now!"

Belle looked up, tears glistening on her eyelashes, studying Carson Garrett. Then she smiled. "I guess that is true—now." She squeezed his hands, "You're so wonderful. I don't know what I'd do without you."

He shrugged, "Probably keep on making pin curls."

Belle took a sip of coffee, and then put her cup back in the saucer. "I wonder why Kurt was on the porch. He wouldn't be going to a place like that."

CHAPTER 38

Kurt found himself driving out by the lake. He couldn't still his fury. Wait for her to come home, that's what he would do. He drove around the lake, and then drove toward her house and parked his truck in the shadows of the trees. He walked to her back porch where he always saw her. The screen door was open. He sat in the swing, waiting. Waiting for what? To know she was home?

A young girl opened the back door, walked through the shadowy sun porch and on outside. She didn't see him in the darkness, seated in the swing. He watched, following her white robe in the moonlight, saw her kneeling in the distance, and set something down.

Kurt got up and walked down the brick walk. She must be Lillian's child.

"What is it?" he said softly.

Startled, she looked up. "Who are you?"

"Oh, somebody your mother knows. I do things for her sometimes. I made the boathouse for her. Why are you out here? It's cold."

"I buried McAnnelly."

"McAnnally?"

"A doll. My doll. And over there is Buttons. My cat died last summer, but McAnnally died in the snowstorm. I've always had McAnnally. She slept with me all my life, and I miss her."

"Your doll died?"

"Well, not really, you know, but it feels like she died. It feels like when my Grandma left us—you know?

"How come you didn't go to the dance?"

"Oh, I don't know. Mama said the dance was for people her age and Daddy's—not for me. I still feel bad about McAnnally."

"How old are you, anyway?"

"Sixteen."

"Sixteen! He couldn't see her well in the moonlight, but he had thought he was talking to a child. Her long hair, so like Lillian's, fell loose over her robe collar. "You'd better go back in. It's cold out here."

When she stood up it surprised him. She was tall, above his shoulders. She flipped her long hair back and began walking with him to the sun porch. She sat down in the swing and he sat by her.

"I'm sorry about your cat—and McAnnally. What if I bring you something special? Out where I live there's a white squirrel. I'll bring it to you. Maybe you can call it McAnnally."

"That would be good," she answered. "But there can never be another McAnnally."

Kurt couldn't think of what else to say. "So," he began, "do you go to school...what's your name, anyway?"

"I'm Coralee. I used to go to school, but my Mama decided to get me a tutor. The tutor said I was very smart, and I could get along fine, but he doesn't come anymore, so I'm done learning—I guess."

"Aren't you cold out here?" Kurt asked.

"Kinda, but I like to talk to you."

"Do you have...people you talk to?"

"I got cousins," she added brightly. "And I got lots of dolls. You just name a kind of doll, and I got it. I got a new one—a Harlequin doll. You know what kind that is?"

"No, don't think I do."

"It's a clown doll, kinda. It's got all colors in its coat. It's pretty. But not my favorite doll."

A new revelation hit Kurt. Coralee was the reason Lillian kept the back door locked when they were together on the porch, and why she would never let him in her house. And with that came the stunning reality of something he had heard once, that one of the Allison's had a child that was not quite right. He was talking to that child.

"What do you do with a white squirrel?" Coralee asked, as they went to the swing.

"It's fun to put peanut butter on bread and when the peanut butter gets on their paws they like the taste, but they get confused about the sticky stuff on their paws."

"That sounds funny," Coralee laughed. "Bring me a white squirrel."

Headlight beams filled the drive and died as the car went into the garage. "Mama and Daddy are home!"

Kurt and Coralee rocked quietly in the swing, hearing loud steps on the stairs inside the house. "Mama'll have to help him up to the bedroom." Coralee giggled. "But it won't be his rheumatism."

"Coralee!" It was Lillian's voice echoing through the house. "Coralee, where are you? Are you out there with that doll? You should be asleep. It's late." Lillian burst through the back door, but Kurt and Coralee sat still, swinging slowly.

"Evenin', Mrs. Powers." Kurt's deep voice drawled in the darkness. "Did you have a good time tonight? Better than Saturday nights usually are?"

"You? Why are you here?" She snapped on the light. "Cora...my God. Get away from my daughter. Don't you dare ever..."

"Ever...what, Ma'am?" Kurt taunted.

"Mama, we were talking about McAnnally. He's gonna bring me a squirrel—a white one."

"No, he's not. No. No. No. He is not. Coralee, go to bed. And close the door. Just go. You're out here talking to this— strange man. I've told you about the riffraff that's come in. Won't you ever listen to me?"

"This riffraff didn't come 'in' as you say, Mrs. Powers. I've been here all my life. Maybe I have riffraff demeanor."

"Shut up," Lillian hissed.

Coralee obediently left. Lillian locked the back door and turned off the light.

The swing creaked as Kurt slowly moved back and forth. "Nice daughter."

"Get out of here. Don't you ever go near my daughter again. I know you. You'd screw anything walking."

"Not anymore—since you." The swing creaked in the darkness. "I don't do them others now. But I hate being pushed aside—while you twist your pussy against Logan Webb."

"You crazy idiotic fool—staring in the window."

"His hands were all over you." He came to her, pulled her to him. "I don't like other hands on you."

"You're insane."

He began kissing her even as she pushed him away.

"No, Logan just got you warmed up—now it's my time. This is my night, remember?" He pulled her coat from her, slipped the satin straps off her shoulders and pushed the dress over her hips to the floor and kicked it aside.

"It's cold out here," Lillian said. "I'm going..." His mouth covered hers, stifling her words, but she didn't resist.

"Remember me, Lillian." He whispered through his kisses. "Remember how *I* feel?" He kissed her harder then drew back. "Don't ever think you can pass me off—ever."

He pulled her down to the floor and they gasped and twisted, down on her coat, panting, then lay quietly in the darkness.

"You can come to me whenever you want," Lillian finally said, "but if you ever come near my daughter, again, I'll kill you."

CHAPTER 39

It had been more than a month since Robert St. Pierre came into Dutch's. The morning was grey outside, bitterly cold, dark clouds above, with snowflakes in the air. Three men bundled in heavy work coats, hunched together at the end of the counter, hands warming on their coffee cups. They had worked the night shift and were still trying to thaw out. The door opened and cold air poured in. The parrot piped up, "Howdy, Mister." But St. Pierre ignored the parrot and all others whose eyes followed him. He slid onto a distant bar stool. Annie looked up and smiled. Then she felt self-conscious remembering his compliment about her pretty smile. Did he think she was flashing it on purpose? Flirting? She carried breakfast orders to the three oil workers. Somehow one of the eggs she was serving slid right off the plate and onto the counter.

"Whoa there." The customer stopped the egg with his fork. "Big night last night, huh, Annie?" one of them teased. "I know all about them whollopin' morning-afters."

Robert St. Pierre, still burrowed in his zipped leather jacket and plaid scarf, turned on his stool, tight lines forming between his eyebrows, his face stern. The men grew quiet, paid attention to their breakfast.

"St. Pierre," one of the men called down the counter, "we're gonna be settin' up on your place startin' Tuesday."

St. Pierre nodded.

"We're gonna make you a rich man when we bring that gusher in. We'll be expecting a fried chicken dinner right out there under a tree." He punched the shoulder of the guy next to him. "Won't we, Roy?"

"And a keg of beer to wash it down," Roy answered.

St. Pierre said nothing.

"Fried chicken and apple pie."

Annie watched St. Pierre. Would they taunt him into a conversation?

"And mashed potatoes, and gravy and baked beans," Roy continued.

They kept on, trying to get a response. "And cornbread and biscuits."

"That's right, we make you rich, you gotta lay out a feast before we tear down that derrick. No way you're gonna get rid of us,'til you do."

Annie studied St. Pierre's face, clean shaven now, lean with prominent cheek bones, and eyes that showed not a spark of spirit.

He began to talk but didn't turn toward the men.

"I had a lot of land once, downstate," he began. It was as if each word was hard to bring to the surface. "The oil companies came in down there, too. I couldn't wait to lease up—like all the rest." Everyone stopped and listened as if a mute had just started talking. "We were all eager. I got oil. Oil wells pumping all over." He looked down, took a sip of coffee, "Money poured in. Easy money. So I quit working. I never had so many friends." A cynical smile twisted his lips. "Why not? A rich man. Important."

He was silent for a while, but no one spoke.

"Had a wife, too. Always thought she had the soul of a saint, but then when I'd come home from my partying, I begin to think she wasn't so much—kind of a plain-looking woman.

"It was about March, I think." Robert St. Pierre was talking out loud to no one in particular, but once started, the words flooded out. The three men who sat listening seemed to forget to eat. "She set in to do spring house cleaning," he went on. "She cleaned and cleaned and cleaned and then she began mending. Mended everything we had on the place. She even pulled out old socks I had stuck back in my drawer and darned them."

He settled his attention on Annie, who leaned against Dutch's back counter. She slipped her hand quietly behind her and turned the radio down.

"I told her there wasn't any need to do that. We'd just buy more, but she kept on fixing everything. She put out a big garden and one day she spent the whole day cooking. She fixed up a cake and pies, a platter of fried chicken, homemade bread. She filled that kitchen full of food."

He looked again at Annie yet seemed not to see her.

"The next morning while I was gone, she walked into town. Took both our children. There was a note propped against the cake cover on the kitchen table. She said she knew I didn't want her anymore. Said she didn't want anything from me. Not a cent. Just to leave her alone."

He looked down at his coffee for a while. "I found them in St. Louis. When she saw me coming up the walk, she quickly closed and locked the front door. I stood at the open porch window and called her. She closed the window without a word in answer. Then she pulled down all the window blinds."

Weariness shown in Robert St. Pierre's eye, as he spoke. Annie wanted to comfort him, as you would a child to make some life come into his dead spirit. She looked out at the dark chilled morning. But how could she help anybody? She could barely take care of herself and the baby.

"You get a divorce or what?" One of the men down the counter called out to St. Pierre.

"I signed the papers and sent 'em back to her."

"I had a wife once," Roy said. "She divorced me, but she was different than yours. She wanted the house, the garage, the car that was in it, the truck in the drive, the road in front of the house, the money in the bank, the change in my pocket; and the shirt, pants and shoes I was wearing."

St. Pierre didn't react to the comment. It was Annie he talked to. "It took about six years for the oil to completely peter out." He took a drink of coffee. "It had seemed like some kind of fountain that would never run dry, but it did. And then it was over. Family gone. Land wasn't worth much after the salt run-off from the wells. I sold it and bummed around the country for a while."

The men were quiet while they finished their breakfast.

"So," St. Pierre turned to face them, "if there's oil on that twelve acres out there where you're getting ready to drill, that's fine, but if there's not, that's fine. Either way, don't count on celebrating with me. I'm not laying out a fried chicken feast or anything else for an oil well.

Dora and Emma hovered close to the heater, their heavy coats pulled tight. Hattie and Sophie moved the quilting frame near the heat, and then joined them. It would be another twenty minutes before the chilled basement was warm enough for their cold fingers to thread a needle.

Even with the basement door closed, the drill of the derrick, just outside the churchyard made conversation a chore.

Sophie rubbed her hands together over the top of the heater and raised her voice, "Last Sunday, Pastor Wendell started his sermon, but no one could hear him, so he stopped, and we sang hymns through the whole service. I think it says a lot that that man'd let them drill nearly at the church door knowing we can't have a prayer service with all that racket."

"How long will this last—this boom." Dora spoke over the din. "Oil wells popping up all over—more by the month."

"The price of oil is going up, and I don't have to tell you why," Hattie spoke up over the noise.

The ladies were silent.

"The war," Sarah Emma said. "The swastika flies over Belgian and the papers last week said bombs had fallen on Paris. Now Italy's joined with Germany."

"I've got two sons just the right age," Hattie called. "If war comes to us."

"Congress is not favoring the draft," Dora said.

"—for now, it said," Hattie corrected. "Anyway, as long as the price of oil is going up the oil companies will keep drilling, and we'll have the noise. I hear there's two more wells in the works for that St. Pierre man. I tell you, he's a strange one. Not a bit sociable—really puts you off from speaking to 'em."

"Everybody speak up," Dora said. "You can't hear yourself think."

Hattie unbuttoned her coat.

"Didn't hear that last, Dora." Sophie cupped her hand behind her ear.

"Wasn't anything, honey. Go on Hattie," Dora leaned close.

Sophie slipped out of her new coat, put it across the back of the chair, and sat down in her usual place at the quilt frame.

"Somebody said they're talking about putting another well in the church yard." Hattie sat down and took out her needle. The others sat down, too and began stitching—In silent disapproval.

Robert St. Pierre came into the truck stop a couple of weeks later. He nodded toward Annie as he found a booth by the window.

"How goes it?" Annie tried to be light with him, but his presence was always so heavy and somber. Still, she noticed, he looked better each time she saw him.

"Not bad." He smiled at her briefly.

She handed him a menu and slid in the booth opposite him. "I hear they're drilling on your twelve acres."

He unzipped his leather jacket and folded it up beside him. He had on a bright blue checked shirt that looked to be new. "Started about a week ago," he answered.

Annie wasn't sure whether she should congratulate him or keep quiet.

"The people at that church out there—what's it called? Bethlehem? They're upset with me. An acre of land was given to the church, but the mineral rights stayed with the original owners and with the deed, so the oil company wanted to drill in the church parking lot. If I agreed, the church would not get the royalties. I'll get them. They'll just get the nuisance."

"You could promise them money from the well, for compensation."

"They're so angry with me, they don't want it." He handed Annie the menu. "Biscuits and sausage gravy." He leaned across the table, his hand around the coffee cup. She realized while he was talking to her, his conversation came easy, now. "You see they were all for it when they thought the well was entirely theirs. They would rebuild the little white church and make it bigger, but when they found they could get nothing or, as you say, some of it, depending on my generosity, they decided they didn't want any part of it."

"You could have stop the company from drilling, if you wanted to."

"The Board of Trustees at the church was adamantly against a derrick being set up, even if I compensate them from the royalties, assuming there are any. You know it could be a dry hole." He shrugged. "It's not going to stop them having church, and the derrick won't be there forever."

"There's the noise and trucks everywhere—blocking the drive..." It was Annie's childhood church and she felt loyal to it, but she could imagine which obstinate heads had decided—all or nothing.

When she came back later with his check, Robert looked up, a question in his serious eyes. "Annie, do you ever..." He stopped.

"Ever, what?"

"Nothing." He stood up. "Nothing." He pulled a bill from his wallet, folded it and pushed it toward her. "Keep the change." He left, ignoring the parrot that hadn't heard the cash register ring, calling out, "Money, mister. Money, mister."

When she unfolded the bill, it was a twenty.

CHAPTER 40

Maxwell Porter sat on the stump in his front yard, his rifle across his knee, and watched as Carson Garrett's black Buick rolled slowly up the bumpy drive and pulled to a stop. Garrett peeled out of the car and slammed the door.

"I hope you're not aimin' to use that gun anytime soon?" Garrett nodded toward the gun.

"Not 'less there's a need," Porter's jaw was set.

"Well, Porter, I thought I'd come by and tell you we'll be setting up on your property in about a week."

"That right?" Porter was not to be a joke again. The rifle stayed put. "Where's that supposed to be?"

"It'll be over by that hedgerow. There, about fifty yards from the road."

Porter nodded his head, satisfied. Everyone could see it. John Malvern could see it.

"I'm obliged you took the time to clear this up. Shore it ain't some joke on old Porter?"

"No joke, Mr. Porter. We'll be out there drilling before you know it. You don't need to do anything special. The men are used to all this." The story had widely circulated about Porter moving his outhouse to accommodate the crew he thought was coming earlier.

"If you're funnin' me…" He looked up at Garrett and patted the gun. "Nobody makes a fool of ole Porter twice."

"It's the real thing, this time." Garrett tipped his hat and left. Porter watched him drive down the lane and turn onto the main road. He walked down where the well would be. He stood there, digging his toe into the crumbled white clay, pondering. Maybe this was gonna be his beginning. They'd find a pool down there and on over there. He'd have to tear out that hedgerow, so's they could have access to that field from the road. In town he'd be linin' up with the big boys. They'd all nod to him when he walked into the Blue Moon. "Here, Porter, you ain't leavin' without a game over here with us," they'd say. And they'd regret they'd made him out the fool. He kicked a clod of frozen clay. "Ole Porter won't be nobody's joke no more."

The crew came in and began setting up the derrick and Porter shut down his sawmill.

"What's that thing for?" Porter sat on his haunches, watching Bill Anderson wind the cable to sink the drill.

"That's what goes down into the earth digging for the oil."

"How's come this is the spot you fellars picked to sink that drill?"

"You gotta ask somebody smarter'n me." Anderson squinted up at Porter. "I just do as I'm told. I reckon Carson Garrett knows why. He's the man with the drillin' savvy."

"It's his money so he ain't gonna pick some place just because it's pretty. He's got to know more'n he's tellin'."

"You'll have to ask him, Mr. Porter. I mostly just see bolts are good and tight and such like. Them serious estimations, I leave for the big shots."

"Big Shots?" Porter leaned forward, watching Billy Anderson strain to tighten a bolt. "Well, this here's my land. I reckon if they's something to be knowed, I'd qualify to be in on it, wouldn't you think?"

"I 'spect so, Mr. Porter."

"When you think Garrett gonna be out here?"

"I couldn't say, but when we're puttin' in a new well, he's not scarce. You're gonna see him here anytime—night or day."

Porter stood up and rolled a cigarette. "I'll be speakin' with him when it's convenient for *both* of us."

"That'd be fine Mr. Porter. He's an easy man to talk to."

Porter struck a match, cupped his hand, and lit the cigarette. "Looks to me like he knowed just where to put this well, so he knows something from all them charts they read, and then he's gonna have an idea where the next one'll be drilled. Like he knows where the pool is and—they can tell that kinda stuff from them electric logs."

"Could be." Anderson moved to another bolt on the metal lattice of the derrick.

"I heard Malvern talkin' about that—the formation down there. They lay out one of them shocks, and it comes up and draws lines on a chart that just about tells you for sure where that oil is— like some spots is solid hard rock and other parts is not, and that where the oil might seep in."

"That may be, sir. That's for them with more schooling than me."

Porter pulled himself erect, looked down at Billy Anderson, took a drag from his cigarette. "Well, you're a fine boy. You're Sarah Emma's boy, ain't you?" He patted him on the back. "You're a fine lad, I can see that."

"Thank you, sir."

Porter ambled back to the house, but he stayed near the screen door all morning waiting for Carson Garrett's big Buick to turn down his lane. By one o'clock he reached for his hat.

"You just calm yourself down," Pearl Porter drawled. "Sometimes it takes three or four weeks to see if it's a good well— longer if they have trouble."

Porter looked at his wife. "Woman, you don't know about these things. They can tell—they can." Something was alive in Porter and he couldn't get down to thinking about another thing.

On the sixth day of April, Porter marked on the calendar, "Begin to set up."

Soon he could see the derrick out there in his field, lights stretching to the top, shining even into his bedroom at night like there was a carnival out there.

Three days later he marked on his calendar, "Begin to drill." He would listen to the chugging of the drill all night, until he dropped off, exhausted, then wake with a start to be sure it was still running. It was. Day and night. And there were trucks down there coming and going. Every day, he took the red crayon out of the drawer and with Pearl at his shoulder, they crossed off another day on the calendar hanging in the kitchen advertising Colclasure's Funeral Home.

"Sorry Willis couldn't a seen this," he whispered to his wife as he put the crayon away. Then he was sorry he had said it, because Pearl started to cry.

"Oil well don't compare with a boy, Porter."

"I know, Mama, but maybe he wouldn't done what all he did. You know what I mean. Just tryin' to live up to the Malverns."

Pearl turned away from the window, away from the well and wiped her eyes with her long apron skirt.

On May 14, at 4:00 in the morning, Porter was roused from his sleep. "Mr. Porter," it was the Anderson boy outside the screen. "I thought you'd want to know. They hit pay dirt. The well's come in."

Porter grabbed his pants, as Pearl ripped off her hairnet and they rode out, the old truck bumping over dried furrows to the site.

"I knowed it'd come in. I knowed it." Porter kept saying.

They watched the pipe gurgle and finally began to flow. Porter stood still, silent. He looked up long at the twinkling lights of the derrick. It didn't feel like it was his. He watched as the flow grew stronger.

"It's a good one, Mr. Porter. You got you a good well," Billy Anderson said.

Porter walked back over to his old Ford and sat down on the running board. They couldn't make him out a joke now, not ole

Porter. Everything would be different now. Still it just didn't seem like it was really happening. He rubbed his eyes, trying to understand that he was coming into the money now. Hisself.

"I'm kinda sorry it come in the middle of the night. Weren't nobody to see it," he said to his wife sitting by him on the running board.

He cupped her knee in the palm of his hand, "Pearlie, whenever the money comes in, you can have whatever you want. You can. Anything."

He turned to look at her. Tears glistened on her cheeks.

"I can't have that no more. I want my boy, Willis back."

Before the men came to tear down the derrick and put the well on a pump, Porter and his wife did the ritual honors of laying out a feast in their front yard for all the oil workers. Fried chicken was always expected, and it was piled in mounds surpassed only by stacks of biscuits, and alongside that were crocks of baked beans and potato salad. At one end of the table there were chocolate, burnt-sugar and angel-food cakes; and pumpkin, raisin, apple and cherry pies. Meanwhile, down in the field, the lights and constant drone of the pump continued. Sometimes Porter would just stop and listen and smile.

Porter decided to go to town. In his bedroom he put on his new blue bib overalls he had bought right after the oil came in. This morning the first royalty check had been in his mailbox. Once in the bank, he looked about hoping there was someone who would notice him, see him cashing the check. The clerk counted out four hundred and fifty-six dollars and nineteen cents. She used four one hundreds, a fifty and six ones. Porter held the money for a moment, then leaned into the barred bank window and whispered to the girl to change the hundreds into twenties. The girl frowned, took back the hundreds and counted four stacks of twenties.

Porter walked from the bank, a wad of bills rolled in his fist, the fifty wrapped around the other bills. He went into Allison's Store where he'd recently added the boots and overalls to the long list of items on his old bill. He waited impatiently, the stack of money out on the counter before him with the fifty on top. "I'm here to pay what I owe you." He laid his hand over the bills on the counter. "All I owe you." He looked over the clerk's shoulder, hoping someone he knew might be watching. When the girl presented Porter with his bill, he carefully pulled off three twenties from under the fifty, "I think that'll cover it." He put the roll of money in his pocket, smiled, tipped his hat, and ambled across the street to the Blue Moon.

Porter sat down at the first barstool, pulled out his stack of bills and casually put them on the counter, again the fifty on top. "I'm gonna buy everybody drinks in this place."

"Now Porter, you just put your money away," one of the men said. "It's us that'll be buyin' the drinks for you—a new well and all. Come on over here." Porter moved down the bar to join them. Nothing in his life had ever felt so good as this.

On the way home, he stopped to pick up Pearl who was getting a permanent at Belle Dorsett's Kozy Kottage Beauty Shop. When he came up the walk to the shop, Porter noticed a sign in the window, "Antiques for Sale." He went in, although he didn't think it was the place for men.

Belle Dorsett nodded toward Porter as she pulled rollers from Pearl's hair.

"I've decided to buy Belle's china cabinet, Porter." Pearl looked up at him.

"Whatever she wants." Porter laughed, leaned back, pulled out his roll of bills, and held them.

"I'd like to know how much you'd take for that bed in there?" Porter motioned through the door to the bedroom.

"Oh, Mr. Porter, I'm sorry but that's not for sale. I was born on that bed. All of us were."

Porter looked at Belle, studying her. He pushed back the bill of his cap. "You mean that there bed is where John Malvern was born?"

"Well, yes. All of us were, and our papa before that." Belle began brushing out the tight curls.

"I'll give you this whole stack for it." Porter put the money on the table in front of his wife.

Pearl turned instantly in the chair. "Porter, we don't need that bed."

"It is not for sale, Mr. Porter—not that piece." Belle was firm.

Porter patted the money. "I got the money right here."

"Mr. Porter, I couldn't sell that." Belle looked in the mirror at the hair-do she was beginning to shape on Pearl's head.

"You Malverns wouldn't let a Porter have anything if you could find a way to keep him from gettin' it."

"Mr. Porter, no amount of money could make me sell that bed. Not to anyone."

"Get that job done on Pearl, we're leavin', and we ain't takin' the china cabinet if we can't have the bed, too."

"But Porter," Pearl protested, "you said I could have whatever I wanted."

"Well, you can have whatever else besides this you want." Porter grabbed the money off the table, shoved it in his pocket and waited in the car.

CHAPTER 41

From January to April the Malvern family huddled in two rooms, the kitchen and one bedroom with wall-to-wall cots, while the Lightfoots, father and sons, tore out walls, built an upstairs and superimposed a roof over the skeleton framework of a larger house. Hammers rang out from daylight to dark. By early May the Malvern house had been turned from a modest solid house into a grand showplace.

It was a brilliant morning, with the whisper of summer in the air and the eternal awakening of the earth. Wild flowers lined the roadside and thick bright leaves hid the old oak's winter limbs. Eva Mae held her mother in her arms as her father plowed up the dried remnants of last year's garden.

"Now, please don't cry, Mama," Eva Mae said.

"I've fed my family from this garden," Sophie's voice broke, "ever since I married your Papa."

"But we're going to make it a garden with flowers. Just flowers—mostly roses. We'll have walkways through it and a trellis arch," Eva Mae soothed.

"I plant my pole beans along the fence." Sophie pointed past the place Malvern was plowing.

"It's going to be the most beautiful garden in the county, along the side of our beautiful house, full length of the yard. You'll see, Mama. Dannie Allison's mother is president of the Garden Club in town. She has all kinds of roses in her garden."

Sophie pulled a handkerchief from her apron pocket and dabbed at hot tears. "And over there is where the tomato plants go and lettuce goes here."

"Mama, you don't need to do that anymore. You can go to the store and buy everything you need. You know every year you get a rash on your legs and hands when you do gardening. Now you won't have to worry."

Not have to worry! Tears spilled down her cheeks. What would she do with herself? It was like being deprived of her hands. "You're making me an empty old woman. This time ought to be my easy life, but now I have to learn to do everything new," she cried. "When are you and your Papa going to stop and just let things be?"

"Don't be so old fashioned, Mama," Eva Mae scolded. "It's exciting."

It wasn't the first time Sophie had felt robbed of her usefulness. When their big house had been completed and it sat on an acre lawn, like some kind of white palace, she thought, John had gone to town and bought massive carved mahogany pieces to replace the furniture that belonged to her own Mama. She had complained that the dark furniture caught dust more when oil trucks rumbled by and that she always had to dust.

"We'll just get somebody to come in and take care of the house," was Eva Mae's cheery solution.

"Take care of the house," Sophie stormed. "I will not have someone taking my place in my own house as long as I can put both feet on the floor when I get up and put one foot in front of the other all day." She had shaken her finger at Eva Mae. The very idea! A strange woman putting Malvern things away, doing her work. What would there be for her to do? Who would she be? Put in a rocking chair out of the way? But Eva Mae and John had just soothed her and cooed over her, then went right on and hired the young Walters girl to come—ignoring her.

Eva Mae looked down at her unhappy mother, who was watching the mutilation of her garden. "We've got lots of money, Mama. Don't you understand that?" Her mother still looked miserable. "Isn't there ever anything you wanted, Mama?"

Sophie thought for a moment, watching John turn the tractor at the end of the row. "There was something I saw. It was some time back. A beaded lampshade. It was real pretty. There was strings of beads hanging down, something like fringe—different color beads—some were amber and there were rust color and brown and gold ones. There in the store window...the sun was shining through them and they were so pretty. But we didn't have electricity, so I put that nonsense out of my head."

"Oh, Mama, you shall have all the lampshades you want."

"No. That's not necessary. Let's don't waste money on that kind of foolishness."

"Mama, you are a sweet darling angel." Eva Mae hugged her mother. "I love you to pieces, but..."

Sophie didn't want to watch the destruction of her garden anymore. She went into the house to her magnificent new kitchen, where she couldn't find a thing, sat down by the table, and stared at the floor.

Tuesday was usually Annie's day off, but the other waitress was sick, and Dutch had called her to work the late shift. It was ten o'clock when she picked up Hannah, and she was exhausted from a long hot day. As she turned off the highway onto the country road, she noticed headlights in her mirror. They came close, following at each turn. Her heart began to pound in her chest. Were they going to harass her as they did Willis? When she accelerated, it kept up with her. Then it was gone, turned off. Relief drained through her. People had a right to drive on the roads, she told herself. It didn't mean anything. But she couldn't calm herself. Flashing through her mind again, was Willis's bloody body slumped across the steps. Annie turned in her drive, gathered up the baby in her arms and got out. The headlights were there again, coming in her drive.

The car rolled slowly on the gravel, stopping at the back of her car. Two men got out and blocked her way to the house.

"That father-in-law of yours," one said, "has been all over town with handfuls of money, showing off to just about anybody that'd listen to him. Remember, Mrs. Porter," moving toward her was a man with light curly hair, heavy jowls, and a paunch that hung over his belt, "there's a lot of money owed us." Moonlight and gas flares lit up her yard except for black splotches under the trees. The other one stood back, the one with black hair, the one who had threatened Willis.

"You killed my husband," Annie cried. "You took everything from me. Don't you see I got nothing?"

"What we know, Mrs. Porter, is your husband never paid what he owed. Now it's down to you."

"Me? If I could've gotten anything, don't you think I would? Willis wouldn't be dead, then."

"Oh, you can get the money, all right. You got a father with all them oil wells and now your husband's father is parading around with his money. We want what's due us." He leaned forward, his warm breath on her face. "You can see that, can't you, Mrs. Porter?"

"Leave me alone. I have to work every day just to get by."

He moved closer. "And you have to leave your kid out there at the Porter place—the very same Porter that's got the money to show around town!"

Her heart hammered, the back of her neck knotted, a tightening crawling on her scalp and gripping her temples. They knew what she did every day! She held her child so tightly, the baby began to whimper.

"I'm going to the sheriff and tell him how you won't leave us alone." She felt the impotence of her threat, like a powerless child.

The fat face smiled down at her. "Yeah, that's the thing for you to do. Talk to the sheriff."

Moving out of the dappled shadows, the other one cut in, the one she knew killed Willis.

"Your husband's old man. Talk to him. He's the one to make your troubles go away."

After they left, Annie walked back and forth, the length of the house, distracted. She didn't want to go to the Porters. She hated the very thought of it, but—she had to get these dangerous people to leave her alone. It was Willis who got them in this mess. Maybe, his father *could* take care of it.

Early the next morning, with Hannah propped beside her, she turned down Porter's lane, surprised to see a crew setting up another well back in the woods behind his house. An oil truck was coming toward her so she pulled over on the narrow driveway to let it pass.

Annie pounded on the screen door. Finally, Pearl came, greeted her, and took the baby from her arms. Porter was glued to the back window, watching the activity around the new well site.

Annie sank down in a chair by the kitchen table, her elbow resting on the checked oilcloth. A warm breeze poured through the house. "Gonna be another hot one," Pearl said as she bounced the baby on her lap.

Maxwell Porter rubbed his hands together, chuckling. "Reckon you see ole Porter's gettin' another well?"

"I need to talk to you." Annie hesitated. "I've got to get the baby to a safer place."

Porter turned toward her. "You got some problem, girl?"

"Those men that taunted Willis. Remember? In that car? They're back, threatening to hurt the baby…threatening me."

"My, God!" Pearl whispered.

Porter came back and sat at the table opposite Annie. "What they sayin'?"

"They followed me home last night…wouldn't let me in the house at first."

Porter leaned in. "They go for you?"

Annie frowned, confused. "No, no. They were just there…said you got money now, with the well, and they want what Willis owed them."

"Owed 'em?" Pearl spoke sharply, her eyes moistening. "Willis paid all right...they took his life." She clutched the baby tighter and tears brimmed her eyes. "Oh, dear God help us."

Annie looked up at Porter, begging. "I'm scared to death, what they'll do to this child."

"They ain't gonna do anything to you and that baby." Porter stood and stretched himself.

"I can't see how you can say a thing like that, Porter." Pearl argued as if Annie were not there. "They took and killed your only boy. They ain't to be messed with."

"What they said, Mr. Porter," Annie's voice quavered, "is that you could get the money and make my troubles go away."

A truck rumbled slowly by outside the back window, carrying the top section of the derrick. Porter jumped up and went to the back screen door. "You see that?" He turned to the two women, "Pretty soon your ole pappy Malvern ain't gonna be braggin' much to Porter."

"Give her the money, Porter," Pearl begged, tears tracking down her gaunt cheeks. "There's the baby to think of."

Porter turned about, scratched the back of his head, and squinted his eye as if he had a troubling decision to put up with. "You tell 'em, to come and see me and I'll make *their* troubles go away. You just tell 'em ole Porter said that. You tell 'em I got what they need if they just come out here and get it." Porter hurried to the front screen door. A parade of trucks was moving between the sawmill and the side of his house, hauling in more sections of the derrick.

He came back and put his hand on Annie's shoulder. "They're just tryin' to scare a little money out of ole Porter now that he's come into it, and they're gonna find out I ain't to be trifled with."

Annie left as fearful as when she came. She took her child to her aunt, Belle Dorsett. Hannah was nearly a year old now. She could play around the shop, and The Kozy Kottage was across the highway from Dutch's Truck Stop. Maybe, she thought, they wouldn't go to such a public place.

CHAPTER 42

Robert St. Pierre walked through Dutch's Truck Stop Cafe, looking neither right nor left, and as always, sat in a far booth. He came often now. Two wells pumped on his twelve-acre strip of land. The men sitting at the counter in Dutch's said nothing as he walked by. They knew better.

"Morning." He looked up briefly at Annie, and snapped the menu closed. "The usual."

"Everything all right, Mr. St. Pierre?" She poured him coffee.

"No, things are not all right."

She put the coffee pot on the table and sat down in the booth opposite him.

"Magnolia wants to drill across the road from the church," he went on. "The church people are already angry about the noise. Some of them were at my house last night complaining. And Magnolia's pushing me to let them drill."

"What'll you do?"

"I don't know." He rubbed his forehead with his index finger. "I'm going to see a lawyer today." He sighed and looked out into the parking lot. "Oil has brought me more grief than anything in my life."

"I could say the same, and I've never had any."

"It seems to pursue me."

She left to serve a crew just coming off a night shift. When she brought his usual biscuits and sausage gravy, she sat with him again.

"You know, Annie," he tackled the biscuits. "It's not really the oil that's brought us such misery. Oil's just oil." He took a bite and looked at her, deadly serious. "It's the power of it that's bewildering. In a matter of months, maybe weeks, you got more money than you ever imagined. You never even knew anybody with so much money. It's spewing out of the ground and it feels limitless, then you feel limitless. You feel you're on a pedestal twenty feet high above everybody, but you don't know what to do next. What all you used to do that had meaning you don't have to do anymore. You got too much money to work. He dug again into the biscuits and gravy. "You're not sure even who you are or what's the truth about anything."

"It infects other people, besides ones standing on that pedestal," she said. She looked around to see if anyone noticed how intently St Pierre was talking to her. "When Willis saw people as poor as he was getting rich, it made him crazy."

"The thing is," St. Pierre said, "You can't build something grand, expecting it to stand when it doesn't have a foundation. Wealth on poor folk's foundation don't work."

She leaned forward, closer to him, "I am so scared."

He looked up. "Why?"

She didn't know why she said it. He had troubles enough of his own. She just had to have someone to talk to.

"What is it, Annie?"

"A car follows me. Parks in my drive—the same one that followed Willis. I know they're the ones that killed him—but the sheriff won't do anything. He's as scared of those people as everybody else."

"He's in their pocket."

"They threatened my little girl." Everything began to pour out of her. "I had to take her to my Aunt Belle's place. It's an inconvenience for her, but then I can see who drives in over there."

Annie shoved her hair back behind her ears. "I don't know what to do. My parents were so fed up with Willis and my problems I don't want to go to them—and Willis's father..."

"If you ever need me." St. Pierre stopped her, paused himself as if considering his words. "That is, if you need to leave your house, you can stay with me."

"Thank you."

"I mean, you understand...just to be safe. Nothing else. I wouldn't..."

"I know. And it's good of you to offer." She smiled at him, and then looked out the window. "Willis's father says he'll take care of it, but," She shook her head and sighed, "he won't." Heat waves rose off the highway, and it was only nine in the morning. "It's going to be another blistering day."

"Annie." He spoke so softly she hardly heard him.

She turned back to St. Pierre. "Yes?"

"Would you...go out with me?" He looked directly into her eyes. "I mean if it's too soon after losing your husband. If you said no, I'd understand. I didn't know if you were going out...or if...." He looked as if his life hung in the balance of her answer.

She had really never been asked out on a date. Since seventh grade she had been Willis's girl, and they went everywhere together. She felt self-conscious. "Yes," she answered, twisting the corner of her little waitress' apron under the table. "I think I'd like that, Robert St. Pierre," she said formally. "I'd like to go out with you."

He smiled with the first real hint of joy she had ever seen in his spiritless eyes. A happy buoyancy poured through her like a gentle spring breeze, whisking away somber workaday burdens.

"Maybe, Friday night?" His eyes were serious, expectant.

"That would be fine—better than fine."

Annie watched through her window as Robert St. Pierre drove up to her house in his shiny '38 Chevy, irritated with herself for being so nervous. It had taken her twenty minutes to decide what to wear.

"I can't be gone long. I left my baby with my aunt," she said when he came to the door and then decided that was an abrupt thing to say. "It's just that Hannah's with my aunt," she tried to explain as he helped her in the car. "I'm sort of imposing on her anyway,"

"I understand," he said.

They drove through the country roads, yellowish lights from the flares covering the fields, country music on the radio, and cooling air splashing over their faces on the hot summer night.

"Where would you like to go? Sarah Emma's, maybe?"

"No, not a restaurant. That's too much like work. Let's see…" She looked at him trimmed and spruced up like she had never seen before. "Take me to see your new well—the one by the church." They drove for ten minutes or so before they stopped in the churchyard. A derrick was standing on the east side of the steepled church within twenty feet of the building, decked from ground to tip with bright lights. The grinding drill, deafening.

"I see why the people are upset," Annie yelled over the roar.

"Let's go in the church so we don't have to shout."

They walked up the three steps to the little church, and he opened the double white wooden doors.

The church doors closed, the noise muted, they stood near the back. Annie thought she felt his fingers brush hers. She noticed he had carefully kept from touching her.

Inside, the derrick lights came through the windows splashing the dark interior of the church with stripes of brilliant horizontal patches of light.

"What can you do about this?" Annie said, "You say you don't care anything about the money?"

"It's not me. The church was given the land, but the mineral rights under the ground stayed with all the rest of the land. When I leased the land the oil company decided where they wanted to drill. If I had known all this before I signed the lease, I'd have signed the mineral rights under the church property to the church. Now I'd have to fight the oil company to keep them off this property."

She turned to face him. "Is this Carson Garrett's Company?"

"No. I could reason with him. Not these guys . . ." He didn't finish.

She decided not to go on with this, felt he could resolve it if he wanted to, then thought maybe she was too personally involved knowing all the people in church as she did. The silence seemed to reverberate off the dark walls. Annie turned to him and tried to see his expression.

"Do you mind if I ask you a personal question?" She hesitated. "Have you gone out since your wife left?"

He stood just outside of the long splashes of light that lay across the pews in the dark church. "This is the first time," he whispered.

"Oh." She felt suddenly awkward and for some reason responsible. She couldn't see his shadowy face, but his voice sounded earnest.

"When you asked me—I felt—a sudden rush of happiness like I hadn't felt for a long time. I haven't laughed in months." She stopped, looked out at the well, felt she had said too much, perspiration was popping out under her clothes. "I have to ask, Robert, why me?"

"Why you? Because you have a beautiful smile. It started something in me. Every day the thought of it crept in, whatever I was doing. I began to wonder about you—not just the waitress. It seemed to call me."

He put his arm about her, but it seemed uncertain. She moved closer to him, feeling the strangeness of it. She had been in no other man's arms but Willis's in all her life. She lay her head against St. Pierre's shoulder, moved close to him. It was comforting, easy to lean against him. His arms tightened about her easy, in a loose gentle embrace as if he held something fragile.

She felt his warm breath on her forehead. Finally she whispered, "I promised my aunt I wouldn't leave the baby long."

"Yes." He stepped back, part of his face still in the deep shadows. He tentatively stroked her hair. "It's good to feel a woman's hair against my cheek."

"We could talk a little," Annie ventured and sat down on one of the wooden pews.

He sat by her in the darkened church. "Ah well, don't listen to me," he whispered. "You shouldn't listen to me. I had a woman walk out on me—never wanted to see me again."

Annie found his hand, held it, feeling the warmth. It had been months since she'd felt Willis's touch. But it was not the same. Wounded as he was, she sensed Robert was a stronger man.

"I'm not sure I should tempt myself or involve you," he said. "She said I'm not a fit person to live with."

Annabelle looked up into his shadowed face and raised his hand to her cheek. "Surely that can't be true."

He stood up. "We have to get you back." He took her hand, and they walked down the three steps of the little church.

At Belle's house, they stood outside The Kozy Kottage Beauty Salon, the air filled with night sounds. Annie smiled. "I enjoyed being with you, Robert. I really did. I'm glad we talked."

He looked at her for a moment in the moonlight. "Me, too."

CHAPTER 43

The day was sweltering; billowing dark clouds hovered low with deep rumblings in the east. Dutch had every fan he owned turned on. Annie was exhausted, tired of sweat-soaked men at the counter who were impatient and rude because of the heat and she was impatient, too. Her only thoughts were of celebrating her baby's first birthday. She looked at her watch. Finally time to leave work.

Her parents were busy with their new friends and never called. Hannah's other grandmother, Pearl Porter, didn't drive at night. So Annie had invited the Patrick brothers who sheepishly came regularly to see Hannah with the most flimsy of excuses. She had thought often of Robert St. Pierre and considered inviting him, but after their first date he had not called or come into Dutch's. She felt he was avoiding her.

Hannah, dressed in a white dress with little red valentines and a bright ribbon in her brown ringlets, was perched on a kitchen chair with two pillows. Otis and Henry Patrick sat on either side of her. Annie placed a small chocolate cake with thick icing before Hannah. She grabbed for it with her tiny fists, put a handful in her mouth, liked it, and reached for more and more. Then she began to pat and pound the cake remnants like it was a mud pie, licking her palms, and then rubbing them on her white dress. In a short time, her face, arms, hair and dress were covered with chocolate.

"That is so cute, I wish I had a camera," Annie said, but she noticed Otis frowning and then go back to his job of steadying Hannah in her chair. Henry was sober-faced.

Finally Annie said, "That's enough fun, let's clean you up." She lifted the baby out of Otis's arms and took her to the sink, washed her and changed her into a fluffy pink dress and stood her before Otis. Both brothers brightened and smiled.

"Annie," Henry spoke up, "it's not our business, and we know that, but we want to say our piece. We don't like to see her get that dirty or messy. It's not the way she should be."

Annie looked from one brother to the other, amazed. They were gazing down on the baby as if she were some sacred object. They simply adored the little girl.

She served the meal and then brought out the real cake with one candle. Henry showed Hannah how to blow out the candle but wouldn't let her touch the cake. Otis took her on his lap and carefully fed her with a spoon, one bite at a time.

Otis brought in a long box from their truck and helped her open it. It was a doll almost as big as Hannah. Annie smiled, realizing what it meant for these shy brothers to go to town, ask about the toy department, and make a purchase so foreign to them.

By eight o'clock they were hiding their yawns as they watched Hannah with her doll. "I think it must be past the baby's bedtime." Henry said. "We better be going,"

"You have to work tomorrow, Annie," Otis added, backing up his brother's attempt to escape for their own bedtime.

As they started out the back door they saw the three locks Annie had had Glenn install. "What's all this. You got trouble, Annie?" Henry asked.

"Oh, no." She shrugged it off. "Lots of new people around we don't know, and I have the baby to consider."

Both brothers seemed to wake up. "You got 'em on the front door, too?"

"Yes, but I'm all right." She didn't mention that with the heat she had to keep the windows open.

"You need anything, just ring us up." Henry said.

"Anything." Otis was suddenly alert, too.

They seemed satisfied as they took one last look at Hannah sitting on the floor, busy with her new doll.

After they left, Annie, balancing Hannah in her arms, awkwardly locked all three locks to her house. As she drove into town for the fireworks, she thought again of Robert St. Pierre and puzzled why he hadn't called, or even come into Dutch's.

She found a place among the crowd and spread a blanket on the grassy banks of the lake just as the first orange sunburst of fireworks filled the sky, mirrored in the lake. The baby clapped with glee each time the sky lit up. Once while the light illuminated the crowd below, Annie glanced about. She saw him! Robert. Standing by a tree, alone. Darkness followed. Then a blast of three volleys filled the sky, again. Hannah stood; spread her arms wide like the giant umbrella of light above. Robert glanced toward the baby, then saw Annie, and nodded. When the next light came, he had turned, looking toward her. Their eyes met briefly before the light dimmed completely.

Why had he not come back? Maybe he didn't want a woman with a child in his life, or maybe he just didn't want another woman. As a bright light rocketed into the sky, she saw he was gone. He was avoiding her. She was surprised how sorry she felt—empty, alone. Hannah was so exuberant people around them laughed at her antics, but in the darkness, Annie vowed she would not look in Robert's direction. The light came again, and she saw him threading his way through the islands of seated people, moving toward her. He slipped down on the blanket beside her; put his arm around her shoulders in a hug just as the brilliant sky faded. But in that instant, she saw something else, a lively spark in his eyes as he looked at her, so different than the spiritless eyes she remembered when she first met him.

"I've never seen your little girl," he whispered. "She's having a great time."

When the light came again, she looked into his eyes and she knew he was happy to see her.

"It's her birthday," she said, as the friendly darkness enveloped them. She felt the warmth of his arm touching her.

"It's good to see you," he said softly.

"Yes," was all she could say. The stubborn thought would not go away, that he had taken her out, then avoided coming into the restaurant, leaving her feeling uncomfortable and ignored. Light bathed over the crowd, the lake, and the tall trees on the other side of the water with the fireworks finale.

Then it was over, the crowd on the grassy lake bank thinning around them. Hannah, exhausted, crawled into Annie's arms and settled heavily against her.

"I suppose you wonder why I have not been back in…"

"No," she lied, "I knew you were busy, the new well and …"

"That was part of it."

"I hear about the problems with the well and the church."

"They moved the services to a tent," he said. "Having a regular tent meeting. Making a statement, I guess."

Cars were honking, along the roadway, trying to get out of the traffic jam. "I've moved into a house near my twelve acres…" the noises on the road drowned him out. "It's…"

"I know the house," she answered. "I've been in that house many times when I was a child."

"Let's go there. We need to talk." He looked across the park, now dimly lit only with car lights.

Robert had just put his car in the garage, when she drove in the drive. They walked up the steps to his porch, and he carried Hannah inside where she nestled drowsily on the couch. Annie followed as he showed her through the house, which was furnished with a kitchen table and one chair, an old couch and a cot in the bedroom. Not a single picture or personal extra to suggest a home.

"Let's go out. It's cooler," he suggested. They sat on the edge of the porch, in the semi-darkness, fireflies floating in the air.

It nagged at her, why he had not called, but she said nothing.

He sat apart from her a bit. "Annie," he stopped and looked across the darkened lawn to a mountain of light from a derrick protruding in the eastern sky. "I don't know how to say this. I'm not afraid of much but meeting you and what you awakened in me..." he stopped. "I need time to think this out. I want to be...well, I can't be anything but straight with you." He looked at her in the shadowy light. "I'm not doing this very well..."

"You don't think we should see each other again. Isn't that what you're trying to say?"

"No, not at all. You know," he hesitated, "I had a wife...I had complete faith in her, that no matter what I did she would be there. I never imagined she could leave me. But she did. I was devastated, but mostly I was shocked. If she could leave, I've wondered, who can I ever trust again?"

He was so deadly honest, nothing like the perpetual shallow flattery she heard all day from the men at Dutch's.

"And, Annie, I thought of you too, seeing your murdered husband. The shock you've had. It's not easy to believe in life again. I care about you, Annie, enough to be sure neither of us gets hurt like that."

She wanted him to take her in his arms as he had before, but she didn't move closer. Maybe he did want to end it.

"Since we were together, I've not thought of the past so much. Sometimes, I've thought what it might be with *us*." He put his arm about her shoulders. "It feels wonderful with you...but I want to be sure. Know what I'm doing."

He was older than Willis probably by twelve years, and a hundred times more cautious. She sensed he was crowding through oceans of doubt, struggling to come back from the walking dead. "You have to go on—have some faith in the future," she said.

"I've learned how fast it can change. It's a fragile thing."

She turned to him. "No it's not. It's what people determine to make it."

"You're a sweet soul."

"I did nothing to cause my grief, Robert. It was my husband and the cursed oil that made him associate with those thugs..." She broke off. It wasn't for him to know about the men still threatening her.

"And what?"

"Nothing." She reached down and pulled up a blade of grass and split it with her fingernail. "Robert" she began. "What did you think about when you imagined life with us?"

"I don't know." His arm dropped from her shoulder. He put his hands on his knees and looked out at the busy fireflies. "Talking to you about things I wouldn't say to anyone else. Feeling your warmth by me in the night. Knowing you would be there, to reach for—to touch, and that you loved me."

She trembled, feeling his capacity to love. He would expect much more than Willis ever understood and give much more. "Anything else?" she whispered.

"There isn't anything else. Loneliness is a hard teacher. Too much money, too little money—that's only the window dressing of real life."

She moved closer and nestled her head on his shoulder. "What about us?"

"I don't know."

"You were right to stay away, think things through," she whispered. "I'm glad we had this talk." Then she sat up straight, turned to look at him, "Let's do that. Not meet for two weeks. If we can't stay apart, we'll know."

He smiled at her and nodded.

"I really need to go home, I have a ten-to-six day tomorrow. Dutch is short of help."

"I'll follow you. You won't want to go in a dark house alone."

At her back door she fumbled with her purse, holding the sleeping baby, and opened the locks.

"What's this? Three locks?" Robert said. "Most people don't even lock their doors."

"Just being careful," she said offhanded. She flipped on the lights, walked to the bedroom, and put Hannah in her crib, then turned around.

Robert was staring at the kitchen table. He put his arm around her as she gasped. Hannah's new doll sat on the table— decapitated. The head rested on a note. Shock turned to horror.

Robert picked up the paper. "It says, 'Get the money.'"

"They got in the house! With all the locks, they still got in. Oh, God, Robert, what'll I do?" She cried, terror clutching her. "They can come in anytime." He held her close to him for a long time.

"What's this about?" he finally asked.

They sat down, and she told him about Willis, the money still owed and the threats.

He held her into the night until she finally calmed and went to sleep in his arms.

In the early morning, they woke as dim light filtered in the room. She made coffee, fried bacon and eggs. While she was busy Robert took the broken doll to his car.

After she dressed, fed Hannah, and got ready to leave for work Robert came to her. "I'll go to the sheriff and tell him he has to look into this and patrol your house on a regular basis, so the word'll get around, and I'll be back tomorrow night."

"This is dangerous, Robert. You shouldn't get involved. They're killers and the sheriff is nothing but their pawn. There's no law here and this is not your problem. You don't need to stay with me."

He looked at her for a moment. "Yes, Annie, I think I do."

CHAPTER 44

Annie lay with the pillow hugged to her, hungry for someone to hold her. The shock of losing Willis had been so intense and abrupt; it was as if there had been no part of her left to grieve. She still couldn't believe she was alone. She fingered the lacy pillowcase she hugged to her. Moonlight and flare light from the wells streamed in the east windows of the house. Robert St. Pierre came into her thoughts.

Night after night he came and stayed with her, kissed her goodnight and napped on the couch, until he was sure the sheriff's car did drive by at intervals. When she joked about their plan to stay apart for two weeks on a trial separation, he smiled but became evasive. "I like watching a woman make breakfast for me."

Still he came into Dutch's daily and they talked when she had free time. He had never asked her out again but she knew he was beginning to care for her. She saw how he looked at her.

The fan feathered across her warm body. She glanced at Hannah sleeping peacefully nearby in her crib then looked at the clock. Three-thirty.

There was the crunch of gravel outside the window. She sat up. A car moved slowly into the drive and stopped. She slipped from the bed and crept to the side of the window. That car! She stood there wadding her cotton gown at her throat, her skin crawling, tightening. She couldn't leave, they could see from the drive both the front and back doors of her little house. The doors were bolted, she told herself. They couldn't get in.

She saw a man open the car door and walk to the kitchen window. She watched a knife rip into the window screen. Her heartbeat thundered in her ears. But he would find a locked window. He couldn't get in. Terrified she watched him score a square in the window glass and punch a hole in it with the butt of the knife. She stood transfixed, unable to move. No place to run. No place to hide--herself or the baby. He reached inside, unlocked the window, pushed it up and crawled through. She backed into the bedroom, into the darkness of a corner between the wall and a dresser, praying the sheriff would drive by now. Her knees turned to jelly. He was coming though the kitchen, and into her room. He stopped at the foot of the empty bed. She hoped the baby would not wake up. Make him notice her.

"I know you're in this house. If you don't answer, I'll take the kid."

"What do you want?" She heard her own weak voice.

"You know what I want. Eight thousand dollars."

"You murdered my husband."

"He owed me eight thousand dollars. He's dead so it's down to you."

"I don't have anything like that. Surely you know I would..."

"Your husband's ole' man can get it. He's swelling all over town about what he's got. There's your ole man, too. Got plenty. You got ways, girl, if you're interested, and I'm gonna see that you're interested."

"I got nothing," she cried. "Leave me alone." Hannah roused and whimpered briefly.

"I'm gonna stick closer to you than a bad habit, girl." He moved toward her. Annie backed further into the darkness of the corner. "I'm gonna live in your head, in your skin. You're not doing nothin' without me being there—just outa the corner of your eye." He stood not more than three feet from her, in the flickering flare light.

There was silence except for the ticking of the alarm clock by her bed.

"You don't look half bad for one of these country girls," he said.

Annie's hand clutched at her gown almost wringing it, but he came no closer.

"You're gonna pay me what's owed me. You may as well get that worked out in your mind. It's gonna happen. That's a promise I'm making you. You're a smart girl and you've got the places to go. You'll figure out how to get it."

He moved to the back door, turned the three locks inside. She saw him silhouetted in the doorway. It was the man who had threatened Willis.

"Get the money," he said and went out.

CHAPTER 45

Eva Mae Malvern sat in the center of her bed, a Good Housekeeping magazine on her crossed legs, studying the article "How to Plan Your Wedding from Announcement to Honeymoon."

"An Engagement party as an afternoon tea," was one idea. She wrote that down on a pad.

Dannie Allison had asked her to marry him shortly after she graduated last June. Eva Mae's attention drifted out the window, still not too sure about Danny's resolve.

Once while he was discussing the wedding of a friend he would have to attend, the subject had moved into something about marriage. She remembered it all very well. She had said, "I think we should wait, don't you?" Then he said, "we could," but he seemed a little distant. She had said, "Of course, we don't have to." And he said, "No, we don't have to."

She told him she liked summer weddings better than fall ones, and he said either one was okay but he hadn't said any more about it. A couple of weeks ago she said they might just as well go on announce their engagement this summer. When he said, "Okay," she knew he wanted to marry her.

She hopped off the bed, moved to the vanity, and looked in the mirror. Suddenly she felt like a rock had developed in the lower part of her stomach. How would the Allison family expect someone to handle a marriage announcement? She had no idea. And her mother would be no help at all.

Also, and she had thought about this a lot, she needed Danny to give her a ring pretty soon. How would she go about that?

Eva Mae went to the Clay County Library and checked out a book from the back section, called, *So you're Getting Married.* As she sat in her bedroom, she began thumbing through the book, making notes. It would be on a Sunday afternoon, a lawn party by the new rose garden, and tables with white cloths. The book said you didn't have to have tea at a Tea, but maybe she would. And cake. She would have Glenn make large trellis arches—maybe several side by side and cover them with ivy. She had to find something to hide that terrible ramshackle shed in the back. Her father simply would not pull that thing down. He had built it, he said, and that was one thing he would not change. It was where he kept that old F-12 International Harvester tractor he liked so much.

She began to envision the party. She would be wearing a flowered chiffon dress with a wide-brimmed picture hat and Danny would be by her side. She would be very gracious, and they would all think how nice it was that Danny was marrying that lovely Malvern girl. Once her father announced the engagement, she and Danny would step through the trellis. They would stand briefly while the guests applauded. They would applaud, wouldn't they? She would then sweep her hat to her side. Then Danny would kiss her—and they would applaud again.

An oil truck rumbled by and brought her back to reality.

But what to do about inviting her family? If she asked Glenn to make the trellis, she would just about have to invite him? Eva Mae put a question mark beside that. Not Kurt or Annie. What if they talked about when they went to school without shoes? She would simply crawl with humiliation if that happened. Danny knew they were her brother and sister, but she had taken pains to let him know they had lived a different life.

Joey was—little, Glenn was...? She'd think about what to do with him. She would keep her mother too busy with refreshments to talk much. The quilting ladies! Some had oil wells and Eva Mae had noticed that Danny's mother and father were fascinated with the people who had just come into oil. There was a skeptical assessment in their manner as they measured the newly wealthy.

Kurt idled his truck, waiting. His pulse always pounded when he drove out on the dirt path that encircled the lake. The road then cut off and wound through the great oaks and cedars of Walker Preston Park. He turned the ignition off and waited. Malcolm Power would not be gone this weekend. When Kurt last talked to Lillian, she told him not to go near the house. He was to wait while she walked around the lake to meet him—after Malcolm was asleep.

So now he waited. A creeping insecurity began to steal over him. What if she didn't come!

His eyes focused on the house—a light upstairs. Malcolm's room. Lillian had never let him in her house, but he had watched the house from every angle, knew every room. Kurt could imagine her now, slipping into a gown, pretending to go to sleep. Soon, when Malcolm was asleep—Kurt smiled at their little deception— she would come to him, hungry, almost vicious in her ravenous passion. He could feel her flesh; feel her breath on his neck, her whispers in his ear. She seemed to live inside him.

All lights were off now upstairs and down, except one. That was Coralee's room. He could see the glow out her window from the side. He imagined Coralee sprawled under the sheet, her long dark hair spread across her pillow, those long legs, those plump breasts on the grown-up body of a child. He shifted his thoughts quickly away from that and stared at the darkened house. Why hadn't Lillian come?

Kurt had picked away at a strip of loose welting on the seat in his truck—pulled open a patch of padding and picked at it before he realized what he was doing.

He checked his watch. Twelve-thirty. What was she waiting for? There was a breeze off the lake, moonlight shimmering on it. He stretched, tried to doze off, imagining her coming up to the window, seeing him asleep, confident she would come. Sleep wouldn't come. He couldn't even fake it. He got out of the truck and impatiently kicked a rock into the lake. One o'clock. He pictured her in her fancy house over there, laughing at him—knowing he was here in this truck waiting for her. She must be looking out those upstairs windows, searching and finding his truck across the lake and laughing at him, knowing he was waiting, and she was not coming to him. Bitch!

He got back in the truck, leaned his head back. Bitch! Bitch! He hated her! She was just a woman, after all. She needed to understand a little respect.

As the long hours passed a plan took shape. He would make Lillian see she couldn't turn him on and off at her whim. He'd go away. He could walk away anytime. Let her see that. Yes, he would leave her to stew and think of *him*. As he started the truck, he saw the faintest glow of light low on the eastern horizon. She would never know he'd waited all night, tormented, hoping she would come.

By six-thirty he was at the crossroad at the edge of town. Should he go north or west? Or back east? Did it matter? He pulled to the left lane and headed west.

CHAPTER 46

On the day Kurt left town, Eva Mae sent out the invitations for her engagement announcement.

It was the custom when a girl announced her engagement, her girlfriends would give her a handkerchief shower. Eva Mae liked the idea and suggested it to her mother. Sophie was appalled. "You are not to invite people to come share in the happiness of your engagement and then ask them to bring you a present. The very idea," Sophie had said.

Eva Mae decided after the invitations were written, and her mother left her to finish addressing them, she would just add a note at the bottom that there would be a handkerchief shower. If people came with presents, what could her mother say?

The day came. The August afternoon was perfect, the sky an azure blue with white fluffy clouds drifting slowly above. A bee buzzed about near the roses. In a grassy space by the house, a long table had been set up with tea, punch, cookies and a cake, surrounded by round tables with bright white table clothes on which she and her mother had embroidered "E.M. and D.A." Nearby was a rose-entwined trellis that she and Danny would walk through after her father made the announcement.

Danny and his parents came first. She showed them the embroidered monogram on each tablecloth she had taken so much time to design.

She turned to Danny. "It will be our signature monogram--on everything we do. Do you like it?" Danny nodded absently. His mother smiled on her future daughter-in-law.

Sheriff Logan and his wife, then Danny's Aunt Ella Donnelly came. Eva Mae had not invited her Aunt Belle who, as the absolute entire world knew, had dyed Ella Donnelly's hair pink and had been on the receiving end of Ella's wrath ever since. Of Eva Mae's family, she had invited Glenn, little Joey, her parents and her mother's quilting friends. And as her father met guests and Joey seated them at tables, she thought, please God don't let anyone bring up to Sheriff Logan that embarrassing business of Willis's unsolved murder.

By mid-afternoon the lawn party was filled with cousins, aunts, uncles, nieces, nephews and all sorts of connections to Allisons, Donnellys, and Powers families, plus the few on Eva Mae's side—all sporting their finest afternoon tea attire and manners. Sophie was busy bringing out cookies and her special burnt sugar cake. Lillian Powers asked Sophie when she served her a thin slice of cake, how on earth she made such a concoction. Eva Mae held her breath hoping her mother would not say something totally ridiculous as Sophie went through every bit of the recipe, and Lillian listened as if she were terribly interested.

At the appointed time, John Malvern stepped forward took his place near the trellis and began the speech Eva Mae had rehearsed with him through the last week. "I have the pleasure of announcing the engagement of my beautiful daughter, Eva Mae Malvern to Daniel James Allison."

They stepped through the trellis. Eva Mae blushed and acted shy as she surveyed the crowd. It was just as she had planned. She smiled sweetly, pleased with herself. Everyone was looking at them, clapping—as she knew they would. She swept off her wide flower-trimmed hat as she had planned, but when she turned to Danny, he simply stood there, staring. He was supposed to kiss her now. But he just stood there. Panic swept through her. She lifted up her hat, held it before Danny and kissed him. Everyone cheered and clapped as she knew they would. It was done. It was done! Just as she planned. She would be an Allison. She was sure they were thinking 'what a sweet, gracious thing that Malvern girl is—just perfect for our Danny.'

At that moment, Hattie stepped forward and snapped a picture with her Brownie camera. After that, Eva Mae seated herself in a white folding chair while a flurry of little packages was presented to her. With Danny sitting by, looking a little swept along by the dynamics of the proceeding, she opened the first box and slowly lifted a pink lacy handkerchief. "What a surprise," she breathed and read the card. "From Sarah Emma Anderson."

John Malvern stood aside, watching as each box she opened drew applause and exaggerated thanks from Eva Mae. He was growing more pleased by the moment as he recognized this excellent match his daughter was making. He came forward, by her chair. "I want you to know that my beautiful daughter has a brother--my young son, Joey. You're gonna hear more about this boy as time goes on. He's gonna be—a doctor or lawyer or somethin' way up there like that." Joey dropped his head, a little embarrassed, and Eva Mae looked irritated at her father's interruption.

She reached for another of the fancy little boxes at her feet. "This one's from Danny's grandmother, Marthursa." Eva Mae spoke loudly, calling attention back to herself. As she was untying the bow, the worst possible thing happened. She held the half-opened present in her lap, her eyes froze, and a deep sinking sensation fell through her.

Kurt drove past in his dusty truck and began steadily honking as he turned into the half circle drive in front of the house. You idiot, Eva Mae thought; you fool!

Slowly, he got out of his truck and closed the door. All eyes turned on him. He hadn't shaved in days, his hair was long and matted, clothes rumpled as if he'd slept in them. He walked through the tables. Conversation stilled.

Anger, disgust, and embarrassment flashed through Eva Mae as he came to her chair by the trellis. He nodded toward Danny by her.

"Don't let me stop the show." Kurt looked out at the guests, seated at the round tables. "You see my invitation got lost in the mail. That's probably what happened. It got lost."

Danny's parents look away, embarrassed.

"I didn't hardly know this was the right place—and a party and all."

Eva Mae fiddled with the unopened present, her face flushing hot with fury.

"Anyway, I'm here and this is the big event." He looked around, scratched the back of his head, then looked down at Eva Mae. "I used to climb that old tree right over there—take the hoe out there in that garden for my mama." He stood for a moment looking at the guests, the picture of exhaustion and defeat. "I guess they put in roses sometime." He signed. "But like I said, don't let me stop anything."

Kurt ambled to a table and settled slightly behind Lillian and her husband, Malcolm Powers. He leaned forward, within a few inches of Lillian's ear. "I reckon it was my demeanor that kept me off the invitation list. You reckon that was it, Mrs. Powers?"

Lillian moved her chair a little forward as far away from Kurt as possible, ignoring his presence.

"I'm sure I don't know why you weren't invited, Mr. Malvern," she hissed.

"Oh, I know it must be. It's the demeanor thing."

Kurt cleared his throat and gave feigned attention to Eva Mae. Eva Mae, once again composed, opened another box, and showed off a dainty flowered handkerchief with cutout work in one corner.

"Thank you, Lillian, that is so lovely," Eva Mae cooed

"My that *is* lovely, Lillian," Kurt whispered near her ear. "That's just so sweet of you to do such a thing for my little sister. If you want to meet a genuine, authentic bitch, there she is right up there opening her little presents." He whispered. "Course, I do like bitches—no matter where you find 'em."

Lillian adjusted her chair further away from him.

Kurt got up and walked before the crowd again. "Reckon you'll have to excuse me. It's not that I'm not welcome here, you understand." He cleared his throat and looked up into the sky. "It was sure a different place when little Kurt played around here. Reckon that's what caused my demeanor problem."

Lillian looked away, trying to ignore him. "I wouldn't have missed this thing for the world, what with Eva Mae latchin' herself onto an Allison—or something like that."

Kurt turned to his father. "Did you make the speech about little Joey being the prince of the family? You see," he turned to the guests, "I'm his son, too." Kurt's voice seemed about to break. "Well, here's to a great union, oil and—Allisons." He bowed elaborately to Eva Mae and Danny.

Then he looked out into the crowd, again.

"Where's Annie? Did her invitation get lost, too? I s'pose she's too busy because she's got to work since her husband got murdered." Kurt singled out Logan Webb in the crowd. "You heard about that, Sheriff? Willis Porter gettin' murdered right here in your county?"

"That'll do, Kurt." John Malvern stepped forward and took his son by the arm. "You need to move on—get on outa here." He led him to his truck.

Kurt jerked free. "I'm goin'. I got done what I came to do."

CHAPTER 47

Kurt honked as he passed the party on the lawn and speeded up to create a cloud of dust. At that moment he hated Lillian, hated his father, his sister and the whole Allison outfit. But he knew now how he would get his revenge. It had been right there all along. He stopped by his place in town and picked up something he had been saving. Then he went to the park and circled the lake. It was the perfect time, with Lillian gone.

He drove into the drive of Lillian's house. He had never gone to the front door, never once.

Coralee opened the door slowly, then backed away fearfully.

"My mother said I was not to see you."

"I know that, but I made a promise to you, remember?" She smiled and nodded. "I promised I'd bring you a white squirrel." A covered basket dangled from his left hand. "Do you have a place to keep him where he'll be safe?"

"I think so," she hesitated. "Let me see him."

Kurt opened the lid of the wicker basket.

"Anywhere your mother won't see it?"

"I could keep him in my old play house, I guess." She knelt down still in the doorway to look at the squirrel.

"Bring him bread with peanut butter," Kurt instructed. "Can you do that?"

"Yes, I can do that."

"Show me where," Kurt whispered as though they were involved in some nefarious conspiracy, "and I'll put him there for you."

"Okay." She whispered back and opened the door wider and let him in. He followed her through the house taking in every detail of the layout; to the back yard; and on down by the lake to a little imitation log cabin. When they stepped through, both had to duck their heads.

"I don't play in here any more. It's too little for me now."

"Well, I can see it was a nice play house. Best I ever had was some boards in the crotch of an old tree."

"Crotch of a tree? What's that?"

"It's where the limbs split as they grow up out of the trunk."

"Oh," she said and looked into the basket. "He's little." She looked up, her eyes gleaming. "I'll call him Biscuit."

The afternoon sun was dropping low over the lake. Kurt looked across to where he had waited all night for Lillian to come to him. He could feel his face burn just thinking of how she liked to toy with him.

He turned his attention to Coralee and smiled. "Tell you what, Coralee, you keep Biscuit in this little cabin—locked up, and I'll make him a big cage. After you've fed him for a while, we'll let him out sometimes, but we'll keep him in the cage to be safe."

"When will you come back—I mean, with the cage?"

"Oh, in a few days. Sometime when you mother's not here. I like to keep a secret with you, Coralee."

"Me, too." She giggled.

"You're very pretty, Coralee."

"My mother's pretty."

"Yes, she is."

"She's got pretty earrings."

"Does she?"

"And she smells pretty all the time."

Kurt kept his attention on the summer sun dropping lower over the lake. Lillian and Malcolm would soon be home.

"Try to keep Biscuit fed until I get back with the cage. You can slip something out, can't you?"

"Course, I can."

"Remember, your mother said I couldn't give you this squirrel, but I promised you and that promise was important to me. I didn't want to disappoint you. You're important to me, too, and our secret is important to me, too."

"We have two secrets, don't we?" Coralee whispered. Kurt stared at her, then turned and hurried to his truck.

The following Saturday night Malcolm was gone on a fishing trip with Bucky Allison. As Kurt came toward Lillian's back door, he wondered about many things. He hadn't seen her since Eva Mae's party. Would she be furious at his attempt to make their acquaintance public? Would she care he'd been gone for three weeks with no word? Would she even acknowledge it? If she came to meet him after that, he knew he owned her.

His steps grew softer, slower, more uncertain as he neared the door of the screened porch. What if she wasn't there? How could he live, not having this? Embedded in the back of his mind was the sweet feeling that he was taking back some of his own with this developing alliance with her daughter. Lillian was dangerous, vindictive but maybe that was part of his attraction for her. But the one thing she could not endure was for him to win Coralee's affections.

He touched the latch, heard the faint familiar squeak of the door and stepped inside.

She stood in the shadows. As she moved forward, her white robe slipped away.

"Kurt," she whispered softly.

"Yes," he came to her and all fears, insecurities, and vindictiveness melted away. She loved him savagely. Soon they were on the floor on the robe and she was hysterically in need of him, digging into his back with her fingers, clutching him to her.

"Mama? Are you out there?" Coralee called from inside the house. "Why did you lock the back door, Mama?"

They stopped, and Kurt started to get up, but Lillian held him.

"I couldn't sleep, Coralee. Go back to bed. I'll be in in a few minutes."

"Why did you lock the door, Mama?"

"Go to bed, Coralee," Lillian commanded her.

"I can't. There's something I need to check on—outside."

"What?"

"I can't say, now."

Kurt felt himself chill. Again, he started to get up, but she held him to her.

"Everything is fine, dear. Go to bed."

"Okay, Mama."

They lay still for a long time not talking. Crickets, singing their chorus outside the sun porch. She kissed him, finally, as quiet behind the door continued. Then suddenly in spite of himself, he turned off. The whole thing was revolting. This vicious haughty bitch—*and a mother.* She made him sick. He stood up, unfinished.

"What's the matter? I can't imagine that distracted you. Not you."

What he hated was not this. He loved this. He hated the woman, when publicly she humiliated him with her arrogant attitude, but could hold him to her and rut like an animal on the floor, when it suited her. How could she be these two people? What about the mother part? What about that? Coralee was slow, he saw that, but he wondered how much she was locked down into a child to accommodate her mother. She had robbed her daughter of her freedom to have a mind. He hated Lillian. He feared her, demon that she was, but he hungered for her.

"You left without telling me," she whispered, still lying on floor where he left her. They were the words he'd waited to hear.

He'd cracked her selfish armor. She would never humble him again.

"Did you need to know?" he answered absently.

"No," she answered slowly after a long time. "Will you be back next week?"

"I don't know," he said, but as he closed the screen, he knew he would.

As a child Kurt had been fascinated with the striking clock that sat on a shelf in his parents' dining room. He had taken apart and put back together several clocks, intrigued with their intricate mechanism. When he left home, he found work at a jewelry store in town working mostly, however, on the broken watches oilmen brought in.

Kurt busied himself all week in his apartment making a cage for the squirrel, the clocks he'd brought to his apartment to fix, now pushed to one side on the table. Sometimes at work in the store, when he was putting a watch together, memory of Lillian would crowd in on him. He would get another beer from the icebox in the back of the store and sit there, lost in his moments with her. But now, when he thought of Lillian, Coralee also came to him. He felt sorry for the girl. She was trapped. Lillian could do that to a person, own them, possess them, and infiltrate their mind. Didn't he know what she could do?

Kurt had taken great pains to make a clasp on the cage secure, but still easy enough for Coralee to open. He'd have to get it to her, into the playhouse—somehow. He sat the finished cage aside, picked up a piece of a clock, and began to work. Two weeks later, he found his opportunity.

For over a hundred and twenty-five years an annual event occurred that not even the Allisons started or directed. It was held in a grove of trees north of town, where a grandstand had stood for at least half that time. Each year the story was told of the original county settlers who came together on a day after the summer field work was done and before harvest time. Women still came in costume, long skirts and bonnets and men in black hats and suspenders.

Throughout the grove on The Old Settlers' Picnic Day, the aroma of frying chicken, barbecued pork, and chili simmering in black kettles filled the air. There was a square dance, old time fiddling, speech making by politicians running for some office, singing and sometimes a horse race across the road. As night came, tubs of fire dotted the grove and people stood about with sticks toasting marshmallows. It was an event not to be missed and few people did. But Kurt knew one person who would—Coralee. Lillian would not take her daughter to such a public place.

Kurt drove slowly up to Lillian's house, saw no signs of her, and rang the doorbell. Coralee opened it.

"I brought your cage for Biscuit," he said.

Her hands went to her cheeks, her eyes dancing. "Meet me in back at the playhouse."

He put the cage on a table inside Coralee's playhouse and showed her how to open it. It was early dusk, crickets already singing near the lake. Kurt knew Lillian would not be home for hours. Coralee leaned over near the clasp and studied it. She tried it. Kurt helped her, and when inadvertently he touched her fingers, she looked up, smiled, a little sparkle in her eyes. She watched him work the clasp and then she moved closer to him. Coralee was wearing her mother's earrings, but mostly he was overwhelmed with the excessive fragrance she had doused on herself. Lillian's perfume. No mistaking that.

"It was nice of you to bring this to me," she said almost inaudibly. She kept looking at him, expectantly, and then timidly her hand stroked his.

Kurt froze. Of course, he wanted to make Lillian pay for taunting him. He gloried in the idea that he was betraying Lillian by using her own daughter. But now he looked down at Coralee, her eyes, her lips—tremulous, curious, hungry. He stepped back. He felt sorry for the child—no, woman. No, child! It was cruel for a mother for her own vanity, to make her daughter remain a child, especially when this child could never fight for real independence. It was worse than old Porter who used to beat his son. At least he'd grown up strong enough to hate. Coralee hadn't been allowed that.

Suddenly, her arms were around his neck, kissing him, clinging to him. He felt her firm breast against him, her warm arms encircling him, her quick breath on him filling him with fearful, trembling sensations. He gently detached her arms from his neck.

"Coralee, I—you're very young."

"Not so young. Seventeen, now." Her eyes were filled with worship.

"Well...in other ways."

"I love you." She ran her finger over his forearm, delicate as a feather touching him.

"Coralee—I don't know..." How *did* he feel? Sure, he'd set out to do vengeance on Lillian, but..." he looked down at Coralee, so close. What did he want? Not this girl—this sweet simple girl.

"I've never had a boy kiss me," she whispered. "Will you kiss me?" she whispered.

He leaned forward and kissed her forehead.

"No, no, not a little kid kiss. I mean..."

Slowly he moved forward, took her in his arms and gave her a gentle chaste kiss. He sensed passion rising in her.

"Coralee, I think this is a bad idea."

He began to back away. "I hope you have fun with your squirrel—with Biscuit." He ducked his head to leave the playhouse door.

"Bye," she whispered, and clung to the side of the door. "Now, we have three secrets, don't we, Kurt?"

CHAPTER 48

From Carson Garrett's upstairs office, Belle Dorsett looked down on the courthouse square, a big green expanse in the center of town. She raised the window and leaned out. On the south lawn by the courthouse, the band was playing as it did every Saturday night. Farmers and their families sat on the grass around the brilliantly lighted bandstand. Musicians were turned out in white summer uniforms, light glinting on their gold instruments as they raised them.

"I need the work schedule for a new well on Porter's place." Carson had told Belle, so they stopped by his office.

Saturday night was the week's entertainment for the farmers as well as those who lived in Amsley. Along the street around the square, parked at angles were Model-As, dusty trucks, and anything else that would run. Farmers came to town with eggs, cream, and butter to exchange for what they could not grow. Belle watched a couple of kids chasing each other through the bushes surrounding the great white structure of the courthouse, colonnaded at opposite entrances. She smiled. She was once one of those kids.

Carson Garrett sat at his desk working for a few minutes, then flipped off the light and came to the window beside Belle. She slipped her hand inside his arm and held his hand.

"It's been like this as long as I can remember. Saturday night—everybody in town, streets packed, watching the band concert. It sort of punctuated the week. When I was a kid, if the store had bananas, my father would buy John and me one. We would sit on the courthouse step and eat the first half all at once, then we would wrap the peel around the other half, and just take a bite now and then—making it last."

He moved closer to her, watching below as if looking down on a little kingdom. Small groups congregated on the sidewalks before stores; Allisons' store was busy as a beehive; and across the square, customers streamed in and out of Aunt Nora's Ice Cream Shop and Holmier's restaurant.

"It's nice," Carson whispered, "an insulated, dependable life."

"My brother doesn't come into town on Saturday nights. Since they rebuilt their house, they entertain all the time at home."

"It looks like the concert's breaking up." Carson said. They watched band members begin to stow their instruments in cases, fold their chairs and stack them against the courthouse building.

"Now the movie'll start," Belle said. Below, a great frame with a screen was being rolled into the street. People scurried to find a seat along the curb or on the courthouse lawn before the movie started.

"Why doesn't your brother come into town anymore?" Carson looked at her, questioning.

"They don't have to trade, now."

"How about you?"

"I still think it's charming, but it's poor man's entertainment and I'm still one of the poor ones. In fact, poorer!" She glanced at him. "After that fiasco with Ella Donnelly and the pink hair, my business has fallen off—a lot. I came to the bitter decision I have to sell some of my antiques."

He turned to her and stood back in the semi-darkness. "You know, Belle, all you have to do is say the word and I'll take care of you. I've told you that." He put his arm around her waist and kissed her. "You don't have to sell those antiques you love so much."

She started to speak.

"Don't say it." He put his finger on her lips. "You'll go with me—if I leave. You have to. Please, don't argue about that."

She slipped easily into his arms and felt them envelop her. Outside, the crowd cheered and clapped, the movie was beginning. Belle glanced past him, at the jerky movements on the screen in the center of the street.

His lips came closer to hers. "I've lived a long time to get to this place and know for sure," he whispered. "I'm sure about you, Belle."

She looked up at him. Her arms came around his neck and their lips were together. She tried to move closer to him, as close as she could, taking him into her. He fumbled with the top buttons of her dress and she helped him while they still kissed. Slowly he undressed her until she stood before him, trembling, unclothed.

"It's been a long time," she whispered, but he didn't answer. She drew in her breath and closed her eyes. She had been alone so long.

He stopped and stood back. "I love you, Belle, very much."

She moved into his arms, and they clung together and then they went down on the rug. She helped him with his clothes as he came over her. Her head fell back over his arms, as they kissed trying to absorb everything there was in the other. Her back arched against him, remembering the insistent need so long pushed aside, trying to forget, forget when there was no one to give her love to. Slowly, they gave themselves up to each other, crowding away the grey loneliness she had accepted as her life. Resurgence came over her again, her passion rose, to encircle him. Barriers fell away as she opened her soul. She seemed not able to give enough of herself, to love him enough until there was—gentle peace.

Outside the open window above them, the crowd screamed and clapped as the sound of a chase scene came through the window. Belle lay quietly in Carson's arms, still wonderfully alive in the soft warm cloud of contentment.

They lay by each other quieted by the profound feeling they had found, talking softly to each other until the movie ended. Cars started up and shouts drifted on the heavy damp air. In a few minutes the square would be empty, the stores locked up, the concert and movie over until next week. Still they held each other, warm, touching, not speaking.

"You said," Belle broke the silence, "that some time you would sleep in my big bed. I think this is the night."

He followed her down the back stairs to his car. The town was almost deserted. A couple of boys slouched against a storefront under a street light, smoking. As Carson turned off the square and drove out to the highway, he leaned toward her, "I also told you once that sex in a public place was exciting."

She laughed and shook her head.

A flare of lightning blinked on the northern horizon and a distant rumble floated on the quiet clammy air when they turned into Belle's drive.

They sat up in the bed, their backs against the high ornate headboard. The room glowed briefly as lightning flashed in the distance and Belle glimpsed his bare chest propped on the pillows beside her.

"When you're getting rid of your antiques, don't ever sell this bed." Carson said.

"I've already had an argument with Porter over this bed. When he found out John Malvern had been born on it, he wanted it. Probably wanted to chop it up for kindling."

Carson laughed. "Belle, I only bring this up to quiet your mind, but I wanted to tell you something. There are two places where tests indicate there is deep oil. The wells on the Patrick brothers' land and on St. Pierre's that adjoins it. What I'm saying is that as long there is oil to be found here, I'll be staying, and you won't have to think about leaving. But, Belle," he was watching her when the room flared white with distant lightning, "there may come a time when I will have to move on, and you belong with me. You must believe that now?"

"I've never been anywhere except this little place—and I'm not as young as I used to be."

"About how old are you?" There was teasing in his question.

"Not as old as my antiques."

Trees thrashed in the yard as the wind tore at them. A refreshing breeze cut through the hot night and blew across the bed and their warm bodies. Lightning flashes were closer with thunder crashing immediately, rattling windows.

"If there is to be a war..." Carson said.

"War?" A thundering crash came down outside.

They both were silent.

"If war comes," Carson said, at last, "we'll be looking for oil anywhere it can be found, prices will go through the ceiling, and it'll pay to drill to those deeper strata." He sighed. Lightning bathed the room with light. "Countries are toppling like dominos over there—Norway, Denmark and now France."

She leaned into Carson's arms and put her head on his shoulder. "I need you here," she whispered. "And I have some problems of my own. Annie is being threatened—the people who killed Willis are harassing her. She's scared, and I don't know how to protect her. That's why I keep Hannah. She thinks they won't come into a business where there are people."

"Doesn't that put you in danger?"

"But there is no one else. Her father—my own brother, I hardly know him—is so enthralled with all his new oil and fixing up his place and promoting Eva Mae into that social nonsense, he's oblivious to what's happening to Annie."

"And she's your favorite?"

"Always was. The men hounding her say her father-in-law's got money now. He can pay Willis's debt."

Carson nodded. "Yeah, you should see Porter strutting around town, showing off his money."

"I hear he's getting another well."

"Maybe. Not sure yet."

Lightning flared the room again, and a cool mist drifted in as rain began to fall. Carson closed the window and slipped back in bed as the storm was upon them. Rain pounded the glass and the room flared into brilliance as lightning crashes came one upon the other. They moved down under the sheet and lay quietly in each other's arms, stilled by the wrath of the storm.

CHAPTER 49

Annie hated to be late picking up Hannah, but she'd had to work overtime. She opened the back door of Dutch's to go to her car. An arm that seemed to come from nowhere locked around her neck, a knifepoint at her throat. She felt warm breath on her cheek.

"Don't make a sound. We're going for a little ride in the car over there." She felt the point of the knife press her throat. "Not a peep, you hear."

A car waited beside hers. Annie expected to see the big blond man in the passenger seat of that familiar black car, but it was empty. He pushed her in from the driver's side, the knifepoint always a few inches away. "Move over," he said and stared at her, eyes cold, dead of feeling. She began to tremble uncontrollably, her heart pounding. She was going to die—like Willis. A long scar cut through his eyebrow; the man she knew killed Willis.

"Roll up the window." He stepped on the starter. From the shadows in back of Dutch's, the car rolled slowly forward to the brilliantly lit parking lot in front. He turned onto the highway.

Annie looked nervously across the road at Belle's house, where Hannah was to be picked up. She said nothing.

"Yeah, I know where your kid is," he said.

Her thoughts were darting frantically for escape. If he slowed, she'd jump out.

Once on the road, he picked up speed. Then he turned off on a narrow country lane. Giant trees overhung the road making a dark cave of foliage. He pulled to the side by the dense hedgerow, the car idling. She grabbed for the door and he slapped her hard, again the knifepoint was at her throat. Annie held her head high, straining away from the point.

"You were supposed to have the money last week and then the week before that. I'm getting tired of you."

"I—I'll get it."

"You said that. Say somethin' new, I ain't heard."

"I need more time," she gasped. "Willis's father's gonna get it," she lied.

"See, the thing is, I don't think you got respect for me. You keep putting me off like you don't give serious attention to what I'm tellin' you." He leaned forward into her face.

She tried to turn away, but the knifepoint held her.

"Take off your clothes," he said.

"What?" Annie pulled back cowering in the corner of the seat. "No, I won't do that." Panic poured through her, pounding her temples, pictures of Willis lying dead flitted through her mind. *She* was going to die, too.

The knife tip pierced her skin and she gasped at the pain. "Yes, you will." The words were deliberate and quiet.

Her fingers shook so she could hardly undo the buttons of her blouse.

"The rest."

"I'll get the money," she cried, pleading. "I'll get it."

He stared into her face, eyes hard on her. "You say that, but you forget. Now you're gonna get over this forgetting problem you got, because this is gonna be with you every minute, the rest of your life. You see it's gonna either be the money, which you don't want to get, or your kid or—you. Take off your clothes."

She began to sob, trembling, slipped out of her skirt. Her shaky fingers, like wood, fumbled to unhook her brassiere.

He stared at her naked breast in the dashboard light and she felt the knifepoint relax.

She grabbed for the door and ran alongside the thick trees on the shoulder of the roadside. He caught up with her and threw her down. She pushed and kicked at him. He seemed to have dropped the knife, but he held her down below him, ripping at her panties.

"Don't do this," she screamed and fought at him, but he pushed her knees apart wedging himself in. He crawled over her, his knees between her legs, hard at the crotch. His hand spread tight on her throat.

"Don't!" she shrieked.

He looked down on her. "Nobody can hear you."

"Oh, God." Heaving sobs came. How could this happen to her?

She stared into his face and began to scream.

"Shut up."

She felt him drive into her hard. "No, no, don't," she cried in her sobs. "No. No."

"Shut up." His hand clamped over her mouth and he kept up the feverish, savage pumping into her body. Then he was done, dazed with satisfaction, he took his hand from her mouth.

"I'm gonna kill you, you pig," She hissed into his ear.

He dropped his head forward over her, his hand at her throat again.

"Remember this, remember the money, which you never got for me. Now I had you so..." His hand still choked her throat. "So what does that leave? Oh, yeah. The kid." He stood, and she was instantly at him, clawing at his face. He picked her up and threw her by the hedgerow like a dead animal he found beside the road, then turned quickly and ran toward the car.

"Give me my clothes," she screamed.

He laughed. The car door slammed. Gravel sprayed as tires spun into the center of the road and he was gone.

Annie crawled to where he had pulled her panties from her. Slowly she worked her legs into them, then found the other shoe she'd lost. Then she lay down again, convulsed in sobs. Her neck hurt where he had cut her. She ran fingertips over it. Blood was running down her neck and over her left breast. She sat up, numb, straining to see her wet fingers in the dark.

Annie raised herself and looked through the thick growth of hedgerow to a field and saw a gas flare by an oil pump. In the distance there were others. Only her mind worked, her senses turned numb. She recognized where she was. Beyond the field, a white church steeple stood out in the night, lighted by the derrick behind it. "Robert's well," she realized out of her dazed thoughts. Maybe she would go to his house. She sat down again and ran fingers through her matted hair, feeling like a discarded piece of garbage. She could hardly stop whimpering and shaking. Finally she got up and started walking, her arms shielding her bare breast. Walking wasn't so bad—it actually felt better. She could still feel some pain inside her, but she didn't think he had torn her.

Then the high beams of an oil truck turned onto the road. Annie rushed to the black shadows of the hedgerow and dropped into the high growth by them. She didn't need any more trouble— some strange man finding a naked woman walking on a dark road. She hunkered among the snarled branches until the truck was out of sight. She walked for about twenty minutes and then came into the yard of Robert's house.

The house and yard with its tall trees lay like a dark island in the field lighted with gas flares.

Robert's car was gone.

Annie went to the screened-in back porch and pounded on the door, but she knew he wasn't there. She sat down on the bottom step, the cement cold to her bare flesh. She couldn't stop shaking. She hugged her knees up tightly to her breast, gripping hard to control the trembling. Blood still trickled at her neck. She felt the inside of her leg. Blood was leaking down. Had he torn her? Strangely there was no pain.

She got up and went into the open dark garage, felt about and found an old jacket on a nail. Annie slipped it on. It went half way to her knees. She pulled it tight around her and leaned against the doorframe of the garage. She felt like a person she didn't know, like she was watching someone else. She had never before felt like this—like nothing, not person at all, but a disposable piece of meat.

She stepped out into the drive, considering what to do. From the church, it was less than a mile to her parent's house.

She wanted her mother, to feel her mother's arms around her and for her to tell her things were not as bad as she knew they were. She stumbled on down the road, mindless, wanting her mother. Her throat was beginning to throb where the knife had cut.

"Cars?" Annie said outloud as she came over the rise in the road that obscured her parent's house. "So many," she whispered. Through the open front door, she saw people talking, laughing. She stood in the road, staring numbly. She went to the backdoor and pulled on the screen. Locked. Maybe someone would hear, bring her some clothes. She leaned her head against the door.

"Somebody help me. Come out here!" she called. The kitchen was filled with trays of food. There was an ache in her back—and crotch. Her legs felt rubbery, like they would give way. The baby! She hadn't thought of Hannah since she left Dutch's. My God. Aunt Belle must have the sheriff out looking. THE SHERIFF! The idea hit her like a bolt. The sheriff! There was no one to go to! No recourse, no law, no safety—nothing, nobody.

Eva Mae came bubbling into the kitchen, calling back over her shoulder. "You don't want cookies, when you can have champagne! I can understand that."

"Evie." Annie called through the screen. "Let me in."

Eva Mae set the bottle down and came to the back screen door.

"I need some clothes, Evie. Something. I can't come in like this."

"My God! You look awful." Eva Mae's hand went to her mouth, her eyes widened then she looked back at the table. "No, don't come in. You can't, now. We've got a party…"

"Eva Mae, I've been raped. I have to…" Annie pleaded. "I want to see Mama. Get her, Evie."

"No, Annie, I won't. This is their wedding anniversary. I made a big party for them and invited—everybody."

Annie stared at her sister and gasped. Breath seemed to lock in her throat. She clawed at the door. "Eva Mae—Iwant Mama."

"Well, you can't have her. This is their night and you're not spoiling it for them. Every time you come here you upset them with another mess in your life."

"Evie!" Annie begged. "I've been attacked. I'm bleeding."

Eva Mae didn't seem to hear. "You know how Mama always wanted a beaded lamp shade, but we didn't have electricity? I got her beaded lampshades for every room in the house. She was so thrilled, but she didn't want to let on."

"Eva Mae, for God's sake."

"This is their silver anniversary."

"I'm coming in." She yanked the hooked door open.

"No, you are not!" Eva Mae blocked her. "You went out and got yourself raped and you come draggin' in here like a cat that got the worst end of a scrap. You're not going in there and embarrass me in front of the Allisons—and spoil Mama and Daddy's anniversary party."

Something came through the fog of Annie's thoughts. "An anniversary celebration for my Mama and Papa! I didn't know. I didn't hear. Kurt and Glenn?"

"They couldn't come."

"Like I couldn't come?" Annie began to sob. "I want Mama."

"Go to the sheriff. Let him help you."

"He did nothin' when Willis was murdered." Annie sobbed. "Do you think he'll pay attention to a rape?"

"Willis, Willis. That's the evil seed that this family's had to put up with. Go to the basement, Annie. Lick your wounds down there. I'm gonna talk to Papa about taking that baby of yours. You can't take care of yourself. How you gonna take care of a child?"

Annie stared, breath left her as if she'd been punched in the stomach. "You rotten bitch," she whispered. And then she began to whimper like a wounded animal. Hannah!

"Bitch? I'm not the one standing out in the world naked. Who was it, one of the oil guys? When this gets out, they're gonna pass you around like dessert. We're gonna take that baby so it'll grow up with something behind it besides a tramp for a mother."

Annie backed away from her sister, awed, as if she were standing before Satan. "I'll die before I let anybody have my baby," she hissed, then closed the door. She stumbled along the house to the side door leading down to the basement. Downstairs, she curled up on a rug by the washing machine, her knees folded to her chin. Her numb body was beginning to know the assault and her thoughts, jumbled as a fevered dream. The trembling would not quiet. She fell into a drowsy semi-sleep, but it didn't last. Annie kept trying to sort things out, but she couldn't clear her head. She had to go somewhere. She couldn't go home, couldn't stay there—even when she got her baby back. She looked about the basement for something to put on. On a nail just outside the coal bin, hung a pair of bib overalls. Her father had kept them. The ones he wore when his first well came in, kept them still soaked with the new oil. Shivering, she put them on, hiked up the straps, rolled up the pant legs, then put on Robert's jacket, and forced herself up the basement stairs to the outside door.

Walking was painful now. When she got to the rise in the road, she looked back at her parents' house, their great new house, now filled with people, happy sounds carrying on the night air. She turned away and kept walking. Once over the little hill, light from the house faded, the laughter gone, only distant gas flares relieved the darkness.

Annie stopped at the church, sat down, and leaned against its white weatherboarding in the dark shade of the building opposite the bright oil derrick. Across the road, back in the field, sat the tent Robert had told her about. They were having Wednesday night service. The end of the tent was open, and the sides rolled up halfway. She could barely hear voices over the noise of the well. Annie hovered by the building. A crew was working at the well on the opposite side. Her body was beginning to ache.

There was nowhere to go. No one to turn to. She didn't dare go to her house. That animal that attacked her might be waiting. She lay down on the hard dirt and cried. She pounded the ground with her fist.

"Damn you," she swore at God, "for letting this happen. Damn you, damn you. You hear me, damn you. I didn't do anything. Why are You doing this to me? What did I do?" The people in the tent began to sing. She looked up, watched, curious. Anger growing. She knew all of them.

"Oh, yes," she whispered bitterly, "Show me how happy you are. What right have you got to be in there singing? Look out here, outside that damn tent. This is where God should be, not in there." She wanted to run down the aisle, screaming at them to see what had happened to her. She heard Oran Nesbit's loud bass booming over everyone. Oran, with half a dozen oil pumps whose tireless arms dipped wealth out of his fields. Oran, fat, self-satisfied. Safe. Her whimpering began again, and she curled against a bush by the church like a wounded animal. Only in the east did the glow of derrick lights interrupt the broad star-filled expanse above. She felt as if some dense layer covering her soul had been torn off, leaving her more exposed than her naked body. Finally, quiet came as she lay on the soft grassy ground, the distant sound of a hymn lulling her.

Then she sat up. "You listen to me, God. LISTEN TO ME. There's nowhere for me to go—no body anywhere—no place. What can I do? What? If you're there. . ." She stopped, stared at the bright tent, "You have to be. You have to be there." Her heart felt it would break from the pleading. "Come out here. Outa the damned church. Why should you be in there? They don't need you." She stood up and put her arm against the building to steady herself. She laughed, felt foolish. Talking to God like she did when she was a child. Like He was real. A person to talk to. She bit her lower lip, shaking her head. Maybe everyone did that when there was nowhere left to run.

She started walking as if in a dream. No cars came along, although it was usually a busy road. At the first crossroads, she turned right. She couldn't hear the hymn singing now. She kept walking, thoughts sifting through her mind. Willis lying lifeless across the steps. Eva Mae at the screen door threatening her. The animal over her. She pulled Robert's coat tighter over herself. Free fall now. No one to save her. No one cared if she perished.

Annie was at the Patrick Brothers' lane! Their house was dark? Maybe they had gone to bed. What time was it? Time felt endless, floating, out of its dependable reality.

She knocked on the door of the two back rooms where the brothers lived. Finally, Otis came, a kerosene lamp in his hand. He held the lamp high and squinted through the screen to see who it was.

"Annie?" He pulled a suspender strap up over his shoulder with his left hand. "Annie, what you doin' out there at this hour?"

"Otis, let me in. Something awful happened."

"What is it, Annie?" Otis opened the door, and she followed him in. "Why are you dressed like that?" He put the lamp on the table.

Henry was pulling on his shirt.

"Lock the doors—all the doors," she said.

"Well, now Annie, we don't usually lock up," Otis said.

She sat down at the table and pulled the jacket close to her.

"You got a cut on your neck. What's that?" He reached toward it, but she flinched and pulled away. "No," she cried. "Don't touch me..." Her fingertip moved to her neck. A little blood still oozed but she felt no pain, only a sickening shame that she had been forced to be like animals.

She couldn't bring herself to look at Otis. "I been raped," she whispered.

Otis dropped his eyes, embarrassed, and sank down in a chair opposite her at the table. Henry sat down by him.

CHAPTER 50

In the pale lamplight she told them everything. Otis didn't look up. When she finished only the ticking of a clock by Henry's cot filled the room.

Henry got up. "I'll get you something so's you can get out of them dirty overalls." He came back with a ragged quilt.

She went into the small bedroom where Hannah had been born, stripped and wrapped herself. She couldn't stop shaking.

Otis came into the room, his face a sober mask, "I made you some warm milk. It'll help you calm down."

She took a sip. "Did you lock the doors?" She looked up at him, the cup by her lips. "That monster's out there."

"We locked up." Henry nodded.

"I put cinnamon and sugar in the milk," Otis said.

"It's good." She took a drink. "Did you close the windows?"

"Annie, it's too hot," Henry said, "You're not yourself, now. We'll watch out for you,"

"I got to get my baby." Her hand went to her mouth. She stared at them, terrified. "He threatened Hannah."

"The baby!" Henry blanched. "What do they want with that child?" he demanded, then pulled back timidly, "I mean what can they do with a little baby?"

"They might do anything," Otis talked to his brother as if Annie were not there, his eyes wide, his face intensely sober. "See what they done already, murdered her daddy and ra... did this to her mama."

Henry stood up. "She's got to hide."

"Yes," Otis nodded. "That's just it. We'll keep Annie right here in secret."

Henry added. "Yes, Annie and the baby."

"That's the very thing. We'll keep her right here," Otis echoed.

"We'll put her way up there in one of them dormer rooms on the third floor." Henry said.

"Her and the baby." Otis nodded, as if they had just decided together to plant alfalfa rather than corn in the south forty.

"But how we gonna get the baby?" Henry asked.

Otis didn't have a quick answer for that. He looked down at Annie.

Henry dropped down on his haunches before her. They had decided the best thing to do, as they did all things. Now it was time to tell Annie what the plan was. "The thing for you to do is just disappear. Questions will be asked. The sheriff will have to look into it."

"We'll get the baby somehow." Otis said.

"You have to tell my Aunt Belle why you're taking the baby," Annie whispered.

Otis stood before her, puzzling, his two index fingers across his lips. "You write her a note about this and tell her to say the baby was picked up as usual. The only person who would call her a liar is that—man that ra...attacked you and he's not gonna say anything."

"We'll tell Miss Belle we're takin' the child to you, but we won't tell her nor nobody where you are," Henry said.

"No matter how hard she asks." Otis nodded, soberly.

"You can trust her," Annie spoke listlessly, a sense of defeat stealing over her.

"But the thing is, just disappear." Otis took her hand, "like something happened to you. Leave your house open and your car where you left it. Don't go to work, don't talk to nobody, just disappear—like you were abducted or drowned in the river." Otis repeated it as if having made the plan, reiterating it made it firmer and safer in their minds.

They handed Annie a tablet and pencil and she wrote:

"Aunt Belle, I am safe. Let one of the brothers bring Hannah to me and send me a couple of your dresses and a gown. If someone asks you about me just say, Hannah was picked up as usual. Do not tell anyone about this—no one. Remember Willis. Love, Annie"

Henry stood up. We got to get that little girl tonight, before people notice you're gone. Otherwise they'll be watching Miss Belle's—place.

"You go, Otis," Henry said.

"Me?" Otis's face sobered to a stare.

"Yes."

"I don't know," he said tentatively.

"You do it like this. Go when it's good and dark, but before she goes to bed. Go on the back road, not the highway. Drive towards the back of her house and when you get to the Prather crossroads, leave the truck and walk to her back door. Tell her what your business is and get out as quick as you can, with the child."

"What if the little girl was to be too scared to leave with me and won't come?"

"She won't be scared of you. You just bring her to her mama and not tell Miss Belle where Annie is. Just say she's safe but she won't be unless this is kept secret."

Otis looked down at the linoleum floor for a minute, and then stood up. "I'll do it." He drew up his plump body and reached for his cap in the closet. "I'll just go into that back crossroads and walk to the house, get the baby and hurry back and I won't say nothing 'bout where Annie is."

"That's right. And bring back the note after Belle reads it."

"But what if I was to be seen, say from across the road at that Dutch's place?"

"Just be careful," Henry counseled.

The brothers sat down in straight back chairs and cast glances at Annie from time to time as the three sat in silence.

"Reckon, it's time to go?" Otis said after a few minutes.

"I'd wait 'til it's later. Be good and dark," Henry said.

They continued in silence.

In about ten minutes, Otis stood up. "I'll be goin' now."

Henry settled Annie upstairs while Otis was gone. Within the hour Otis, flushed with pride, knocked on Annie's dormer room and delivered her frightened child to her.

"It wasn't no trouble atall," Otis said, thoroughly pleased with his successful mission.

CHAPTER 51

For the next month, Annie crawled into a cocoon provided by the gentle brothers who felt almost parental to the baby. At night and sometimes all day, she lay rolled in the quilt staring at a lantern Otis had provided for her. The lantern was black with cutouts in the tin that sprayed light about the dim room from the distant, dark corner where she placed it. Dark green blinds were pulled over the windows. Her world was two rooms. She felt reduced to the level of a hurt animal, shorn of her pride—purpose and direction.

Time after time, she rehearsed a ritual in her mind, closing and locking each door and window on the ground floor. She imagined locking another door that closed off the second floor and again locking the door that led to the dormer rooms. She went through this several times a day, each time reassuring herself she could not be found, could not be touched or violated again.

Both brothers came when they brought food. Henry and Otis fussed over Hannah making sure she ate her stew or cereal.

The two upper dormer rooms were covered with long woven rugs sewn together and nailed to the floor at the ends of the woven strips. There was padding under the rugs. The brothers were so odd; maybe they had put down straw, underneath it, for warmth. She had heard of people doing that long ago. Sometimes at night, when nightmares came, Annie walked the length of those rooms, the crunch of straw underfoot, wondering what there was to live for—why everything had gone so horribly wrong.

Annie thought her parents might be wondering about her, but then, Eva Mae could tell them what had happened, if she wanted to. What if they disowned her after they heard what Eva Mae might say? What if they wanted to take Hannah from her?

Each day her mind cleared a little, but still she drew into herself and hid, rolled in her quilt, and staring at the light from the lantern. It quieted her raw, unsettled spirit.

One day she saw the sheriff's car drive down the long lane. She hurried downstairs to the first landing and crouched, concealed in the corner. Henry, Otis, please don't give me away, she prayed. The back door opened. She could hear Otis talking. Annie sank down to the floor of the landing clutching her knees to her chest. She wondered if she would always imagine that someone was about to betray her.

"The Malvern girl." It was Sheriff Logan's voice, "She's gone missing. You seen anything of her?"

"Which one of 'em? There's three or four and I can't keep 'em straight," Otis said.

"There's two girls…" The sheriff was impatient with him. "You say one's missing?"

"About a month, now."

"A month, you say. Well, I never knowed them kids to tell 'em apart."

"She's no kid. She married that Porter boy that got himself shot. Some people's afraid she might of done away with herself, maybe her baby, too."

"You don't say." Otis was quiet for a minute. "Done away with herself? I declare. Henry," he called back inside. "One of them Malvern girls done away with herself."

"I didn't say that" Sheriff Logan sounded disgusted. "She's missing, is what I said."

"Well, I can't imagine she'd kill herself." Henry had now joined in. "How do you think she done it?"

"She didn't. I mean we don't know that…"

"Well, that's a terrible shame." Henry's voice sounded concerned.

"Listen, if you hear anything…" Annie could tell the sheriff was trying to make his escape.

"Say, Sheriff." The squeaking back screen opened. They had moved out onto the porch. "I knowed of a case where this woman just threw herself down in a cistern." Henry was talking now. "They went to draw up some water and there she was just rollin' around down there. Drown. Dead."

"Yes, well, Henry, I thank you for…" the sheriff was abrupt.

"You ought to look in all these old cisterns around here," Otis added. "Don't ever'body cover 'em up like they ought to, and they're a hazard."

"We used to need 'em," Henry joined in, "but now folks has got indoor water. It's different now. Hope you don't find her dead like that other woman was, swishing around down in a cistern."

Annie peeked through the curtain at the second-floor window. Otis had followed the sheriff to the car and was leaning in the window on the passenger side.

The Sheriff slammed his door and accelerated backwards as Otis jumped aside.

Annie went back to the dormer room and checked her baby who had not awakened for the day. Then she sat down on the bed, leaned back against the headboard and smiled. She began to hear Otis's words again and she started to laugh. She laughed and laughed. All the time she thought it wasn't that funny, but she couldn't stop laughing. Then tears came, streaming down her cheeks. Annie thought again of Otis and how he played the sheriff and the tears gave way to laughing again.

I'm feeling! It came to her like a revelation. I'm not frozen numb and scared. I'm living again. She raised the dark shades and the sun splashed in. She pushed the window open and warm October air poured over her. She felt free like a child.

But as she looked down into the world below, Annie knew sometime she would have to go out into that world. Sickening fear began again to spread in the pit of her stomach. She pulled the shade down quickly, went back to her bed, rolled up tight in the quilt, and stared at the lantern, and its spray of light in the corner.

CHAPTER 52

While the Patrick brothers secretly sheltered Annie, Kurt was pushing the sheriff to do his job and try to find her. Kurt, also, went to well sites asking questions. She seemed to have just vanished. He heard from Glenn that his parents were asking questions and pressing the sheriff to look for her as well. He imagined they were worried, but he did not speak with them. He did see in the paper that Eva Mae and Danny Allison had been named King and Queen for the coming Harvest ball, and John and Sophie Malvern had attended that event at a Country Club dance. After about a month of searching for Annie, however, Kurt began to take up some of his own unfinished tasks.

He had not seen Coralee or Lillian for weeks. One day at the jewelry shop he noticed Lillian across the street. It was his opportunity. He left work and drove out to Lillian's house to see how Coralee was doing with her pet squirrel.

He knocked on the front door. Coralee opened the door a crack and looked out.

"Oh," she sounded gleeful. "It's you. I thought...never mind what I thought. Come in."

"I think I'll just go around to the back—to the playhouse," he said, tentatively.

"Okay." She closed the door and was at the back door before he was. They walked to the playhouse, where she kept the squirrel.

"Every time I feed Biscuit I think of you telling me about him."

Once there, Kurt felt uncertain about the whole situation. "I just came by to tell you that you could let him out. He'll stay, if you keep putting food out and then if he's playing around your yard, you won't have to be so secretive with your mother." Secretive. The word rang through him. Why did he feel he shouldn't have come out here?

She came close to him. "You're a nice man," she whispered.

"Coralee," he started backing through the low doorway, but she caught both his arms.

"You were about to bump your head." She looked up at him, tenderness in her eyes. "I think about you all the time," she said softly. Then her arms were around his neck, kissing him, a moist, sweet kiss.

For a moment he held her, and then he pulled away. "You are not for me. Do you understand that?" He hardly recognized his own fierce voice. "You just must not do that. I have to go."

She looked bewildered. "Did I do something so wrong?"

"No, well...not wrong. I don't know." He left quickly, swung into his truck and sped away from the house.

All night Kurt lay staring into the darkness seeing those wide questioning eyes when he had left her. She was a child, so innocent, and so dwarfed by her mother. He felt sorry for her. He wanted to do something for her. Something kind. But he felt her moist lips and her hand on his arm. He got up, walked to the door. He had to put those thoughts from his mind.

Kurt did not go near that house for two weeks. He alternated between the tormenting hunger to have Lillian and the real fear that somehow Coralee would discover him with her mother. It would break Coralee's heart. No, not break her heart but turn her against him. No, it wasn't even that. It would tarnish her innocence and that was more important than anything to him now. Seventeen, and still a child—a hungry child.

He hated the mother as much as he lusted for her, but what he felt for the daughter was something very different. It made him regretful he had tried to use her.

CHAPTER 53

Annie lay each night rolled in a quilt, not caring or knowing if anyone was looking for her. She fixed her eyes on the lantern—a beacon, drawing her. She stared at it, trance-like, imagining its warmth, feeling that only. It was as if safety and security and spirit and healing were encompassed in that light.

Once she awoke with a start. Something was moving on the gravel outside. She froze. Sat up. Couldn't calm the terror that crawled over her. She slipped from her bed and looked down from her third story window. It was a big red oil truck, moving to a new well site. She looked through the narrow slit at the edge of the dark green shades she kept pulled. She had developed a hunger to focus on the lantern with its spray of light spreading about the room. She didn't understand its soothing balm. The light that made her feel peaceful.

She felt she was moving aimlessly in a subterranean world without identity, shorn of dignity—trust. What was real was a world of brightness in other people's lives, but she lived in grayness. She couldn't go back to sleep. She began again the game she constantly played, imagining the back door, the one from the kitchen to the back porch, locked and bolted. She saw herself locking and bolting the front door, locking windows, and then climbing the two flights of stairs to the third floor. There, a white door with a square black lock opened to narrower stairs leading to the two dormer rooms. She imagined locking and bolting that and finally alone. Hidden, secure she rolled herself in the tight quilt cocoon and stared at the lantern light that washed over her like the gentleness of a prayer. Constriction at the base of her neck relaxed when she felt locked away—relaxed into the seductive glow of the light, which touched her spirit as sunlight touching a flower.

She spent hours playing with Hannah, grateful for unlimited time with the baby. Only one piece of furniture stood in the other dormer room where Hannah liked to play, a dresser with an oval mirror above. Annie studied her familiar reflection, through the dark tarnished spots at the edge of the old mirror. She looked the same. But she would never be the same.

Tomorrow she would do something about her hair. It had grown into an unkempt mass in the weeks she had slept and tried to rise above what ravaged her mind. Tomorrow. Maybe. For today she would play with her child.

One day she looked down on the drive to see Robert St. Pierre's car crunching slowly along the drive beside the house. "Robert," she breathed. What must he think of her? Disappearing like she had? So attentive had she been to her own wounds there had not been much left over to consider others' feelings.

Henry was on the back porch immediately. Annie cracked open a window. She was surprised at the joy she felt just seeing Robert. She wanted to run down to him, tell him she was safe, and how much she missed him. It was the first spark that had touched her spirit in weeks.

"Have you seen Annie Porter?" He stood by the car, looking so earnest as he questioned Henry, she could hardly keep from going to him. "I've looked everywhere. You boys know anything about her?"

"What name was it you said?" Otis cupped his hand behind his ear, acting confused.

"Annie Porter. John Malvern's daughter."

"Can't say we know nothing about her," he said.

"She's missing. Over a month."

"You don't say."

Annie looked down on the back of Otis's white head. "Missin' a month, Henry." He looked at his brother. "Goodness gracious me. You reckon she run off with one of them oil people?"

"No," Robert countered quickly. "I don't reckon that. I'm afraid those men who have been hounding her did something to her and the baby."

"Baby? You didn't say nothin' about a baby."

"She's got a baby. Now Henry, you know it." Robert was on that instantly. "She told me you helped deliver it." He studied Henry for a moment. "How come you're not inviting me in? What have you got inside there?"

"Oh," Otis looked up. "It was *that* Malvern girl that's missing you say?" Henry continued his addled charade.

"Yes," Robert St. Pierre almost bellowed. "I'm worried sick. I know about the threats. I was there when..." He stopped again and stared past Henry. "Annie," he screamed. "Annie, if you're in there, I've got to know. Are you all right?" He pushed past the brothers. "I think you're in there, Annie."

Annie flew down the stairs, "Robert. Robert, I'm here." She ran to the back screen. "I'm all right," she called. He bounded up the steps as she opened the door.

Henry stepped back as Robert came inside the kitchen and held her.

"They've been hiding me," she whispered as she clung to him. "Oh, Robert. I..."

"Why are they hiding you?" He looked at Annie and beyond at Otis.

"I...I can't tell you." She had worried about how he might handle the rape. "I...I went to your house, but you were gone and I ...I am so happy to see you, Robert." When she stepped back out of his arms, she noticed the expression on Otis's face. Crestfallen. Henry turned from her and dipped himself some water from a tin cup.

"Robert, you must tell no one where I am." She looked into his eyes, pleading. "They threatened my baby. Promise me."

"A lot of people are looking for you. They're worried. They're gonna keep looking."

"You've got to keep this to yourself, Robert, and you must go and not come back." She kissed him as he stood in the open door.

"I don't see why I should go now that I've found you."

"Because," Henry drew himself up to his full height and glared at Robert, "someone might see you here and wonder why you would stay so long," Henry was more emphatic than Annie had ever heard him.

Robert nodded, looking down at Henry. Clearly he was not welcome. Robert tilted her chin up, kissed her. "Good bye, Annie. Take care of yourself. I see that I can't."

She watched as his car moved back down the drive.

Annie turned to face the brothers. Otis, sober, downcast, kept his eyes away from her. His shoulders drooped helplessly. She had injured their gentle feelings. She saw that. They had saved her sanity and maybe her life. They had protected her baby and she had betrayed the secret they had tried so hard to keep for her.

She went to each of them and hugged them. "I am so sorry."

Henry gave her a wistful smile, but Otis was a lumpy unresponsive heap in her arms. She laid her head on his shoulder.

"Annie," Henry spoke at last, "to keep a secret, you tell no one."

CHAPTER 54

The Lone Star Oil Company was drilling a well at the corner of the brothers' lane and a road leading to the pasture. Oil trucks ground in and out of the lane at all hours. Neighbors came every evening as was the custom and parked their cars in the glow of the derrick. It was the most exciting of social activities in the county, especially when a well was expected to come in. Annie stayed upstairs, her light off, but the two attic rooms on the third floor were bright as noonday from the lighted derrick.

She looked about the dreary house and wondered again why the brothers didn't use some of their money to fix things up. The stair runner was so ragged it was dangerous. Of course, they weren't at all domestic. Still why didn't they trade in that old truck or get a new tractor? Even that. Why did they still go to the field every day and work just as though they didn't have money pouring in? But today Annie had bigger concerns than the brothers' housekeeping.

Hannah was fussy. Annie put her down for a nap, but she couldn't sleep. Her breathing was short, her chest congested. Annie walked the length of the two rooms, the child on her shoulder, trying to soothe her. Evening turned to night and Annie began to worry. She had no medicine to help the wheezing in her chest.

Hannah whimpered in her fitful sleep and then woke. Her eyes were watery and her body feverish.

The brothers were working in the field. Only last night they had talked of the unpredictable fall weather and wanting to get the hay cut and in the barn. She heard the hay wagon lumber into the backyard and into the barn. She hurried down to the kitchen.

"Otis," she called. "Hannah's real sick."

Henry, hot and dirty from his day's work in the field, looked at her for a moment, then took charge. "We'll see what we can do."

In a few minutes Henry and Otis hovered over Hannah's bed, their faces telling their concern.

Otis came up the stairs carrying a black pot, steaming, obviously just off the fire. It filled the air with a putrid smell.

"What is that? You're not giving that stuff to my baby."

"Not giving, rubbing." Otis bustled about in a businesslike manner. He pulled Annie's ragged quilt over the ends of the bed exposing one side. As the substance in the pot cooled, Otis began to rub it on Hannah's chest and throat.

"What is that?" Annie asked.

"It's onions cooked in grease and mixed with two kinds of liniment."

"Otis!" Annie protested.

"Ma used it on us."

Henry came in the room with a small tub of boiling water. "Now," Annie moved near her baby, "what are you planning to do? Tell me."

"We're gonna break down that fever," Henry said, his thick brows knit as he dropped a towel into the hot water, fished it out with a wooden spoon, and rolled it in a dry towel. The brothers' round, thick bodies at opposite ends, their heavy arms wrung out the excess water.

Hannah cried, and looked to her mother. "Not too hot," Henry admonished as he and Otis squeezed out another wet towel. "Just enough she can stand it." They wrapped it around Hannah's chin and the top of her little body. As Annie stood by, the brothers went silently about their job through the night, applying the wet cloths to her chest as the foul, stifling odor filled the room. They continued putting the hot wet towel on the baby into the night.

"There, Henry." Otis was in his element now. "You see that, there's some bubbles of sweat on her lip. Give me another towel."

Henry studied the baby and felt her forehead. He nodded approvingly.

Annie looked over their shoulders. Hannah, eyes still drowsy, looked helplessly at Henry. A noisy, rattling cough escaped her throat. The brothers stood up and looked at each other—a wordless understanding.

"It's breaking." Otis smiled through his week-old whiskers.

Hannah looked relaxed, about to drift into sleep. Annie changed the baby's damp bedclothes, wrapped her in a dry flannel sheet and put her in bed. The brothers came back with two thick comforters and piled them on the child. "Need to keep her sweating."

"The fever's been beat down," Otis informed Annie.

Henry picked up the tub and wet towels then came to stand by his brother. Still in their work-stained overalls, they looked down at the baby, saying nothing--a gentle adoration in their eyes. They had helped her come into to the world and now, tonight... Annie realized that Hannah must be the most precious thing to have touched their lives in a long time.

She and Hannah slept late into the next day. In the afternoon, there was a timid knock at the bedroom door. She opened it to find Otis with Henry behind him.

"We just wondered...we didn't want to go to the field 'til we knew." Both freshly shaven, they wore clean overalls and caps.

"You waited all this time?" Annie looked at them, touched by their humble consideration.

"We came up, but it was so still we didn't knock."

"Hannah's doing fine." The child was banging tin cups Otis had brought up for her to play with. "All thanks to you two. I think she's hungry."

Within minutes they were back with hot cereal and milk. Otis held Hannah on his lap and seemed to enjoy helping her while she ate. Annie gobbled down her own cereal as she sat on the edge of her bed.

"What was it you used on Hannah last night?" Annie asked.

"Liniment we use in the barn."

"You used horse liniment on my child?" But as she said it, she watched Hannah giggling on Otis's lap.

"It always works," Henry said.

"It smelled like manure." Immediately she knew she should not have said that. The brothers looked away, a gesture she had come to know meant disapproval. They were uneasy about a word like that coming from a woman. Henry walked to the window and watched the beehive of trucks and equipment down by the oil well.

"How's the well coming?" Annie said quickly, "I mean, Henry, do you think it looks like it's good?"

He turned, "I talked to Garrett yesterday. He said they're expecting to top the Glen Dean formation at about twenty-three hundred feet. They'll see how that looks."

The words had become familiar to her at Dutch's, these strata the drill penetrated before finding pockets of oil.

"You can tell by that sometimes," Otis explained, "if there's Cypress or McClusky pay."

Annie nodded.

"Otis, Garrett said you can't always count on that as a guide around here. Said we'd have to go a little deeper in the well," Henry said.

"He told me once the Glen Dean is the first marker to have any real value. He said that, Henry, to me."

Henry pulled off his glasses and glared at his brother. "You have to go deeper, Otis. That's what that Garrett said to me right out there in front of the barn, and he knows."

"How many wells have you got?" Annie cut in.

"Twenty-two," Otis answered without taking his eyes from his brother.

"That's not so, Otis, it's twenty-three."

"I get twenty-two."

"You always forget that one, back there close to the branch."

"All right! Twenty-three."

Henry looked satisfied.

Otis, huffy, grabbed up the cereal bowls and left.

"Don't let on," Henry whispered to Annie as if the walls might hear, "I'm thinkin' my brother's getting forgetful. You saw that. Completely forgot about an oil well."

That afternoon, the brothers went to the field to shuck corn. Annie heard a scrape at the back-dormer window. She froze. Maybe the wind blew something against the glass. She had begun to feel secure in these third-floor rooms, locked safely away from the world. There it was again, like a pebble. She moved slowly toward the window, peering down through the narrow slit by the green window shade.

Robert!

He shouldn't be here! Oh, but she was so lonesome. Lonesome for him. She ran down the stairs and opened the back door. He stepped inside, and he took her into his arms.

"You came here in broad daylight," she whispered. "You shouldn't do that."

"I wanted to see you." He held her close. But she wanted to back away, retreat into herself as she had these last weeks. She was different. She looked at him trying to understand this new feeling in her—wanting to get away, like a skittish animal. But this was Robert!

"I came to tell you something," he said not noticing her withdrawal. "The people parked down by the well last night thought they saw light and movements in the attic. One thought there was a light and people moving around."

"Hannah was sick...Oh, God!" Her hand went over her mouth, thinking of the monster who was looking for her, the monster who promised to attack again... What if someone suspected she was here? Then she continued. "Otis and Henry, oh, they were so wonderful... They brought Hannah out of it. She's much better today."

"You know how talk goes, Annie. Your disappearance is a big mystery. I wanted to warn you." He looked at her. "You can't stay here forever. You'll have to come out sometime and... I...miss you."

"It's not just hiding, Robert." She faltered, looking away. "It's something more." She fixed her eyes on the red checked tablecloth nearby, unable to look into his eyes, unable to say the words. Dreading how he would feel about her. "This is going to be hard," she whispered, still looking away. After a moment she went on. "You see I needed a quiet nest, somewhere to heal."

She raised her eyes to Robert's. "I was raped."

The words hung in silence.

He looked at her, as if trying to comprehend what she had just said. A mask came over his face. He swallowed, his jaw tightened. The hard silence came on him like when she first met him. He had been hurt once. Could he handle this? She felt panicky, but once started she went on.

"He held a knife to my throat." She stepped back and closed her eyes. "I fought, but he threatened the baby if..." A gentle fragile trust had grown up between them and it had been dirtied. It was she who had been dirtied. She felt sick.

"Who was it?" he said finally.

"Listen to me, Robert." She looked up into his eyes and held his arms. "I saw my husband lying in his blood, three bullet holes in his body. I don't want you to...Oh, God, Robert, don't try anything. Please, please."

"The black car?" he asked.

"Yes."

She saw the old hard expression on his face. "Both of them?"

"One."

He walked slowly to the back door, reached for the knob as if in a trance.

"Robert, they'll do anything—rape, murder. He is a beast...there's my baby and—there's you."

He said nothing.

"There's no law here." Annie heard herself pleading. "You know that. They know that. No law for me, for most of us."

She knew he was still staggering, feeling now a sharper reality of the violence about them.

"I'm so lonesome to see you," she whispered, "but you can't come back. There's a monster looking for me."

She couldn't read how he was feeling. He seemed frozen. Desperation began to crawl over her. If he lost affection for her, would he betray her? No, he wouldn't do that...she didn't think he would.

He stared about the room, not seeing. After a while he spoke. "There's something else—a lottery for the draft. And your brother Glenn, along with some others, went off to join the Navy."

"Glenn!" she echoed. "But why, there's no war?"

"Not yet." Robert looked at her for a moment. "I'm sorry, Annie, about this—about you." He opened the screen door, looked about like someone lost, then walked slowly down the steps.

She went to the second story landing, sat down and cried for a while. 'I'm sorry about this—about you.' That's what he said—detached. 'about you.' It was her problem, not his. She pounded the floor with her fist. Everything went back to the cursed oil. After a long while, the tears dried, and she leaned back against the corner on the landing. What Robert had to tell her, he could have told the brothers, but he wanted to see her. It was then she knew whatever he thought of her now, she had fallen in love with him, and her heart was breaking.

CHAPTER 55

Throughout the month of October, oil trucks had used the Patrick brothers' driveway, then veering off into the field behind the garage to the well site. Annie had remained concealed behind closed windows and dark blinds even when afternoons grew sweltering. But the well had come in—the twenty-fourth—a good one, and although the derrick still stood, the crews had moved on to work other sites.

Annie opened the windows to let a balmy breeze blow through the dormer rooms. Tomorrow would be The Harvest Carnival and Parade—the anniversary night of Willis's murder. Nightmares had sometimes come—Willis lying on the steps. At other times she woke with a start, the monster over her, hurting her. When she looked from her windows down on the world below, she turned away sick, because someone violent still prowled free, waiting for her.

Just when she felt safe to open her windows, another oil truck came up the drive and stopped by the back step. Mitchell Dillman, the head driller, pounded on the screen. Annie heard Henry greet him.

"Listen," Dillman said, "you boys laid out so many spreads for us, what with all these wells, my crew says they're gonna give you guys a treat."

"Well, now," Henry drawled, "that won't be necessary, atall."

"Sure it is. We've ate chicken dinner off of you boys ever' time of the year. The men always like a feed after they finish up so we're gonna set up right out here in the yard, kinda pay you back."

"Well, now, I wish you wouldn't do that," Henry protested. "It might rain or something."

"Don't you give it a thought. We'll take care of ever'thing."

No matter how the brothers protested, Mitchell Dillman meant to do them a good turn, and would not be deterred.

Saturday morning, they came. At the edge of the yard they set up two great iron kettles over fires and filled them with every kind of vegetable that came from the fall harvest.

Annie peeked through the thin crack between the blind and window. She looked at Hannah wondering how she could keep the baby quiet in the long hours that stretched ahead. As the day wore on, kettles simmered with corn and vegetable chowder.

Annie showed her toddler how to draw pictures with crayons on the wallpaper. By late morning they had decorated both rooms. She looked again through the window blind. Men were bringing in sawhorses and wood planks for long tables under the wide ancient trees. If they just stayed outside! By mid-afternoon the chowder was done. As the party got going, trucks pulled up under the trees and a couple dozen men now working on other wells bailed out to get their share of the chowder.

Writing on walls having lost its attraction for Hannah, Annie sat down on the floor stacking up blocks for her. The baby grew sleepy, so Annie began rocking her. There was only the distant murmur of voices in the yard below. A sharp wind rattled against the windows. Then she heard pounding on the front door. The front door! She had never seen the front door opened. Boisterous voices became louder as the party spilled from outside into the house.

"Better get some more bowls and make up some coffee in there," Mitchell Dillman's voice boomed from the ground floor below. "Don't ever' body want beer?"

Hannah roused and cried out.

"You hear that, Mitch, sounded like some kid a squallin'." one of the men said.

"Hey, Henry," Dillman called out. "You got a youngun nobody knows about?"

There was silence below. A breeze pushed through the house and a door slammed. Hannah flinched in Annie's arms. She put her hand over the baby's ear.

"Was it you boys that kidnapped that woman?" Dillman kept up.

"Bet you took her up them stairs and had your way with her. That right, Otis?" Another voice taunted.

Annie could hear the jibes going back and forth from the lower rooms. She was terrified for herself, but she felt sorry—even guilty for what Henry and Otis were going through.

"Never thought you guys needed a woman, but then you can't never tell." Guffaws and snickers followed. Men were traipsing around in the kitchen, the forward rooms, through the front door and into the yard, disrupting the brothers' quiet regulated life.

"You're all wrong, all of you." It was Henry, angry and defensive. "That's that cat we got. He can sound just like a baby cryin' sometimes."

"Yeah, Henry, sure. It was a cat. I'll bet these boys has got some kind of a harem up there and maybe younguns, too."

"That's right. Women go for money, don't they, boys?" Dillman came back. "And here you are, two fancy bachelors with plenty of money." That brought on boisterous hoots of agreement. Annie could imagine the agonies the shy brothers were suffering with backslapping and insinuations.

"This is not true." Otis's voice was earnest and indignant. "We do not have…"

"Come on ole Buddy, we was just joshin' you a little. Got to have some fun. It's a party, ain't it? Hey Tom. Bring out some more beer from the kitchen."

"'Sides," a voice called from the kitchen, "we don't care if you got a harem."

"We do not have..." Otis stammered trying to defend himself, but the brothers could never be liars.

Annie's heart ached for them. This was too much, too many men coming at them. Never in their lives had they done or said anything dishonest.

The front door slammed with a crash in the rising wind. Hannah's drowsy eyes opened briefly but she settled back into sleep. The conversation was shut off below with everyone outside now. Annie held her child close, slowly rocking, praying the men would stay outside.

Finally, the chowder was devoured. Annie put Hannah down for a nap and took another careful look at the party below in the front yard. A black cloud was moving in and the wind upset one of the improvised table. Men hurried to their trucks. Annie sunk down in a chair and closed her eyes, the day's tension had drained her. A question had been raised, she knew, and suspicion would come out of it.

The wind continued to rise, roaring at windows and doors in the old house. A mammoth cloud billowed low across the sky. The rooms darkened like an early dusk. Treetops near the dormer windows thrashed. Annie sat on the edge of her bed, as the small windows caught the vicious wind. The old house creaked and rattled. Then she heard a loud crack outside and ran to look out the window in the other dormer room. A twister. She watched, paralyzed with fascination. Tree limbs dashed through the air and settled to the ground. Then she saw the top of the oil derrick, ripped off, and flying through the air across the lane to a hedgerow. The twisting cloud uprooted a row of old trees, making a westerly path of destruction where it leapfrogged over fields. She ran back to pick up Hannah and go to the lower floors. Then she heard plodding sounds on the stairs. Henry, at her door, was carrying a steaming black pot and bowls, and Otis behind him a kerosene lamp held high.

"Shouldn't we go to the cellar? This old house...a tornado..."

"Nawh." Otis put the lamp on a tiny table. "Beams in this house is hard as rocks. We got some chowder for you."

Henry set out four bowls, spooned out the chowder as they huddled together in the pale circle of lamplight. The wind howled as if some mighty devil wanted to break into the creaking house.

"There might be some talk." Otis leaned forward, wiping his mouth with his fist. "Nobody knows anything for sure."

Annie, the stress of the day returning, tightening every muscle in her body, listened to the furious storm, imagining the high dormer rooms ripped off like the oil derrick.
"We should go to the cellar."

"We never moved to the cellar before," Henry said. "We got a bigger problem than that storm out there. We'll have to take you somewheres else. The sheriff..."

"No." Otis stood, challenging his brother. "We're keeping Annie and the baby."

She had never seen the shy Otis take such a firm stand.

"We hid her so far, and we'll keep on taking care of her. Ain't nobody else gonna know."

Henry nodded and for once didn't argue with his brother.

The rain hit, unleashing torrents on the windows and roof. A tremendous crash hit the house and pieces of a shattered tree limb splattered hard against the window; but the glass held. Annie looked at her child on Henry's lap, trembled, remembering the derrick flying through the air and praying that another flying limb wouldn't crash in on them. "We're not safe here. We must go downstairs," she pleaded

Henry tilted Hannah's bowl to get the last spoonful of soup for her. "Them warm days was a weather breeder," he said and wiped her mouth with a cloth.

"There's a tornado out there, Henry," Annie whispered as if loud talk would attract fate. "We're just lucky as saints we weren't in its path." The screaming wind drove rain against the windows and the roof.

"We was in for a weather change." Otis leaned back in his chair, his hands clasped across his thick middle. "October and all."

In the morning, the storm had calmed, but water stood in the yard, and the sunken driveway was a stream. The house was cold and damp, and Hannah still sniffled. Sitting at breakfast in the kitchen with the brothers. "Do you think," Annie began, "I could move to the second floor, the bedroom over the kitchen. Then heat from the cook stove can come up through the grates in the floor?"

Henry looked down at his cereal and poured thick cream over his oats and pursed his lips. "I don't like it," he finally said.

Otis cut off generous slabs of butter, laid them in sections on his bread, carefully covering it to the crust, and then applied two heaping spoonfuls of blackberry jam, meticulously spreading it to the edge. "They got to have heat, Henry."

Henry stirred the oatmeal and poured sugar over the mixture. "The baby cries sometimes. People come to the back door. Easy to get careless."

"We'll have to be on the lookout," Otis replied.

"Well, I don't like it." From the back window, Henry noticed men taking down the remaining skeleton of the derrick. He could hardly finish his oats. "I might just go see that they pick up all the litter scattered in the fields from that derrick. Don't want to tear up a plow next spring when we go to put out a crop." He reached for his boots behind the stove. Pulled them on. Annie watched as he sloshed through the back yard, down to the well site.

Everything was so strangely quiet outside, the ground soggy with standing water, no traffic on the roads. Annie felt a freedom she had not felt since she came to stay with the Patrick brothers. That morning, Otis helped her move to a bedroom just above the kitchen.

The low slanted ceilings of the dormer room had once seemed a safe cocoon to her, but now felt confining. Maybe her old confidence was returning. She missed being with people—and most of all, she missed Robert.

Annie and Hannah came down again to the kitchen for the sociability of the noon meal.

At lunch Henry reported his morning conversation with the oil workers. "The Little Wabash's a rushing river, overflowed its banks and washed out the bridge over on the main road." He forked two pieces of fried ham, laid them by his mound of potatoes, and then covered it all with white gravy. "Can't get to town 'less you go all the way around by the Hackett place and come in from the south. Surprises me the bridge on our road didn't fall in, rickety as it is."

"Didn't used to be rickety," Otis said. "All them oil trucks goin' over it day after day, shook loose every nail and screw in it." He cut off a chunk of ham and savored it. "They'd just better got all the pieces of that derrick picked up out of the field. Salt water runoff done enough damage to the land."

Annie smiled, thinking how much money these two men must have, and still they carped about how the oil operation had ruined their fields and bridges.

CHAPTER 56

The next morning in her new second story room, Annie quietly dressed to go down for breakfast while Hannah slept. She looked out the window to see if the water had receded and froze in disbelief. The black car sat in the drive! The man who raped her sat on the passenger's side. Her heart began to pound. The driver, tall with gray hair, bailed out, came to the back door, and banged on the screen.

Annie sat down on her bed, shaking. Hannah moved but didn't wake. Annie grabbed the blanket and clutched it to her chest. She had felt safe for the last two days, water standing everywhere—as if the world had stopped.

She heard Henry at the door. "What do you want?" he said.

"I think you got somebody in there, somebody we need to see." It was a strange voice.

"My brother and me live here." Henry said. "Just the two of us."

She heard him in the kitchen now. "Where's this brother you talk about?"

"Well, he ain't here just now."

The voice grew louder. The intruder had pressed on into the house. The voices seemed louder. Shaking uncontrollably, Annie felt like trapped prey.

"This brother you talk about that's not here. Is this him, behind the stove?" The man's accusing voice boomed. "That right?"

"I don't think you should be pushing into our house uninvited." She heard the quaver in Otis's voice.

The baby cried.

"Now, what was that? Tell me again how this brother standing before me, ain't here and you ain't hidin' nobody." He had pushed past the kitchen.

Through a slice of her open bedroom door on the second floor, Annie could see him in one of the forward rooms, towering over Henry, pushing him aside, and heading for the stairs. "Tell me how you're not lying to me."

She held her hand over the baby's mouth to keep her from crying out. Her heart thundered in her chest, fear pulsing to her fingertips. She thought of running to the top floor but if she opened the door, he'd see her.

Henry pushed himself in before the intruder and stood at the foot of the stairs.

"Answer me, old man! I hate a liar more'n anything."

Henry stood on the bottom step blocking the way. The intruder started forward.

"How much does she owe you?" Henry quietly asked.

He stopped, studied Henry for a moment. His eyes narrowed. "I'll settle for fifteen thousand dollars.'

"Fifteen thousand dollars." Otis, standing alongside the stairs, glared at him. "You took the very soul of that woman for fifteen thousand dollars?"

The man turned to Otis, sized him up. "So, old man, you have got the woman here."

"I never said that," Otis got out.

"She owes fifteen thousand dollars. Her old man's got it."

"Come tomorrow." Henry spoke up with solemn authority. "You'll get your money and she'll be shut of you once and for all."

He moved back from the stairs, bore down on Otis, grabbed the overall straps together under Otis's chin, and pulled tight. "You're not playin' tricks on us are you, old man?"

"I got a nephew that works for the FBI, up there in Chicago." Otis gasped out, his plump face reddening.

"Yeah," the intruder grinned, "you call that nephew that works for the FBI up there in Chicago. Call him, right away." He let go of Otis's straps. "Tomorrow! The money."

After he left, Annie ran down the stairs, watching the car leave the driveway. The wrenching terror she thought was over throbbed through her, pounding at her temples..

"Fifteen thousand dollars, Henry!" she cried. "Willis only owed them eight thousand!" She ran frantically about the room, peering out the window from time to time. "And anyway, that's not the one that—raped me. Oh, God please don't let them near me. It was the other one...the one in the car." Her fears, her nightmares were happening, but it felt unreal, dreamlike. She stopped before Otis, "I thought it was over." He came to her and put his thick arms about her shoulders. She could hardly breathe she was so scared.

"It's gonna be all right, Annie," Otis soothed, stroking her hair. "Gonna be all right."

The next morning, she sat with them, Otis and Henry, at the table, silent, watching the drive, waiting. In the center of the checked oilcloth on the table were stacks of hundred-dollar bills. She stared down at it. Where did they get that money? She looked at them, questioning but she felt she should not ask. They had not gone to the bank. The truck hadn't been moved.

"Willis only owed eight thousand dollars. Henry they're lying to you."

Otis patted her hand. "These are people who will lie, Annie."

Shortly after, the black car pulled to a stop in the drive. The same man stepped out. Alone, this time.

"That's not the one, Henry—."

"We know, Annie." Henry gathered up the money, went to the back porch, and stood at the top of the steps.

"Well, old man." The man smiled down at Henry. "You said 'tomorrow' and its tomorrow."

Henry clutched the money in his fist. Without saying a word, he began to count it out in his palm. "One hundred, two hundred…" When Henry finished, he pulled a wadded paper from his pocket. "I want you to sign…"

The man laughed, pocketed the money and patted him on the head.

"You there, now git," Henry called after him. "Don't come back. You just git."

Henry watched the car back out, then came in, slammed the door, and sat down in a chair. Annie saw his hands quiver. None of them said anything. She poured Henry a cup of coffee, but when he took it, he spilled it on the table. He stood and began to pace.

"There is nothing I can ever do to repay you," she said. "You delivered my baby, saved my life, you are... the kindest…I just can't tell you what you mean to me…there's nothing…I can ever do for you." She went to Henry and buried her head on his shoulder. She felt him shaking as much as she was. "You're a gift from God," she whispered. "Thank you—both,"

Henry pulled back quickly from the embrace. "Well, you're shut of them for good,"

Otis looked to her. "They got no hold over you now that the money's been paid. You don't have to hide no more." He got up and poured them all coffee. "Let's us have breakfast."

That night another storm raged. Annie imagined the black car in the drive, but there was nothing to see in that blackness. She sat back on the edge of the bed and ran fingers through her hair. For two years she had lived with this torment Willis had brought on them. Now she was free. She would have to make plans to leave this hiding place one of these days.

The next afternoon she decided to make a special supper for them. Otis was asleep on the cot in the kitchen where he often napped. Henry was still outside.

A knock came at the door. She hesitated but thought there was no need for fear now. She opened the door.

Standing before her was the man who had raped her.

She screamed. "Get away from me." The screaming continued. She swayed unsteadily. Behind the heavy mustache, scar through his thick eyebrows, and cigar-stained teeth, was a monster named Lee.

"Get away. Get away," she kept screaming. Otis was by her side. She grasped his arm. Annie felt again the weight of that wide body on her, the hurting, the helplessness, the cruel hard eyes.

"You come up with that money pretty easy. I think you got some more where that was." Lee said.

Annie ran behind the stove. She saw a poker and picked it up but Lee only laughed at her outside the screen. She hung far back behind Otis. Through the open door, she saw Henry coming through the back yard on his tractor. He plowed through a corner of the garden fence, over an outside pump, moving toward the porch. Henry kept coming, his head down just above the steering wheel of the tracker aiming at the old wooden porch steps where Lee stood, coming at him. Lee got distracted and jumped off the porch just in time. Henry was upon him, taking out part of the porch with the tractor. Otis grabbed his rifle as the man ran for the car.

In the car, Lee started to back, but mired in the mud. His tires spun in the soggy ruts. Henry rammed the front of the car with his tractor and spun the car to solid ground. Otis shot out his front and rear tires. The driver started to get out, but Otis shot again, shattering the back window. Lee dived to the floor.

Otis eased himself from the porch that now had no steps. He hurried to his truck as Henry rammed the hood of the car again with the tractor and shoved it several feet backward. Otis came in behind the car with his truck and drove hard into the back end, rumpling the trunk lid and sandwiching the car between them.

The driver tried again to open his door, but it was jammed. Otis leaned out the truck window, leveled his rifle and fired into the back window of the car. The driver tried for the other door, saw Otis aiming at him and dropped down in the front seat. Otis backed the truck up and Henry pounded and pushed the hobbling car backward.

Annie ran through the front room, pried open the rain soaked front entrance, stood on the porch, watching as the hated black car was forced with pushes and jerks to the end of the lane. Otis fired again. With his truck, he forced the crumpled heap to head north on the main road. Henry continued to push and gouge it with the tractor. She heard Otis's rifle ring out again.

Hannah stood by her mother and watched with questioning eyes.

"They can't go that way," Annie said out loud. "The bridge is about to collapse..."

Then she smiled.

Henry still pushed at the car with his tractor and Otis, in the truck, hovered near the back ramming the wreck over and over into the center of the road.

The distant hedgerow blocked her view. Annie waited. She heard another shot. Finally, she saw Otis's truck return and move slowly into the lane toward the house. He looked neither right nor left, as he passed. He put the truck in the garage and closed the door, something he seldom did. Soon Henry's tractor lumbered past, and he put it in the shed and closed the door.

She wanted to know what had happened, wanted desperately to know, but she knew she must not ask. They came in and sat by the stove, saying nothing.

At supper the brothers were silent, absorbed in their food, hardly lifting their eyes. Not even Hannah distracted them. Annie put things away after the meal, washed the dishes and took Hannah to their room.

A wall of silence hung there as surely as if it could be touched.

After Hannah was asleep, Annie's curiosity had eaten at her. She had to see them, had to know. Maybe they would say something—anything.

As she came down the stairs, she could see only a narrow slice of the kitchen through the doors. The lamp spread a yellow circle of light over the table. The old Bible lay wide before them. Henry's index finger traced words as he read. Otis, seated at a right angle to him, listened. In the lamplight their rounded heavy cheeks glistened, wet with tears.

CHAPTER 57

Annie walked down the Patrick brothers' long lane to the main road, the first time she had retraced this path since she stumbled down it a lifetime ago—the night she was raped. But today—today she was reborn, free now, the old fear-filled time over.

"I want to tell my mother I'm all right and..." Annie had announced to the brothers as she fixed breakfast for them

"Take the truck over," Henry said.

"I'll just walk. It will be wonderful to just be out, walking, breathing the air."

"Won't be very scenic, all the crops have been brought in," he continued.

"We'll keep the little girl for you," Otis quickly volunteered.

Annie had watched the brothers with Hannah and she saw they felt almost a father's responsibility for her.

"Thank you. I won't be gone long."

Annie's hand trembled as she knocked on the door of her parents' newly remodeled house, remembering the night of her attack when Eva Mae refused to let her in. What had Eva Mae told them? She felt like a pot of jelly from her stomach to her knees as she waited on the porch. A sharp chill in the wind, whispering the coming of winter. Don't let it be Eva Mae, her heart begged.

When the door finally opened it was Glenn. Sober, gentle Glenn. "Annie," his eyes brightened.

"Glenn, I thought you were gone to the Navy."

"I'm home. Got a furlough 'til after Thanksgiving." He held the door for her to enter. "Annie, I reckon you know our folks was real worried."

She looked at him, puzzled. "No, I don't know that." He knew how his father had changed.

"Well, Mama was about outa her mind and—me and Papa, we all been worried."

She stepped into the new kitchen and looked around but said nothing. "I-I'm doing fine. How do you like the Navy?"

He dropped his head. "Can't exactly say I love it."

"Glenn," she whispered overcome, and rushed to wrap her arms around him, full of love for the old family. Tears came. Glenn would always be the old family. He held her close briefly, but Glenn was awkward with displays of emotions. He pulled away and went to the hall door

"Mama," he called. "You better come here and see who we got."

Sophie Malvern came into the kitchen. She stared as if not seeing. "Land sakes," she whispered, wiping her hands on her apron, tears slipping down her cheeks. "Oh, my lands. We thought you was gone from us. We prayed every night and now here you stand. Land sakes." She pulled Annie to her and held her. "My dear baby daughter. Oh, thank you, my good Lord." Annie could feel her mother's heart against her and the old lady's tremble.

"You come on in here and sit." She took Annie's hand. "This here's the parlor or living room or whatever they're callin' it. I don't hardly think I live here no more. This is Eva Mae and your Papa's doin'—all this new furniture and re-doin'"

"It's pretty, Mama. I'm glad you got something nice."

"Oh my, just let me look at you. I'm so thankful you're all right. Where on earth was you? I just thought of everything that mighta happened—I put in terrible nights."

They settled on a blue velvet couch, Annie clasping and unclasping her mother's hand while she told her all that had happened. Annie watched her mother, wondering if she would disown her, think she was responsible.

Sophie sat in silence for a while, staring at the floor. Finally she began stroking Annie's hand. "You all right now?"

"Yes, Mama." It was what she answered. But from the bottom of her heart she ached to bury herself in her mother's arms and cry it all out. Her mother, she knew, could not understand the pain, the fear and the fury she felt. She would only understand the shame.

Sophie's face sobered. "You haven't told anybody that you was—attacked, have you?"

"Well, the Patrick brothers, of course."

Sophie dug in her apron pocket for a handkerchief and wiped her eyes, then took Annie's hand again. "There's no good reason to tell it. And there's just no good that come out of this oil business. It just makes misery."

"It's not the oil. We knew how to live life before it came, but now...things are different."

Sophie shook her head. "They plowed up my garden, you know. Won't have me puttin' one out. I raised you children on my garden and now I can't have it no more. Tell me," she turned to face her daughter, "what am I good for anymore? An old woman that's not supposed to do what she knows how to do? Now we got them roses. Eva Mae's set on changing things, and her father's right there with her."

"Where is Eva Mae?" Annie asked.

"Joey took her to town to some doin' at the Allison family."

"Danny Allison may go, too." Glenn said. "to the Navy when I go, but Eva Mae don't know it yet."

A car turned into the drive and they watched it stop in the circle driveway.

"That'll be Joey now in his new Roadster," Glenn volunteered. "Papa thinks he's teachin' him to drive, but Joey don't need much teachin'. Drives seventy miles an hour out there on the highway when Papa ain't with 'em."

"Joey's got a new car?" Annie repeated almost to herself.

"Papa bought it for 'im," Sophie put in.

Annie stared at Glenn sitting across from them. His head was down and his finger fussing with a loose thread on the worn knees of his overalls. Glenn did not raise his head.

"Your Papa's puttin' a lot of store in Joey. Gonna send him off to college next year. Least ways that what your Papa's sayin'."

"What about Kurt, Mama?"

"He don't come around much," Sophie whispered.

Glenn looked up in his sheepish way. "He don't like it here no more."

Sophie began to cry. "I wisht my children was little, and they was here, around me. Glenn, here is gonna be gone off to the Navy, and you was gone, and we didn't know where you was, and Kurt, he don't come here no more cause he hates the way Evie's got. And Eva Mae, she and Joey are like people that don't even belong to me."

Annie picked up her mother's hand and held it to her own cheek. "And Papa?" she asked.

"I reckon he's happy. He and Eva Mae are always busy at something—changin' things." She looked through the window where Joey and his father were wiping mud off the new car Joey had just parked.

John Malvern came into the room first, Joey behind him. "Annie!" he whispered. He ran to her and hugged her, "My little girl." He held her at arm's length. "You look...all right. Where you been, girl? Half the county's been looking for you."

She looked at him and stepped back. She couldn't tell him what she'd been through. Maybe she couldn't even forgive him. If he had given Willis the money, which he could have done, all of this wouldn't have happened. "I'm all right, Papa," was all she could muster.

Sophie quickly spoke up. "I'll tell you later, John, what it was that happened."

He looked at Sophie and knew it was not something she would say in mixed company. "You're comin' back is like a prayer been answered," he whispered.

"Hey, Annie," Joey spoke up. "You want to go for a ride in my new car? It cost more'n any other car in town. Ain't that right, Papa?"

Glenn straightened out of his chair, slipped from the room, and out the front door.

"That's right, son, but don't be sayin' 'ain't'. Eva Mae got on you about that. You can't go sayin', 'ain't' and the like. You hear what I say, Joey?"

Joey smiled widely at Annie and spoke importantly. "You're ready for a spin, ain't you, Annie?"

They breezed down the country roads to the highway. Joey stepped down on the accelerator as they pulled onto the pavement. The car lurched forward and gathered speed.

Annie looked across at her little brother. She hadn't really paid attention to him in the last three years, not really looked at him. He was nearly grown now, full of over-blown self-confidence.

"Got to pick up my new watch at the jewelers—where Kurt works."

She nodded and smiled, then leaned her head back against the new upholstery. She had never smelled a new car before.

Joey wheeled into a parking space angling the curb.

"Think I'll walk down the street," she told him, "see how it feels to be among the living." That's how it felt, like she had stepped out of a long, sinister dream into the sunlight and the living world again. Feeble November sunshine bathed over her and a cool breeze brushed her face. As she passed Barney's café, the aroma of fresh coffee and frying hamburgers wafted out into the air. Even the lively noise of traffic brought exuberance. She looked in Allison's window at the new fall dresses. There was maroon wool, with square hobnails across the shoulders like a general's uniform, bias cut to cling across the hips. In the window's reflection she saw traffic behind her, red oil trucks and cars streaming by. How long had it been since she had had a new dress? Before she married Willis, she guessed—years.

A woman came out of the store. "Hey, aren't you that girl that everybody was looking for?" A matron with tight curls capping her head and a buttoned up brown coat that stretched tightly over bulging breast. "We all knew your husband was shot to death, and we just figgered they got you, too. Where was you, anyway?"

"I was..." Oh, God she didn't want this. There was no explaining it all. "I had to leave..."

The door of Barney's slammed closed, and another reflection appeared in the store window behind her, taller. "She had to take her daughter away, you know, for a vacation. Kind of away from here."

Annie turned, amazed to hear Robert St. Pierre explaining to the woman her whereabouts and surprised, too, at the excitement that pounded through her as she looked up at him.

"It was because her husband was murdered, wasn't it?" The woman turned her attention to Robert. "I knew it had to be because of that murder."

"Well, there you have it," he continued, not looking at Annie. "I guess you figured it out."

Annie was speechless as she looked up at him. How long had it been since she'd seen him? She couldn't be sure, so much had happened. It seemed long. She had wondered a thousand times why he hadn't come back after she told him of the rape. She was awkward, and unsure with him. How did he feel about her now? It wasn't her fault the enchantment had been broken...but then it wasn't his, either.

"You came to my rescue," she said. "Thanks." Did she sound too friendly? Flirtatious?

"The last time I saw you, you were burrowed in like a mole in the dormer rooms, and now, walking down the street?"

"It's over." She studied the lines of his face, wondering what thoughts lay behind those eyes. He could have come to comfort her, she thought, but then she reasoned, wanting to excuse him, he hadn't had as much time as she to deal with it, to absorb it.

"You thought it was over before."

The cafe door behind them slammed, and they both looked away. Did he think she was somehow responsible for the rape? Men thought that sometimes in spite of themselves. Nothing showed in his face. Maybe he was angry…or disgusted.

"I still have your jacket. The…" She said.

"My jacket?"

"I took it from your garage—that night…to put on."

"I am sorry I wasn't there."

It prickled at her that he had abruptly stopped coming to her once he knew what happened. "It had nothing to do with you," she answered.

He turned on her. His eyes were steady, intense, "I guess not," his words were slow, "if you don't want it to be." He walked away. People passed by on the street, but Annie hardly noticed as she watched him go. Trucks ground noisily to a stop at the new light in the center of town. Robert stopped, came back to her and leaned close. "Some animal tore into your body, and you say it has nothing to do with me?"

"I don't know, Robert, does it?"

Joey came out of the jewelry store. "Look here," he flashed the new watch back and forth on his wrist in the sunlight. "Ain't that a cute thing?"

She and Robert turned back to each other, so much aching to be said.

CHAPTER 58

That evening after supper with Otis and Henry, she stepped outside. Fog filled the yard rising over the saturated ground. In the distance a tower of muted light—a derrick—gave indistinct substance to the tool shed and garage. She walked to the end of a rock-embedded path, stood there feeling the chill in the light breeze, feeling the freedom to stand outside unafraid. It was over. The horror of the last weeks, the years of worry with Willis, over now. Now she needed time to think. Time lay before her, a life to begin again.

Hazy light from the kitchen splashed across the broken porch. Henry had driven the tractor into it—on that day! The day the monster died. Even in this eerie night, with leafless black tree limbs etching into the grayness, she was not afraid. Was she a new person? She thought of the night she had crawled up those porch steps, naked, scared, wounded, both cursing God and begging for help, and the brothers had opened their door.

Tomorrow she would venture out again. She would look for work. She would begin a new life. Willis's neurotic shame before her parents' new wealth would not be part of it. Hannah would be her life. At the end of the walk, she looked back at the house that had sheltered her. Those dear gentle souls had given her her life back.

But Robert? What of him? Today she had seen his eyes, sometimes indifferent, sometimes eager, but what she remembered was the anger. She understood him. One dream in his life had been broken, and now when he dared to dream again, another had been shattered. What they had had was only a fragile warm promise—but was it strong enough? Was he angry with her for the damage the monster had done to them both? She had to know.

When she came inside, Henry sat by the stove whittling on a piece of wood. Otis was on the floor playing with Hannah

As she sat with the brothers after supper, she was quiet, thinking of what she must do next. Go back to her house, go to work for Dutch. How would these men who had cared for her, react when she told them she was leaving? She looked down at Otis on the floor playing with Hannah, giggling with her, like a child himself. Maybe they were ready for her to go—thought they had done enough, that she had caused them enough trouble. They had murder on their conscience because of her.

Her throat was dry as she started to speak. "I think I will see if Dutch can take me back. I need to take care of myself—and Hannah, not impose on you anymore. There can never be a way to thank you enough or pay you back..."

Henry went to the cook stove, lifted the lid, and lit his pipe with a piece of kindling. "Annie," he turned, took the pipe from his mouth. "You don't need to pay us back...you and Hannah..." He looked down at Hannah, his forehead tightened into a frown. He didn't finish. He sat down again and continued whittling on a piece of oak, shaping it into the head of a walking stick. "It ain't for the two of us to hold you back if it's goin' you want, but no need to be in a hurry—winter comin' on."

She looked at Otis's wide back, hiding his face from her. There was going to be more to this than just leaving. They had never known a father's responsibility. But they brought Hannah into the world, nursed her when she was sick, sheltered them both, and destroyed the monster that preyed on them. They could never go back to the way it was before Hannah came into their lives.

Henry's head was down, silently working his knife over the wood. "Dutch probably gave your job to somebody else. I 'magine he did. Might not need you anymore."

Otis turned to face her. "There ain't many jobs around, Annie. Just oil jobs. None for women."

"I suppose not," Annie whispered. Hannah came to Henry and he took her hand to smooth over the wood he'd worked on. What would she and her baby have done without them? Where would they be? Maybe dead. But it wasn't gratitude Annie felt. She loved them.

"You don't need to make no fast decisions," Henry said.

CHAPTER 59

Sarah Emma pushed the bedcovers back and looked outside. Still dark. She went to the kitchen, shoved wood into the cook stove, struck a match and started a fire. The boarders would be down soon for breakfast and then she'd get busy on the pies before that crew from the Colclasure well came in for lunch. She rubbed her eyes, stretched, and then went back to her room to dress.

Quietly she slipped the ledger she'd been working on last night into a drawer, careful not to wake her daughter, asleep on a cot across the room. If she could just keep things up like they were going, she could pay off the note by this time next year and make a dent in the doctor bill her husband left. The shock of finding herself buried in debt after his death had given way to anger. He had kept her ignorant of all financial matters. Now confronted with this mountain of bills, she had had to learn by stumbling forward, feeling her way, trying to recover. She'd never on her own have owed a penny to a soul on this earth if she could've helped it.

After the men had eaten breakfast and gone off to the wells, she put some of their grimy clothes to soak in a tub on the back porch, then went to the pantry, took down four jars of canned apples, two jars of cherries, and two of blackberries, from the stock she had put up last summer. She turned the radio on, listening to the music while she made her pies. She smiled; the men said she was becoming famous for her pies. Finally, she put the last berry cobbler in the oven, sat down with a cup of coffee, and a newspaper one of the men had left.

"CAN THE ILLINOIS BASIN HANDLE THE BIG OIL BOOM?" Headlines questioned.

She took a sip of coffee and scanned the article. She was doing her part, housing and feeding eight boarders. The towns were all filled—every extra room, apartment, house or garage rented. Some of the men brought families from Texas or Oklahoma. The article said there were shacks of corrugated steel hastily thrown up near the Halliburton headquarters. Saturday nights, when everyone came out for shopping and the band concert, the streets in town were so full you could hardly make your way down the sidewalk—and there were so many she didn't know now.

She folded the paper and dropped it in the wastebasket. The men working on the Ellis well would be in soon, ready for lunch. And there was quilting this afternoon.

About one thirty, Sarah Emma headed out to Bethlehem Church in her 1937 Ford. She topped the overhead and made the big curve just past Dutch's Truck Stop when she saw a young woman alongside the road. Poor thing, she thought, hobbling in them high heeled shoes, no coat in this November chill. She shouldn't be out there on the road—a young girl like that. An invitation to trouble if there ever was one. There were men here without their wives, tempted to do wrong. Sarah Emma pulled over, leaned across the passenger side and rolled down the window.

"Honey, you okay?"

"What?" The girl did not come forward.

"I mean, is there a problem? Can I take you somewhere?"

The girl smiled. What a sweet little face, Sarah Emma thought. In that little skirt and sweater, she could be one of the schoolgirls.

"I got no problem," the girl answered, but did not come to the window.

"Well, honey you be careful out here. Whose child are you? I know about everybody around here."

"I'm kinda new."

My goodness, she was younger than her own daughter. "You sure I can't help you none?" The girl ought to get off the road to somewhere safe. She heard how her boarders talked about women.

"I'm waiting for…my husband."

"Well, you ought to find a better place to meet." Sarah Emma rolled up the window and drove slowly forward but was continually drawn back to the figure in her rear-view mirror. Just then a truck came down from the overhead, around the curve and pulled over. The girl got in.

As Sarah Emma arrived at the last basement step of the church, Sophie met her, all smiles. "Praise God, Sarah, Annie is all right. She's alive as you and me."

"Oh Sophie…" Sarah took her into her arms. "Annie's back? What happened?"

"I was never so shocked in my life." Sophie pulled back. "Glenn called me in the kitchen and there she stood." Sophie felt in her pocket for a handkerchief, blew her nose. "It was like she come back from the dead."

"Where's she been all this time?"

"This is not for everybody to know," Sophie dropped to a whisper, and they all gathered close, "but the Patrick brothers have been hiding her from those people that was after Willis. Annie said she couldn't tell nobody where she was so's they wouldn't have to lie. Goodness knows when the sheriff questioned me, I was sick with grief. I couldn't even talk."

Hattie frowned, looked past Sophie. "But how does she know she's safe now?"

"Annie said they're gone. Went away. Joey took Annie to town, and then back to the Patrick brothers. He saw the baby but...." Sophie looked up at Dora. "I want to hold my grandbaby again."

"Well, course you do," Dora soothed, "and you will. It'll be just like before."

"No," Sophie shook her head, "it'll never be like that again." She moved away from them, took her accustomed seat at the quilting table and they found theirs.

"Reckon you heard about the drowning?" Hattie said. "The Little Wabash River's been swollen so bad from all the rain but when the water went down, they found a car washed up against an outcropping of rocks about fifteen miles downstream and," she leaned close, "it had a body in it. They first thought somebody just went off the road but then they saw bullet holes. It was so smashed up it was hard to tell much. The body was so bloated they couldn't make out who it was."

"It was one of them mob people," Dora said. "Everyone says so. The bullet holes and everything. That's how they settle things."

The ladies fell silent, staring down at the quilt block they were stitching.

"It's them people that come in... God knows, the oil outfit is bad enough, but these people are different still." Sophie looked down. "You get in debt to 'em, they just kill you."

Sarah Emma stopped stitching, broke the silence. "There was this young girl just walking along the highway when I came out. A child really. I offered to take her somewhere, but she said she was waiting for her husband."

"She wasn't waiting for no husband, Sarah," Hattie said. "There was young girls seen out along the McAllister Road, when they were drilling so much out there."

Sarah Emma stared at Hattie. "You mean a prostitute? She's younger than my Betty."

"They bring 'em in and put 'em out on the roads to get the money from the men before they get to town. That's what Raymond McAllister told my husband."

"Who brings those...children in?" Sarah Emma was appalled.

Hattie didn't look up. "I don't know that I can say exactly who, but it's them that runs the gambling."

"The gambling they swear's not happening," Sophie said. "But we know it does,"

"It's them that's in with the man who drowned in the river...his car riddled with bullets and it's the people that killed Annie's Willis. It's them. The sheriff knows who they are but he don't do nothing. He's either scared to tangle with 'em or he's gettin' paid off."

That night Sarah Emma washed the dishes after her boarders finished their supper then went out to the porch, picked up the wash board and went to work on oily clothes that had been soaking all day. In the feeble glow of the porch light she hung them on the line outside to dry.

It was eleven when she crept to her room. She looked down at her daughter. Betty's dark hair fanned across the pillow, her face innocent and unmarred with care. Sarah Emma wondered about the girl she had seen this afternoon. Where was *she* at this very moment? She dropped to her knees at the foot of the bed. "Thank you, God," she whispered, "for helping me through all this bad time, for the customers you bring me, and for your protection of my family." She crawled up onto the bed, slipped under the covers, and fell into a deep sleep.

CHAPTER 60

Annie woke the next morning to voices drifting through the grate in the floor from the kitchen below.

"It's gettin' ready for winter, sure enough," Otis said to someone that had apparently just arrived. "Sit down here and let me pour you a cup of coffee. You want to see Annie?"

"If she's here…"

Robert! Annie pushed the covers back. Don't be too anxious, she thought.

"Course she's here…where else would she be." Otis sounded indignant.

Annie slipped into her best sweater and took some time with her hair. She glanced at Robert's old coat hanging on a hook behind the door. Don't take it. Let him ask for it.

All night she had seen his face hovering by her wanting to know…know what? Where things stood between them. No matter. They couldn't go back to where they once were.

On the bottom step she paused, a hard knot in her stomach. She looked at the closed kitchen door and willed herself to walk in.

"Morning." she nodded to Robert, sitting by Otis, hand wrapped around a mug. Something made him stand up, but she doubted it was courtesy. He fumbled with the chair nervously, and sat back down, seemingly surprised at himself.

"Did you sleep well?"

Formal, she thought. Was he was exploring to see if his words disturbed her. "About as usual."

She topped off their coffee, made toast for herself, and then she sat down opposite him, thinking how awkward he must feel. She couldn't think what to say. Henry was gone, probably doing the chores. Otis was reading the farm news.

Hannah came in, standing in the door in her flannel gown, rubbing sleep from her eyes.

"Robert," she cried, ran to him and cuddled against his shoulder and he rumpled her hair.

Annie got up, made another piece of toast, searching for words that didn't want to come. But there was so much to say, words pounding to be said.

She looked toward Otis. "I thought I'd take Hannah down in the woods this morning. There's a persimmon tree near the creek," she ventured. "We could gather up a few and I'll make a pudding."

"You'll have to shake the tree some to get the high ones down." Otis didn't look up from his paper.

"I could go shake the high ones down for you," Robert volunteered.

She smiled at him. "You can come with us, if you've got the time."

So they set off for the woods, Annie carrying a basket and Robert holding Hannah's hand. Crisp red and brown leaves crunched underfoot, the woods damp and pungent, mist rising in the treetops. They walked along saying nothing, until they came to a rickety footbridge.

"Bet those Patrick boys walked across this to school more'n half a century ago." Robert said.

"I walked on it, too," Annie said. "In that direction is a hollow oak that's always had bees around it. We used to dare each other to run over, tag the tree trunk and not get stung. It must be loaded with honeycomb. I'm sure the brothers haven't touched it in years."

"Maybe we can challenge the bees one day when it gets warmer," Robert answered.

They filed across the bridge uneasily as it creaked underfoot. On the opposite side stood the persimmon tree. Annie and Hannah began to fill the basket with mushy persimmons lying on the ground. Robert shook the tree limbs and Hannah held the top of her head, giggling, as the soft fruit rained down on them.

Annie and Robert stepped back and let Hannah fill the basket.

He turned to her, solemn, "Annie, I don't know how to live with this…what to say to you. How to be with you."

She kicked at the bed of leaves with her toe. "I've got nothing left over to give…to anyone." She felt the anger—hysteria rising. Someone pressing her about what happened. "I've been hardly alive."

He lifted her chin, "How is it now?" It was an earnest caring question.

"Better, by the grace of God and the Patrick brothers."

"I want to kill that bastard. I think about that—killing him."

"He's dead."

He stared at her. "How?"

An image flashed through her mind of the tearful brothers sitting in lamplight reading the Bible after forcing the rapist to drown in a rushing river. "He was found dead," she said.

He held both her shoulders, searching her eyes. "I have to know what he did and about you. I see him clawing at you…"

"Are you asking me to help *you*?"

"No, no. But I want to know one thing…did you…that is, was there anything that could have stopped…?"

She slapped him squarely across the mouth with all the fury and force she had in her. "You want to know if I let it happen…"

"No, no…Annie. I shouldn't have asked that. You're not yourself."

"No, I don't know who I am now." She grabbed the basket of persimmons and heaved it at him. She began to cry, a whimper first then in the open freedom of the woods a scream came and another and another from some deep spot in her, a furious primal protest at the mean, sickening toll that had been taken out of her.

"Mommy!" Hannah began to cry, too, as she picked up some of the lost persimmons.

Robert came to Annie, standing before her. He started to put his arm about her shoulder but stopped. "I'm...sorry. I think too much about it...all of it." A red bubble of blood oozed from his lips. "I don't know how it is...between us." He took her in his arms, but she pushed him away, ran across the footbridge, and stood facing him on the opposite side.

"Robert." Her throat burned from the screams. "I don't want us to be like this, but I don't think we can go on."

"Do you want to kill what we had...hoped we had?" he said.

"Remember the first time I saw you—so troubled? I wanted to do something for you, make you smile. That girl is gone, Robert. Now, I only want to tend my own wounds." She pushed her hair back and pulled her blue sweater tighter over the swell of her breast. "I don't want to kill what we had but I'm not sure I can make it live...that I have it in me. It makes me heartsick about..." She looked into the mist-shrouded black limbs of the woods. "I love you. I don't want you to be unhappy again."

He stood at the end of the footbridge, absorbing the impact of what she said—a puzzled expression on his lean, weathered face. Then an unjoyous smile twisted on his lips.

She turned back to him. He needed a haircut, his dark hair curled over the collar of his leather jacket. Why did she see these things, see he needed care? "You say nothing, Robert. Have I been...immodest, saying what I feel?"

"No, Annie, you can always say what you want to me."

He picked up Hannah and her basket, and walked across the bridge, then stopped by Annie, his hand touching her cheek, soft as a feather, a warm light in his eyes. "I don't think anyone was ever very concerned about whether my life was happy or not."

At the porch step, he put Hannah down and turned to Annie. "Can I come back?"

She looked into his questioning eyes. He still cared? The wonder of it!

"Yes."

Annie ran a match across the wick of the kerosene lamp, replaced the globe and put the lamp in the center of the table against the darkening evening. The single bulb hanging over their kitchen table brought them an electric bill in the mail box to which they were not accustomed, so the brothers did not use the electricity often.

Wind whistled through the loose windowsills of the old house. A knock came to the door. Her hand gripped the chair; she tried to still her rising anxiety. It's over, she told herself. She cracked open the back door. "Robert?" A sharp breeze poured in, as he stepped inside.

"Can you come with me for a while?"

She looked back. Henry was dozing on his cot and Otis reading while Hannah played on the floor. "I suppose. Why?"

"We need to do some talking."

She slipped into a jacket and pulled a sock cap down over her head. "I'll have to put Hannah to bed soon."

His car was warm as they backed out the long lane and onto the road. They passed white steepled Bethlehem church, with the oil well behind it, Robert's house, and turned onto a dark road going toward the highway. Annie's heart began to pound. She braced herself against the back of the seat. It was the road where the attacked happened. She hadn't been there since. She looked at Robert. What did he want? What was he trying to do? Fear tightened through her.

"I want out! Stop this car."

"I'm not going to hurt you, and no one else is." He stopped and pulled to the side of the road. He seemed surprised at her terror. "And no one else is," he said again.

She didn't answer.

He lit a cigarette, half turned toward her, his left hand on the steering wheel. She looked away from him into the darkness of the hedgerows. "I've thought about this for hours. There's something I have to say to you." She saw his handsome, serious face in the dim dashboard light. "When I met you, I was--dead to everything. I didn't know the world could be so cold. One day a woman smiled at me. She gave me something *free* in a restaurant and said, 'Merry Christmas'. That's all. In spite of myself I began to think and make little plans, like what I would say to you when I came to Dutch's the next time. I kept thinking I ought to know better than to build dream castles. They come down hard on you. Then there's the cold world, again. But you were there, and you were warm and kind. Annie, this attack wasn't just on you. It was on us." He took a drag on the cigarette, leaned forward, and put it out in the ashtray. "All you went through over Willis and I...well, you know about me. But we got some hope, both of us, a little bit of hope that things might just...be good for us."

"Yes," she whispered. Her eyes began to feel moist.

"I want to hang on to it, like it's my life."

"Yes," she said. "I understand."

But she stared away from him out the dark window. Fear-filled memory was beginning to throb through her and she began to talk--as though he weren't there.

In the black space of the dark window, the sinister dream was coming alive to her. "There was a knife at my throat," she whispered, almost to herself. "The edge was sharp. He pushed me in the car and drove. The car stopped...I don't know...somewhere. He pressed the knife into my throat harder, cutting my skin." She continued to whisper, living it again. She stopped, still staring into the blackness. "I screamed and screamed but he just laughed. I raised up and the knife edge sliced at my throat. He went on about Willis... and the money. I was outa my mind with terror. I knew *I'd* be dead in a few minutes...after.

"He said that there had been two chances to pay back the money...Willis and he hadn't, and I..." She was seeing it all again. "Then he said, 'what's left? Oh, yeah, the kid. You'll get the money before that.'"

She turned to Robert as if coming out of dream. "Then I knew he wouldn't do any more than rape me. He was out for Hannah." Her heart still pounded hard. She looked back at Robert, but he was staring across the steering wheel, seeing it, too.

"They don't make empty threats," she said.

She buried her face in her hands, quiet for a while. "What came later, I won't tell anybody, ever."

"It wasn't your fault, Annie, none of it."

She looked up at him puzzled, that he didn't know that already.

"You had no responsibility in this." He seemed to be settling this point in himself. Robert began to move the car forward, until they came to the cross roads, then he turned and finally parked the car under a tree in his own front yard. In silence and without touching, they walked around the house to the back door and went through the screened-in porch to the kitchen. He flipped on the light.

"Would you like something?'

"Hot tea, maybe." She was still shaken and exhausted.

Later he poured the hot liquid into a mug. It warmed her as it went down. He opened the kitchen cabinet and took down a bottle of Seagram from a top shelf. He set a flowered water glass before her. Some of the daisy design had been chipped away from the glass. He filled it to half full and swallowed some of it.

She studied him, as he sat across from her at the table. "I can't believe you would take me to that place, tonight, where it happened. I hate you for that."

"This morning you told me you loved me."

He looked down into his drink. "I thought if you went to the place where the worst thing in your life took place and you were safely there with me, you could let go of it...let go a little."

She shook her head. "Oh, I don't know what I think or feel. I don't know what I'll do. I hate myself for being this way. It's not me."

"I've never known a woman who actually had it happen..." he got up and went to the window. Orange light from the oil flares flickered in the blackness, "and now," he turned back to her, "it has to be you."

"You want me to help you get over this, Robert? I need you to help me," she spit out. "I need you to hold me and...and I don't know why you want to know about it. Are you jealous?"

"Maybe there's some of that in it."

"Of an animal?"

"That animal intruded into my world with you. What do you expect; I'm going to like it? That I'm not going to want to know?"

"Leave it alone. I want to forget."

"You won't forget."

"Not if *you* can't leave it alone."

He sat down again, elbows on the table, his chin in his hands. "We used to talk, Annie, about things...how money turned your family's head. I cherish the times when we used to talk."

He was opening a door, an old door. Okay, she thought, maybe this was the way back. Talk of old things.

"I thought when I met you, I'd found my best friend," she picked it up, trying too, to weave a bridge back between them. "I couldn't have said to anybody else that my own family looked down on me. That I knew I was an embarrassment to them in their new life--Kurt and I, and Glenn."

"Not your Mama, surely?" She saw the old spark come into his eyes.

"No, but she fumed about me marrying a Porter. She said they were no-quality kind of people. That was the beginning— when I married Willis." It felt good to remember what they used to talk about.

"I never thought your Mama was one to worry about 'quality'."

"Oh, quality is important to Mama, but it has nothing to do with money. It's about something you don't need to show off, like being solid and honest," Annie moved her tea cup around, outlining a scroll design in the oilcloth table cover, "like having pride in your character, and a charitable nature."

Robert took a drink from the daisy glass, letting her talk.

"Willis just kept trying to keep up with Papa's money," she looked across the kitchen at the sparse cabinets, wondering unconsciously how Robert cooked for himself. "But Willis didn't know how. That's the bottom line of it, Robert, for all of us. None of us know how. We don't know what to make of something we've not been used to, something that came too fast. Mama's a lost soul wandering around in that big house. And the truth is, though they don't see it, Evie and Papa are more lost than Mama."

"I know who's not lost because things have changed." he said.

"It doesn't matter if you got oil or not," she went on, not really hearing him. "The Allisons used to be the richest family in the county but no more. It's changed for the likes of them and they never got a drop of oil."

"Who do you suppose is the wealthiest person in the county now? Your father?"

"Maybe. But the Patrick brothers have more wells."

"Ah, they're the ones." Robert leaned back against his chair; relaxed in the jacket he still wore. "Nothing is going to change those old souls."

They both smiled at the thought of the two round old bachelors who lived in complete contentment, nearly oblivious to their wealth.

Then there was silence again. Back to where they started. The invisible monster between them. She realized that being with Robert tonight, some of the sadness had lifted; some of the bitterness was softening. He had cared enough to take this time with her, hoping he could make her feel safe.

He took another swallow from the flowered water glass. "I had begun to think about plans again, maybe even, if God was willing, to trust...."

She knew where he was going. Trying again to build something between them. She leaned across the table, "Do you still think you were wrong?"

"Not with you and never more than this morning when you tried to tell me you had become so selfish you couldn't love me anymore. Annie, I don't think you understand genuinely selfish people."

She didn't answer. She had traveled over strange terrain without him. She was not now the girl he had known before.

Robert sat back, looking down at the linoleum. "If you keep this a silent wound, wrapped deep in yourself, it will always be between us."

CHAPTER 61

Kurt Malvern sat in his truck, across the lake watching Lillian's house, waiting for Malcolm to leave. It was gray dawn, and cold. Waiting. Damn he was always waiting—waiting for the way to be clear. Now, that daughter was a presence to watch for. Truth was, she'd always been there.

Coralee. Kurt smiled. A pretty thing. The wind outside rocked the truck a little. He hunched in his jacket, waiting.

There he goes. Malcolm in his truck—a hunting trip this weekend with Sheriff Logan, Lillian had said, leaving early. Kurt started his truck. Bits of snow swirled before his windshield when he parked in the trees a short distance from Lillian's house.

She met him at the back door and took him into the warm kitchen, dim in early dawn and smelling of the coffee brewed for Malcolm's thermos.

"I'll go in and talk to Coralee, if Malcolm awakened her," Lillian whispered. "You go upstairs to my room—the one at the top of the stairs. Close the door. I'll be there." She kissed him hungrily and left. She had never invited him in—all the way into her house and now he was to go into her room, and in daylight. He was getting closer to her. She was giving him more of herself.

He went through the kitchen and the big dining room with more look-alike chairs than he had ever seen at a table. He heard their voices, Lillian's and Coralee's. He began step by step to move up the stairs. Almost at the top he saw Lillian standing in the doorway of her daughter's room, her legs apart, light shining through the thin gown and robe she still wore. His breath quickened.

Coralee was apparently awake, mother and daughter talking. When he was in Lillian's room, he softly closed the door. A purple satin cover was turned back. Kurt took off his clothes and lay naked on the rumpled sheets where Malcolm had slept. He liked that, lying down where Malcolm lay beside his wife. He could still hear the distant murmur of conversation from Coralee's room, and the wind driving against the windows. He ran his leg over the satin, savoring it. This is how it is to live rich, he thought, lying warm and snug under a purple satin cover while the wind outside chilled the rest of the world.

He sat up on the edge of the bed and picked up an orange sheet of paper from the nightstand on Malcolm's side.

TURKEY SHOOT
THE GROVES AT WALKER PRESTON COUNTRY CLUB
NOVEMBER 19, 1940
MEMBER FEE $15, NON-MEMBERS $75
RIFLE AND ARCHERY COMPETITION
SEE IRWIN PRESTON

Kurt lay back on the bed, fingers clasped under his head, his eyes searching the ceiling. He'd heard of the turkey shoot. It happened every year, but those who participated were people he only knew by name, the ones who belonged to the Walker Preston Country Club and he would hardly know about that. He wondered how they went about getting into the competition, and he wondered, too, if any of those dandies in the competition could hit the ground with their hat.

He put the paper on the table, stretched back on the bed and allowed himself to sink deep into purple satin. The door opened. Lillian stepped inside, closed it, and pushed the lock. She stood there outlined by the doorframe, untying her robe. It dropped to the floor, the filmy gown veiling her body and the shadowy triangle between her legs. Kurt slid up against the headboard. "God," he whispered. That was more than Malcolm could handle! He came to her, kissed her and caressed away the gown until she stood, a golden temptress in the firelight. He continued to kiss her, lingering over her entire body and then he carried her to the bed, the bed, he pictured, where Malcolm loved her—or did he? He held her gently in his arms, loving her a long time because he knew it was really love she needed. Then his own need became intensely insistent, and his mind again numbed to all but that velvet oblivion that addicted him to her.

Later, she turned on the pillow to face him. "You could stay a little." Her words were soft and sweet as honey. "Coralee likes to sleep late and Malcolm is gone for three days." He looked at her, hunger gone now, only reality, and again was overcome with that hatred in himself for what he was. And what he realized could not be.

"I think I better go." He stood up and pulled on his jeans. His eyes picked out lines on the flyer; "TURKEY SHOOT", he buttoned the top button of his jeans, "NON-MEMBERS $75," "SEE IRWIN PRESTON."

The next morning, Kurt drove slowly along the land that once belonged to Walker Preston, looking for the entrance to the Preston grounds. He turned in and drove down the lane toward the two-story house with a sculpted roof that somebody had said was French style. Old Walker Preston had been the banker in town, but when the '29 crash came, his bank closed. He sold his land to the city for taxes with a request they make it a park, which they did, and still later, part of it, a country club.

Irwin Preston came to the door.

"I understand you're the one to see if I want to be in that Turkey Shoot?"

"Yes-s," Preston said. "It's $75 for non-members?"

"I've got the money."

"Why don't you just come in?" He pushed away at the clutter, found a place for Kurt to sit, and extracted a paper from a stack on a nearby desk. "Now, you just put your name down, here." He watched as Kurt wrote out his name on the top line.

"Kurt Malvern." Preston eyed him for a moment. "I've seen you around."

"I 'magine so. I've been here all my life."

"Malvern. Yes." he looked again at Kurt's name. "That's the family that's got all those oil wells out there, isn't it? How does that feel? Rolling in money?"

"I'm not much used to it yet, besides the money's in my dad's pocket."

"You ever been to the Turkey Shoot before?"

"This is my first time."

"Well, this is how it works. We meet over by The Grove. It'll be Saturday at 9 a.m. Bring your own rifle, of course. You got one?"

"I got one."

"We take our turn, best shot takes home half the purse and a turkey."

"Half the purse?"

"Well, yes. There's this club, mostly the young guys that got into hunting with bows and arrows. The Archery Competition takes the other half of the purse and the winner gets the other turkey."

"Sign me up for that, too. The archery part."

"Now you are a comer, aren't you? Ever shoot with a bow before?"

"Now and again."

"The archery is a little different, usually there's ladies around, cheering on their husbands or fathers or boyfriends. Like I said, its mostly young men. The custom is for the winner to give the arrow to some lady. Competition gets pretty lively."

"I'll bet. Who's the winningest?"

"Who's the man to beat? Oh, that'd be Sheriff Logan with the rifles. He's got to keep up target practice, you know. There's others that have a good day but Logan's probably the best."

"Logan?"

"He's not into the bow and arrow stuff, though." John Preston stood up. "The one there would be Bucky Allison. I'll have to take your seventy-five dollars now, sir."

"Right here." Kurt pulled out four twenties and laid them side-by-side on the table. "Any more for both competitions?"

"No. That gets you in for either one or both." Irwin Preston handed Kurt his five-dollar change. "You much of a hunter, Mr. Malvern?"

"Depends on what I'm after." Kurt pocketed his five dollars and left.

CHAPTER 62

Kurt pulled his truck under the bare limbs of an oak tree, a short distance from what was called The Grove. A crowd was gathering. In the distance they were setting up the target, the grove of trees behind it. Early morning had been foggy, and a mist still hung in the dense woods, a dark overcast day with a damp chill in the wind. Thanksgiving was four days away.

Kurt thought there were probably twenty-five men standing about, rifles in the elbow of their arm. As he neared the group, he noticed two crated turkeys to one side.

A truck came past him, stopped, and unloaded a couple of dozen white folding chairs. Malcolm Powers sat at a table by Irwin Preston taking money from those who had not yet paid. A couple of men bailed out of a truck and begin placing the chairs in a double row to watch the competition. Behind the chairs was the check-in table. Kurt walked to the table.

Irwin Preston looked up. "Mr. Malvern, morning." He looked down his list. "There you are, paid in full. Got you down for number five. You'll be up right after Alex Bunnell." Kurt took his number, pinned it to his left sleeve, gave a perfunctory nod to Malcolm and walked away.

Others were arriving, some spectators slipping into their chairs. Ella Donnelly and one of the Allison women were with a couple Kurt didn't know. Several men who weren't in the competition took seats. Then he saw Lillian with Coralee walking toward the chairs. She had not seen him. He turned away, moved in with the competitors. Something of a line was beginning to form.

Sharply at 9 a.m. Irwin Preston shot a pistol in the air. "Number one in the shooting competition is Dorance Allison."

Dorance stepped up to the line carrying his new Remington. He carefully poised himself. Gun to his shoulder, setting his sights. Took it down, took a sighting again. Squeezed the trigger. Three men ran forward and checked it with a ruler. "On the edge of the red ring outside the bull's-eye," they called. "Four inches off."

"Stand aside, son. We'll see how the rest goes," one of the judges instructed.

Next came Thomas Donnelly, who after some sighting and consideration, centered his sights and fired.

Again the judges came forward, "You got on the target, Tom, but touching the outside rim." This shot eliminated Dorance Allison, so he took his seat while Thomas Donnelly stood aside as the man to beat.

Sheriff Logan stepped quickly to the line, raised his rifle to his shoulder and immediately squeezed off a shot. The judges rushed forward and began measuring.

"Bulls-eye," Harley Brown, one of the judges, yelled, "About three fourths inch off center. Good work, Sheriff."

The audience cheered and clapped.

The sheriff stood to one side, smiled and nodded to the spectators, as Thomas Donnelly went to his seat.

Alex Bunnell raised his rifle over his head with both hands as he walked to the line. "Been practicing for this, folks."

Somebody called out, "You nail it, Alex boy." He leveled his rifle and set his sights. Kurt saw the barrel waver. Then he fired.

"Good shooting, son, but way over to the side of the Sheriff."

Sheriff Logan patted his shoulder as he passed by. "Next year, I'm gonna watch out for you. You're getting dangerous."

Kurt was next. He walked forward. He could feel eyes boring on his back. He raised his rifle, an old Springfield he'd carried into the woods since he was thirteen. He leveled the barrel and for a brief space stilled it, raking his index finger over the curved metal. Again he took his sights, finger curling lightly over the trigger. He pulled quickly. The judges rushed forward.

They inspected the target, talked softly, and huddled together. One pulled out his ruler and measured both ways across the yellow center. Then they turned, glanced briefly at Kurt, before apologetically addressing Sheriff Logan. "Looks like it went square in the center, Sheriff."

The Sheriff started to walk toward the target, and then apparently thought better of it. He dropped the butt of his rifle to the ground, grasp the barrel, pursing his lips. Without saying a word, he took his seat.

"Sorry, sheriff," one of the judges tentatively called out.

Kurt stepped to one side, the place the others had stood; the place of the one to eliminate. Those in the gallery said nothing. He didn't look their way, knew they were looking at him standing there waiting to be bested, knowing there could be no better shot.

The others came forward, but with the sheriff out, the challenge was gone. Kurt Malvern lacked the stature, in their eyes, to be of much consequence.

After all contenders had taken their turn, the judges stepped before those seated, the contestants milling behind them, and announced, "Kurt Malvern is our new sharpshooter. Just new this year and acquitted himself with great skill. He takes home a turkey and half the purse."

There was a light smattering of applause.

"Now, we'll move on to the Bow and Arrow people," Irwin Preston announced. "They can show us how they got those turkeys for the first Thanksgiving. That'll be starting in about twenty minutes when we get set up. We're gonna need a little help moving these chairs."

Kurt went over to the caged turkeys, picked one up, heaved it onto his shoulder and walked across the space where the gallery was reshuffling itself. Lillian caught his eye, a frown gathering across her brow. Kurt tipped his hat to her and to Ella Donnelly and old Mrs. Mathursia Allison in an impersonal gesture just before he dropped the gobbling bird into his truck bed.

"Hi, Kurt," Coralee called out a cheerily greeting, as the gallery reseated themselves. "You did good."

Her mother pulled her down to her seat, "Don't make a fool of yourself."

"But Mother, Kurt just won…"

"Be quiet, Coralee. Why do you care what he won, anyway?"

"Because…he's Kurt, and look how good he shoots."

The competition for the archery contest was much smaller, a different composition, primarily younger than the riflemen, but with some overlap. Sheriff Logan did not compete.

Bucky Allison came first, the one they were all waiting for. He took his sights, slowly pulled back on the belly string and let go. The arrow caught at the edge of the red ring around bulls-eye center. Bucky stepped to one side.

Davey Preston, Irwin Preston's son, came forward, pulled on the bow and let go.

"Not too bad, Davey, for a learner," Preston said. "Now let's see." The judges began to measure. "Off center about one and half inches."

The next contestant's arrow whizzed past the target and stuck in a tree some distance into the grove. Five more contestants stood in line before Kurt. One hit the blue band and another the outside white band. Finally Kurt stood at the line.

The audience rose, hushed, watching. They had seen him with a rifle.

"Good luck!" A voice called from behind. Coralee!

Slowly he took aim, as he had since his father had made bows out of hickory limbs for him and for Glenn when they were children. He pulled back with the arrow between his fingers, until he felt the string go taut, sighted the imaginary trajectory of the arrow and let go. He knew before the dead thud of contact it made the mark. He stood back, sure of his ability. The judges moved to measure and record. "Well, it's a perfect center for you again, Mr. Malvern." It was a grudging remark. There were no jubilant smiles this time, no cheers or applause. "Come get your arrow. There may yet be a tie." Kurt walked briskly forward and pulled out his arrow.

Most did hit the target and Adam Donnelly broke into the edge of the hole made by Kurt's arrow. Finally the judge turned to Kurt, "Well, Mr. Malvern, looks like a sweep for you. You're going have to eat two turkeys this year." There was soft applause from the gallery.

"Just a minute." It was Sheriff Logan, "I'd like a re-match on that shooting competition. That was pretty damn close. It's a dark day, a little foggy."

"Well, now Sheriff, we never have done that before. It was pretty clear." The judge turned to the other two. "Didn't you boys think it looked pretty decisive?"

Harley Brown looked down, evasive, scratching at the short hairs on the nape of his neck.

"Fine!" Kurt stepped forward. "Let's do her over again. Get this settled. Sheriff can go first. Whatever he likes."

Everyone moved back to their original positions.

The Sheriff ambled up to the line. "I'll follow you."

"Suit yourself." Kurt loaded his gun and waited by the sheriff while they set up a new target.

"What the hell are you trying to pull off here, Malvern?" Logan growled under his breath.

"Sheriff, I can take the prize any time." Kurt's voice was low, "The turkey and anything else I want and what's more I'm a free man. The mob don't own me."

The sheriff was six inches from Kurt's face. "Don't say what you can't back up," he hissed.

"Where you s'pose all these rumors start, then?" Kurt kept his eyes straight ahead.

The sheriff was about to answer but was cut short, as they called Kurt to shoot first.

Kurt moved to the line, fitted the stock to his shoulder, took a slow sight and fired.

The judges measured. "Perfect bulls-eye. Right where it went before. Can't do no better'n that, Sheriff."

Logan went up to the line, silent. Carefully, this time he took sight. He raised his head up, sighted it again, and squeezed the trigger.

"That un dead center, too. Can't even see where it changed Malvern's."

"Well, we've not got another target." Harley Brown said. "This sort of thing never happened before."

"We'll call it a tie," the other judge announced.

"No," Kurt said, "we'll make a target and keep this up 'til one of us misses. Whittle off some of the bark on that tree yonder. Draw a circle on it. That's all we need to decide this."

The two stepped back while the judges made an improvised target.

"You're mighty good, Sheriff." Malvern whispered, his eyes on the men drawing a target on a patch of tree trunk scraped of its bark. "Course when you shoot at trees, they don't shoot you back. It's another thing, trackin' down a real killer, like the one that killed my brother-in-law. 'Member him, Sheriff? Willis Porter? Dumped him on his door step, three bullets pumped into him." Kurt smiled but looked straight ahead. "Same number as you're getting ready to shoot off now. 'Magine how that'd feel. Three bullets hittin' your body."

"You're gonna mess up one of these days, Malvern," His breath was warm near Kurt's ear, words drilling into him. "And I'm going make it the worst day you ever lived."

"OK, Sheriff," Harley Brown called, "we're ready."

Logan took aim. Kurt saw the barrel waver. Logan steadied himself, fired.

"Just inside the line, Sheriff," Harley yelled. "Sorry, Logan."

As Kurt stepped up, he heard the silence. They wanted him to miss. They wanted to know that their tight little world had not been challenged. Everything was as it always had been.

Kurt slowly took aim, never feeling so defiant in his life. He pulled the trigger. Loose bark flew from the tree on impact. "It's right there, Harley," one of the judges said. "It's in the middle." He turned to the crowd. "It's got to go to Mr. Kurt Malvern."

Coralee stood up clapping, then ran to Kurt, threw her arms around his neck and kissed him. "I am so-o proud of you." Coralee's adoring eyes were on Kurt. "Can I have that arrow?"

"I guess," he stammered, watching Lillian walk toward him, glaring at them both. "I'll bring it…excuse me."

"I told you to stay away from my daughter," Lillian hissed under her breath.

"She just said she was proud of me. Aren't you proud of me?"

"I was embarrassed for you. Humiliated."

"I beat everyone of 'em in everything. Now how embarrassed do you think I should I be?"

"You are arrogant…"

"Mama…" Coralee protested.

"Yeah, and that's why you like me…" He leaned close to her ear. "and my ass."

"Stay away from my daughter."

She started to walk away, but he followed her and caught her arm. "Why don't you let that girl out of the cage? You don't need her for a pet. You've got me."

"That girl is none of your business, and you're way over the line telling me how to raise her"

"Lillian, look at her. She's raised."

He let her go as she pulled away, then picked up the crate with the second turkey, and loaded it onto his truck bed.

CHAPTER 63

He drove around town with two turkeys in his truck. One he'd take to the Patricks' for Thanksgiving with Annie but be damned if he'd take the other one to his parents. Eva Mae would want to know where he got it, and how the Allisons looked, and what they said to him.

Then it came to him. Sure, why not. He drove up to Lillian's house, took out a crated turkey and knocked on her door.

It was Malcolm who came.

"Mr. Powers," Kurt stammered, feeling awkward. "I got two turkeys today. I guess you saw that. Can't use but one. You might as well have the other. Your daughter seemed real excited when I won."

"What a generous thought, Mr. Malvern. I have to say that was a mighty fine shooting exhibition you treated us to this morning. About time Logan had some real competition. Step on in here. If you could just take the turkey to the kitchen, we'll take care of it from there."

Lillian, sitting at the table, looked up startled to see Kurt standing in her kitchen, wooden crate in hand.

"A turkey, Madam, for your table."

She drew back in her chair as he held the big crate with a cackling bird before her. "Why did you bring that thing here?"

Malcolm took the crate and placed it in the middle of the table. "Mr. Malvern is offering us one of his prizes, Lillian. Says he can only use one."

"Kurt," Coralee appeared at the door. "Oh, Kurt, did you bring me my arrow?"

"Right here." He pulled it from the edge of the crate.

"Give that thing back, Coralee." Lillian snapped.

"I want it. I will not give it back."

"You are not keeping it, young lady."

"I will keep it."

"Your daughter was the only one to congratulate me this morning." Kurt put the arrow in her hand. "She gets the arrow."

Lillian stared at him. "My daughter never talks like that to me." The turkey in front of her began to fill the room with its loud gobbling. Lillian looked at the bird with disdain.

"Lillian." Malcolm was frowning, confused. "I've never seen you so ungracious."

"Don't be cross with Kurt, Mama. He's nice. He gave me my white squirrel, Biscuit, and now this turkey and…"

Lillian stood up so abruptly her chair almost tipped backward. "You gave her that squirrel? We hired you to build a boat house, then you got a little bit of money…you people think that's all there is to it."

"No, I know there's more to it than that," Kurt mocked with feigned seriousness. "There's demeanor."

"Daddy, make Mama be nice," Coralee said.

Lillian's eyes blazed. "You people think now you can just bull your way in anywhere."

Malcolm stood by, puzzled at his wife's outburst. "Lillian, this is hardly the way to treat this man. He not only built our boathouse … he painted our house. I am sorry, Kurt…isn't it…my wife can be abrupt, but we are not snobbish people."

"Mama doesn't mean any of what she's saying, Kurt," Coralee said. "We like the turkey, don't we Daddy? I'll walk you to the door."

Under the questioning eyes of her husband, Lillian gathered her dignity about her. "No, Coralee, sit down. I'll see him out."

At the door Kurt turned, smiled and whispered, "Does that mean I am never to come here—my sweet little darlin'?"

"No Malvern is going to have my daughter. Do you understand?" Her sharp words ripped him.

"I do," sobered, he nodded. "You want my ass all to yourself. No young stuff."

"You are the most despicable…trash—an animal…anything that's female. You think I am jealous of my own daughter?" Her eyes bore into him, her cheeks flushed, even in the cold November day. "How can you imagine I'd think that?"

Then her gaze softened. "…after all we have had together?"

She studied him for a moment. "You absolutely cannot come into my life, Kurt. Do you understand me?"

"I do, Ma'am, perfectly. My place is on your back porch."

She slammed the door in his face.

Kurt sauntered to his truck, whistling as he crawled in the cab and the other crated turkey cackling beside him.

CHAPTER 64

A couple of hours later, back in his apartment, Kurt heard a noise outside--a crunch in his driveway. "Lillian," he whispered, excitement building in spite of himself. Back to say she was putting on that show just for her husband, and she didn't mean it. He moved to the door. Then she'll want to get laid. It was not going to happen this time, he decided as he opened the door before she could knock.

"Coralee!" He looked beyond her; to the bicycle she left lying in the drive. "Does your mother…"

"No, Mama does not know where I am." There was a certain resolve in her voice he hadn't noticed before. "I want to apologize to you for my family. Well, just Mama."

Kurt felt a cold sweat inside his clothes. He hadn't thought of this happening. "You don't have to do that. I—maybe went a little too far."

"You gave us Thanksgiving dinner and Mama ordered you out of the house. That's just wrong." Her eyes, simple and beseeching, were on him.

He began to retreat reaching for some kind of safety.

"I'm very sorry, Kurt. I know how nice you are."

He looked at her honest, serious face "Well, your Mama made it pretty clear that money in the pocket don't take seediness off the coat."

"May I step inside?" Coralee asked.

"Of course. Sure." He grabbed his jacket and dirty shirt off a straight back chair and pulled the chair forward. "There's a seat for you."

"Mama... It's like she puts people on pegs, high pegs, low pegs."

Careful now, Kurt thought. This is treacherous ground. "I don't know your Mama too well, but she seems..."

"Oh Kurt, she doesn't like you one bit."

"How so?" Kurt stood awkwardly in the middle of the room, feeling that to sit down with her was too inviting. Too receptive.

"You're part of the trash that got the new money, she says, and they're all trying to take over."

"She says that, does she?" Not much news there, he thought.

"I think if people are nice, that's enough."

Kurt studied the girl. She had always been so timid, childlike. Coming here was probably the first thing she had ever done without her mother's direction—knowledge, even. "I think you're about right on that," he nodded. There was something new in her manner, stronger maybe. He couldn't decide what it was. How had she got away from home?

"Well whatever... just keep thinkin' for yourself. That's what you should do." He noticed her eyes were a little watery and cheeks pink from the chill outside. "You've got lots of thinkin' to do," he said quickly, wishing she would leave. But she looked fresh and young; and he had never seen her so bright and alive.

"You're the nicest man I've ever met."

Wisps of unruly dark hair curled on her temple. He wanted to push it back. He felt sorry for her, tempted even to comfort her, but he must not do that. He heard Lillian's hard words, "anything female." He must not! He hoped she would not come to him, as she sometimes had. But she sat composed in the chair, head down, and fingers buttoning and unbuttoning her sweater. "I guess you can see I care for you," she whispered.

He pulled out another straight-back chair, sat down opposite her, and took her hands in his. "Coralee, you're like a little flower in the woods, starting to break through to the sunlight...just starting. It'd be cruel to step on it, wouldn't it? I mean before it breaks through and gets to grow." He knew he was talking all around what he meant. She couldn't understand, anyway.

She looked confused for a second, and then said, "You are my very best friend, Kurt." A gleam came into her eyes, "Do you think I'm pretty as Mama?"

Kurt pulled back in his chair, studying her with affected concentration, then he leaned forward. "I think you're a beautiful person."

"I'd rather have a pretty face."

"No you wouldn't." He stood up. "I told you, you have a lot of thinking to do." Her hands were still in his. He gently raised her to standing before him. "Coralee, you should not come here again. I live here alone and the neighbors, well, Mrs. Celteaux has a mean tongue. I wouldn't have harm come to you on my account."

"But Kurt, I...like you."

"Please. Don't come here."

CHAPTER 65

"Dear Father, God," Henry Patrick began as they sat around his kitchen table, "we thank You for all these people seated here with us, and for the fine bird Kurt brought to our table and the fine food Annie cooked. We ask You to look after Glenn, who will put on his country's uniform and will leave us soon. Bring him home safe. Thank you, too, most graciously for…Annie and…the little girl…" Henry's voice quavered, then he stopped, swallowed and finished with his hasty "Amen."

Robert had come by several times in the last two weeks and readily accepted Annie's invitation to join them today. His hand found Annie's under the tablecloth and closed over it when they all looked up.

Otis broad face was beaming, "Not even when Ma and Pa lived, we never had people at the table like this—seven people. It's a great day." He looked gleeful as a child.

Roasted turkey sat before them, its savory aroma filling the downstairs rooms. "Annie's a real good cook," Henry added.

Beside the turkey, sat dishes mounded with sweet potatoes, beans, onion pie, hot biscuits, a cut glass bowl of churned butter and honey in a white enameled pitcher. The kitchen stove warmed the room until windows were covered with steam. At the edge of the stove, a hickory nut pie and persimmon pudding waited to be served with steaming coffee.

"Thank you for thinking of me," Glenn spoke quietly.

"How come you're not at your own Ma and Pa's house?" Otis blurted out. "Its Thanksgiving, and you're fixin' to leave. Seems you ought to be there in a special seat with them."

Annie looked first to Glenn, who seemed to concentrate on his sweet potatoes, then to Kurt. No one spoke.

Kurt blew across the top of his coffee, silent for a moment, and then said. "Papa and Mama went with their new friends. Glenn's leaving don't come until Wednesday. Plenty of time for social climbing till then." Kurt's voice rang with sarcasm. He put his hand on Glenn's shoulder. "Anyway, Glenn's special every day with Annie and me."

"Danny Allison's goin', too." Glenn looked about. He was still tanned, and his hair sun streaked from working in the oil fields all summer. "Right up there alongside me at the Great Lakes Naval Base. He's not such a bad sort."

"Allisons always shine out big wherever they are," Kurt said.

Annie watched Kurt and Robert, whom she had never seen together, each man taking the other's measure. "Glenn is here with us now," she smiled, "and maybe we won't even get into the war."

"That's right," Robert said. "No telling how things'll turn out."

Otis wore new bright blue overalls for the occasion. "There's gonna be war." He sounded irritated. "Everybody knows there's gonna be a war. Any day now."

"Now, Otis." Henry did not look up from the turkey he was carving, knife and fork in hand. "We don't know that. You get some mule-headed idea going, Otis, and that's all you can see. You're gettin' worse every day. Here, Glenn give me your plate."

"Glenn probably won't have to go anywhere dangerous." Robert smiled, trying to smooth things over.

"War'll make the price of oil go up and up. Already has," Otis kept on, undeterred.

"What do you care about the price of oil, Otis," Robert passed his plate to Henry, "you don't spend the money you've got."

"Yeah," Kurt teased, "how many wells did you get last month, Otis?"

"Never got none last month," Otis answered solemnly, his shiny baldhead bent over his plate. "One's probably comin' in next week. The price goes high enough it'll pay 'em to drill deeper like they keep sayin'. They'll need oil—the war and all."

Annie watched Glenn staring, eyes frozen wide, at a salt and pepper set. He had not taken a bite.

"I don't like this talk," Annie cut in. "It should be about what we're thankful for. Thanksgiving came at just the right time, because I am so thankful for Henry and Otis. And we're all here together."

Glenn seemed relieved at the change in mood.

"Annie," Henry held his fork midway to his mouth, "we never knew how empty it was here before you came to us."

"Thank you." Annie looked across at Henry. "I'm grateful the bad times are over and for my brothers who remember our old times--and for you and Otis."

"What about you, Kurt?" Glenn said.

Kurt looked up with a grin, "I'm thankful for being a crack shot."

They had gone around the table, and now attention was on Robert. He turned to Annie, looked at her and smiled. "I thank God I found Annie...and someone to love."

Annie caught her breath at this unexpected declaration before her family. She trembled, looked away from him, glanced at her brothers, then back to Robert. A surging thrill poured through her, lifting her. "Robert..." she whispered, startled by tears smarting at her eyes, looked at his lean, handsome face watching her expectantly.

She didn't know what to say. She stood up finally. "We need some light," she said. Feeble sunlight had faded, the room darkening although it was only late afternoon. She got the lamp and lit it, wondering, unsure now, as she placed it in the center of the table, if she was capable now of giving love to anyone.

Finally she said, "I am thankful for Robert..." she stopped. "He cared enough to...not leave..." She couldn't go on.

Seeing his sister's awkwardness, Kurt turned quickly to Henry, "Why don't you boys get electricity in this house? At least turn on that lonesome naked bulb up there."

"Can't do that." Otis came back. "All them people would want to come in here and get warm."

"You mean the oil guys?" Robert's hand sought Annie's under the table as she sat back down.

"Not them. Not the oil guys. The others. Them, out there, in the trees. The ones on the garage."

Everyone turned to Otis, silently questioning, watching him as he ate unaware of their attention.

"There ain't anybody there, Otis," Henry corrected gruffly.

"They're there." Otis reached for a biscuit and buttered it. "All the time, all over."

Annie went to him, enclosed him in her arms, tears sliding down her cheeks. Otis looked up, confused.

Thanksgiving dinner lasted long past the last cups of coffee, and on into the evening. Both brothers, with no afternoon nap, were unabashedly yawning before the clock struck eight. Glenn stood ready to leave. Everyone, they were all painfully aware, was planning to be at the train station on Wednesday to see him off, along with Danny Allison and Bill Anderson.

After Glenn and Kurt left, Annie walked out into the darkening evening with Robert. "Do you have to go, too?" she asked. Lamplight cut into the darkness, splashing from the window in a square patch of light near them on the demolished porch. In the pale glow, bits of snow drifted and tumbled in the lazy breeze, the ground already wearing a variegated blanket of grey and white.

"Yes, it's been the best day I've had in a long time."

"Robert," he stood close not touching her, "my mind is in a tangle," she said. "I should leave; go to work but now..." she glanced back at the window, "when things were so bad for me for so long, those two were my only solid ground. Now Otis... poor old sweetheart."

"And if you don't take care of them," he searched her face, "what then?"

"I don't know. I owe them my life. My daughter's life."

"They're lucky to have you."

"It's me that's lucky. They are the most innocent, honest... They..." She looked at him and stopped, dared not finish. She would never tell what they did, betrayed everything they believed was right, preformed the ultimate act for her—took another's life to give hers back for her.

Robert pushed a long lock of her hair back from her shoulder. "What about us?" he whispered.

"Us?" There was so much pouring through her mind. "I don't know."

He reached for her, held her. "You have become *my* life."

Her first impulse was to pull back, the body's memory freezing her with fear. But she didn't. Then slowly, willing herself, she parted his unzipped jacket, moved close to him, felt the warmth of his body against her, the rise of his chest, beat of his heart. She leaned into him, felt his warm breath on her cheek, felt a safe fortress inside his arms.

"Just hold me." She laid her head on his shoulder for a long time, feeling part of him, at one with him. "Please, understand me for a while." She drew back and looked at him. "Can you? For a while?"

He picked a snowflake from her hair and then another and another, then cupped her face in his hands and kissed her lips softly. "I'm not going anywhere."

CHAPTER 66

The morning was desperately cold, snow covering the ground and beginning to drift along the hedgerows. Annie dressed Hannah in her green snowsuit for the ride into town. Robert would come by soon.

Otis hovered by the stove. "Glenn goin' back to the Navy, today?"

Annie nodded as she pulled on her coat "Along with Bill Anderson and Danny Allison. When they'll get back is anybody's guess." She swallowed away a hard knot in her throat, "what with the news and all."

"It's a raw day." Henry turned from the window. Robert's car had just come to a stop in the driveway. "Dunno if Otis's up to a trip to the train station."

Otis grabbed for his boots drying out under the stove, "Nothin' wrong with me."

"Well then, if you're bound and determined to go, Otis." Henry scowled. "We got some business in town that ought to be took care of."

"I'm goin'," Otis groaned as he stood up.

Henry looked over the top of his glasses. "Robert's out there in the car, waiting, Annie."

Henry nodded as she opened the door. "We'll be along later."

Robert and Annie dropped Hannah off at Belle Dorsett's beauty shop before they went to Dutch's for hot soup and coffee. When she walked in, it felt like old times, Dutch's parrot called out "Pretty Baby," and oil crew workers sat along the bar laughing at some joke. That hadn't changed, Annie thought, but she didn't know any of them or the new waitress.

They slid into a shiny green leather booth and Robert leaned forward. "This feels something like a date."

Annie smiled. "The first time I saw you sitting where you are, you looked like you crawled out of a rat hole. I'll never forget how everybody stopped and stared."

"That feels like a life long ago."

When they got to the train station, Glenn sat on a wooden bench with Kurt. Sophie looked up at Annie and smiled. She had her arm locked in Glenn's, holding him close. "You got to write to us, son. Tell us what you're doin'—all that's happening."

"I will Mama, I promise," Glenn said.

John Malvern turned to Annie. "Guess this is St. Pierre."

"Yes, Papa this is Robert and..."

Robert extended his hand. "Everybody knows John Malvern."

Sophie smiled at Robert, but there were tears in her eyes. "Those boys are so young..." She looked away, as if searching for something else to say. "Eva Mae's coming with Danny pretty soon." It had been two weeks since Annie had spoken with her parents even though they lived less than ten minutes apart. Annie looked at her father and wondered if this wall would always separate them.

John Malvern turned to her. "I guess you care enough for the Malverns to see your brother off."

Anger shot through her. She saw Kurt's eyes flash, and Glenn looked down. "It wasn't me, Papa," Annie said, "that was put aside…it was the other way." She pulled at her coat, felt a hot coal in her chest.

"Please," Sophie begged. "Not today. I don't know when I'll see my boy again. I want my children to get along."

"*You* left us," Malvern came back, "changed your loyalty to that Porter family. That's the beginning of it all. You know that, Annie Porter."

"Papa, you're just putting this on me because you changed—the oil has changed you. You hate to think of the old life—and how it was when we were your life." Hot words spilled out. "You blame me because you don't want to see it."

John Malvern's face reddened, and his jaw worked. She had seen it often in her childhood when he was angry, his jaw locked—his mind made up.

At that moment Danny Allison opened the door, while Eva Mae pushed a wheelchair inside, carrying Marthursa Allison, Danny's grandmother. Eighty-seven years old, erect as an empress, swathed in rich brown mink, she ruled the Allison family and the Allisons ran the town. Eva Mae leaned forward, solicitous, as the old lady spoke. Eva Mae then removed the lap robe from Marthursa's legs, folded it and carried it. The door opened again on the windy day. Danny's parents had arrived. John Malvern sauntered over to greet them, all smiles, and was soon charming the group with his latest story.

The day was growing darker; through the windows of the old brick depot she watched snow churn in the wind. Wide wooden floorboards creaked as people came to greet each of the boys. Sober-faced newcomers found their way to one of the long benches along the wall.

Sarah Emma Anderson arrived with her Bill, and her quilting friends, Hattie and Dora, all bundled, cheeks red from the cold. They nodded a greeting and moved close to the roaring stove in the center. Annie went to them, wished Bill well. Eva Mae, occupied by Marthursa, kept apart from Annie and Robert, as well as her mother and Glenn.

They stood about in little groups. From time to time Annie glanced at the clock over the ticket counter. The train was due at 9:46. Nine minutes. Snow was building up on the platform by the tracks.

A blast of cold air poured into the room when Otis and Henry blustered in. They gave a bashful nod to Sophie, shook Glenn's hand, and made their way to Bill Anderson. They kept their distance from the quilting ladies, and then came to sit in safe territory, on the bench by Annie and Robert. Henry slumped tight against the corner of the bench, earflaps on his cap pulled down, jowls of his round face escaping over the high-buttoned mackinaw.

Annie studied the little islands of people, huddled in their own world, knowing each other, here for a common reason, but separated. Separately mostly by—oil.

Maxwell Porter opened the door. He stood for a moment, framed against the busyness of falling snow, then brushed flakes from his coat sleeves. Conversations lulled to a stop. The Allison and Malvern families glanced at him, and then turned back to their own interests.

Bill Anderson walked over to greet him, "It's mighty fine of you to come, Mr. Porter. Real nice of you. Come over here by the fire."

Porter yanked off his hat, shook off the snow. "They said over there at the tavern that the Anderson boy was leavin' for the service. You worked that well of mine. 'Member that? It was you that come up to the house and said we had a good 'en."

"I remember, Mr. Porter."

"Well," he extended his hand, his manner awkward, "good luck."

Sarah Emma touched him on the sleeve. "Thank you, Mr. Porter, for coming. We appreciate it." The train whistle sounded in the distance. "Why don't you wait? See him off."

Everyone stood and gathered up their things from the benches, glanced at the clock.

"You got your ticket—everything?" Sophie Malvern asked her son once again.

"I got it, Mama," Glenn whispered, and looked embarrassed at having attention drawn to him in this group.

The crowd fell silent. Maybe it was the darkening day that made a soft melancholy fill the room. It was parting, and they didn't know for how long.

They crowded about the double doors leading to the platform, waiting as the train squealed to a stop on the icy rails, then they moved out into the blizzard. Eva Mae dutifully tucked the lap robe about Marthursa's legs before pushing her outside.

Amid hugs for all three boys, the young men stepped up onto the train. Through the train windows, the tearful group watched them walk down the aisle, find seats, then peer out, smile and wave back. The train jerked forward. Slowly it picked up speed. Only Sarah Emma and Marthursa Allison stayed out, watching through the blizzard until the train crawled far in the distance, a long curving black line.

Sarah Emma pushed the old lady into the depot and joined the somber crowd around the stove.

"I shall never see that boy again." Marthursa Allison stared out the dirty window of the depot.

"Course you will." Dora Cook patted her shoulder. "Them boys'll be back in no time."

"I will never see him again." Marthursa spoke more emphatically, and no one answered.

Then Marthursa Allison looked across the circle crowding around the stove to Maxwell Porter. "You're that Porter person whose boy was killed by the mob, aren't you?"

Everyone in the room stood silent, looking at Porter.

Porter dropped his head.

"I have to say, Mr. Porter," Marthursa Allison spoke, confident in her enormous prestige, "it takes a big man to come here and see these boys off after what you lost."

Porter's head was still bowed. "Thank you," he whispered.

For a brief few minutes at least, Annie thought, there were no differences here. Marthursa Allison and Maxwell Porter both understood an aching heart.

Eva Mae was not in the group absorbing warmth from the stove. She sat by herself in an old wooden chair, softly crying. She wore Danny's engagement ring. She had planned a summer wedding and it had been an abrupt surprise, an embarrassment, when he told her he was enlisting in the Navy

Annie reached for Robert's hand and walked toward the Patrick brothers, who still sat on the bench, apart from the group by the stove. They're so uncomfortable, Annie thought, with all this emotion.

Henry stood up, deflecting any show of affection Annie might have. "Otis and me got something we need to do. We'll be out home after a bit."

Joanne Hardy

CHAPTER 67

Robert stood at the foot of the stairs as Annie came down from tucking Hannah in for her nap.

"Annie," his eyes sparkling as he looked at her, "we're alone in this big old house. A dark day," he motioned to the window, "a snow storm outside." He took her in his arms. "How many bedrooms did you say?" he whispered in her ear.

She pulled back, something tightening in the back of her neck. "Nine...I think." She knew this moment would come, and she didn't know how she would handle it.

"Seven empty..." His lips brushed her forehead. "If we don't like one we'll try another."

She could feel his warm breath on her cheek, the rise of his chest against her and a longing to be loved, but there was something—a stubborn, angry spot in her that didn't yield. Memories of a savage animal. She reasoned with herself. Robert cared for her. This was different. She wanted him. At least she did once. She loved him, yet now she wasn't sure. She took his hand, and with bravado she did not feel, turned in his arms, put her foot on the first stair step and said, "Let's go up—to the dormer rooms."

They stopped on the top landing and he reached for her, stroked her face, and then kissed her. His kiss grew more insistent, pulling her into him. She felt a glad release in herself. A fire began to rise building, that hunger she hadn't known for a long time. Her arm slid around his neck as his lips moved down to the cleft between her breasts. He pushed her sweater and blouse away. She felt the cold of the drafty hall on her bare shoulder and breast. His warm hand slid over her skin, and she trembled.

They moved toward the old dormer room where she had hidden so long and stood in the door. He kissed her again.

"No, no." she felt the hard knot of resistance began to tighten, "not here…in this room."

"All right," He pulled the covers off that bed, carried them to the opposite room, and they made a pallet on the floor. The room was empty except for a dresser.

They pulled a quilt over their naked bodies against the chill. Outside the snowy day gave the room the room a pale grey light.

His skin was warm, and she moved closer to him, feeling sheltered, something she had once thought she found in Willis's arms. But this was Robert and he was so very different, a man she could lean on, go to, had known more of life. There was a certainty with him. Love swept through her as she looked into his eyes and reached to kiss him. For a long time, they lay in their warmness, gently loving. He moved over her and looked down into her eyes, and she pulled him to her. He kissed her slow and long, gradually holding her tighter. Slowly, they began to move, rising quickly to the joy, but she could not give over completely. Then a wave of panic hit her. She couldn't breathe. She began to gasp for air, felt she would burst out of her very skin.

"You're heavy," she cried out, "like him…over me. I can't breathe. Get away." Her fingernails dug in the floor by her sides as he pulled away. She drew the quilt around her and huddled across the room near the corner, heaving for breath and shaking. She buried her head in her arms on her upraised knees, sinking into herself.

He wrapped himself in a blanket from the pallet and moved across the floor to sit by her.

She did not raise her head, still trembling. Into the wad of quilt, she gasped, "He broke me... that night, Robert. I'm ruined," she sobbed. She raised her head and looked across the room at the tilted mirror over the dresser that framed them both, huddled against the wall in the dim room. "My life is over...after that night." She spoke to Robert's reflection in the mirror. "I just didn't know 'til now. I didn't know what he did to me. Every day's going to be the same forever. I'm dead as ashes."

"Nonsense! Do you love me? You say you do. Do you need me to be with you?"

"I do, Robert, but this other..."

"This other will fade away." He stood up, shed his blanket, pulled his clothes on, and looked down at her. "Twenty-two years old and your life is over! Dead as ashes! Get dressed. We're going downstairs. It's cold up here."

Down in the warm kitchen, they didn't talk, didn't look at each other. The blue enameled coffeepot sat on the back of the cook stove. Robert poured them each a cup, and he pushed it to her across the table.

The clock struck three.

"I thought Otis and Henry would be back by now." Annie broke the awkwardness.

She went to the window, peered out, coffee cup in her hand, and then Robert came to her and put his hands on her shoulders. "I'm quite a lover," he whispered. "You won't be able to resist me long."

"We'll see." She smiled instantly, turned to him, and surprised herself with her natural coquettishness. Maybe, she thought, the spirit *is* alive—then thought, she should not tease if she couldn't...go on.

They watched through the darkening afternoon, expecting anytime to see the brothers' old truck come down the lane and stop behind Robert's car.

"Maybe they were blinded by the snowstorm and drove off the road," Annie said.

"If they're not here soon, I'll go looking for them."

"We'll all go. I'll wake Hannah."

The clock chimed 4:00 as Annie finished bundling her daughter. Robert picked up the child, and they went out into the storm.

Robert hunched forward over the wheel trying to see the edge of the road as snow churned into the windshield. It seemed they were driving in a cloud.

"This is the only road they ever use, coming from town," Annie said.

"It's the only way they could come, the bridge is out the other way." Images of the brothers pushing a wreck of a car off a broken bridge came to her. She was frantic to find them.

Annie strained to see anything stranded along the roadside. "Where can they be?" She was on the edge of her seat.

"They've been out hundreds of times when it was like this, Annie," Robert soothed

"But they're not the same anymore."

They turned onto the highway, which made driving easier because oil trucks with chains had already left the road sloppy with loose dirty snow. They drove into the parking lot of Dutch's Truck Stop looking for the truck. Nothing. They passed the overhead and saw lights of town already on in the early dusk.

"Maybe, they decided to stay in town?" Robert suggested. "The blizzard..."

"Oh, no. Not them. They don't like town people and they would never spend money for a hotel room."

They drove slowly through town. A sparse dozen or so cars and trucks were parked along the three blocks of business buildings. "They're so helpless anymore," Annie whispered. "Henry said they had business to take care of."

"There's that other bank out by the depot?"

"They don't trust banks. Won't put a cent in them. I'm really getting scared, Robert." Annie hugged her daughter to her.

"Maybe they never left the depot this morning. Maybe something happened there." Robert drove to the back of the depot.

Henry's truck was pulled in close to the building.

"Thank God." Warm relief melted through her. She bailed out, Hannah in her arms as soon as the truck stopped.

Inside the depot, they found them sitting on opposite ends of a bench, caps pulled over their foreheads, earflaps down, mackinaws buttoned to their throat, feet planted on the floor. Not speaking.

Otis looked up and smiled, eager as a child to see her.

"Are you all right?" Annie hugged him.

"I been lookin' all over town, for that old fool," Henry exploded. "Just found him thirty minutes ago, sitting out there on that bench waitin' for the train. He liked to scared me to death." Henry began to unbutton his mackinaw. "We had to see this man and Otis was anxious to get it done and get goin' so's I says, 'just sign your name here and go on down stairs and wait in the truck.' I told 'im I'd be down directly. When I got back to the truck—no Otis..." Henry's eyes began to water. He pulled out a red handkerchief and blew his nose soundly. "I begin lookin' everywhere. The snow was comin' on. I asked about him when I saw people. Then Elmo Cox said he saw Otis wandering down in this part of town. I tell you, I'm just wore plum out chasin' after this simple-minded old fool." Henry shook his head.

"Where were you going, sweetheart?" Annie sat down and cuddled Otis against her chest.

"Said he was waitin' for the boys to come back. Glenn and them others." Henry growled. "Dummy."

Otis turned his dull eyes on Annie, "That woman said they'd be back in no time."

"Silly old fool, sittin' out there on a bench in this blizzard." Henry blew his nose again. "I'm just give out."

Robert stood up, "We've got to get you home. I'll drive your truck, Henry. Otis can ride in my truck with Annie. She can follow my tracks."

At home, they built a roaring fire in the kitchen. Henry moved closer to the stove. "I'm just chilled plumb to the bone." Annie brought a small blanket and put it around his shoulders.

She fixed dinner and they ate in silence as the wind howled against the window. "Robert, you best stay here tonight." Henry said. "It ain't no night for man nor beast out there."

"Yes," Annie echoed, looked around the kerosene lamp in the center of the table and smiled. "There are so many bedrooms here." Robert smiled back. Quickly, she drew back into herself, realizing she was flirting again, in spite of herself, teasing and tempting in her old natural way. "I think I'll put Hannah to bed. Please, excuse me, Robert," she spoke formally, "you should stay."

"I think I will." He matched her formality.

As she sat on the bed brushing Hannah's hair, Henry knocked on the door that was slightly ajar. "Can I come in?"

He pulled a chair forward. "I been thinking about this for some time. Otis and me talked about it. It's about when Otis and me is gone. It's that business we had in town." He watched her brushing Hannah's hair, then looked up at Annie. "We, Otis and me, want you to have this place."

Annie stopped with the brushing, looked at him dumbfounded. She could hardly believe what she heard. She stared at Henry trying to understand what he was saying?

He handed her an envelope with the name "Oscar Nathan," written across the center. He reached for Hannah, took her onto his knee, and hugged her while Annie opened the envelope and scanned the two pages.

"When the time comes," he leaned close to her, "you are to go to him. He'll tell you what to do about us and what needs to be took care of. We're giving you this place, Annie, and what's in it. It's a place for you to live all your life and raise this little girl. The rest'll go to our nephew in Chicago. We got nobody to help us. Poor ole Otis's gettin' to be a perfect blank. You see that. I'm worried about 'im. He's gonna be an awful care, Annie." Henry's face was flushed pink. He had changed to his older dry mackinaw, but Annie saw him shiver under it even though it was completely buttoned up.

"I'll do whatever you need," she said. "You know I will—I love you both so much." Still frozen in disbelief, she looked across at him. "Thank you," she whispered. "I don't know what to say. Are you sure?"

He nodded over Hannah's sleepy head.

She came to him, but just as she put her arm around him, Henry quickly stood up and placed Hannah on the bed. "It's for this here child, too," he said brusquely.

"Henry, you're burning up."

"We don't never want her to have a need." He ignored her comment, replacing the chair.

"I think you've got a fever."

"Well that's all I wanted to talk about." Then he left the room.

CHAPTER 68

Much later, Robert and Annie stood in the broad hall upstairs that separated their two bedrooms, each carrying a lamp in their hands, Robert leaned forward and kissed her cheek. "I'm just across the hall, you know."

"I know."

"It's a very cold night. It's nice to sleep warm, close up by somebody."

She smiled, "Good night, Robert."

"The door'll be open," he whispered.

In bed, lying by Hannah, she stared into the blackness. 'I'm quite a lover,' he'd said. She smiled, turned, bunched up the pillow under chin. Maybe he was—a good lover. How would he know. It takes a woman to decide that. She'd be the judge. Sometime. Maybe. She turned again, snuggled deeper, imagining she was lying by his warm body. She thought again of the afternoon, his hands moving over her... She closed her eyes. No. One failure a day is enough.

But her senses were so alive she couldn't sleep. I'll just rest, she thought, but the idea toyed with her. She had but to slip across the hall into his bed, into his arms and feel him against her skin warm, inviting. She made a firm resolve. She would not walk across that hall. She would not. She would rest peacefully in this bed, comforted by her imaginings. She turned again on her pillow.

A noise down stairs broke the silence and light show up through the grate in the floor. She sat up.

"Annie. Annie."

She threw on her chenille robe and hurried down the cold hall and stairs to the kitchen.

"I got myself sick..." Henry spoke through a fevered breathiness as Annie hovered over him. "That silly old fool." He motioned to Otis standing at the foot of the bed in his long underwear, helplessly looking on. "He got me sick, that's how it is." He turned his head to the wall, "silly fool," he muttered.

"Now, now," Annie soothed, "we'll build up a fire and get some steam for you to breathe." She pulled the comforter up to his chin.

"Can you get me some sheets, Otis, to drape over the bed?"

"Sheets?"

"They're in the stairs closet, Otis."

She shoved sticks of wood into the kitchen stove. When Otis came back, they adjusted the sheets to make a tent. Then she turned to him. "The mixture you made up when Hannah was sick—can you do that, again? It was so effective."

"Mixture?" Otis looked confused.

"Were there onions?" Annie prodded.

"Onions?"

"And grease? And what else?"

"Grease?"

"The ole dummy can't remember nothin'." Henry's voice was raspy. "You're gonna need that horse liniment in the barn."

"I'll get dressed and go get it." Annie turned as Robert came into the kitchen.

"That old fool over there can get it, if he can remember where the barn is." Henry said.

"I'll go," Robert volunteered.

Within an hour the house was hot as an oven. A kettle of steaming water sat on a chair at the head of Henry's cot with the odious vapors from the special Patrick mixture filling the room. The clock struck midnight, and Henry was still hot with fever.

"I'll call the doctor," Robert said. He went to the phone, rang two longs for the operator, held the receiver to his ear. "It's dead."

Henry was sleeping fitfully with short breaths.

"I'll make us some coffee. It's going to be a long night," Robert said. They took turns replacing the steaming kettles of boiling water by Henry's bed. She watched Robert as they ministered to Henry. When Robert handed her a cup of steaming coffee she smiled, thanked him, and quickly turned back to Henry. But it was Robert she was thinking about. This is an all the way grown up man. Something flooded through her. Admiration, maybe, or hope or joy. Or excitement or all of that, but it was beyond what she had ever felt for anyone, something wondrous. As all these thoughts tumbled through her head, she didn't take her eyes from Henry.

She looked at the clock. 3:30 a.m. She wondered, when they replaced another kettle of steaming water, if she looked as tired and haggard as Robert.

"He's breathing better," she said to Robert. "Otis, sweetheart, go on to bed. We'll be going soon, too." Annie kissed his cheek.

Robert felt Henry's forehead. "He's cool now. I think the fever's broke. He's resting now."

They waited a few minutes, saw him drop off to sleep, looked at each other and nodded. He would be all right.

Lamp held high, Robert took her hand, as they climbed the stairs. At the top they stopped before his open door. He looked at her saying nothing, an invitation in his eyes.

"Listen," she began awkwardly, knowing she loved him— knew that now, but fearful, too. "Thank you for helping…"

He dropped her hand from his. "You're giving me gratitude, Annie?" He gave her a chaste kiss on the forehead,

"Sleep well," then turned, went into his room and blew out the light.

She stood in the drafty hall, staring after him. She called into the dark room. "All I said was 'thank you.'"

A faint drowsy voice came through the dark, "Okay."

She started to her room, blew out the light, and then turned back. Nobody goes to sleep that fast! He hadn't closed the door. She started toward it. She should not cooperate with this ploy. She should not, she thought. The hall was absolute blackness. She felt along the wall for the door casing, and then she crept into his room, her hand extended forward searching for the footboard of the bed. Very softly she ran her fingers along the cover, until she found the edge.

"Hello, Annie," Robert whispered, as he threw back the covers for her.

"You fraud."

"I heard your footsteps."

She slipped in by him, into his arms, against his warm body. He was naked! She pressed closer, sinking deep in the soft cloud of a feather bed. He kissed her slowly, warming the cavern around them. All weariness was forgotten in the exhilaration sweeping her along. He helped her push away the gown. A feverish hunger, long silence, made her reach for that ecstasy she had once known, that had carried her whole being to some lofty promontory, exposed and wildly open. But a knot of control still held her. More certain of him, she opened some of her trust to him, and with it her body as they came together. She felt he was holding back, allowing her the lead and after a time, she took it. And then there was no separateness between them, just a fusion of intense need that she felt through him as much as in herself. All night they lay in each other's arms, at peace, like finding that rare, special place when you both feel at one.

As she lay against his shoulder, some of her fragmented impulses seem to gather into focus and with that she sensed she could move on. She could *live*. A miracle, she felt had just happened. To know she could build on life again.

"Now how did that go?" Robert whispered. "Every day will be dead as ashes. Your life is over."

She turned to him to kiss him. Then a crash in the room below shattered the dark morning stillness.

They both sat up. "What in the hell was that?" Robert said.

"No telling." Annie wrapped her robe around her naked body and hurried down stairs. Otis stood by the wood box, fully dressed, cap pulled down over his ears and brushing wood chips from his mackinaw. Hannah came running down from her bedroom. "Mommy, Mommy," she cried clinging to Annie's long robe, eyes wide and fearful.

"Brought in some wood, Annie. It ain't snowin' now but can't hardly open the door."

"It's... the middle of the night, Otis. Why on earth are you up?" Robert asked.

"Everybody's up."

"Nobody's up, Otis." Annie yawned.

Otis looked about puzzled. "They're all up. It's time to fix breakfast for people."

"No, dear," Annie began to unbutton his mackinaw. Henry sat on the edge of his bed, bare legs dangling over the side. The bed, still draped with the sheet, loomed in lamplight.

"Lock that ole fool up somewheres." Henry's voice was husky, breathy.

Annie hurried to him, felt his forehead. "Henry your burning up." Robert held the lamp over her shoulder.

"We can go on with the steam and hot towels. It worked last night," Annie said.

For hours they worked applying the hot wet towels to Henry's chest and he seemed to relax, drift off from time to time, but when the first feeble sunlight came, revealing the thick blanket of snow outside, Henry's fever still held.

"I'll go find a doctor." Robert reached for his heavy coat. "Maybe I can get out with the truck." He pushed hard against the drifted snow at the door and went out. She watched Robert struggle to open the shed door for the truck, but her attention came back to

Henry. He became agitated, turning this way and that, arms flailing about— crying out, scolding, uttering meaningless sounds. Hannah came back from her room with a stuffed dog. "Uncle Henry want Buttons?"

He shoved the toy away, calling out, "Ma." Annie washed his flushed face with a cool cloth, and he calmed. He grew very still, drew one deep sigh…and he was gone. She dropped to her knees, "Oh, Henry no." She put her arm across his thick middle. "No…sweetheart…no." She laid her head on his silent chest.

Hannah stood by her, patting his arm. "Henry sick?'

"No, honey," Annie sobbed, not looking up. "Not now."

CHAPTER 69

The church basement was cool and damp after spring rains. Sarah Emma felt the clamminess through her thick sweater.

"Ladies," Sarah Emma pulled a magazine from her purse. "I brought something. It's a project. It might work for Bible School."

The other ladies gathered around.

"It's a vase," Hattie said. "Looks like mosaic and done up with paper flowers. The third grade could do that."

"There's a problem." Sarah Emma turned to them, the magazine folded in her hand. "The base of this is really a glass beer bottle. You glue these tiny pieces of paper all over the bottle, sprinkle some gold sparkle, and coat it with varnish. Then make up these paper flowers. What do you think?"

No one said anything.

"It's attractive," Sarah Emma persisted.

Dora searched in her purse for her package of needles. "How could we ever get that many beer bottles?"

"The preacher won't hear of us bringing beer bottles to Bible School." Sophie shook her head.

"We can make up a model of it and tell him we're in need of a lot of bottles—for the students." Sarah Emma said.

'Still, where we gonna get that many beer bottles in time?"
Dora didn't look up from the magazine.

"We'll go ask for them somewhere," Sarah Emma said.
"Maybe the Blue Moon!"

Sophie stared at her. "You'd go in there, Sarah?"

"Well—yes... I would. We need the bottles, and it's for a
good purpose."

"Maybe you'll see something." Dora and Hattie chorused
almost at once.

Dora handed the magazine back to Hattie, leaned close to
the others and whispered, "And I'd just like to see in that Blue
Moon, wouldn't you?"

"Did you see the newspaper this morning? Another so-
called raid on that Blue Moon Saloon." Hattie said and took her
place at the quilt frame.

"And nothing again," Dora added. "But did you see the
last line of the article? 'No gambling found last night, or maybe
we should say, so far'. "Beebite" Cantrell wrote that.
'...so far.' "Beebite's" an honest reporter. I've known him since
that time when he was a little boy—running down the street
holding his back end and screaming, 'bee bite my bottom, Mama.'
I know if he saw something, he'd write it."

"Well, if he keeps reporting that stuff, it looks like he's in
with the sheriff and his Chicago cronies." Hattie sat down at the
quilting frame.

"I just wish somebody could slip in there and see what's
going on, when nobody's expecting anything." Dora said.
"Somebody they wouldn't think a thing about."

"The whole town'd like that," Sarah said. They fell silent,
as they settled into their customary places at the quilting frame.

Sarah Emma stopped stitching and rested her elbow on the
quilt frame. "You know what we can do? We can make sure we
see something—if there's something to see." Everyone leaned
forward. Sarah Emma spoke softly as if the rafters above might
betray her. "We'll go in. We'll act nervous and embarrassed but

one of us will walk up to the bar and show the model of the project for Bible School. At first we'll all be there, then one'll ask about the restroom and the other one'll say she wants to go along. There's got to be a stairs somewhere. Maybe it's by the restroom. One'll just stand around like she's waiting outside the restroom."

Dora eyes widened. "Like a lookout!"

Sarah nodded. "…while the other one tries to find the stairs and slip up for a peek."

They were silent for a moment, sensing the gravity of this plan.

"I don't know." Sophie Malvern shook her head. "How are you gonna see something without you being seen yourself? It's dangerous." She stood up, walked about nervously. "What if we get the wrong people against us, and they follow you everywhere and threaten your family, kill you, maybe. They'll do that."

They were quiet again; the ticking of the clock filled the basement. It was a dangerous mission they were considering.

"Well, I'm for doing it." Sarah Emma said.

"Me, too," Hattie pulled a needle through the quilt and looked up. "Let's do it. Now whose gonna go with Sarah Emma?"

No one spoke.

"I'll go with her," Dora said. "She can do the talking at the bar. She's good at that. I'll stand watch out, if Hattie'll take her Brownie Kodak and try for the stairs."

"Yes, do that, Hattie. Take the Kodak. You'll need that big purse of yours," Sarah mentioned.

"This is dangerous," Sophie warned.

"It could be," Dora whispered but there was excitement in her voice.

"First off, no talking about it," Sarah Emma said.

"Absolutely not. No talking about this," Dora echoed, and all four grey heads nodded in agreement as they went back to stitching.

It was a hot afternoon in early June as Sarah Emma, Hattie, and Dora approached the open door of the Blue Moon. They stepped tentatively inside. The room seemed dark. A neon sign behind the bar blazed "Pabst Blue Ribbon."

A couple of men, obviously from an oil crew were at a corner table. Three men sitting at scattered spots along the bar, looked up, craning to see the three prim ladies, in printed silk dresses, hats pinned to their curled hair, and gloved hands clutching white purses, who just came in. One of the men was Maxwell Porter. Sarah Emma nodded to him as she walked forward, and placed the adorned bottle, the example of a vase made from a beer bottle, on the bar.

"Have you heard of Bible School, sir?" Sarah Emma heard the quaver in her voice.

The bartender nodded, "Bible School? Sure."

"We're planning our activities for this year, and we want the students to make up this little vase." Three heads of the men down the bar leaned forward in graduating degrees, like the opening of an accordion fan.

"This pretty little vase is really a beer bottle with tiny papers pasted all over it." She took off a glove and ran her hand over it. As she talked, she felt more relaxed. "We need a lot of them. In about three weeks."

The bartender picked it up, looked it over and put it down. "The thing is, ladies, we sell full bottles to people who pay for them, so I don't see how we can help..."

"I'll give you my empties," the man in the middle spoke up.

"You can have mine, too. Which church is it?" The first one echoed.

"Well, ah, the one at Woodcrest and Second Street." Sarah Emma warmed to their friendliness.

"I know that one. I went to a revival there oncet and got saved."

"Sir," Dora came up beside Sarah Emma. "I'm embarrassed to have to ask, but do you have a Ladies?"

"A toilet? Yeah," The bartender nodded, "just before the back door."

Hattie and Dora smiled and excused themselves.

"Let me see that little vase," Maxwell Porter said.

Sarah Emma walked down the bar for the men to have a look. "Bring the bottles around to the side door of the church facing west," Sarah Emma continued, "I'll put a box there. Did any of you gentlemen ever go to Bible School?"

"I went to Sunday School." The first one still looked over the vase.

"I did, too. My Mama took me." He shoved a hand out for Sarah to shake. "Johnny Bob Curtis, Ma'am. You ever go, Porter?"

"Naw."

"He don't know about church, Ma'am," Johnny Bob explained, investing himself with sanctified authority. "I used to stand right down in front in that very church and just let her rip, 'In my heart there rings a melody...' He stopped and took a drink. "My Mama used to set there in the second row and look at me singing and just smile like she was so proud, and I'd smile back and rear back and sing." He wiped the foam from his upper lip. "Been a long time since I thought of that."

"Well, you ought to think of it." Sarah Emma spoke. "You ought to think of things like that, your immortal soul, and where you're gonna spend eternity."

"An immortal soul?" Johnny Bob had wonder in his voice.

"Everybody's got an immortal soul," Sarah Emma persisted, "If they make provisions for it. That is if they're saved from eternal damnation."

"I was saved at a revival meetin' once." He looked up, thinking. "maybe twice."

"It just takes once." Sarah Emma smiled, took off her other glove and retrieved the vase.

"That is if it takes," Johnny Bob answered.

"What's this thing about an immortal soul?" A man in the middle asked, sliding to a nearer stool.

"It's what you are without your body, Harry." Johnny Bob explained as a source of reliable knowledge. "It's what goes on when you die and you ain't got a body to live in. That's what your immortal soul is."

"No," Harry pulled back. "I ain't never heard of that."

The bartender put down the mug he had been drying. "Well, you probably don't have one of them, Harry,"

Johnny Bob stared, unseeing into the mirror behind the bar. "I used to stand up there on that platform at church, and just sing with them other kids."

"Shut up, John," Porter got up and moved away from Sarah and the men. "You're always runnin' off at the head. I don't believe in that foolishness. When you're dead, you're done. It's over. There ain't nothin'."

"You don't know that," Johnny Bob came back. "You ever die before to find out?"

"There's nothin' to it." Porter said. "All that nonsense is 'cause people are scared to die, so they get ready all their lives, with that foolishness."

"Well now," Harry began, "how are you gonna know without dyin'?"

"You don't, Harry, but you're a bettin' man." The bartender picked up another mug and began drying it. "Maybe it's like Porter says and maybe it's like this lady says. You don't know, but you got to pick one, there's no middle."

"We don't have to pick now," Johnny Bob said.

"No," Sarah Emma answered, "but you need to think about it. It's important."

Porter turned to Sarah Emma. "I don't like this here talk. When my boy was shot to death all them church people run the other way 'cause they didn't want to have nothin' to do with ole Porter."

Porter stood up, slapped his cap on his head. "The preacher came out to our house right after we buried our boy. Me and the boy's mother was sittin' in our chairs, tender and hurting like an open wound. That preacher says Willis brought it on hisself, on account of the way he learned at home. It probably wouldn't a happened, he said, if I'da lived a better example. Divine retribution he called it. Divine retribution, hell! I run 'im off with a shotgun. I don't want to hear nothin' about church."

"Mr. Porter, I am genuinely sorry about you losing your child. I have a son. I don't think I could stand it if something happened to him," Sarah Emma soothed.

"Well, I thank you for that. I knowed your boy—Billy Anderson. Worked out there on one of my wells before he went to the Navy. He's a good person and you may be too, but some religious people ain't. I know it." Porter ambled to the entrance and slammed the door.

"Hey," one of the oil crew called from the back table. "What I want is to hear Johnny Bob sing that song that makes him proud of hisself. Maybe the lady can help 'im with the words."

"I know the words. Whatta you think, I'm dumb or something?" Johnny Bob stood up and moved away from the bar.

"Well, let's hear it." Harry turned on his stool. "Let 'er rip, John,"

While Sarah smiled and cheered Johnny Bob on, Hattie was carefully slipping up the back stairs. They found the stairs when Dora and Hattie had walked down a dark hall toward the back door. On one side of the back door, was the toilet, and opposite that, another door. Hattie reached for the knob. Unlocked. Stairs. Hattie glanced at Dora, and then stepped on the first stair step. Carefully she closed the door behind her, leaving Dora outside. She pulled out a box-like Brownie camera from her purse, took off her glove, fastened the purse, and began silently moving up the steps. No sound. She moved cautiously, silently up three steps more until her eyes were level with the second floor. She ducked quickly down but she had glimpsed a vast unfinished storage room with open rafters and a row of slot machines along the west wall. Crouched down, she opened the camera shutter, then raised up again. Several tables. Two men in a game. A woman by the upstairs window. A gathered curtain angled across a dim corner at the end of the row of slots, creating a private enclosure.

Hattie slipped down, again. She was beginning to tremble. What if they looked in her direction? What if one of 'em started down the stairs? What on earth were they thinking when they planned this?

What if she took a picture, and they heard the click? Maybe she better go back. Leave well enough alone. But here she was. Evidence right before her eyes. All they ever expected to get. She had to try. She checked to be sure the flash was off. That wouldn't do, for sure. Down stairs they started on a new song, and she could hear Johnny Bob's voice rise on the high notes. Hattie stood up on the stairs to take the picture. She froze. The woman by the window was walking toward her. Did she see her? But the woman stopped and looked down through a grate in the floor in the middle of the room. "Hey you guys, they're gettin' religion down there," she said.

"They're doin' better'n I'm doing up here," one of men at the table scowled at his cards.

This was the time! Hattie steadied the Brownie against the stair railing and snapped a picture of the slot machines. She slipped down below the second-floor level and rolled the film forward. Again she took another peek.

The woman was on her knees at the grate now. "You guys oughta see this."

"Just a minute." One of the men threw down a card and got up to look through the grate.

Hattie steadied her camera, waited for Johnny Bob to hit a loud note, and then snapped it—just as Sheriff Logan stepped out from behind the curtain shoving his shirt into his pants.

"What's going on down there?" he asked.

Hattie sank down on the step, terrified at what she had done. She was simply overwhelmed at her unbelievable success, but now fear began to come over her. What she had was dangerous enough to get them killed. Sophie had warned them. She shoved the camera into her purse. She tried to hurry down the stairs but her knees were spongy rubber. Slowly, she turned the doorknob and peeked out. Dora stood blocking the entrance. "Dora, move. Get outa the way," she whispered. "We gotta get outa here. That liar of a sheriff's up there."

"He's no threat."

"He is now." Hattie's eyes were wide.

Hattie tried to affect casualness as they strolled toward Sarah Emma, but she couldn't still her trembling. No one seemed to notice. Sarah was helping to remind Johnny Bob Curtis of every song he had ever sung in church.

"Sorry, we were so long," Dora said to the bartender. "Thank you."

"We have to go, Johnny Bob. I enjoyed your little songfest." Sarah Emma patted his shoulder with a gloved hand.

Once outside, Sarah Emma said, "I thought you'd never come back. What did you see?"

"Keep moving, don't talk," Hattie said, "Let's get out of here."

"I want to know," Sarah insisted.

"Well, I'm not gonna tell you 'til we get way away from here."

They went to Sarah Emma's restaurant, sat down, and cut one of her rhubarb pies into thirds. "Now, Hattie, what made you so scared?"

Hattie leaned forward, whispered, "I was just simply stupefied at what I saw. Then I began to get scared when I realized what all it could do."

Dora leaned forward, "Well, get it out, Hattie."

In hushed tones Hattie related in detail what she had seen.

"You saw the sheriff with one of them prostitutes?"

"Well, more'n that. The slot machines, the game tables. and that other woman. Probably one of those kind, too."

"My God." Dora settled back, her eyes full of fear as she looked at Hattie. "What'll we do with this? It'll blow things wide open, show the sheriff for a liar and a front for the mob."

"We could get killed just like poor Willis," Sarah Emma said.

"We'll get the film developed and give it to the paper," Dora said.

"No," Sarah Emma whispered, "We've got to get this right. We'll get these developed out of town and wait 'til the time is right. Maybe after one of those fake raids showing nothing, we'll have them run these pictures in the paper. It'll show them up for liars. We'll take 'em to "BeeBite." He'll love a scoop like that. But we got to be careful. Remember what happened to Annie's Willis."

"I got a sister in Springfield. I'll mail the film to her. We can have 'em back a week from Thursday when we quilt," Dora said. "But we'll always keep the negatives hid somewhere."

"We'll have to tell Sophie. She'll be dying to know."

"Yes, but nobody else."

When they leaned back, they realized they had polished off the whole pie in five minutes.

Hattie and Dora stood ready to leave. Their eyes met Sarah Emma's. A sobering mission had fallen to them. They might yet bring life back to the way it used to be.

CHAPTER 70

Sunday morning Sarah Emma dressed for church in a new flowered print she had just bought. Standing before the oval mirror, she pinned her hat on, and pulled white gloves over her calloused hands.

At church she walked down the center aisle, slipped into her accustomed seat, three pews back from the front. A soft breeze blew across from the tall open windows while the pastor delivered his message. As they were ready for the last hymn before the altar call, the preacher stepped down from the platform away from the pulpit.

He cleared his throat and waited for a minute; then in a less formal tone asked, "Does anyone know why there is a three-foot-high pile of beer bottles against the church by the youth entrance?"

Sarah Emma's hymnal trembled in her hand. She looked down at the words but didn't see them. Something very heavy seemed to be collapsing through her to about the area of her stomach. She would have to explain. But what would she say? She stared at the bald head of Ivan Thompson in front of her. She was about to raise her hand to explain when a cheery voice from the back boomed over the congregation.

"I brought 'em."

Johnny Bob! Sarah Emma knew that voice.

"Brought 'em for Bible School." Johnny Bob looked sheepishly pleased with himself. "I told folks the church needed their empties and to bring 'em over here. Johnny Bob Curtis the name."

The preacher looked across the room. "I'll talk with you later, Mr. Curtis, about this." He quickly nodded to the pianist. "Now, Hazel, number 47. Let us sing"

For the first time in all her adult life Sarah Emma did not stand in line to wish the pastor a good morning and compliment him on his sermon. She slipped out the side door by the pile of beer bottles. Sarah Emma was guarding a secret, an important one, and she felt if she looked into the honest face of that preacher and revealed any part of what she knew, the whole thing might just unravel right there in front of him. Whatever Johnny Bob might say, he didn't know the half of it.

On Thursday, quilting day, when they met, all thought of their raid on the Blue Moon was overshadowed by much more important news. Two of them had received letters from their sons in the Navy.

"I knew something was up," Sophie Malvern said, "as soon as I read the postmark. It usually says Great Lakes Naval Training Station. Glenn wrote to us and Eva Mae got a letter from Danny Allison. They're all up there in Bremerton, Washington. Getting organized to ship out."

Sarah Emma pulled out her letter, "Bill says they requested to be assigned to the USS Ranger. He wrote he'd loaded ammunition all week. Said he didn't think there was that much ammunition in the whole world. He's in the Quartermaster Corps."

Sophie opened her quilting bag, pulled out a spool of thread and tiny scissors, and placed them on the quilt. "Glenn filled up the whole letter telling me about what he's learning. He's in the Navigational Division, and he's learning different codes."

Hattie glanced at Sophie, "Being up there, in Washington State, it don't look like they'll be going over towards Europe."

"We can be thankful for that," Sophie said quietly. "Danny wrote to Eva Mae that they're shipping out this week. Said he hadn't got his assignment, yet."

"I 'spose they might be out there on the ocean now." Sarah looked away, seeing her Bill walking along on some strange ship deck, endless ocean wherever he looked. "I hope he wrote again before he left," she glanced at the others, "so we can know where they're going."

"Well, let's get back to quilting. I need to keep myself busy," Sophie said.

They were quiet for a while, each moving their needles back and forth through the circles in straight even stitches on another Wedding Ring design.

Sophie finally broke the silence. "What's it look like inside the Blue Moon, Hattie?"

After Hattie told her all she had seen, Sophie said, "We've got to be careful how we use this. We don't want one of us dumped on our front step."

"Let's get the pictures first," Sarah held up a needle and ran thread through the eye, "Then we'll decide what to do…and by the way, I do think we've got enough beer bottles for Bible School.'

Sarah Emma was eager for Thursday afternoon to come. They had not met for quilting for two weeks because Hattie and Dora were both Bible School leaders at the church. Even Sarah Emma had given two mornings a week to help out, but when they had met at the church, they did not speak of what they knew, and what they would do. Today, though, she knew Hattie would have the pictures back from her sister in Springfield. When Sarah Emma arrived, the other three were already there, Hattie at her usual place, with the pictures spread on the quilt before her. The others hovered over her shoulder, soberly looking at this shocking evidence.

"They're a little dark," Dora bent close to them, "but you can sure make out that those are slot machines and that's the sheriff, right there by the slots."

They passed the pictures back and forth studying them in detail. Sophie looked up. "What if they say it's not the Blue Moon? Say it's somewhere else, another county or something? What then?"

No one spoke.

"Well," Sarah Emma finally said, "when they run pictures in the paper, we'll get these in the next issue and people can see for themselves it's the same room."

"Right," Dora said. "That will prove it."

Sarah Emma ran her finger along the edge of a picture, "This is more than we ever hoped for." She put the picture down by the other five on the quilt before her. They each took their seats saying nothing and began quilting, but Sarah's hand shook as she tried to stitch.

"Do you think we should really go through with this? It's dangerous."

"I think we have to," Hattie said and again they worked without speaking.

An awesome burden had fallen on their shoulders. Sarah knew they all felt it. They could get rid of that sheriff. They could help bring in some real law. But what of the mob?

"I was real sorry for that Mr. Porter," Sarah Emma finally said, "losing a son like that and no one seemed to care."

"That sheriff's got a lot to answer for." Hattie eyes narrowed as she worked.

"The preacher said it was the Porter boy's own fault," Sarah continued. "That's double edge."

"That boy was mine, too," Sophie Malvern flared, "my son-in-law, and it *was* his fault. He wouldn't stop the gambling. Put my Annie through hell. You know that. Put all of us through hell tryin' to keep him out of debt." She stared down at the quilt, shaking her head. "I'm sorry they killed 'em, of course, but we knew he was headed for something."

They all glanced at Sophie then went quietly back to their stitching.

Sarah decided it was time to change the subject. "I've got something to show you," she pulled a woven grass mat from a paper bag and placed it on the quilt. Then she brought out two miniature imitation palm trees, standing on half coconut shells that resembled sand dunes. "Bill sent this to me." She brought out three small figurines—girls with black hair, flowered pieces around their necks and skirts of imitation green grass. She placed them on the mat.

"He said he wasn't much of a hand for describing things, but he wanted me to see how it looked where he was."

Tears spilled over the rim of her eyes as she unfolded her letter. "He said he was glad to be in the Quartermaster Corps. Said that he had General Quarters at 18:30 so he'd go up in the ships's nest and look for lights and other ships." She pulled a handkerchief from her purse and wiped her eyes.

"That was real nice of him to send that to you, Sarah. Makes you think of all the places in the world we don't know about," Hattie said.

Sarah folded the letter and put the grass mat and figurines back in the paper bag. "I sure do miss them."

Sophie Malvern didn't answer; her head was bent low over her work.

"Well, course you do," Dora soothed. "But they're seein' things none of us'll ever see. You gotta think of it that way."

"I s'pose. Bill said when they arrived in Pearl Harbor, he had never seen so many planes and ships in his life and the rest of their fleet had not even arrived yet."

CHAPTER 71

Lillian lay across a blanket near the lake's edge, moonlight through the tree dappling over her body. Kurt loosened his clothes, his eyes intent. It seemed to him she lay at the bottom of a cave, waiting for layers of obscuring shadows to be pushed aside. Waiting for him. Shading covered one of her breasts, but moonlight bathed over the other and down her abdomen and beyond, to where her legs lay slightly apart. Crickets shrieked a tumultuous clamor in their ears, but there was no talking between them. Kurt dropped down beside her; naked also. Leaves starting to fall from the wide oak above crunched under the blanket. He smoothed his hand over the white satiny flesh and could feel her come alive under his touch. He leaned forward and gently kissed her. Lillian cradled his head in her arms as his hand caressed over the supple contours of her flesh. He felt her begin to move slowly, then the fire burned hotter in him. She reached for him with both her arms, reaching for him, growing frantic. And then he entered that soft, timeless heaven.

"I'd go through hell for this," he whispered.

"You may," she gasped in his ear, pressing up to him.

When it was over, she stood up, shook out the blanket. He watched her while he put on his clothes. She folded the blanket carefully. Finally, she dressed, and he followed her, expecting to kiss her goodbye, but she showed no interest. She placed the blanket in the boat and stepped in beside it.

"I'll see you here next week." She began rowing away to the opposite side of the lake.

Moonlight spilled in on the sun porch where Coralee sat absently swinging. She saw something moving along the road that rimmed the lake. It gleamed into full light. Kurt! Kurt's truck. She stepped out the door, but it was gone, traveling without lights. It turned off into a grove of trees, and she lost it.

"Mama," she called as she went inside. "Kurt's doing something across the lake. Mama. I know it was his truck. Mama!" She went through the house and then upstairs. "Mama." She looked in Lillian and Malcolm's room. She stepped out into the hall, "Mama."

No answer.

Coralee went to her room and dropped across her bed. Kurt. She pulled a pillow to her and put her head on a corner of it as she would his shoulder and hugged it to her. She melted into the imagined circle of his arms. But what if she really were with him? Maybe she would be. Then came another idea, one she'd had before.

She went back into her mother's dimly lit room and opened the fourth drawer of the tall chest. She slipped out of her dress and cotton panties and took from the top layer of lingerie peach satin panties and brassiere. Coralee pulled the panties on, and for the first time slipped her arms through the straps of a bra, slid her breasts into the cups and fastened it. She touched the crease between the fleshy mounds overfilling the garment, ran her hand over the curve where the panties flared over her hips and saw herself as she thought Kurt would. She changed from one set of lingerie to another, luxuriating in the filmy material soft against her skin, each time replacing the garments almost reverently to their place.

The room was suddenly bathed in brilliant light.

"What are you doing?"

Coralee stood shocked and quivering, from long-time fear as she faced her mother.

"Standing there in front of the mirror admiring your own nakedness. Shame on you." Lillian screamed at her. "Why are wearing my brassiere?"

Coralee, sick with humiliation, the pit of her stomach churning, felt her face grow hot. "I need to wear a brassiere, Mama." Her voice quavered.

"You do not. You are a growing child. There's time for that." Lillian threw the blanket she still carried on the bed.

"Where you been, Mama? There's a leaf in your hair."

"You answer me first. Why are you in here doing this foolish thing? Wrap yourself up."

Coralee grabbed the blanket. Broken leaves fell to the floor as she threw it over her shoulders."

"Where were you, Mama?"

"It's none of your business where I go. I'm your mother, and I don't have to account to you, and you are not ready to wear grown-up underwear." Lillian softened, "You're just a child, Coralee. My child."

"Why do want me to...to put you up more high than anybody else?" Coralee's voice quavered as her eyes searched her mother's face.

"Stop this talk. It's disrespectful. Remember, I am your mother."

"You want me to live...like a little person beside your big life, but I don't want it to be like that. I want to do things I like."

"I will not hear this," Lillian moved toward her.

Coralee's eyes were level with Lillian's. "I don't think you're higher than other people and I don't love you."

"I won't have this from a child of mine." Lillian slapped Coralee's cheek. "I won't stand for it."

Coralee whirled about and slapped Lillian. The blanket she clutched fell to the floor. She ran down the stairs, clothed only in panties,

"Where do you think you are going?" Lillian cried from the stair railing. "Come back here."

Coralee jerked the front door open, dashed out into the night, and around the house. Lillian was soon following behind her.

"You impudent child," Lillian called. "When I get my hands on you…"

Coralee ran to the playhouse, slammed the door, and braced it against her mother who was immediately pounding on it.

"You forced me to chase you. You come out this minute and receive your punishment. I won't have this. Do you hear?" Her mother pushed hard on the door but Coralee held it firm.

"You won't never slap me again," Coralee called through the crack in the door. There was a long silence. She leaned her head against the door, listening. "You didn't have to chase me," Coralee said, and waited for an answer. She looked down at the floor, still listening. Maybe she had gone, gone back to the house, but then Lillian pounded on the door again.

"Coralee, baby, you don't want to treat your mother like this. Open the door." Lillian pushed the door, again.

A crash sounded behind Coralee, startling her, as she realized the squirrel had scampered into some of her toys.

"Is that squirrel in there with you?" Lillian's voice again demanded.

"Biscuit? Yes. He's here with me."

"I won't have you keeping it. *He* gave it to you. Coralee, *wh*y did he give it to you?"

"Because he's my friend."

"What did he do to you?" Her voice still had its demanding ring.

"Do to me?"

"You can tell Mommy. You won't be in trouble." The voice was softer now. "You wouldn't know it was something wrong."

"Kurt talks to me, Mama."

"Leave him alone. He's a bad man."

"I like him… I love him."

"Coralee," Lillian exploded, pushing again on the door. "You are never to see him again. Do you hear me? Never." The demanding voice. "Baby," the soft voice again. "Baby, listen, I just want to protect you. Open the door for Mommy. Let me hold you. Make everything all right, like we always do."

"No…I'll come out when I please."

"Coralee, you are breaking my heart. Baby, do you want to see your Mommy crying because you've hurt her so? Do you want to see your Mommy with a broken heart?" The voice was soft again.

"No," Coralee wavered, "I don't want you to cry."

"I am crying, baby. You're my dearest treasure. What would I do if I couldn't count on you to love me?"

"Mommy, I was looking for you to tell you I saw Kurt's truck across the lake."

"Kurt, again. Forget Kurt."

Coralee did not answer.

"Maybe he was fishing in the lake," Lillain said. "Who knows what he might do. That family is not like us. Promise me, Baby, you won't see Kurt again."

Coralee listened intently at the door. She thought she heard sobbing.

"I'll stay here until you promise," Her mother's voice was soft again

"I promise, Mama." She was sure she heard sobbing. "Let me be by myself."

"One more thing, Baby, I want you to get rid of that squirrel." The demanding voice again.

"All right, Mother." Coralee smiled. "Whatever you want. I'll take it to him in the morning."

"No. No, don't do that. Just let it go."

"But the wolves might get it. Don't you trust me to give it back to Kurt."

There was no answer for a long time, then a halting voice. "Of course, I trust you... but you're... such an angel of innocence and..."

"It's good manners to take it back, Mama. You said I should have good manners."

"Yes... " Lillian answered.

Coralee opened the door and stepped out into the moonlight. Lillian took off her sweater, wrapped it around her daughter and smiled the benevolent smile Coralee so often saw when people did what her mother wanted.

Through the night, Coralee tossed in fitful sleep. Her argument with her mother disturbed her less than it had at other times. She knew she could not keep her promise, to not see Kurt again. She never intended to. At first light she dressed, slipped downstairs, out to the cage where she had penned up Biscuit, put it on the back of her bicycle and rode quietly out into the gray dawn.

Still in the haze of sleep, Kurt pushed back his disheveled hair as he stood in the opened doorway. "My God, what time is it, Coralee?"

"I had to see you. It can't wait."

"What? This squirrel?" Kurt stifled a yawn, looking down at the cage dangling from her hand.

"Mama and I had an argument. We... Oh, Kurt, she says I should have nothing more to do with you."

"Is that it?"

"And she wants me to get rid of this squirrel, too." Coralee's eyes were tearful, and she bit her lip. "I promised not to see you but," she timidly smiled up at him. "I didn't mean it."

Kurt slipped on his shirt and smoothed back his rumpled hair.

"Mama's friends treat me like I'm her pet, like I'm a Biscuit."

He took her arm, brought her inside and closed the door. "Coralee, it's a risk for you to come here. I told you that."

"She treats them bad, but they want to be with her, with the Allison's. Kurt glanced at her. She seemed to be pouring out something that wouldn't stop. "We all do what Mama wants."

Kurt looked up, drowsy, but finally interested.

"I can't not see you again," she whispered, tears rimming her eyes.

He looked down at her but said nothing. He felt sorry for her; he understood how it was to be one of Lillian's throwaways. Coralee's eyes were big, her lips tremulous. She had everything—and nothing.

He put his arms about her shoulders and took her to the door. "Don't ever come back."

"But, yes, I got to. You're my friend. You talk to me..." He closed the door and left her on the front step but watched her through the curtained window, standing there, staring, arms hanging. She started to knock, but didn't, then turned, and went to her bicycle. A milk truck across the street pulled past Mrs. Keltoux' house. As Mrs. Keltoux' reached out her front door to pick up two quart bottles of milk, Coralee looked up, smiled, and waved.

CHAPTER 72

Kurt drove to Sarah Emma's restaurant, slid onto a stool and ordered a piece of cherry pie. One end of the room, which was actually an enclosed porch, was now exposed. Maxwell Porter hammered with a vengeance on the last beam of the frame for an extension to the restaurant.

Porter got down from his ladder, went behind the counter, poured himself and Kurt a cup of coffee, and leaned across the counter.

"I'm re-making this porch café into a real restaurant for Miz Anderson, over there." He nodded to Sarah Emma who was serving her boarders at a separate table. "You know that there woman is one of the finest people I ever met, 'less it's her son. He's gone to the Navy, you know."

"I know that, Porter. He's with my brother, Glenn." Kurt's mind was in a fog, what with meeting Lillian last night and Coralee on his doorstep this morning, and he didn't know what to do about this mess that was developing.

"She started out deep in debt," Porter went on, "my woman told me how it was. Her husband got up out of bed and just up and died, right there." Porter leaned close, speaking low. "He had debts, don't you see, and she bein' just a woman didn't have no idea how she was gonna pay off them folks. They wantin' their money, and she herself with still two young ones to bring up. Well, she went to work makin' these pies and takin' in boarders. She got herself free and clear. Now she's makin' money hand over fist. The oil boys like to come in here. They're makin' her business. The funny thing is, don't you see, she's gettin' rich offen the oil, and she ain't got airy a well."

Kurt eyed him, knowing Porter still had just the two wells, and felt like an underdog in the countryside where dozens of dirt-poor farmers around him were becoming wealthy.

"Yes sir, she's doin' all right. I got me an agreement with her that soon as I finish up here, I'll begin re-makin' her house into a big roomin' house. You know, nobody's got enough space around here for all these people comin' in to work. Yes, sir, she doin' all right and got that fine family, too. Bill's off over across the ocean with your brother."

"They're in Hawaii, Porter."

"Yeah, over there." Porter pushed aside his coffee cup. "How many wells your Pa got now?"

"I heard twenty-four." Kurt smiled inwardly, thought, now we're getting to the heart of this conversation.

"Don't reckon he knows how much he's worth?"

"I imagine he knows about to the dime what he's got, but he don't tell me nothin' about it. Eva Mae and Joey get in on that."

"Shame how your family's gone."

"What do you mean?" Kurt stiffened.

"Well, the trouble and all."

"What trouble?" Fire was building in his chest.

"Folks see it. How John Malvern treated Annie when Willis died and you and her and Glenn sort of set off to one side while he struts out tryin' to be what he ain't never been raised to. Folks see it. It's what the oil does to some people. Some it don't. Look here at Sarah Emma, not a drop... "

"Shut up, Porter. If you think so damn much of her, get back to work and do what's she's payin' you for."

"Well, now I's just passin' the time a day with you and you get riled..."

Kurt tossed a quarter on the counter, went out to his truck and his own dilemma. He closed his eyes, remembering the ecstasy he tasted last night with Lillian and then her daughter's worshipful eyes.

He sat in the cab and thought about how it had started—four years ago. He still was at home then. His father had turned to him, put his hand over the receiver of the phone and said, "This is John Allison's daughter, Miz Powers it is now, and she says she wants some farm boy to come in and chop out some dead limbs from her trees. Reckon you'll do. We could use the money."

So he had gone and when he finished the job she came to him, still in her white terrycloth robe, with a check in her hand. She looked up at him with a hint of a smile in her eyes. "Does a good-looking guy like you do any other services for lonely ladies?"

He stuttered a bit and then she put her hand on his arm. He could still feel that hand resting on his arm and remember exactly what she said. "My husband is always gone on Saturday nights. Come by, I'll be on the sun porch, waiting. I might have something else for you to do."

The next three days had been an agony of indecision. A woman like that. Maybe the most important woman in town. He had wondered at it. Worried about it. Who was he anyway? A farm boy, for sure. Married women he'd always stayed away from but still, a woman like that! So he had gone. And it began. Then she asked him to build the boathouse on the lake—and he came each day for months. Then he couldn't leave her. Sometimes he thought about girls his age, and what he might be missing, but it was Lillian he hungered for. It was why he took her scorn and the scorn that had grown more bitter as he changed from the farm boy to the son of the wealthiest man in the county.

And now Coralee! How Lillian had kept her daughter away from their relationship he never considered.

CHAPTER 73

It was more than a month before Kurt came back to Sarah Emma's café. Porter had finished his work and the room was now a spacious restaurant filled with twenty tables and booths around three sides. Sarah Emma was not behind the counter. From somewhere he heard a radio playing music. Spread across the counter was a newspaper someone had left, with blaring headlines, "Raid on Blue Moon Finds No Gambling." In the column between the European war news and the latest update on the oil activities, it went on to say that the persistent rumors of gambling and prostitution do not have any factual basis.

Kurt put the paper aside and looked about. "Anybody here?" He called out. A couple of oil workers were at the far table, but they had been served.

Sarah Emma came bustling in from the inside of her house. "Sorry, Kurt, I had to call your mother about this thing in the newspaper." She said, pointing to the paper. Kurt wondered what his mother could have to do with gambling in the Blue Moon, but he didn't pursue it.

"I asked her to come by my house on Sunday." Sarah Emma put a menu before Kurt.

Soon after Kurt left, Sarah Emma was on the phone calling her quilting friends. "You saw the paper, Hattie? It's time to take those pictures to the editor. Meet at my house on Sunday afternoon. It's time we got the truth out to the people."

Sarah Emma left church at ten-thirty on Sunday. She went directly into her restaurant, where she served her boarders and a couple dozen other customers. She could hardly get through the routine of the day, knowing great things were coming to pass and she and her friends would show that worthless sheriff for what he was, a liar and a puppet for the mob. It was Sunday, so she served up pot roast to her boarders, sat down with them and made them say grace.

Later she took her apron off, turned the restaurant over to her daughter Betty, and went into her living room. When the quilting ladies all arrived, Hattie spread the pictures and negatives out on the dining room table.

"These need to run in the next issue," Sarah Emma said. "We'll get them to "BeeBite" tomorrow." She looked around. "Now who's going?"

"Sophie, your son-in-law was murdered and nothing done. You got reason," Dora said.

"We all got reason. We'll all go," Dora said.

They studied the pictures again—treasures, they felt, that would change their town, their lives back to the way it used to be. They nodded. "We'll all go." Sarah said.

"Mama." Betty burst in. "Come listen to the radio. Something's happened." They hurriedly gathered up the pictures and followed Betty into the restaurant. The radio was on the second shelf behind the counter. Six customers had already gathered about, solemn, intent.

"The Japanese have bombed..." static. "War imminent..."

"But where?" Sophie asked.

The static cleared, "Wave after wave of Japanese bombers pounded the U. S. Pacific fleet moored in Pearl Harbor turning the whole harbor into an inferno..." Static. "...waters in the harbor are filled with bodies,"

"Oh my God," Sophie cried. "Pearl Harbor...no, don't let it be..."

The radio announcer went on. "We are told smoke pours from flaming battleships. It's hard to assess the exact damage, but..." static. "We know the West Virginia, the Tennessee, the Arizona and the Oklahoma..." everyone leaned close to the radio, straining to hear."... "have all been severely..." static "... and are going down."

"Oh, my God," Sophie kept saying, bracing herself against the counter.

"... there may be more," the voice continued, "...but these four have been confirmed. The Japanese attack was first seen as planes cleared the morning haze..."

Sophie slumped against the counter. One of the roustabouts picked her up and carried her back to Sarah Emma's living room couch. "Turn the radio on," Sophie whispered. He turned on the console in the corner. Sarah Emma followed him and collapsed in a chair, sobbing. "Our boys, Sarah," she gasped, "our poor boys. Oh, my God, my poor Bill." She shook her head, crying, protesting. "This is just too horrible."

All afternoon they sat in the darkening room listening to the reports coming. Hattie gathered up her pictures which seemed so important a few hours ago and put them in her purse. When a knock came to the door, Hattie let John Malvern in. He sat down by Sophie.

"Glenn's gone," Sophie whispered to her husband and took his hand. "He must be. He was on the Arizona. Oh, my dear God how can we ever get through this?"

"Does Eva Mae know?" Hattie asked, "Danny..." her voice trailed off.

"She's gone to St. Louis," Sophie said at last. "She'll be back on the four o'clock train.. We should go home, John." Slowly Sophie and John made their way down the walk to their car.

It was late in the evening when Eva Mae came home and found her parents sitting close to the radio, both crying. Annie and Robert had come, as well as Kurt, all hovering near the radio, soberly hanging on every word.

"What's this about?" Eva Mae stood inside the door, peeling out of her coat.

"We're going to war." John Malvern's voice faltered, "Pearl Harbor was..." he couldn't go on.

"Pearl Harbor! What Papa? That's where Danny's..."

"Yes, Eva Mae," Kurt spoke, "it was bombed, and ships have gone down..."

"The Arizona?"

"Yes, Evie," Sophie spoke through sobs, "probably with our Glenn and Bill and..."

"And Danny?"

"We don't know yet." Malvern's head was low, by the radio.

"No, Danny was not on it," Eva Mae began, "he was probably in Honolulu. He goes there. He writes he does. He's all right. It's not him. We're going to get married as soon as he gets back. It's not him... Oh, God no, this can't be happening." She stopped and listened to new reports of the waters filled with dead men and others screaming in agony. Eva Mae stepped back and walked to the front door, staring out at the chilly winter day. She turned back to the group by the radio. "No, no, I don't want this." She walked aimlessly through the room. "I don't want this," she began to scream over and over. "Why is God doing this to me? Why? I don't want this."

She turned to Annie sitting by her mother "You've had one husband already and now you're going to get another. There's no one else here I would marry, but Danny." She began to gasp for air. "Don't you see, I'll be left out?" She picked one of her mother's potted African violets and threw it crashing to the floor. "I don't deserve this." She collapsed on the sofa, in hysteria. Kurt tried to help her up, but she pushed him away. She finally stood, pounded up the stairs, raging and crying and slammed the door.

Sophie and John Malvern, Annie, Robert and Kurt did not go to bed that night. Time stopped. Simple activities seemed a distraction. They turned to different stations on the radio, but the reports were all the same

Exhausted and heart weary, they still couldn't stay away from the radio. Glenn couldn't have died in that massive inferno they reported. It just couldn't be—not one of their own. It was too horrific. Finally dull morning light filtered in from the east and Annie made some coffee.

In town Sarah Emma left the restaurant closed. No one came anyway. The town was empty except for the unremitting oil trucks. Everyone sat by their radios.

Sarah Emma made her way up to the attic. In a trunk at the top of the stairs, was the black wreath she had hung on the door when her husband died. She did not actually know if Bill was gone. Maybe, maybe, by the grace of God he was not on board. Maybe.

For the next few days during which time war was declared, everyone sleepwalked through their day's work, but for Sarah Emma and the Malverns there was no night or day, just shock and fear and desperate hope flowing together in some timeless terrain.

CHAPTER 74

The next Sunday, in church Sarah Emma sat quietly holding her daughter's hand. Somehow they had made it through the week. The preacher stepped to the pulpit and gave a short prayer that some, who were thought to have perished, might by some miracle have survived and those that didn't were now in Heaven. The rest of the service, he said, would be given over to hymn singing, the best way, he said, to soothe breaking hearts.

"Wait a minute," Sarah Emma stood up. "I want to say a word." She walked to the front. "I don't know where my son Bill is. I don't know. Maybe he's well, or in a hospital or... he's gone to be with God. I don't know, but I had him for 21 years to light my life and I cherish those 21 years... and I hope, dear God, I hope there will be more years..." she couldn't finish. The preacher put his arm around her shoulder and helped her back to her accustomed pew.

The next morning a telegram arrived. Bill was "missing and presumed dead." All that day she sat with her memories and bouts of uncontrolled grief. The next day she took out the black wreath from the upstairs trunk, unlocked the restaurant, and hung the wreath on the door. It seemed half the town came by to offer their sympathy. She kept the coffee brewing and served them free coffee. No one said much, they just sat with her and listened to the radio behind the counter, the war news, then took her hand, offered their respects and left.

The following day, Sarah hung a white satin banner with a gold star in the center of her window. Oppressive grief was constantly with her, intruding into the daily routine she tried valiantly to maintain. The second week melted into the third and the week before Christmas she asked Maxwell Porter to resume work on her rooming house.

Sophie Malvern lay in her room, with the shades pulled. Days had run together. She relived memories of Glenn, but the tears had dried. She went downstairs where John constantly sat by the radio obsessed with the news.

"Don't think I'm going to put up a tree and make Christmas for you two," Eva Mae said as Sophie came into the room. "You act as if you're the only ones that lost somebody. Well, I miss Glenn, but Danny was my life and he's gone. You don't seem to notice what I have lost. I'll never marry and have a family."

"Eva Mae, please." Sophie implored.

"I won't, Mama. I'll never be proud to say I'm 'Mrs. Danny Allison'. You'll never know what that means to me. You don't understand those things, Mama. You're just an old countrywoman. You don't see what I've lost."

John Malvern roused from his trance by the radio. "Your mother lost a son, Eva Mae. You don't know what that is."

"You are both too backward to see anything." She ran upstairs and closed her door.

The next day Joey came home from college. There would be no gifts this year, no decorations for the holidays. On Christmas Eve morning John and Sophie Malvern rode into town with Joey and brought back a white satin banner with a gold star. On Christmas day they tearfully hung it in the window although no telegram had come about Glenn as it had about Bill Anderson and Danny Allison. They knew it was coming; the boys were together on the Arizona.

Joey sat for a while in the somber, silent house, then got up and stretched. "Think I'll go for a spin. Want to go for a spin, Eva Mae?"

She stared at him, "No, I do not want to go for a spin, Joey. Don't you understand anything? My life is over, done. There's nothing left."

Joey bundled up against the December cold and left. John Malvern looked up from his gloom when he saw Joey gun the car and speed up over the hill west of Eva Mae's rose garden.

"That boy is a spoiled, selfish idiot." Eva Mae pronounced. No one had the spirit to argue.

Sophie went to the kitchen and made oyster stew for dinner and Joey was back in time to join them. "Think I'll be getting on back pretty soon." Joey broke the silence of the meal. "I miss Glenn, too. We had good times together. I understand you're grieving, but why is everybody else so sad...even uptown everyone is sad."

John Malvern leaned back in his chair and studied his son, puzzled, the youngest, and his dearest hope. "Because, Joey, everybody's been wounded—the whole country's wounded," he said with disgust.

Joey didn't answer for a while and then he said, "Think I'll just pack up and go on back to school. Bound to be somebody hangin' around the dormitory over Christmas."

Heaviness that pressed in on Malvern weighed more even than the grief. Nothing, he thought, turns out the way you plan.

It was late January before a letter got through from Glenn. He had been on shore when the attack came, but a piece of shrapnel tore into his arm. He had been in a hospital, but no one had had time to help him write.

CHAPTER 75

Annie stepped outside, stood on the porch, breathing in the sharp cold air. The snow—covered countryside, under brilliant sunshine, and a bright blue sky was so striking it made her eyes ache. A beautiful day. Valentine's Day. Her wedding day.

Inside, she built fires in the kitchen stove and carried coals to the two fireplaces into what Otis and Henry called their "forward rooms."

She and Robert, with Otis helplessly looking on, had spent days clearing away cobwebs and debris in the cavernous rooms where the brothers had stored potatoes, onions, sometimes bales of hay and on occasion a puny pig or calf, if the weather warranted it. Now the rooms sparkled with something of decayed elegance, an echo of what had been.

They had moved the kitchen table to the room that once was a dining room, opened it with many extensions, and covered it to the floor with a white tablecloth. In the room that had served once as a parlor, they had placed chairs in a semicircle around the fireplace.

By four-thirty the guests were in their seats, Carson Garrett with Belle Dorsett, Kurt, and Sarah Emma Anderson. Hannah was perched on a seat near Sophie and John Malvern wearing a white lace dress and new shoes that absorbed her attention. She was to come forward with a ring on a little pillow. Eva Mae, Sophie explained to Robert, was too much in grief to attend.

"Can't see her sister marry a second time when she never got even one husband," Kurt responded, in a whisper that could be heard in the next room.

Stationed at the bottom of the stairs, Otis looked severely uncomfortable in a black suit and blue tie. Robert and Annie had taken him to Allison's Department store and bought him the first suit he had ever owned. It had been a fearful event for Otis as he walked through foreign territory filled with racks of suits.

"Never had one and never wanted one, but..." he had scratched his head, then looked sheepishly at Annie and said, "if you want me to wear one to the wedding, reckon I can."

Knotting a tie was another hurdle. When Robert finished tying it, and stepped aside, Otis beheld himself in the mirror.

"That'll do," he said emphatically, and began to grab at the knot of the tie.

"But don't you want to try another suit." He and Annie looked at their reflection in the mirror. "You might like it better!" Annie suggested.

"Nope, this un'll do."

Now today, for Annie's wedding, he suffered to don it again but only for the ceremony.

When the clock struck five, Annie slowly came down the stairs, wearing a midnight blue satin suit with a hat angled over her forehead. A wisp of blue veil feathered over her eyes. At the bottom of the stairs, she linked her arm through Otis's and they walked toward the fireplace where Robert stood waiting by the minister. As the winter afternoon faded into evening, light from six candles on the mantel and the fire glow bathed over the three of them. Three, because Otis, after delivering Annie to Robert's side decided not to sit down, but remained standing by Annie, intrigued as a child watching how this marrying business was done. Sophie helped Hannah down from her chair and she came forward, her head down, intent on the pillow with a ring in the center. When the ceremony was concluded, and the minister said Robert could kiss his bride, Otis curiously looked on. Then the minister said, "I now present to you Mr. and Mrs. Robert St. Pierre." Everyone clapped, except Otis. He bowed.

"A sweet, lovely ceremony," Belle Dorsett said as she kissed her niece. "Be happy. You've both earned it." Everyone surged about the newlyweds, everyone but Otis.

They went to the dining room, gathered around the table and after the first three toasts Otis stood, raised his glass, said nothing for a long embarrassing moment, then he burst out, "I don't want Annie to leave me."

She went to him, "I'll always be right here, sweetheart. "Don't worry."

He seemed pacified, looked down at the overabundant wedding feast. "Think I'll change out of—this." He looked down at his suit and left the room.

Belle Dorsett raised her glass, "I want Robert and Annie to come pick out any one of my antiques they want for a wedding gift."

"Except the big bed." Carson Garrett spoke up quickly. "That's already been spoken for."

Everyone laughed as they sat down to a candlelight dinner. "Aunt Belle, you caught the bouquet at my wedding to Willis. Now when are you going to be a bride?"

"It's entirely her fault," Garrett said, "she's afraid I'll take her away from here—and I just might."

"But I've heard you say," John Malvern knew what he meant, "if they find deep oil, you'd stay here."

Garrett nodded. "Then this would be the place to be."

"Looks like it might already be showing. Sohio drilled on the Shelby farm and found a deep run of saturated sand at 4,500 feet. They're doing a drill a stem test tomorrow."

Annie found Robert's hand under the table, leaned close to him, "This is not fit conversation for a wedding dinner."

"There's no getting around it, when oil people get together," he said softly.

They sat at the end of the long table, a line of candles

down the center. Candlelight, with the fireplace behind them, created an island of light in the great room. The brothers had only put electricity in the kitchen.

Robert enveloped her hand in both of his. The fireplace crackled nearby. A little world had grown between them. Even in a crowd they had their own living universe. "Annie, I thought my life was over," he whispered, twisting the ring he had just put on her finger. "I didn't think I could fall in love again."

She nodded, knowing that desolation.

"It's costly to drill that deep," someone was saying at the other end of the table, "unless you've got a pretty good indication you're going to hit pay."

His shoulder pressing against her, Robert spoke softly near her ear, "I didn't know I would ever find someone so... nice as you."

She looked at him, her eyes filled with tears and joy. "God let us find each other," she smiled, whispering. "I think this is the happiest day of my life."

"They couldn't identify the formation on the Shelby well." It was her father talking and Annie realized she hadn't been paying attention to guests.

"Some say it's in the Cypress series," Malvern went on.

"That's not deep enough," Garrett said. "I have to weigh quite a few things before I begin drilling to those levels even though the market for crude is getting strong now."

Now! The word echoed beyond the soft yellow light at the table into the dark recess of the room.

No one said anything. He meant *since the war*. Annie stole a glance at Sarah Emma, saw her head down. The war had already become excruciating real for those at the table—Sarah Emma and the Malvern family.

"It's raising prices by the month," Carson went on.

The papers had told of factories in the cities gearing up to work shifts around the clock, producing war materials and, as everyone knew, all needed fuel.

Oil production, which had captured everyone's attention for

the last four years, could not now put the incredible war news from their minds for long. Daily Otis and Annie had listened to the war news on the radio, hearing of U-boats sinking American ships, the Japanese's continuing assaults on Hong Kong and the Philippines. Just last month, Manila had fallen. American troops, in retreat, were reeling from severe losses. Names of strange places, Malaya, Luzon, Bataan, had become common knowledge to them, as they were to everyone.

Otis came back, stood framed in the doorway, dressed in his overalls and blue plaid shirt. He was smiling. "When are we gonna eat the cake, Annie?"

CHAPTER 76

By spring planting time, life had been transformed. Comfortable, routine living seemed set aside "for the duration" as everyone was saying. Gasoline rationing had started in some states.

Otis came back from one of his wells and slumped into a kitchen chair. "Gotta git goin' in the fields. One of the men says gas rationing'll be here 'fore the summer's out. Sooner we get out the corn, the better off we'll be."

"Otis, dear," Annie said, "maybe you should let this year slide by. It's time you took your summer under the shade tree."

Otis stared down at the floor. "Always put out a crop, ever since Pa took Henry and me to the field when we was boys."

"You'll be getting an oil check or two, Otis. It'll be all right."

"I don't know 'bout them fields now," he rubbed an index finger over his brow, looked worried, "there's so many people out there, I don't see how I can run a tractor without bumpin' into 'em."

"Listen, Otis," Annie set a cup of coffee before him, tried to distract him, "we're going to ride over to Aunt Belle's in the truck. She gave us one of her antique pieces for a wedding present. She's called twice for us to come over. I think Robert will need a man to help him load it."

As they rode, Annie between Robert and Otis with Hannah on his lap, she noticed how quiet Otis was. The countryside was sprinkled with oil derricks, pumps, interspersed with sodden fields cultivated and ready for planting.

"Time to get the corn out." Otis said, as he watched a tractor cultivating ground around two islands, each with an oil well in the field.

"I think the oil might be enough to keep you in jingling money, Otis." Robert said.

"Always plant corn and beans come May, if the fields ain't too wet." Otis kept his eyes on the tractor moving down the furrow.

"Gasoline rationing has started. Let the farming go this year. It's your patriotic duty." Annie patted his hand.

Otis didn't answer but his attention was fixed on the farmer and his tractor moving along, overturning soil, readying the ground for the yearly cycle of planting, cultivating and harvesting.

Soon they pulled into a parking spot before Belle Dorsett's Beauty Shop.

Otis slowly moved down from the truck. The last time he was in this house, was the night he came to take Hannah to her mother, when she went into hiding after the rape. Daytime was another matter. Otis looked askance at a woman under a strange apparatus, like a giant hood with wires coming down and attached somehow to rollers on her head. Another had her wet hair covered with some kind of red coloring. He edged closer to Annie and moved quickly out of that room.

"I'll be with you in a minute," Belle said. "Go on in and look around. Anything you pick, is yours."

Robert and Annie holding hands, looked at her dining room table. "But she needs that," Robert whispered. They looked at a desk and finally decided on a long buffet. "Maybe someday we'll have our own place," Annie said and kissed Robert on the cheek.

Later, Belle fixed them coffee. "Have you decided?"

"The buffet, Aunt Belle. It's so generous of you to give it to us. What a beautiful gift."

"It will stay in the family. After you, maybe Hannah. The continuity of family. We've always celebrated that."

Annie didn't respond but thought that used to be true before the oil came in.

Robert brought the truck to the side door and as the men pushed, slid and rolled the buffet into the truck bed. Annie turned to Belle, "We are so wonderfully happy. I never thought I could ever..."

"I am happy for you, darling."

Robert and Otis came back and as they were about to leave, Otis stepped to the doorway leading into Belle's shop and stood there for a moment, taking one last look at the woman with wires going into her head.

CHAPTER 77

This Fourth of July there would be no fireworks in town. However, a parade, band concert, and chowder festival were planned; the day was given over to a war bond drive. It was also, Hannah's second birthday. Annie had promised a celebration that evening.

Otis couldn't wait. He came to breakfast with a wrapped present under his arm and placed it before Hannah who was dawdling over her toast. "Here, little Birthday Girl." She grabbed it, ripping off the paper. A very round, pink piggy bank straddled the rumpled paper. She turned it over looking confused. Otis fished in his overall pocket, pulled out a nickel, and dropped it in the slot. Hannah giggled.

"Wait a minute." Otis disappeared into the front bedroom and returned with three fruit jars filled with silver coins. Annie had seen the jars before, a double row on the top closet shelf. He opened the jars, grabbed a fistful from each, and piled them on the tablecloth, then handed her a quarter. "Money make piggy fat." He held her plumb little hand and helped her drop it in the slot. She laughed and clapped at the sound and grabbed for more.

"Make piggy fat with money," Otis said, as they took turns, laughing and clapping, like two children playing a game. Otis said. "Make piggy fat. Make Hannah rich."

"The parade starts in an hour," Annie said. "We'll have to leave soon."

When they got into the Robert's car, Otis refused to go. He had stationed himself in a chair under the big oak in the front yard. "I'll sit right here and watch the oil trucks go by."

The town was alive with excitement, the sidewalks so packed it was hard to walk. Robert picked Hannah up and put her on his shoulders. On the south side of the courthouse square the band played, each member dressed in white uniform and brass instruments glistening in the sun. Flags hung from second story buildings around the square and storefront windows were covered with signs written in colored Bon Ami, "Buy Your War Bonds Here."

The west side of the square had been roped off to traffic. Six huge kettles of chowder simmered over fires in the middle of the street, filling the air with the aroma of corn, onions, tomatoes, beans and pork. The president was now talking of conserving food to stave off rationing, even a "meatless Tuesdays," and there were posters showing an empty plate, with the slogan "A cleaned plate is a patriotic plate."

Robert and Annie with Hannah spread a blanket on the grass in the square. The band left their seats, filed out into the street, and reformed into lines to lead off the parade. The mayor came next, followed by dozens of floats. The finale was a flatbed truck with six men in uniforms sitting in rows. Before them dancing girls, who were also men, with hairy legs under abbreviated skirts, stuffed bras over hairy chests, garishly made up and sporting excessive wigs, jitterbugged to the blaring strains of "Boogie Woogie Bugle Boy of Company B." Hanging from the flatbed was a long sign, "Do it for our boys."

The parade over, the band returned to their usual positions on the courthouse lawn and began playing again.

Long tables had been set up by the courthouse steps, where lines had formed to buy bonds. Not far from the tables selling bonds was another booth, with eight of the prettiest girls in town. Sarah Emma's daughter Betty was among them. As a reward for a bond purchase you could collect a kiss from one of the girls before you moved on to get a bowl of chowder. Robert nudged Annie as they watched a bearded oil-rich farmer in filthy overalls who had just bought 20 bonds and was collecting kisses from one girl after another.

Behind the tables selling bonds, new signs were constantly being posted in the courthouse window, 300 bonds sold, 500 bonds sold, 900 bonds sold. When the sign read 1000, a great cheer went up, cymbals crashed, and the band launched into Sousa's *"Stars and Stripes Forever."*

The day wore on and grew sultry. Barry Cogswell arrived with two cartons of cardboard fans from Cogswell's Funeral Home, on which was written, "Cogswell cares in your time of sorrow." They were grabbed up instantly.

Shadows began to lengthen, and the hot day grew oppressive. Robert and Annie went to the car and as they drove home, white light flared on the eastern horizon and a rumble sounded in the distance.

"Looks like we're going to have fireworks after all," Annie said, remembering the night of Hannah's birth. Soon jagged lightning streaked across the darkening sky. Flashes lit the full canopy of the heavens above them and the rain came with a fury. When they turned in the drive, lightning lit up the grounds.

"Annie, the shed door's open," Robert said. "The tractors gone. That ole man's got the tractor out!"

Annie hurried Hannah through the rain to search the house while Robert went to the shed and barn.

He came in, shaking the rain from his jacket. "The tractor's gone and there's no Otis."

"We've got to find him." A horrific crash of thunder rattled the windows. She gathered up Hannah, and they ran for Otis's truck. They drove through fields, past lighted derricks, around oil pumps, straining their eyes through the pouring rain, but saw no tractor.

"The fields are getting muddy," Robert said. "We'll have to stick to the roads the drillers made."

They stopped at one of the derrick sites, "We're looking for the old gentleman that lives up there." Robert said, as the rain misted in through the window.

"Yeah, saw the old boy this mornin' on his tractor, had a plow hitched on, too." The roustabout in a yellow slicker leaned on the car window. "These old farmers just can't let go. If it was me, I'd sit on the porch and wait for them oil checks to come."

Annie was impatient. "Which way was he going?"

"Well, think he was headed south, driving across the field lickety-split like he was in a big hurry. There's no field over there."

"Oh, God," Annie whispered. "Just the Little Wabash River."

They drove south, to where land began to drop away to the river. They stood above the ravine peering in the dark. Lightning flared again, and they saw the tangled heap of an overturned tractor and plow. Annie ran down to it and found Otis. His thick torso was pinned under the tractor and his head protruded from the wreckage. "Otis, talk to me. Otis!"

What she heard was faint gibberish. "He's alive." Rain was pouring over his face. "We shouldn't have left him, Robert."

"Stop that now. Get your wits about you, Annie. We've got to get this off him and get help. You and Hannah get one of the men to bring an oil truck and some chains. We'll try to pull the tractor up and get him out."

In a matter of minutes, a red truck angled slowly down the slippery descent to the wreckage. They disconnected the plow, chained the tractor to the truck and the truck began to pull. Slowly the tractor lifted. Robert and Annie pulled Otis free.

Otis was babbling unintelligibly. Robert and the driver put him in the front cab of the oil truck. Annie with Hannah crawled in beside him.

"Go to the doctor," Annie told the driver. "Fast." She turned her attention to him. "Otis, this is Annie."

He slumped against her babbling, his arms waving about.

"It's going to be all right," she whispered, trying to control his arms. "We'll get you help,"

At the doctor's house, Robert, who had followed, and the driver, carried Otis inside. They put him on an examining table and waited in the next room. Otis still muttered and seemed to have no control over his arms. The doctor opened Otis's clothing and listened to his chest. Through the open door, Annie saw Otis grow quiet. The doctor continued to minister over him then turned, and came out. He stood before them for a moment. "I'm sorry."

Annie looked through the door at Otis's thick body on the table.

"The doctor looked down at Annie. "I am so sorry. He was about gone when you brought him in here."

Annie found Robert's hand.

The doctor shook his head. "He's still got on his long winter underwear. He was out there trying to farm on a 95-degree day like this one. He apparently lost control of that tractor and got pinned under the wreckage, probably hemorrhaging internally. He laid there in the sun for hours."

Annie went to Otis, smoothed her hand over his cheek and pushed back wet hair plastered to his forehead. "Poor old sweetheart." She reached beneath his thick body and gathered him in her arms and laid her head on his still chest. "They were the goodest two people I ever knew. The world never touched them. I loved them…"

The doctor put his hand on her shoulder, "They were one of a kind."

When they came back home, the jars of coins still open sat on the table, and the piggy-bank beside them. Annie dropped down in a chair, took the piggy bank in her arms, held it to her chest. Tears came. Then wrenching sobs. Hannah looked up at her mother, her eyes wide, little face solemn. "Don't cry, Mommy."

The next day she and Robert pulled out the suit Otis had worn to their wedding. They looked at each other and at once said, "no".

"He should sleep in comfort." They went to Allisons store and bought him a new pair of overalls.

The following Sunday, Annie stood between Robert and Kurt, holding Hannah's hand as Otis was laid to rest next to Henry, their parents, and those who had died long ago in the influenza epidemic. Through the service Annie thought of the night, just outside this church when she railed in fury against God and uncaring religious people. The night she was raped and bleeding and these lonely bachelors had entered her life. She might have died without them—Hannah, too. The impact of what they were to her began to slowly unfold in her mind. She was too stunned to cry. There was only a deep hard ache in her heart.

CHAPTER 78

Annie trudged up the stairs to the room she had shared with Hannah and sat on the edge of the bed. She couldn't imagine the dear brothers were both gone, couldn't imagine life now without them. She sat for a long time, then stood and did what Henry had told her to do. She pulled open the top drawer of the chest and took out the envelope he had given her. "Oscar Nathan" Henry had scrawled on the outside. She knew Nathan was a lawyer in town.

Almost a week passed before she left Hannah with Robert and drove in to see Mr. Nathan. She had never seen the inside of a lawyer's office. Behind him, below a wide set of windows were four shelves of books. The sidewall was lined with wooden file cabinets. An electric fan on his large wooden desk oscillated, moving hot air around. She felt intimidated. This man had read all of those books, she concluded, and carried around in his head all the collected knowledge of the ages. A lump came into her throat.

"I'm here because…You probably know, Otis Patrick died…a few days ago." She sat down and fixated on a bee trying to get through the window screen behind Mr. Nathan. "His brother Henry gave me this letter to keep." She pushed the letter forward across his desk. "He said you would direct me on what to do about their affairs…"

Nathan took it, opened the envelope and studied the letter,

not speaking. He got up and went to a file drawer and took out a brown folder and studied it for some time. Outside there was the grind of traffic, and creaking of the fan as Annie watched with curiosity the bee hovering and buzzing outside the screen.

Finally, Nathan sat down. "Are you Annie Porter?"

"Yes sir. That is I was but I remarried. My name is Mrs. St. Pierre, now."

"Well, Mrs. St. Pierre, they stipulated that you are to receive the house they lived in and its contents."

Annie's hands went up to her cheeks, "Oh, my!"

"And, also the twenty acres on which it sits, which includes the mineral rights. Their nephew will inherit all the rest of the acreage and the mineral rights to that land."

"The mineral rights on the twenty acres!" Annie stared at him, echoing back what he said, trying to understand. But they were just words hanging in the air. She could not get her mind around what he was saying. She clutched at the top of the purse in her lap, until her knuckles grew white.

Nathan leaned back in his chair. "This means mineral rights not only to the wells now producing on those acres but any future production on those acres."

"I don't hardly know what to say."

"Henry told me—they both sat right there last winter, the snow coming down outside---and said, they wanted to provide a place for you and your daughter to stay and some income. They seemed honor-bound to give to this son of their deceased sister the bulk of the land. I'll notify him. There's an address here. I don't think they ever saw him. Henry told me he was their only kin."

"My goodness," Annie could not grasp it. "That old house. Imagine that!"

"And the twenty acres. There are wells producing on those acres now, I believe." Mr. Nathan stood up, signaling the meeting was over. He smiled at her for the first time. "I'll take care of the paperwork and call you. We'll need some signatures before this goes through."

He handed the letter back to her and she shoved it in her

purse, without answering.

"Congratulations." He extended his hand. Annie, somewhat dazed, accepted it. "You're now a woman of property."

She stared at him, not comprehending. "I miss them terribly," was all she could say. Nervous as she had felt when she came in, now she didn't want the moment to end. "... no bumbling around the kitchen in my way."

"They were fine old boys." Nathan followed her to the door and reached for the knob. "Never did anyone any harm."

A fleeting memory came to Annie. The brothers pushing a black car toward the river crunched between the truck and tractor, taking a monster to his death.

"No-o," she whispered, avoiding Mr. Nathan's eyes. "Can't imagine they ever did."

That afternoon as shadows lengthened in the front yard and whippoorwills called in the distance, she and Robert walked through the rooms of the old three-story house. The day had been hot and as they moved up the stairs, closed cavernous room had captured and still held stifling heat. Somehow, though, it looked different to Annie. It felt different as she smoothed her hand over the stair banister leading to the second floor and the bedroom where they had first made love. They climbed on to the top floor and the dormer room where Annie had hid for so many weeks. She pushed open the window and leaned out, a slight evening breeze rustled through the trees

"A lot of living has gone on here," she said as Robert joined her, looking down on the grounds below.

"Our living, too," Robert answered and took her hand. Then he turned to her. "Let's restore it."

She smiled as she looked at him. What a great idea, she thought. "To what it was before those old codgers used it to camp out in the kitchen? It was once a grand place."

They took one of the crayons Hannah had used when she played in the room and began drawing plans over all the faded crumbling wallpaper until darkness closed in on them.

CHAPTER 79

A late summer breeze poured through Kurt's apartment as he pulled out his pocket knife, slit open an envelope and read, "The President of the United States sends you Greetings," it began. His heart began to pump as he scanned the page. "Selective Service…induction…October 21, 1942." He tossed the letter on the table. So it had come. He'd been expecting it. He slipped into a clean shirt. Maybe after he went for lunch, he'd try to see Lillian. He needed her now. Tell her he'd got his draft notice. Would she care?

At Sarah Emma's restaurant, newspapers littered the counter and tables.

"Look here." Dempsey Webster moved next to Kurt and nudged him. "Last Wednesday they raided the Blue Moon and found nothing. Then today, just two days later, the paper explodes with pictures of slot machines and gambling tables all over the front page. And the sheriff's right there, even with a woman." He shoved the paper over to Kurt. "Just take a look at that. Makes out the sheriff might have been lying to ever' body all along."

Kurt focused in on the three big pictures on the front page. "Where'd they get these?"

"Don't nobody know. Paper won't say."

"CAN THE SHERIFF BE A LIAR?" Kurt read with a

scoff, the blaring three-inch letters across the top of the paper.

"Morning, Kurt," Sarah Emma smiled, as she came behind the counter. "Coffee?"

"Sure."

She handed him a menu. "What'll it be today?"

"Got any of that meatloaf? He asked, but before he could find out if she had heard where they got the pictures in the paper, she had bustled off to another table. He turned to one of the men at the counter. "Where'd they get these pictures?"

"Dunno, but they sure caught the sheriff with his pants down, pert' near, anyway."

Everybody laughed.

"They're lookin' hard at the sheriff." Dempsey Webster sidled close to Kurt, reading over his shoulder. "Looks like he's playin' both sides of the fence. Sheriff's madder'n hell. Says somebody's out to ruin him, and he knows who it is."

Webster looked over his spectacles at Kurt. "Course he ain't sayin' this for publication, but he says he's gonna git whoever done them pictures."

"I guess we see he ain't above pulling some things that's not under the badge," Kurt said.

Webster took a sip of coffee. "He's ruined, for sure. It ain't like he can refute what's right here plain to see, or that he was misquoted."

Sarah Emma topped off the coffee for Kurt and Dempsey without looking up, so Webster went on. "There no law here. None atall."

"Sarah, anybody come in here today think they know who did this?" He gestured toward the paper.

"Not that I've heard," Sarah nodded. "Meatloaf's coming right up, Kurt."

At home, Kurt picked up the draft notice, and decided to try to call Lillian. Maybe she would answer. He really needed her now.

The phone rang. "Hello." It was Coralee.

"Wrong number."

"Kurt! I know your voice." Coralee said. "I went to your apartment. Kurt you're in trouble. Really big trouble. You've got to leave town..."

"Why, would I have to leave town, Coralee?"

"This is terrible serious. Kurt, you've got to go. Right now." There was pleading in her voice. The phone went dead.

He frowned as he sat down in a chair. What was this silly kid up to now?

He gave the operator the number again. The phone rang several times. "Hello." It was Lillian.

"Lillian, it's me. I really need to talk to you. I..."

"I knew you Malverns were crazy, but to try this...on us."

"What?" He looked stupidly at the phone after she hung up, wondering what the hell was going on.

In less than ten minutes Coralee was at his door.

"My Uncle Logan, the sheriff and my aunt were at our house this morning when the news broke. Then Uncle Bucky came. They said it's you that exposed him in the paper. Uncle Bucky thinks you're out to humiliate the sheriff like you did at the shooting match,'cause they didn't find who killed your sister's husband."

"He knew who killed Willis." Kurt looked down into Coralee's adoring eyes. "He didn't want to do anything about it."

"They're coming here, to get you. I never saw anybody so mad. I was scared of Uncle Logan, myself. Get out of here," she pleaded. "Kurt, I...I don't want you hurt."

"I haven't done anything. Why should they arrest me?"

"Oh, Kurt, please." She came to him, and timidly put her arms around him. "You gotta go."

The door burst open. Lillian stood framed in the doorway, staring at them. "Why you filthy dog. You animal," she screamed at Kurt. "Mother and daughter. I said I'd kill you if you came near my daughter."

"Mama, I came to Kurt...to tell..."

"Coralee, go home." She pushed her aside.

"Leave, Kurt. You go, now," Coralee cried.

"You filthy dog," Lillian kept repeating, her eyes burning on Kurt. "You Malverns are nothing but...."

"Mama," Coralee stopped and stared at her mother, "what did you mean 'mother or daughter'?"

"Nothing," Lillian turned on her, "nothing. It means nothing."

"Mama, do you like Kurt?" Coralee came toward her mother, her eyes wide. "You say to stay away from him."

Kurt looked from Lillian to Coralee, feeling like a pawn in this game.

"Just shut up." Lillian stood eye to eye to her daughter, her face splotched red.

"No, I don't want to—shut up." Coralee looked at her mother. "I want to know. Do you like Kurt?"

"You don't know what you're talking about. You're just a child."

Kurt watched, thinking anything he would say would only make it worse for Coralee and himself.

"I'm not a child, but—Mama, you're..."

Car doors slammed. Through the open apartment door, Kurt saw the sheriff, Malcolm Powers, and Bucky Allison striding across the grass.

"It's too late." Coralee cringed behind Kurt. "Too late, Kurt. Oh, too late."

"Malcolm," Lillian ran to meet her husband, screaming. "This man has been molesting our little girl. There isn't anything he won't do."

"Looks like that's about right." The sheriff grabbed Kurt and pulled his arms back into handcuffs. Bucky Allison stood before Kurt, bearing his white teeth in a wide smile, merriment dancing in his eyes.

"Get outa my face, Bucky. Tell that stupid sheriff he's all wrong again," Kurt lashed out.

"Kurt never did a thing to me, Daddy." Coralee went to her

father, crying. "Nothing. Mama's lying." She turned to the sheriff. "Uncle Logan, this is a mistake." Coralee ran from one to the other, begging. "Don't take Kurt away. You're all wrong..."

"I don't know what this is about, but you got the wrong guy..." Kurt yelled while Logan yanked him toward the car.

Mrs. Keltoux stood on her front step across the street with two neighbors, watching Kurt being led away.

"Kurt, tell them." Coralee followed as they put him in the back of the patrol car. "Daddy, no. Stop Uncle Logan. It's not true," Coralee stood by the car, her hands over her face, shaking her head and sobbing. "He never did anything wrong."

Kurt pulled back against the cuffs. "I done nothin'," he screamed at the sheriff. "I don't know what's goin' on, but it's a damn big mistake."

Mrs. Keltoux came across the lawn, stood by the patrol car, and looked at Malcolm seated in the passenger side. "It's your daughter that's lying, Mr. Powers." Mrs. Keltoux drew herself up. "That girl of yours was over here. I saw her leaving at six o'clock one morning. It's not my way to be a busybody, but you ought to know. Your wife is right."

"But I did the coming over." Coralee turned on her. "Kurt had nothing to do with it."

"You're—not responsible," Lillian said. "We all know that. Malcolm, that man is not to be trusted in any way."

"What are you gonna do with him?" Coralee peered into the car. Kurt's head was down. Bucky sat by him in the back seat, apparently having the time of his life.

"This has nothing to do with you." The sheriff spoke sharply to Coralee as he backed out of the driveway.

Lillian pulled at Coralee's arm. "You're going home with me. Leave this to Uncle Logan and your father."

Coralee jerked free. "No, Mama." She faced her mother squarely, eyes level on her. "No. From now on, I do what I want."

Lillian looked long at her daughter. "So you've found your will!" Then she shrugged. "What can you do after all?" Her lips curled into a tight smile as she crawled into her car and left.

Coralee ran to her bicycle and followed the sheriff's car at some distance. She was puzzled when they didn't turn toward the jail, but drove on through town. They turned off on a country road that led to the back entrance of the grove, to the place where they'd held the shooting matches.

By the time Coralee arrived, they had handcuffed Kurt's hands behind him around a tree. The sheriff was chopping low limbs off the tree and tossing them to Malcolm and Bucky.

"I heard once about how this was done," Bucky called as he began piling up brush for a bonfire in front of Kurt. "Want it about four feet distant from the tree all around." Malcolm came with another load of tree limbs. "Stack that one behind him then pile the others in between. After a while, it'll catch into a blazing circle, then the tree itself."

Kurt twisted, struggling hard against the tree trunk. "I never done a thing to you, Logan," Kurt screamed. "You're committing murder, you fool. You'll never get by with this."

"What are you doing?" Coralee shrilled as she ran to the sheriff. He kept chopping at a tree, ignoring her.

"Stop, Uncle Logan. Please don't do this to Kurt." Coralee dogged his every step, pulling at his arm. He shoved her away. "Go home. Stay out of this."

A pile of brush began to encase Kurt.

Logan handed the ax to Malcolm and came to stand before Kurt. "You been out to get me because I couldn't find Willis's murderer. I saw that at the shooting match, but you're sure as hell not winnin' this time."

"You knew who killed Willis," Kurt exploded. "You think they're gonna get you outa this…They'll forget you just like you forgot Willis. You're nothing to them hoodlums if you're not the sheriff."

"Shut up, Malvern…" Logan Webb struck a match held it up, looking at it, then held it in Kurt's face. "This is gonna be a slow roast… so you can take your time, thinkin' about how you set out to ruin me. Then think about me taking you down with me— that is, if you're alive."

Kurt stared into Logan's eyes. "I don't know about those pictures," Kurt spit back.

"Maybe it'll come back to you after things get a little hot in there." Logan picked up a long tree branch, struck a match and held it until the brush blazed, and then waved the fiery limb under Kurt's nose. "You feel that? You like it?"

Kurt pulled back. "You're a mad man." Then at the top of his lungs he screamed, "Coralee, help me!"

Logan dropped the flaming limb in the brush. Soon flames began to lick upwards catching quickly where the brush had been piled. Soon the tree limbs would catch fire and he would be engulfed in an inferno. Bucky and Malcolm still dragged brush to fill in the circle.

Coralee stood frozen in disbelief that her father and uncles would really do this. Flames began to leap higher. She jumped on to her bicycle and sped away. She heard Bucky and Logan laughing and taunting Kurt and over that, Kurt's screams for help.

CHAPTER 80

Robert and Annie had begun their grand renovating plan in what once was the parlor. Two feet from the floor, the wallpaper was stained various shades of brown and the pattern above had faded into obscurity. They peeled it down, tearing it loose until they found the bare walls of lathe and plaster. A great mountain of wallpaper fragments filled the center of the room. Hannah spent her days playing in the mound of debris as if it were dead leaves in the yard. That had been two weeks ago. Now all the downstairs had been stripped down to plaster.

"We'll need to replace some of those rotted windowsills before we start refinishing the wood floors." Robert said. "Over by the fireplace, there's black burn marks, where they'd laid hot pokers."

Annie slipped down to the floor, sat cross-legged, pulled the bandana off her hair and sighed when she looked up at the stair banister, thinking of the refinishing job that would be. "This looked so easy when we were sketching it out with a crayon on the wallpaper in that upstairs room."

Robert laughed. "Wait'll we start on that stair runner. Those old boys tacked it and then as it frayed more, they nailed it again and again."

Then suddenly there was a loud pounding on the front door below. Someone was shouting and beating on the door

Robert threw open a second story window. "What is it?"

Coralee Powers looked up, yelling, "Come quick. They're trying to burn Annie's brother to death. At the grove. The sheriff thinks Kurt put bad pictures in the paper."

They hurried down the bare stair steps.

"I'll go to the grove," Robert said, "Get your father, Annie. Coralee, go to Dutch's and get all the men you can."

Annie picked Hannah up from her nap and rushed out to the car. She found her father at a well, talking to Carson Garrett. Garrett turned to the oil crew, "You, Ralph and Clyde, come quick."

Annie stopped at Sarah Emma's café, ran in pleading for for help. Maxwell Porter put down his saw. "You sayin' that sheriff's about to burn somebody alive?"

"Yes! Kurt." Annie cried. "Hurry." Hannah, in her arms whimpered, knowing something was fearfully wrong.

Porter leaned over; grabbed up his hammer from the toolbox; sped past Annie, looking neither right nor left; ran to his truck; and spun out on the road toward the Grove

CHAPTER 81

Kurt writhed, as the intense heat moved closer to him. He turned his head away but faced leaping flames from the other side. His feet were free, and he moved around the tree, trying to find a place he could tolerate, but the circle of heat was growing wider, closing in on him. "I didn't do anything to you, Logan," Kurt screamed. "I'm not the one."

He heard the sheriff laugh. "You want to take me down...I'm takin' you with me."

"Malcolm Powers," Kurt called over the crackling fire, "I never did nothin' to your daughter."

"Don't believe him." He heard Lillian call out. "He'll say anything."

"What in the hell are you doing to this man?" Kurt heard Robert's voice, yelling. "Kurt, we'll get you out."

"You interfere, we'll throw you in there with 'em." Kurt recognized Bucky Allison's voice. "Logan's got his gun on you."

Kurt thought he heard car doors slamming. The heat was searing his face and flecks of fiery airborne debris hit his arm and bored into the flesh and he shrieked.

"Kurt, my God, son, don't give up. We'll git you out." It was John Malvern. His father.

"I'm burnin' Pa. Do something."

"You can't hold us all off, Sheriff." Kurt heard Carson Garrett out beyond this burning wall. "Might as well shoot one of us or give up the gun." More car doors slammed. Loud voices screamed at each other. Kurt could not get his breath. My God I *am* gonna die. His back was baking. His throat was raw from constant screaming. He felt a thousand bits of debris drilling into his flesh. He gasped for breath. Finally he collapsed in a heap at the bottom of the tree trunk.

Then Maxwell Porter's voice roared, "I'm coming over there, Sheriff, and I'm gonna knock a hole in your rotten skull with this here hammer. And it ain't for Kurt Malvern. It's fer Willis. If you're gonna shoot somebody, it's gonna be me. Ever'body's gonna see you murder me. You're a dead man, Logan, just like my boy..." Kurt was not aware of much more—only murmurs somewhere beyond the fire.

Kurt heard water splashing on the fire; sparks crackling. Then there was more water. From the lake he guessed. He felt more than saw an opening in the wall of flames. Hands unlocking his wrists, lifting him up, but he screamed at the touch. It felt like tearing flesh. He was outside the fire now, lying on the ground. There were voices around him. He thought someone said the fire was out.

"They're taking the sheriff away, Son." His father leaned over him. "He's fightin' 'em every step, but he's done for."

Kurt tried to turn his head to his father, but his skin was so seared he couldn't move.

"I want to talk to Malcolm Powers," Kurt whispered.

"He's handcuffed, Son. But I'll get 'em."

Malcolm Powers stood over Kurt. Kurt eyed him, the man who wanted to murder him. Lillian behind her husband was crying. A dozen men stood about. Kurt summoned all the strength he could muster. "I never touched your daughter," Kurt heard his own voice, croaking, "but I laid your wife thirty-seven times."

Lillian turned to her husband. "No, no," she cried, her eyes wild. "He's lying, Malcolm. He's a liar."

Powers bent down, stared into Kurt's eyes, and then turned to his wife. "Why would he lie now?"

"I made a scratch." Kurt could barely find voice to speak, "on the edge... of my truck bed... for every time... thirty-seven times...old scratches...rusty ones."

"That ole boy's not lyin'." One of the oil workers laughed. "That dude's been screwing the Allisons. We're gonna take care of him."

Garrett pulled on Malcolm's arm. "Come on, Powers, we're going to check you in with the State Police. And they're not going to be understanding folks when it comes to roasting people alive."

"Just a minute." Malcolm pulled hard against Garrett as they walked to Garrett's Buick 8. "I want to see that truck."

Garrett walked him to Kurt's truck. Malcolm moved his fingers slowly along the curved side of the truck bed where the scratches were in long succession. He put both hands on the truck, dropped his head between his arms, and kicked at the ground with his foot. "I'm ready." He turned to Carson Garrett. "I said, I'm ready," he barked.

Coralee knelt by Kurt, "We'll get you to the hospital," she soothed. "They'll take care of you. You'll be all right."

Kurt heard other voices behind them, the men taunting Lillian.

"Listen, honey, that half cooked man over there ain't gonna be no good for you now, but there ain't a thing wrong with me. I can take care of you good, darlin'."

"Don't you dare talk to me like that!" Lillian stood her ground. "You're nothing but dirty scum... You come into my town and think you're just as good as my family. Don't you know my father owned half this town? I'm..."

"Oh, honey, I know who you are. I knowed you in Texas, and I knowed you in Oklahoma, and I knowed you a lot of places in Arkanses. I'd know you anywhere."

"Get away from me." Lillian screamed. Kurt sensed they were crowding in on her by the different voices.

"Make 'em stop." Kurt whispered to Coralee.

Kurt turned his head slightly to see Coralee run to Lillian, facing the men. "Leave my mama alone." He heard Coralee's little girl voice. "Leave her alone."

Lillian pushed her aside. "Coralee! You shouldn't be here. You don't understand…"

Coralee put herself in front of her mother and spoke to the man leering at Lillian. "You leave. You just go on…git." She glanced back at Kurt on the ground. "Thank you for what you did for Kurt, but…now…just go on…" Her voice trembled as she stood before the men. "Don't you see, it's my mother, you're talking bad to?"

They turned away, but they were still laughing. Lillian leaned against a tree trunk and began to sob. But it was Kurt that Coralee went to.

CHAPTER 82

For the next few weeks, when Kurt roused from sedated oblivion, he realized he was in a darkened bedroom at his parents' house. Gradually, burns over his body began to heal until only the worst, his face, arms and chest, kept him hurting. The doctor, on one of his frequent visits to the Malvern house, said it was a miracle his vision was not damaged.

His mother's friends from the quilting club came daily to tend his wounds. Throughout the summer, whatever he asked for, they accommodated. Sarah Emma sent meals from her restaurant, and Hattie came by to feed him. His mother sat by his bed. At first he hardly knew who was caring for him, but as he improved he marveled at their gentle care and constant attention.

"The sheriff and Malcolm Powers have both been indicted for attempted murder." Hattie lifted a spoonful of soup to Kurt's lips. "They're looking for a new sheriff." She focused over her bifocals and she dabbed his mouth with a napkin.

One late fall afternoon, Sophie helped Kurt to a chair under the big oak in the front yard. Hattie, Sarah Emma and Dora had come by. They had talked it over at quilting on Thursday and decided that today would be the day. Kurt had to know the truth. They followed Sophie into the yard.

Sarah Emma pulled a chair close by. "There's something

we've been meaning to tell you." She swallowed away a lump in her throat. "It won't be an easy thing for you to hear, but Kurt, you have to know. It was Hattie who took those pictures of the sheriff. We took 'em to the paper. It was us that started everything." There, she had told him! She sat back, relieved but watching for his reaction. "You wouldn't be sitting there burned like you are, if it wasn't for what we done."

Kurt said nothing. He just stared into his lap. Then she saw him tremble.

"There's no words to tell you how sorry we are." Hattie rushed to add. "We just set out to get rid of that sheriff and get things straightened out..."

Kurt looked up at them, his distorted face splotched crimson. *"You* did that? You? You women I've known all my life?" His jaw tightened, and he gripped the arm of the chair.

"We're just as sorry as we can be." Dora's voice quavered.

He seemed to want to get up, out of his chair, strike at something. Then he looked at his mother. "And...you, Mama?"

"That's not exactly all of it." Sophie cut in. "You're not innocent, Kurt, and you know it. A lot of people think a married woman is the property of her husband and you..." Her voice choked. "You brought disgrace on our family with this indecent thing you did... oh, Kurt, I didn't raise you to do things like that. I didn't." She began to cry, and she came and gently put her arms about him.

"I suppose you think I deserve this." Kurt struck out "...retribution." He shook off her embrace.

"No," Sophie whispered. "Nothing like this. But, oh... my boy, why?"

"I didn't do a thing to Logan Webb," Kurt cried, and pushed her away. He laid his head back against the chair and looked up into the trees. "I reckon there was a lot of reasons, Mama."

Sophie ran her fingers over Kurt's forehead and cheek and bit her lip as tears rimmed her eyes. "You're gonna wear them marks all your life."

"There was already marks there, Mama, that didn't show."

The quilting ladies stood about. Hattie began to cry. "I'm heartsick for all the pain we've caused you. Just sick."

"Get out," Kurt yelled and again tried to rise out of his chair. "All of you." Sarah Emma flinched as if she had been struck. "Get away from me," he screamed, clenching his fists in impotent fury, "Do you want me to say it's all right? You didn't mean it and that's it?" He yelled at them. "Do you want that? Look what you've done."

Dora and Hattie, both wiping their eyes with handkerchiefs, stood helplessly by. What was there to say? What was there to do? Finally, they walked across the yard to their cars.

Sophie and Kurt still sat alone. His pain had subsided for some days now. Mostly he felt the tautness of his damaged skin— smooth, slick skin of scars. The doctor had talked of possible reconstructive surgery. Maybe. He didn't want more pain. Not now.

While he sat, the late afternoon growing dim, Annie and Robert came and walked to the chairs by him on the lawn. Annie had come by every day, talking to him about how they were making the old house over, as it once was. He appreciated her company. Pleased she was happy again.

"We've been talking to Carson Garrett," Annie began. "We're going to back him to drill into some of the old wells and go to a deeper level. Price of oil's going up. Reports are good from the stem tests. We'll own these wells, Kurt. Robert and I will. What do you think, brother? Want to go in with us?"

Kurt gave a bitter laugh. "Borrow money when I'm facing military service if I ever get well enough?"

"I'll loan you the money," Annie said.

"I don't think so. Mama's been talking to me about my faulty judgment..." He noticed when Annie talked to him, she looked away. Was he that grotesque?

"It's what you need, Kurt, a purpose to go on. Think about it."

He looked across the wide fields, pumping wells

silhouetted against the twilight. "You're the only one that thinks about my life going on."

"What would you do if you struck it rich, Kurt?" she asked.

He thought for a moment. What would he do? He could hardly put aside this consuming, red-hot fury in him, to find a rational thought. All he wanted was to get well enough so he could feel the satisfaction of revenge. What *would* he do? He remembered the night he stood on a porch looking through a window into an elegant ballroom.

It was a party he had been asked not to attend

"Maybe I'd buy the Hotel Allison."

Annie leaned forward and kissed his cheek. "Think about my offer."

CHAPTER 83

Robert brought the newspaper in from the mailbox, poured himself a cup of coffee, and tasted it. "Too hot," he murmured, sat it aside and spread the paper across the breakfast table. "There's been another murder, Annie."

Headlines blared, "'A COUNTY WITHOUT LAW,' it says," Robert continued, "that a prominent banker in Fairfield was shot in his home, when he answered the door. Retribution, the paper says, because his son left town owing a gambling debt. The article continued, detailing a fracas at one of the well sites and about a prostitute found dead along the road.

"Looks like no one wants the job of sheriff," Robert folded the paper and handed it to Annie. "So what's going to happen here?"

"A least they have something to write about besides my family." Annie retorted.

With the furor that had followed the sheriff's arrest for attempted murder and blaring headlines that graphically explored the liaison between Lillian Allison Powers and Kurt Malvern, suggesting that Kurt seduced the simple child of Lillian's, and had an obsessive determination to ruin the sheriff, Sophie Malvern had nearly collapsed under the burden of disgrace. Annie had stayed on to comfort her mother and help with Kurt. Sophia sat in her grand living room, a King James Bible open and draped over her aproned lap, sobbing her humiliation in Annie's arms.

Annie's father, some months before had gone to the woods, cut a dozen cedar saplings and planted them around his shed. Malvern wouldn't come into the bedroom where, when medication wore off, his son suffered agonies, but spent long hours tinkering in the old shed, behind his wall of cedar sapplings even avoiding the house as much as possible.

Hannah came into the breakfast table, crawled into her mother's arms, snuggled close, for a slow wake up. It was so good to be back home where life was calm, holding her child, talking to her husband—away from the turmoil, shame and suffering. It felt good even to be back working in the "forward rooms" again, doing the mindless job of stripping away paint, wallpaper, age and neglect. To see lost elegance emerge sometimes, was like a happy discovery.

A dismal day in early December, the "forward" rooms done, they decided to tackle the first of the six bedrooms upstairs, three on each side of a wide hall. Carrying a kerosene lamp, Robert with Annie following, climbed the newly restored stairs and pushed open the door to one of the bedrooms. It was dark, smelled musty, with mold covering the east wall. And it was cold. Annie, bundled in a heavy sweater, began scraping wallpaper, but her fingers were stiff, the chill in the room, sharp. Outside, snow drifted in the air, and windowpanes rattled from time to time in the wind. "Robert, it's too cold for us to work up here, now." She rubbed her hands, drawn to the window, watching the falling snow.

"I'll take up the carpet, open the grate in the floor. Downstairs heat'll warm it up." Robert dropped down to the edge of the carpet, slid a chisel under the corner of the rug and pried up a corner the brothers had nailed down. "These big rooms'll take weeks of..."

He stopped. Leaned back on his haunches, then stood.

Annie turned from the window, puzzled.

"Annie," he whispered. "Come look."

Annie gasped, her breath taken away. She stared for a long time. Her hand went to her mouth. "Oh, my," she whispered. "Oh, my God."

He pulled back more of the old carpet. They stood together, stunned to speechlessness.

"My God," Annie breathed, surveying what had opened before their eyes. "Now I believe in miracles."

Little stacks of bills—twenties—each stack about a half inch thick, were tightly laid side by side under the rug. Shaking her head, Annie murmured. "They didn't trust banks,"

She looked at it, trying to absorb the shock.

They pulled back more of the rug and row upon row of bills appeared under the rug. Annie felt a strange presence surrounding her, as if the brothers were with her in this room.

Robert sat back, leaning against the wall, lost in the spectacle stretching across the floor. "I wonder how they knew we'd find it?" Annie ran her hand over the layers of bills with almost reverence. It was eerie. The spirit of the two brothers seemed to be standing over them, smiling.

"Henry probably imagined Otis would go first and then he would tell me, before he died. Otis, the old sweetheart, just didn't remember."

They picked up the chisels again, started loosening more tacks, turning the rug back, foot after foot, exposing the bills.

Annie put the chisel aside, too amazed to go on. "How much do you suppose?"

"I couldn't say." Robert shook his head. "I'm not used to counting money by the foot."

She looked into Robert's eyes and realized he, too, was trying to grasp the sight that lay before them.

"There are four other bedrooms on this floor besides the one we use…do you suppose…" she said.

Robert carried the lamp to the next room. They loosened tacks along three sides and turned the woven strips back completely exposing rows of bills.

"I have never seen anything like this," Robert said.

Yellow lamplight glowed over the treasure that spread at their feet. "When I walked across these rugs," Annie spoke softly as if in awe. "I thought the crunch was a layer of straw. I knew old people used to get these long strips of woven rugs, sew them together and spread straw under them for warmth." She turned to Robert, tears tracing down her cheeks. "But look what they have done!" She was overwhelmed with the sense of the brothers' presence. "They left this to me, Robert—me and Hannah."

She shook her head. "It's beyond belief. They adored Hannah, you know," she whispered.

Robert put his arms around her shoulders. "They adored you, too."

The day was darkening, snow falling heavier, but there was no thought of sanding doors, scraping wallpaper—or even the cold.

Robert picked up the lamp. "I wonder about these other empty rooms?"

"Yes," Annie said.

In the pale light, they again pried loose carpet in the next bedroom, and a sea of money extending out, reaching beyond the circle of light where shadows claimed the room.

In each of the rooms they found stretches of green bills neatly positioned under the rug, except one. There was no carpet in the bedroom where they slept.

Annie's hand went to her throat, totally astonished and overcome, then an idea came to her. "What about the dormer rooms!"

They went up the narrow stairs to the two attic rooms where Annie had hid with Hannah. When they turned back the rug, there was straw. In the other dormer room, they found a few stacks of bills but empty spaces. "This is where they were putting the last money, I suppose." Robert said.

"That's why they put me up here. They hadn't started to use the dormer rooms yet. I remember when I wanted to move down to the second-floor bedroom, Henry objected until I told him the dormer rooms were too cold for Hannah. He couldn't say 'no' to anything Hannah needed."

Annie walked the length of the room where she had lived after the rape, and then she turned to Robert. "Right after we moved to the second floor Henry came to my room and asked me to take care of them. I think he had made up his mind where this money should go to."

"And people called them 'simple,'" Robert said.

They went back to the room where they had made their first discovery, painstakingly prying up every tack and rolling the rug back to a floor of money. They began to laugh and couldn't stop. Annie dropped down into the neat piles of bills and started scooping them up in her arms, throwing them over Robert's head and her own, bills landing in their hair and on their shoulders, laughing as dusty money rained down on them.

In the next week, all interest in house renovations was lost to the consuming business of counting money. They sat on the floor where they first found the money, Robert keeping the tally and Annie counted packets of twenty-five twenty-dollar bills. They laughed as the figures rose to hundreds, then into the thousands, and finally, sobered, past a million and on to almost two million. Finally finished and leaning against the wall, they looked at the ragtag collection of receptacles that bulged with money. Robert had scoured the place for baskets and satchels, then Annie brought out pillowcases and flour sacks.

"We have to do something with this," Annie said.

"Sweetheart, you can't put all this money in the bank at once. The news would be all over town before the day was over. That man, the one who demanded money of the brothers is still out there somewhere. It will be an invitation for trouble, and, as you well understand, there is no law to protect you."

"We have to put it somewhere."

"We could put it in one of the dormer rooms where there is a lock, at least until we decide what to do," Robert suggested.

Annie smiled, "The brothers never locked anything, and they knew what was here."

Robert said, "I doubt if they knew where the key was."

Gazing across the room, still feeling so strongly the brothers' presences, Annie smiled. "Do you realize, Robert, what a strange dilemma we have here?"

He smiled and kissed her on the cheek. "This is what I think, we should open accounts only in out of state banks using a modest sum, then gradually building each one. We can go to St. Louis, Vincennes, Louisville, all an easy day's drive. I also think we should not tell anyone about what we found."

Annie nodded in agreement, then turned to him, suddenly feeling protective and possessive of what was stuffed in baskets and sacks across the room. "But what if there should be a fire while we're waiting to bank it all.

Robert shrugged. "The brothers never worried about that, either."

CHAPTER 84

On Valentine's Day, Annie and Robert celebrated their first wedding anniversary alone.

Only the glow of the fireplace filled the "forward room" where they sat talking late into the night.

The last few months had been devoted to something they both loved, the rebirth of the old house but now Annie felt a new dimension to their work. It seemed like everything she did was a tribute to what the brothers had done for her—protected her, provided for her and even killed for her.

A paperhanger had covered the naked walls with damask paper, which gave off a satin sheen when the newly installed electric chandelier glistened against it. Thick Persian carpets now spread across burnished wood floors. In the firelight, all shined, pristine as new, like the life they were building together.

The house was their creation and working together each day was also a kind of creation but now another creation of their love was growing in Annie's body. What they had found in each other, salvaged from the ashes of damaged lives, others would not understand.

There had been long talks about buying the four oil wells and financing the drilling to deeper strata. They had told no one about the money they had found, just as they decided. The sheriff was gone and the man who killed Willis was gone, but the mob was still very active.

Tonight, one year after her marriage, Annie put her head on Robert's shoulder, cozied against him, warmed by the crackling fireplace. Outside winter moonlight spread over the frozen, snow-covered earth holding growth dormant, but for Annie life was resurging, bourgeoning beyond what she had ever imagined.

CHAPTER 85

It was a brilliant April morning with spring breezes pouring through open windows of the rejuvenated mansion. Annie was with Hannah in the nursery where she had put her well-worn and well-loved teddy bear in the crib so the baby, when it came, would have a toy waiting. A knock came to the door. Annie awkwardly made her way down the stairs and saw her father through the frosted glass in the front door

John Malvern stood, his old black coat hanging on his stooped frame, with Kurt behind him. Her father had not been in Annie's house since her wedding day.

His face was somber, as she invited him in. She expected he would notice the beautiful rooms she and Robert had transformed, but he said nothing, nor did he comment on her obvious pregnancy. Malvern slumped in a chair by the fireplace. Kurt sat down opposite him.

"Glenn is dead." John Malvern said.

"No," she came to him, reached for him in an embrace. "It can't be. It's another mistake, Papa, like…"

"No mistake this time. His ship went down in a battle defending some place called the Santa Cruz Islands."

Annie sank into a chair. All the grief she'd felt when they thought Glenn lost before came back, as if it was just a continuation, only muted now, refusing acceptance. She knew the nightmarish nights that would come, imagining the terror Glenn felt in the last moments of his life.

She glanced at Kurt, her big handsome strapping brother, disfigured, broken and hiding from life. Now Glenn. Tears burned behind her eyes.

Annie watched her father pace the floor, talking mostly to himself. "It makes me mad. It just makes me so damn mad. To think I raised up a boy, my flesh and blood, and I have to give him up to some strange place I never even heard of." His fists were clenched, making motions like he wanted to hit something, but there was nothing to hit, nothing to find a mark for his rage. "My own flesh and blood lying deep in an ocean half a world away somewheres I don't even know about. Family should not be apart like that...when the end comes."

Annie looked up at her father, thinking, family can be apart only a few miles away, but she said nothing.

"I raised up five children." Malvern stalked back and forth. "They were mine." He ripped off his hat and slung it on the floor, "And they took my boy, somewhere and killed him." He dropped down on the sofa, buried his head in his palms, and his great shoulders began to shake.

Kurt sat apart from him, the skin of his face twisted and pulled, slick as satin in places, rough and puckered in others.

Finally, Malvern was still. He raised his head, "Eva Mae's gonna put together some kind of a service for Glenn. Something like they did for Danny Allison, she says."

Annie sat by Kurt, heartsick, almost to revulsion, refusing to understand that her gentle brother was gone from them forever. "Thank you for telling us, Papa," she whispered. "We'll see you and Mama soon."

As they went to the door, Kurt turned and spoke quietly to Annie. "I've not been in my truck for some time. Don't go anywhere since the accident."

Malvern turned sharply on his son, "Weren't no accident, Kurt, and you know it."

"I sold the truck." Ignoring his father, Kurt went on. "Got money from it. Not much, but I want to throw in with you on that oil well you and Robert and Garrett are drillin'." He handed her an envelope.

Malvern faced Annie, his hand on Kurt's shoulder. "This one here is 4F now. Glenn never did nobody a bad turn in his whole life and he's at the bottom of the ocean, but this fucking jack rabbit won't have to risk his sorry hide for nothin'."

"Papa, that's cruel." Annie followed them across the porch to the bottom step.

The service for Glenn was elaborate and completely choreographed by Eva Mae. Kurt did not attend nor did Lillian. They were still the favorite subject of every joke in town.

Eva Mae had written out special invitations to the Allison family to come, and now they filled up one side of the small church. The other side, the Malvern side (Eva Mae had said they were to sit there), was filled with those who came because they had known and respected Glenn. Sarah Emma Anderson, Dora Cook, and the other quilting ladies sat behind Annie, Robert and Hannah. In the back row sat Maxwell Porter and his wife.

"Glenn Phillip Malvern was born . . ." the preacher began to read the obituary, "son of John and Sophie Malvern died fighting for his country near Guadalcanal. Besides his parents he leaves a brother, Joseph Malvern, and a sister, Eva Mae Malvern, to mourn his death."

Annie looked up. She wanted to correct the preacher. Glenn had two sisters and two brothers. She looked at Robert, confused, "They left off my name," she whispered, "and Kurt's! Why? Who wrote that obituary?" She stared up at the preacher. Eva Mae!

Opel Allison stepped forward and began to sing softly, "Precious Memories," then Lawrence Allison's wife recited a poem, she said they had read when they honored their own dear nephew, Danny. "It was entitled 'Immortality.'" After a tearful reading, Opel Allison sang again.

Eva Mae came forward and whispered through her tears

that she wanted to say a few words about her dear brother. "He was the most gentle soul I ever knew," The tears began to flow. "We were so close. Even now..." She had to stop. "I feel his presence near me. I think it will always be so."

Annie watched her sister in amazement. She was putting on a performance. How could she use Glenn's service to do this?

"The loss of Danny has broken more than my heart, it's broken my spirit," more sobbing, "and left me fragile. Now my darling brother..." Her shoulders began to shake, "I don't think I can stand it. Pardon me, please... please understand, I'm so heartsick. It's too much for me." The sobbing grew into convulsive, heart wrenching sobs as if wrung from the depths, and then she slumped down behind the pulpit where she had been standing.

There were gasps from the audience Opel Allison hurried forward and Lawrence Allison picked Eva Mae up, still sobbing hysterically, and carried her down the aisle. The service stopped momentarily, while Eva Mae's parents followed them to the vestibule at the back of the church, lined on each side with coat hooks. They lay Eva Mae down on a couple of the coats.

"You go back in, Mr. Malvern. We'll tend to Eva Mae." Lawrence Allison said. "It is your son's service."

Malvern looked skeptically down at his daughter. He rubbed the palm of his hand across his mouth, and then took Sophie's elbow and they walked back to their pew. The minister began again.

When the service was about to close, Eva Mae, supported by Opel and Lawrence Allison stood framed in the door at the back of the church. "I don't want to interrupt, Pastor," Eva Mae whispered, "but, oh please forgive me and—and thank you for coming and..." She leaned heavily on Lawrence Allison as every head turned, craning to see the girl so broken with grief. "Come to our home...we will have a light repast." She staggered again and seemed to slump against the arm of Lawrence Allison. "Thank you," Her thin voice trailed off.

Annie said nothing as she went to the car. Inside she

slammed the door. "To use Glenn's service like that! I cannot believe Eva Mae feels anything—for anybody."

"Do you want to go to your parents' house for—what was it? 'A light repass'?" Robert started the car.

"She deliberately left Kurt's and my name off the obituary." Annie went on, ignoring him.

"Annie?"

"Oh, yes, I want to go over there." Annie's eyes blazed. "You just bet I do."

They arrived before John and Sophie Malvern got home. When Annie walked into the dining room, it looked as if the table was prepared for a party.

CHAPTER 86

When Malvern left the church, he did not look up as he passed through the rows of people waiting to extend their condolences. He went directly to his car, drove home, and placed himself in the chair by a window in his living room, facing the road. He felt numb, arms and legs wooden, heavy. There had been so much going on. What he would like to have done was go out to his old shed, close the door, and be alone. But he couldn't do that.

Gradually the room filled with somber people. He heard them talking quietly as they took coffee and refreshments from the table, bounty of Eva Mae's party and neighbors who stopped by with food. They came to him, touched his shoulder. He nodded and kept staring out the window. Malvern thought Maxwell Porter had come in with his wife and those people Eva Mae liked—the Allisons. Annie had come. Yes, he heard her voice—and Kurt's. People were talking to him—saying words, sounds that had no meaning. They passed, just scenery to him, like watching a picture show. He tried to think, but there was too much to take in. He felt so very tired. Kurt. Glenn. Eva Mae. Annie. That nonsense at the service. Why was Annie not close to him anymore? He had always loved her best and now things were different. He closed his eyes to shut out the incessant talk, a jangling noise. He wanted quiet. He wanted a peaceful place so he could struggle to understand.

Kurt, able-bodied now, his face grotesquely disfigured and emotions raw since the fire, sat back in the shadows, unspeaking. Glenn's death hit him hard and today, to be excluded from the family during Glenn's service, left him trembling with rage.

Eva Mae, miraculously recovered from her devastating bout of grief, bustled in and busily began serving everyone. Marthursa Allison arrived. Eva Mae met her and escorted her with much deference to the central seat in the living room. "May I get you cake?" Eva Mae asked, as she took her coat. Other Allisons arrived.

Annie and Robert with Hannah took seats near John and Sophie. The room was quiet.

After a time, Joey stood up, "Think I'll saddle up ole Merrylegs and go for a ride. You wanta go with me, Hannah?"

"I wanna go horseback riding." Hannah's eyes brightened, and she slid down off the chair by Annie.

"No," Annie said sharply. "Not now."

"Joey," Malvern was stern. "Sit down."

Eva Mae came to the table laden with food, near where Annie sat.

"Eva Mae," Annie stood up.

Robert tugged at her arm. "Annie, are you sure?"

"Eva Mae you are one rotten bitch." Annie's fiery words shot through the gloomy, subdued mood. Mathursa Allison looked up, ready to take a bite of cake, but stopped. "I can't imagine the kind of mind," Annie flung at Eva Mae, "who would turn her brother's funeral into a self-serving circus, a person who would deliberately leave off his obituary the names of a brother and sister who loved him."

John Malvern looked at his two daughters as if they were strangers to him.

Eva Mae turned toward the Allisons sitting on the couch, her face scarlet.

Annie would not be silenced. "Do you think these people don't know? Do you think they don't know my husband was murdered for his gambling debts? Do you think they don't know Kurt, sitting over there disfigured because he had an affair with their own Lillian? You can't cut us out of your life. We're blood. Nothing can untie that."

Eva Mae turned on her. "I hate what you've done...you and Kurt. I've tried to better myself and you—you want to be trash, both of you."

"And you're better?" Annie said, her hand unconsciously smoothing over her thickening stomach.

Kurt stood up, coming out of the darkened corner. He stalked across the room. All eyes fell on him and conversation hushed. He turned slowly around so all could see his distorted, scarred face.

"I guess you can see why Eva Mae would want to forget she has this for a brother. The thing is, these scars aren't the reason."

"The reason is you disgraced the family," Eva Mae shot back.

"And you turned Glenn's service into a theater performance. That was a disgrace."

"The hell with this," Joey popped up. "I'm goin' horseback riding." His father took his arm and motioned him to sit down.

"I wish I could not claim you as, as anything...Kurt," Eva Mae's face was still flushed.

Annie came to Kurt's side. "Leave him alone, Evie."

"He deserved what happened to him."

"My God, Eva Mae, he didn't deserve this."

"Annie, will you shut up. You brought more trouble on us than anybody."

"Us? Us, Eva Mae? 'Us' to you is staying with Papa where the money is."

"I'm gittin' outa here." Joey said.

"No, Joey," Kurt said, "you're not."

Eva Mae was near tears. "Why do we have to hang our dirty laundry out in front of... everybody?"

Kurt's face was red, his eyes squinted and tears ran down

them. "Why not? We've heard enough about the Allisons. Let them get a look at the Malverns."

"Yes," Annie spoke to Marthursa Allison. "I stood outside the door of this house, after I'd been attacked by a man. I was naked and bleeding and this spiteful little creature wouldn't allow me in—in to see my mother, because..." Annie began to cry.

"Shut up," Eva Mae screamed, "shut up, both of you—all of you. I want no part of you. It makes me sick to look at you."

Maxwell Porter tilted back in his straight-back chair against the wall and leaned near Marthursa Allison. "This here's one damn good show, ain't it Miz Allison? Don't know which is better, watchin' the fur fly in a Malvern cat fight or Eva Mae's hallelujah performance over there at church."

Mathursa Allisons stamped her cane a couple of staccato beats and laughed with Porter.

"See, Papa they're making people laugh at us." Eva Mae said. "We're a neighborhood joke."

John Malvern stood. The somber face he'd worn all day had not changed. His arms hung at his sides.

"Enough. Enough of this." He sounded tired. The room became silent. His two daughters quieted. "I have a son who lies at the bottom of an ocean now... somewhere I'll never know. A good boy. Another one, here, disfigured and disgraced. Annie. My first born...we don't never talk. Eva Mae here wants to forget her blood. And there's Joey! Joey just wants to play at life." John Malvern hung his head. Then after a time he looked across at the people who sat about. He ran the palm of his hand across his mouth. Sophie was crying. "The worse is I had a hand in all this."

The clocked ticked in the quiet room. There was something strange about the way Malvern talked, as if he were looking beyond all of them.

"I always believed family was everything," he finally said. "When I was a young man, Sophie and me moved onto her Papa's farm. We lived happy, and each time Sophie brought us a new child, I planned to buy twenty acres for that child, and when they grew they could live nearby—have their little ones. I'd hold each one as they come along." He looked down at Sophie." I had that dream, and it was a good dream, but I couldn't do it because I was a poor man. Then the oil come, and I couldn't buy the acres because no one wanted to sell their land. Then they drilled on my plots of ground—land I meant for my children when I died. And I got rich. The wells kept comin' and the money kept comin'. I didn't know what to do with it all." He paused and looked about the room, unseeing. "I didn't know this man I was. I'd go to town and everybody knew me. They'd ask how I was, and what I thought about the oil prospect here and abouts and I'd say something."

His hand found Sophia's shoulder. "I lost our dream, Mama." He looked down at her.

He looked up again. "I lost my dream...and my children," his eyes found Kurt. "lost their way. I didn't know what to do...and money just kept comin' in. I couldn't tell what to do, how to do because I didn't know myself."

John Malvern stood in the center of the room, all eyes on him. He looked weary as he turned to Kurt and Joey. "Nothing' turns out like you plan." He got up. "Nothing. And I had a hand in it. I know it."

He stood for a moment, tears tracked down his face, distorted in grief. He turned his back on the group and went out toward his shed.

The grandfather clock ticked in the silent room, then Marthursa Allison, cane in hand, tapped it on the floor. "I'm an old lady, older'n John Malvern. I've been poor, and I've been rich. I raised six children. Some of them broke my heart, but when you're old and all the nonsense of life is pasted up in some crumbling old scrapbook the one thing you see that counts, is family. Some days it's a sorry sight." She looked about for someone to help her stand. "Opel, I'm tired. I want to go."

"Well, I'm goin' horseback riding. Let's go, Hannah," Joey took Hannah's hand. "You can watch me saddle her up," he said. Hannah followed Joey out the back door.

A great flurry of activity began as coats were distributed

and Mrs. Allison was helped into her wrap.

Sophie followed Marthursa to the door, "Thank you for coming," she said. Eva Mae helped her down the front steps and into a car in the circle drive before the front entrance. The other Allisons followed. Marthursa, seated in the back seat, looked straight ahead ignoring Sophie's farewell.

Porter stood up, "We better be gittin' on home, too." They looked out the window as Joey rode by on Merrylegs at full trot.

Hannah came running into the room, crying. "Mommy, Mommy...Papa's..."

"Why aren't you with Joey?" Robert said.

"Mommy, Grandpa's standing in the air." Her eyes were wide, fearful as she pointed to the door.

Robert scooped Hannah up and ran to where she directed.

At the garage door, they stopped! John Malvern's body hung between his black Buick 8 and Joey's Roadster Coup.

"Papa!" Eva Mae screamed and ran to him.

Robert held his body. Kurt cut the rope. Malvern slumped in Robert's arms.

"He's alive," Robert said.

"I'll get the doctor," Annie sobbed, picked up Hannah, and put her in the car beside her.

Robert and Kurt carried him out and laid him on the grass under the big oak. The family stood about, numb as statues. Their strong father was with them a few minutes ago. His helpless body lay before them now.

Robert went back to the garage as Sophie and Eva Mae tried to minister to John.

"Looks like he stood on the hood of his car," Robert said when he came back, "slung the rope over the middle rafter...there's footprints...and he just walked off. Dropped between the two cars." No one was listening.

Eva Mae hovered over her father earnestly begging, "Oh, Papa don't leave us. I'm so sorry. I never would hurt you, Papa. You gotta be all right. You gotta be."

Joey sat down on the ground beside Kurt, plucked up a blade of grass and pulled it through his teeth. "I saw him in the barn when I was saddling Merrylegs. Told Hannah I'd be back for her, after I had a turn. Papa looked at me and said, 'You go on, boy, just have a good time'. That's what he said. I laughed and took off." Joey wiped at his wet eyes with the heel of his palms.

Thirty minutes later, Annie came with the doctor and they took John Malvern into the front bedroom. Annie, Robert and Hannah sat by the table covered with leftover food. The others collapsed in some seat near them, sunk deep inside themselves, waiting for the bedroom door to open, and the doctor to say their father would be all right.

Minutes ticked away and finally the door did open. "Your Papa just may make it," the doctor said. "Can't say yet." He looked about the cluttered room, a quizzical look on his face. "I've known John Malvern all his life. As solid a man as I ever knew. I want to know what made him do such a damn fool thing?"

No one answered. "Maybe I can figure that one out for myself." When the doctor went back into the bedroom, Annie glimpsed her mother sitting by the bed holding her husband's hand. The doctor closed the door.

CHAPTER 87

After Annie had put Hannah down for the night, she put on her coat, went outside and sat in the porch swing. Light splashed on the porch from the front bedroom behind her. She looked in; saw her parents. Tears began to fall, realizing her father was lying there wavering on that mysterious line that could take him from the world of the living. Soon Robert joined her and put his arm around her shoulder. Joey and Kurt came out, too. Kurt sat down on the porch, leaned back against a column and lit up a cigarette. Eva Mae finally left her mother, came out on the porch, and sat in a rocker huddled in a heavy shawl. The night was clear and crisp. Oil flares cast a flickering orange glow behind naked black limbs of the oak tree; limbs ready to awaken for spring

Kurt broke the silence. "'Member the time we went out to get the honey from that old tree in the woods?"

"I remember that," Joey said, "Kurt said he'd get past the bees, but it was Glenn who went in there. Got clothes wrapped around him good, so they couldn't get to him."

"You girls just stood there, scared and Eva Mae kept sayin', 'I'm gonna tell Papa.'"

"But Annie dared us," Joey said. "And we pulled out that great chunk of honeycomb and carried it to the house."

"Papa didn't know whether to be proud of us or punish us,"

Kurt said.

They stopped abruptly as if they had said something disrespectful, then Joey went on.

"'Member them muffins Annie made with the honey?"

They chuckled.

"They were the worse things I ever tasted in my life." Eva Mae laughed.

"Didn't matter we wrestled the honey from the bees." It was the first time Annie had heard Kurt laugh. "But those muffins went flat as pancakes and tasted like leather."

"Mama came in and asked me if I put in the baking powder," Annie said, I said I think I did. 'Well,' Mama said, 'if you did, they wouldn't be flat like that.'"

"'Baking powder makes things rise.' Mama said," Eva Mae ventured out of her sullen silence, and everybody laughed, even Eva Mae. Kurt and Annie went again to the window and looked at their father lying so still on the pillow.

"Annie was getting breasts, what was I supposed to do?" Eva Mae said.

They all laughed again, then fell back into respectful silence.

Annie turned to Robert in the swing beside her. "A couple of nights later after my muffin failure when we were getting ready for bed, I said to Eva Mae 'what is that white stuff all over your chest?' Eva Mae had rubbed baking powder all over her little flat chest. She said, Mama said baking powder makes things rise."

"After that I used to yell down the hall every night when we were in bed. "Hey, Eva Mae how's the muffins coming?" Kurt chuckled.

"Shut up, Kurt." Eva Mae said, but she laughed.

"I think that's what you said then, too."

"Then Glenn'd say, 'Now you leave her alone.'"

Glenn! They fell quiet again. They would never hear Glenn's serious cautions.

After a time Annie picked it up, "Papa'd come in and say, 'You kids stop this and go to sleep.'"

No one said anything for a while. They heard the clock inside strike nine. The dreadful day had been endless and now…now they didn't know what would happen.

Joey got up and peered in the window. "We near killed that old man in there."

They heard Eva Mae crying softly in the dark. "I'd miss him, awful," she whispered, "and I miss Glenn. I don't think I can stand this." Eva Mae sounded like the little sister they once knew.

Joey went to her. She stood up and clung to him, Annie came and finally Kurt. Eva Mae opened her embrace to them, and they held each other. Annie knew they felt the same dark awful dread and the same emptiness she did. For a brief time, they were again the young children John Malvern had loved. Then Annie pulled back, her hand rubbing over on her thick girth. It was hard now to remember Eva Mae as that little sister *she* had loved. "I think I'll go in and see if I can help Mama." She wanted to be by her father, to hold his hand, to remember his touch.

John Malvern lived two more days without regaining consciousness before succumbing to his original wish. Annie, Eva Mae, Joey and Kurt hovered about their mother on the blustery April afternoon, when John Malvern's casket rested above an empty grave. Annie looked at the dozens of flowers that surrounded the grave and covered his casket. Half the county had turned out. He died of disappointment in his family, Annie thought, and once again cursed the oil.

"The heart has just been cut out of this family," Sophie whispered. Annie leaned forward and held her mother tighter, "Yes, Mama." And Annie, too, wondered for better or worse, how life could be without the towering presence of her father in their lives.

CHAPTER 88

Somewhere in misty half sleep, Annie felt it, a pain circling the thick girth of her lower body. She pulled herself up to sitting position on the edge of the bed and ran her hand over her swollen body. Maybe today.

She went down the hall, threw open the doors to the balcony over the front entrance. It was a hot August night, no air moving. In the distance she could hear the grinding drill of the well, her well, hers and Robert's, Kurt's, and Carson Garrett's. It was a gamble, to be sure. You never knew, really knew what was down there until you hit the oil—or didn't hit it. If you didn't hit it, you had literally poured your money into a dark hole. And a deep one this time, five thousand feet.

Another mild pain came over her and she had a dull headache. Probably worry over this well. Daily, she, Robert and Kurt had gone to the well sites. Night and day, they had lived and breathed every detail of the financial transactions and the plans for drilling. The three of them, with Garrett, watched on the day they reopened this old well, the first of four wells they had bought and paid Garrett's Lone Star Drilling company to drill to a deeper stratum.

Carson Garrett had said it would be a couple of weeks

before they could get a showing from the soil samples.

She wandered back into the semi-darkness of the house. There was no going back to sleep. She felt her way down the stairs, went to the kitchen and made some coffee. If the well was good, though, what would that mean? More money, of course! But would the oil boom start over on a bigger scale? With the demands of the war for fuel, it might. She sat down to wait for the coffee. She ran her fingers through her damp hair and gripped the chair seat as another pain came.

By mid-morning the contractions were about the same. Annie walked about the yard with Hannah, talking to her about her new sister or brother who would be here soon. Robert called Annie in for the phone.

"It's Joey," Robert said, and he handed her the phone, "he's in Union Station in St. Louis."

"St. Louis?" She frowned and took the receiver.

"Annie, I'm in a real pickle." He sounded scared. "Eva Mae has gone off somewhere. I've got almost no money, and Eva Mae had the tickets in her purse to get us on the train."

"Gone off somewhere, what do you mean?" Annie felt impatient. Every time she had had a crisis in her life Eva Mae had been in the middle of it.

"Well, we were talking to this man from San Francisco, and he asked Eva Mae to go have a drink with him, so she says for me to stay with the bags and wait."

"Then go over to the bar and get her." Annie snapped, her hand going to her back as a pain stabbed sharply.

"I went there, lugged all these suitcases with me and the bartender said he just come to work and didn't see any man with a woman."

"Joey, I'm in labor…"

"But Annie, I can't get back home. She's got the tickets and the money."

"Joey, I can't stand here. I'm about to have a baby."

"Wait, wait, Annie. Don't hang up."

"Here's Robert, Joey…" She handed the phone to Robert.

"Annie..." she could still hear Joey's muted pleas through the receiver, but the contraction was hard this time.

"Joey, we'll be going to the hospital," Robert said. "You'll have to call us there." He started to replace the receiver then leaned into the phone, "Joey, I can't come in there now. I need to be with Annie." Robert's voice was sharp, "I don't know how long the baby will take. It takes its own time. You're all right, Joey. Go back to the bar. Ask around. We'll not leave you there. Call us at the hospital."

"Let's go Robert." Annie leaned against the door casing. "We have to drop Hannah off."

Annie slid onto the comfort of crisp sheets in the hospital and lay back. A fan spread cooling air over her body. Robert sat with her through the long afternoon hours until their son was born.

"And what will you name him?" Aunt Belle asked that night when she and Carson Garrett came.

Annie held the baby nestled beside her in the bed. "Henry Otis." Annie smiled. "What else?"

The nurse bustled in, "There's a phone call for Mrs. St. Pierre. I told him she can't come to the phone, but he wants to talk to her. Can someone come down to the lobby and calm this guy down?"

Robert left and returned in a few minutes. "It was Joey."

"Eva Mae? What about Eva Mae?"

"Joey went back to the bar, and they had found a note Eva Mae left with a bartender written out on a napkin. Said, she was going to San Francisco with 'Jim,' I guess that's the guy she met. She wrote for Joey to take her clothes home and give them to the poor."

"Eva Mae!" Annie whispered. "She said there was nothing here for her."

"Joey's beside himself. She left him stranded with no money, nothing. I told him I'd go get him."

"Hell," Garrett said. "If that was me, I'd cut out hitchhiking."

"But you weren't raised to be John Malvern's princeling." Belle Dorsett said.

"Eva Mae eloped!" Annie said, "Imagine that."

"If you're thinking marriage, Annie," Robert said. "Think again. We'll hear from her, you can just bet."

"Somebody'll have to tell Mama." Annie turned her head on the pillow and closed her eyes.

Trees had turned from deep green to yellow, orange and red, flaunting their gaudy fall finery. The oak tree at her parents' house, where she now sat with her mother was ablaze with brilliant foliage.

"Eva Mae called." Annie's hand was on the baby carriage, rocking little Henry. Hannah sat in a swing that dangled from one of the tree limbs. "She was in Denver."

Sophie began to tear up, "With that man, I suppose. Jim, she calls 'im."

A light breeze drifted through the tree and leaves fluttered down.

"He offered her a glimpse of the great world, Mama."

Sophie shook her head, "I s'pose."

Robert drove in and joined them. He and Kurt had been with Carson Garrett most of the time overseeing the drilling of their new well. It was an experiment and the entire county waited to see if drilling to a deeper level in the old wells would pay. People like Maxwell Porter, with two wells, which had dried up to nothing, might expect more; indeed the whole community talked of a great resurgence of the oil boom.

Each day the column in the newspaper devoted to oil news, gave updates on the progress of this "deep well" as they called it.

Robert dropped down on his haunches between the women, "The word from the drillers is it might be tonight. Better get the children ready to go. Tomorrow," he said as he stood up, "we'll either be in the oil business or we'll be much poorer." He leaned down and kissed Annie.

CHAPTER 89

A narrow country road, where foliage sometimes overarched them, led to a single strip of black top, through a field, oiled and graveled to bear the oil trucks. Four other cars followed them into the field. When they arrived at the site, trucks and cars were already three deep in a circle around the derrick. "Beebite" Cantrell was there from the newspaper, his ponderous camera hanging around his neck, scampering about trying to talk to everyone.

Annie got out of the car, the baby cradled warm against her. Holding Hannah's tiny hand, she walked to the center of the circle in the blinding light of the derrick, where Robert and Carson Garrett stood. She saw her Aunt Belle, in Carson's Buick, which was parked for ringside viewing, and Kurt was hunkered down in the back seat, ashamed to be seen. Belle got out and joined them. The noise of the drill rendered conversation impossible. Hannah held her hands to her ears and the baby whimpered. Annie watched Robert with Carson, both in dead earnest, trying sometimes to talk, periodically looking across at the derrick, and then going back to shouting and gestures. So much was riding on this, not only their own investment but also what it would mean to the other counties where oil activity had spread.

It was the first deep well Garrett had drilled. If it was good, he would stay and re-open more, for deeper drilling. If it was good a lot people would see larger checks coming to their mailboxes again. If it was good.

Tonight, Garrett had said he would know. If there was oil at the five-thousand-foot level, it would be a profitable venture, if not, Annie looked at Belle's anxious face, he would abandon the project, and go on to another field, and she and Robert would have lost a small fortune. She wondered if Belle would go with Carson if he left. She doubted it. It wouldn't be her way to leave her roots for unfamiliar territory.

"It's close." Robert leaned into her ear, and she looked up and smiled. Across the way in the shadow of a car, Kurt, his cap pulled down over his twisted face, now waited with their mother and Joey. There was something so familiar about this, as if she were seeing again that long-ago night when the Malvern family waited for their first well to come in. Annie suddenly felt intensely the presence of her father. She saw him dancing on the platform, swinging Joey around, "We ain't gonna be poor no more, no more" he had chanted. Sorrow churned in her, thinking of her father and how the oil had raised his life to a towering pinnacle of joy and hope, then left him so disappointed he had wanted to be relieved of that life.

Maxwell Porter leaned against his truck. Annie hoped this well would bring good fortune for him, too. The oil had in effect cost him his son, and then his oil wells had dwindled to nothing.

Her attention shot to the well. It began to sputter. She held her breath. Nothing happened. Robert looked at Annie, a look of distress in his serious face. And then another sputter came. No one spoke. And then oil shot up through the center of the derrick. A wild cheer went up. Car doors slammed. "BeeBite" Cantrell snapped pictures. Annie grabbed Robert's arm. "It's good!" she screamed. "It's good!"

Then it stopped! Nothing followed. They waited, watching, puzzled, expectant. Nothing! Carson Garrett went forward and spoke to the driller. When he came back, he shouted to Robert that he told him to keep drilling deeper, just to see.

Solemn faces stared up at the steel structure, waiting, silent. Even though it was after one o'clock in the morning, half the county had finally turned out, and now stood riveted on the derrick.

Maybe the earth would not give up any more of its treasure, Annie thought. Maybe, the gods were teasing them because they didn't deserve more. They had been tested before and were found wanting and now, they would receive no more.

Then it came, flashing high in the derrick, with intense pressure. Another sputter, it slowed and then oil came again, shooting higher, raining down black drops.

"It's a strike!" Garrett yelled for the entire world to hear. "It's a good one."

Everyone began to cheer and laugh and dance and slap each other's back. "Beebite" Cantrell ran forward, his camera in hand. Kurt came out of the shadows to stand by them. Robert scooped Annie into his arms, baby and all, and kissed her. And Belle hugged them both. "You got a good one, Annie." There were tears in her eyes, and then she ran to Garrett.

"Mommy," Hannah tugged on her mother's skirt. "What is it? Why is everybody jumping up and down and yelling?"

Robert put Annie down by her daughter.

"It's oil, darling. It's oil, and it's ours!" For the first time, Annie understood what so many others had felt, when the strike was really their own. She understood the delirium she had witnessed so often; delirium that led almost to insanity. When the earth poured forth its black riches, lives changed and sometimes they had not the wisdom to handle so great a gift. She sobered as she watched the black gusher. "God has given us a second chance," she whispered. "Let us do it right this time. Please, God, keep us from being fools."

"What's oil?" Hannah watched the spectacle happening around her.

"Something we people can use; we can sell, sweetheart."

"And get money?"

"Yes."

Annie looked down at her daughter; bright innocent eyes, questioned her, eyes that had cried no tears of grief.

"We be rich, Mommy?"

Annie gasped. Those echoing words! In a fleeting she saw her father dancing on the platform, five years ago, calling Joey and Kurt and Glenn to join him. Glenn! Eva Mae, beside their mother, clapping her hands. She had been standing by Willis, her arm linked with his, almost a bride, in love, and filled with dreams.

The warm soft wisp of humanity she held in her arm squirmed against her chest. She wanted to hold it tighter, and Hannah—protect her babies. And Robert and what they had found. She wanted fiercely to gather them all to her, show them what was precious, and let no anguish come to them.

She dropped down to eye level with Hannah and put her other arm about her, encircling her children. "Will we be rich, darling?" She looked up at Kurt and then to Robert. "I guess that's up to us."

The End.

Made in the USA
Middletown, DE
21 December 2021